D0261346

LITTLE STAR

LITTLE STAR

John Ajvide Lindqvist

translated by Marlaine Delargy

Quercus

First published in Great Britain in 2011 by

Quercus
55 Baker Street
7th Floor, South Block
London
W1U 8EW

Swedish original LILLA STJÄRNA, first published
by Ordfront Stockholm 2010

Published by arrangement with Leonhardt & Høier A/S, Copenhagen
First published in English by The Text Publishing Co Australia

A CIP catalogue record for this book is available
from the British Library

ISBN 978 0 85738 510 9 (HB)
ISBN 978 0 85738 511 6 (TPB)

10 9 8 7 6 5 4 3 2 1

Printed and bound in Great Britain by Clays Ltd, St Ives plc

Everyone is actually called something else

PROLOGUE

Solliden, Skansen. June 26, 2007. Ten minutes to eight. The presenter is warming up the audience with a sing-along version of 'I'm Gonna Be a Country Girl Again'. When the song ends a technician asks if all parents could please lift their children down off their shoulders so they won't be hit by the camera cranes.

The sun is directly behind the stage, dazzling the audience. The sky is deep blue. The young people crowding the barriers are asked to move back slightly to avoid a crush. Sweden's biggest music show will be on air in five minutes, and no one must be allowed to come to harm.

There must be these oases of pleasure, where everyday cares are set aside for a while. Nothing bad can happen here, and every possible security measure has been taken to keep this place of enjoyment safe.

Screams of pain, of terror, are unthinkable; there must not be blood on the ground or covering the seats when the broadcast is over. There must not be a corpse lying on the stage, with many more on the ground below. Chaos cannot be permitted here. There are too many people. The atmosphere must be calm and pleasant.

The orchestra strikes up with 'Stockholm in My Heart', and everyone joins in. Hands sway in the air, mobile phone cameras are raised. A wonderful feeling of togetherness. It will be another fifteen minutes until, with meticulous premeditation, the whole thing is torn to shreds.

Let us sing along for the time being. We have a long way to go before we return here. Only when the journey has softened us up, when we are ready to think the unthinkable, will we be permitted to come back.

So come on everyone! All together now!

> Through Lake Mälaren's love of the sea
> a blend of fresh water and brine…

THE GIRL WITH GOLDEN HAIR

I

In the autumn of 1992 there were rumours of a mushroom glut in the forests; it was said that the warm moist weather of late summer had provoked a burst of chanterelles and hedgehog mushrooms. As Lennart Cederström turned off onto the forest track in his Volvo 240, he had a large basket and a couple of plastic bags on the back seat. Just in case.

He had a mix tape of pop hits on the stereo, and Christer Sjögren's voice was loud and clear in the speakers: *Ten thousand red roses I'd like to give you...*

Lennart grinned scornfully and joined in with the chorus, imitating Sjögren's mannered bass vibrato. It sounded excellent. Almost identical; Lennart was probably a better singer than Sjögren. But so what? He had been in the wrong place at the wrong time on too many occasions, seen too many golden opportunities snatched away from under his very nose or heard them zip past behind his back. Gone when he turned around.

Anyway. He would have his mushrooms. Chanterelles, the gold of the forest, and plenty of them. Then back home to blanch them and fill up the freezer, giving him enough for mushrooms on toast and beer every single evening until the Christmas tree was thrown out. Several days of rain had given way to a couple of days of brilliant sunshine, and the conditions were just perfect.

Lennart knew every bend in the forest track, and he screwed up his eyes and gripped the wheel as he sang.

Ten thousand roses in a pretty bouquet....

When he opened his eyes there was something black on the track ahead of him. Sunlight flashed on shining metal, and Lennart only just managed to swerve as it flashed by. A car. Lennart glanced in the rear view mirror to get the registration, but the car was doing at least eighty on the gravel track, sending up clouds of dust in its wake. However, Lennart was pretty sure it was a BMW. A black BMW with tinted windows.

He drove another three hundred metres to the place where he usually parked, switched off the engine and let out a long breath.

What the hell was that?

A BMW out here in the middle of nowhere wasn't exactly a common sight. A BMW doing eighty along the gravel track leading out of the forest was a unique event. Lennart felt quite excited. He had been a part of something. In the moment when the black object came hurtling towards him, his heart had leapt and then quailed as if anticipating a fatal blow, before opening up and settling down once more. It was an experience.

The only thing that bothered him was that he couldn't report the driver. He would probably have given the mushroom picking a miss so he could savour going home and calling the police, giving a detailed description of the encounter on a track with a thirty kilometres per hour limit. But without a registration number, it would be pointless.

As Lennart got out of the car and picked up his basket and his bags, the temporary rush gave way to a feeling he'd been bested. Again. The black BMW had *won*, in some obscure fashion. Perhaps it would have been different if the car had been a beaten-up old Saab, but it was definitely a rich man's car that had covered his windscreen in dust and forced him into the ditch. Same old thing.

He slammed the car door and tramped off into the forest, head down. Fresh tyre tracks ran along the damp ground in the shade of the trees. Churned-up mud in one place indicated that a car had shot away here, and it wasn't much of a leap to assume it was the BMW. Lennart gazed at the wide wheel marks as if they might offer him some evidence, or a fresh grievance. When nothing occurred to him he spat in the tracks instead.

Let it go.

He strode off into the forest, inhaling the aroma of warm needles, damp moss, and somewhere beneath everything else...the smell of mushrooms. He couldn't pin it down to an exact spot, or identify a species, but a faint undertone in the usual scent of the forest told him the rumours were true: there were mushrooms here just waiting to be picked. His gaze swept the ground, searching for a difference in colour or shape. He was a good mushroomer, able to spot from a considerable distance a chanterelle hiding beneath undergrowth and grass. The slightest nuance in the correct shade of yellow, and he swooped like a hawk.

But this time it was a champignon he spotted. Ten metres away from him, a white button sticking up out of the ground. Lennart frowned. He had never come across a champignon around here before; the soil was wrong.

As he came closer, he saw he was right. Not a mushroom; the corner of a plastic bag. Lennart sighed. Sometimes people who were too idle to drive to the tip dumped stuff in the forest. He had once seen a guy hurl a microwave out of his car window. On that occasion he had made a note of the registration number and reported the incident in writing.

He was about to head off along his normal route, searching out the good mushroom places, when he noticed that the plastic bag was moving. He stopped. The bag moved again. It should have been something to do with the wind. That would have been best. But there wasn't a breath of wind among the tree trunks.

Not good.

He heard a faint rustling noise as the piece of plastic shifted again, and all of a sudden his legs felt heavy. The forest surrounded him, silent and indifferent, and he was all alone in the world with whatever was in the plastic bag. Lennart swallowed, his throat dry, and moved forward a few steps. The bag was motionless now.

Go home. Ignore it.

He didn't want to see an old dog that had almost but not quite been put out of its misery, or a pile of kittens whose skulls had almost but not quite been smashed. He didn't want to know about anything like that.

So it wasn't a sense of responsibility or sympathy that drove him on towards the bit of plastic sticking up from the ground. It was ordinary human or inhuman curiosity. He just had to know, or that waving white flag would torment him until he came back to find out what he had missed.

He grabbed hold of the piece of plastic and instantly recoiled, his hands flying to his mouth. There was something inside the bag, something that had responded to his grip, something that felt like muscles, like flesh. The earth around the bag had recently been disturbed.

A grave. A little grave.

The thought took flight and suddenly Lennart knew exactly what had responded to his hand. Another hand. A very small hand. Lennart edged back to the bag and began to clear away the earth. It didn't take long; the soil had been thrown carelessly over the bag, probably by someone without any tools, and in ten seconds Lennart had freed the bag and pulled it out of the hole.

The handles were tied together and Lennart ripped at the plastic to let in air, let in life. He managed to tear a hole in the bag, and saw blue skin. A tiny leg, a sunken chest. A girl. A baby girl, just a few days or weeks old. She wasn't moving. The thin lips were pressed together, as if defying an evil world. Lennart had witnessed the child's death throes.

He placed his ear to the child's chest and thought he could hear the faintest echo of a heartbeat. He pinched the child's nose between his thumb and forefinger, and took a deep breath. He pursed his lips to send a blast of air into the tiny mouth; he didn't even need to take another breath in order to fill the little lungs once more. The air bubbled out, and the chest was still.

Lennart took another breath and as he sent the second puff down into the lungs, there it was. A shudder went through the tiny body and white foam was coughed up. Then a scream sliced through the silence of the forest and started time ticking once more.

The child screamed and screamed, and its crying sounded like nothing Lennart had ever heard before. It wasn't broken or plaintive. It was a single, clear, pure note, emerging from that neglected body. Lennart had a good ear, and he didn't need a tuning fork to tell him that it was an E. An E that rang like a bell and made the leaves quiver and the birds fly up from the trees.

2

The girl was lying on the passenger seat, wrapped in Lennart's red Helly Hansen sweater. Lennart was sitting with his hands resting on the wheel, staring at her. He was completely calm, and his body felt as if it had been hollowed out. Clarified.

He had once tried cocaine, towards the end of the '70s. A fashionable rock band had offered, and he had accepted. One line and that was it, he had never done it again—because it had been fantastic. Too fantastic.

We are always in a certain amount of pain. There is chafing somewhere, and if it isn't in our body, then it's in our mind. There's an itch, all the time. The cocaine took it away. His body became a receptacle made of velvet, and within that receptacle there were only crystal clear thoughts. The mists had lifted, and life was wonderful. Afterwards, realising that striving to regain this feeling could become his life's work, Lennart refrained from taking cocaine again.

As he sat here now with his hands resting on the wheel, he felt something similar. There was a stillness in him, the forest was glowing with autumn colours, and a great being was holding its breath and waiting for his decision. Lennart slowly reached for the ignition key—*His hand! To think that he had a hand with five fingers that he could move as he wished! What a miracle!*—started the car, and headed back the way he had come.

On the main road he was overtaken by several cars as he crawled along. The child had no basket or seat, and Lennart drove as if he were transporting a bowl filled to the brim with a priceless liquid. The child felt so fragile, so transient, that the slightest violent movement might hurl it out of existence.

His back was soaked with sweat by the time he turned into the drive ten minutes later, switched off the engine and looked around. Not a soul in sight; he scooped the child up in his arms and jogged up to the house. He reached the porch and discovered that the door was locked as usual. He knocked twice, paused, then knocked twice more.

A cold breeze swept over his damp back, and he clutched the child closer to his body. After ten seconds he heard Laila's tentative footsteps in the hallway, saw the spy hole darken as she checked him out. Then the door opened. Laila stood there like a massive door stop.

'Why are you back already, what have you got there—'

Lennart pushed past her and went into the kitchen. The door slammed behind him and Laila shouted, 'Don't you go in there with your shoes on, are you out of your mind, you can't go in the house with your shoes on, Lennart!'

He stood in the middle of the kitchen floor, completely at a loss. He had just wanted to get inside, into the safety of the house. Now he didn't know where to turn. He made to put the child down on the kitchen table, then changed his mind and held it close as he spun around, searching for inspiration.

Laila came into the kitchen, red in the face. 'Take your shoes off when you come in, I've just finished cleaning up and you—'

'Shut up.'

Laila's mouth closed and she recoiled half a step. Lennart loosened his grip on the child and unwrapped the sweater so that the head and a tuft of blonde hair were visible. Laila's mouth opened again. Gaped.

Lennart raised and lowered the bundle. 'I found a child. A baby. In the forest.'

There was the faint click of Laila's tongue sticking to the roof of her mouth and pulling free as she groped for something to say. Eventually she managed to whisper, 'What have you done?'

'I haven't done anything, I found her in the forest. In a hole.'

'A hole?'

Lennart explained briefly. Laila stood there motionless, her hands folded over her stomach. Only her head moved, from side to side. When Lennart reached the point where he blew air into the child's lungs, he broke off. 'Can you stop shaking your head while I'm telling you this? It's bloody irritating.'

Laila's head stopped in mid-movement. She took a hesitant step forward and peered at the child with an expression of restrained horror. The child's eyes and mouth were tightly screwed up. Laila began to knead her cheeks. 'What are you going to do?'

3

The range of baby products had increased significantly since Jerry was little. There were bottles with one teat, two teats, smaller teats, bigger teats. Different sized bottles. Lennart chose three at random and threw them into his trolley.

It was the same with nappies. Jerry had had cloth nappies that you washed, but the ICA hypermarket didn't seem to have anything like that. Lennart stood before the wall of brightly coloured plastic packs like a Buddhist at a prayer wall. This wasn't his world. He hadn't a clue.

He almost did the same as he had with the bottles, but then he noticed that the nappies came in different sizes for different ages. There were only two kinds for newborns, and Lennart chose the more expensive ones. Fortunately there was only one kind of formula; he put two boxes in his trolley.

He had no idea what else he might need.

Dummies? Jerry had had a dummy, and look how that turned out. No dummy, at least for the time being. Lennart spotted a giraffe, or rather a giraffe's neck and head attached to a ball so it always popped back into an upright position. He put it in the trolley.

Every single time he picked something up and dropped it among the rest of his purchases, he thought how absurd the situation was. These were baby things. Things for a baby. A wriggling, screaming creature where food went in one end and shit came out the other. A creature he had found in the forest...

Once again that sense of unearthly *calm* came over him. His arms went limp and dangled as his eyes sought out a mirrored dome in the ceiling. He could see little people moving along the aisles, he could see them from God's perspective and he wanted to reach out and tell them all that they were forgiven. Everything they had done to him in the past was unimportant now.

I forgive you. I like you. I really like you.

'Ex*cuse* me.'

For a moment he thought someone had actually responded to his amnesty. Then he came to and saw a fat, pop-eyed woman pushing past him to get to the baby food.

He grabbed the handle of the trolley and looked around. Two elderly men were standing looking at him. He didn't know how long he had spent in his state of grace, but it could hardly be more than a few seconds. That was all it took for people to start staring.

Lennart pulled a face and set off towards the checkout. His palms were sweaty, and he suddenly felt as if he were walking oddly. His temples were throbbing, and the gaze of imagined or actual observers seared into his back. People were whispering about the contents of his trolley, suspecting him of all manner of things.

Calm down. Got to take it easy.

He had a special trick when feelings like this came over him, as they sometimes did: he pretended he was Christer Sjögren. The gold discs, the TV shows, the German tours, the whole lot. People were looking at him because he was so horribly *famous.*

Lennart straightened his back and manoeuvred his trolley a little more carefully. A few more steps towards the checkout and the fantasy was complete: here comes Christer. There was no queue, of course, and as he loaded his shopping onto the belt he smiled at the checkout girl, revealing the charming gap between his front teeth.

He paid with a five-hundred-kronor note, took his change and packed everything into two bags, then carried on through the crowd with confident steps; it wasn't until he had thrown the bags in the back of the car, got into the driver's seat and closed the door that he could drop the mask, return to himself and start despising Christer again.

My very own bloody Blue Hawaii.

He found Laila at the kitchen table. The little girl was in her arms, wrapped in one of Jerry's old baby blankets. Lennart put the bags down on the kitchen floor and Laila looked up at him with the expression that made his stomach tie itself in knots: mouth wide open, eyebrows raised. Helpless and astonished. Which might possibly have worked *in those days*, but not anymore.

He dug out the box of formula and asked without looking at Laila, 'What's the matter with you?'

'She hasn't made a sound,' said Laila. 'Not a sound, in all this time.'

Lennart put some water in a pan and placed it on the burner. 'What do you mean?'

'Exactly what I say. She ought to be hungry, or...I don't know. But something. She ought to say something. Make some kind of noise.'

Lennart put down the measuring scoop and leaned over the child. Its face wore the same concentrated expression as before, as if it were lying there listening intently for something. He prodded the flat nose, and the lips contorted into an expression of discontent.

'What are you doing?' Laila asked. Lennart turned back to the stove, poured powder into the water and started whisking. Laila's voice rose. 'Did you think she was dead?'

'I didn't think anything.'

'Did you think I'd be sitting here holding a dead baby without noticing, is that what you thought?'

Lennart whisked hard for a moment, then tested the temperature of the milk with his finger. He took it off the heat and grabbed a bottle at random as Laila droned on in the background.

'You're unbelievable, that's what you are. You think you're the only one who has any idea how things are, but let me tell you, all those years when Jerry was little and you just—'

When Lennart had poured the milk into the bottle and screwed the teat in place, he took a step towards Laila and slapped her across the face with the palm of his hand.

'Shut your mouth. Don't talk about Jerry.'

He took the child from her and sat down on a wooden chair on the other side of the table. He crossed his fingers under the blanket, hoping it was the right sort of teat. At this particular moment he didn't want to have made the wrong choice.

The child's lips closed around the teat and she began to suck, eagerly drinking down the contents of the bottle. Lennart stole a glance at Laila, who hadn't noticed his success. She was sitting there rubbing her cheek, silent tears rolling into the creases around her neck. Then she got up and hobbled into the bedroom, closing the door behind her.

The child ate almost as silently as she seemed to do everything. All he could hear was quiet snuffles as she breathed in through her nose while her mouth continued to suck away and the level in the bottle fell. When the bottle was almost empty, Lennart heard the faint rustle of foil from the bedroom. He ignored it. He had enough to think about.

With a pop the child let go of the teat and opened its eyes. Something crawled up Lennart's spine and made him shudder. The child's eyes were bright blue, enormous in the little face. For a second the pupils dilated, and Lennart felt as he if was staring down into an abyss. Then they contracted in the light and the eyelids closed.

Lennart sat motionless for a long time. The child had looked at him. It had seen him.

4

When Laila came out of the bedroom, Lennart had placed the child on a towel on the kitchen table. He was turning a nappy this way and that in his hands, trying to work out how to put it on, when Laila took it off him, pushed him out of the way and said, 'I'll do it.'

Her breath smelled of chocolate and mint, but Lennart didn't say anything. He put his hands on his hips, took a step back and carefully watched what Laila did with the flaps and sticky strips. Her left cheek was bright red, striped with the tracks of dried-on, salty tears.

She had been a party girl, a sexy little thing. A pretender to the glittering throne on which Lill-Babs sat, yodelling away. A reviewer had once jokingly called her Little Lill-Babs. Then she and Lennart had teamed up and her career had taken a different direction. These days she weighed ninety-seven kilos and had problems with her legs. The party girl was still there in her face, but you had to look hard to catch a glimpse.

Laila fastened the nappy and wrapped the child in the blanket with blue teddy bears. She fetched a clean towel and made a bed in the big picnic basket, then laid the sleeping child carefully inside it. Lennart stood there watching the whole thing. He was happy. This was going well.

Laila picked up the basket and rocked it gently like a cradle. She looked at Lennart for the first time since she had emerged from the bedroom. 'What now?'

'What do you mean?'

'What are we going to do now? Where are we going to take her?'

Lennart took the basket off Laila, went into the living room and placed it on the armchair. He bent over the child and stroked its cheek with his forefinger. He heard Laila's voice behind him. 'You can't be serious.'

'Why?'

'It's against the law, you must know that.'

Lennart turned and held out his arm. Laila backed away slightly, but Lennart turned up his palm, inviting her to take his hand. She moved closer cautiously, as if she expected the outstretched hand to turn into a snake at any moment. Then she placed her hand in his. Lennart led her into the kitchen, sat her down at the table and poured her a cup of coffee.

Laila followed his movements with a watchful expression as he poured himself a cup of coffee and sat down opposite her. 'I'm not angry,' he said. 'Quite the reverse.'

Laila nodded and raised the cup to her lips. Her teeth were discoloured with gooey chocolate but Lennart didn't point this out. Her cheeks wobbled unpleasantly as she swallowed the hot drink. He didn't say anything about that either. What he said was, 'Darling.'

Laila's eyes narrowed. 'Yes?'

'I didn't finish telling you the story. What happened in the forest. When I found her.'

Laila placed her hands on the kitchen table, resting one on another. 'Go on then. *Darling.*'

Lennart ignored her sarcastic tone. 'She sang. When I'd dug her out of the hole. She sang.'

'But she hasn't made a sound.'

'Listen to me. I don't expect you to understand this, because you haven't got an ear for it, but…' Lennart raised a hand to forestall the objections he knew would come, because if there was one thing Laila was still proud of, it was her singing voice and her ability to hit a note cleanly. But that wasn't what it was about in this case.

'You haven't got the *ear* like I have,' said Lennart. 'Your voice is better and your pitch is more accurate blah blah blah—all right? Happy?—but that's not what we're talking about. We're talking about having the *ear*.'

Laila was listening again. Despite his delivery, the praise was enough. Her talent had been acknowledged and Lennart was able to go on. 'You know I have a perfect ear for a note. When I opened the plastic bag and got her out…she sang. First an E. Then a C. And then an A. And I don't mean cries that sounded like notes, but…*sine waves.* Perfect. If you had set a meter to measure her A, it would have shown 440 hertz.'

'What do you mean?'

'I don't mean anything. That's just the way it was. She sang. And I've never heard anything like it. Not the hint of a slide or a grating sound. It was like hearing…an angel. I can still hear it.'

'What are you trying to say, Lennart?'

'That I can't give her away. It's impossible.'

5

The coffee was finished. The child was asleep. Laila was limping around the kitchen with a wooden ladle in her hand, waving it in the air as if she were trying to scoop up fresh arguments. Lennart was sitting with his head resting in his hands; he had stopped listening.

'There's no way we can look after a child,' said Laila. 'How would that work, the way our life is? I for one have no desire to start that business all over again, sleepless nights and being tied down all the time. When we've finally managed...' The ladle stopped weaving about and made a hesitant sideways movement. Laila didn't want to say it, but as she thought it was an argument that might hit home with Lennart, she said it anyway, '...when we've finally managed to get Jerry out of the house. Are we going to go through all that again? And besides Lennart, forgive me for saying this, but I don't think there's a cat in hell's chance they'd let us adopt. For a start, we're too old...'

'Laila.'

'And you can bet your life they've got information about Jerry, which means they're bound to ask...'

Lennart slammed the palm of his hand down on the table, hard. The ladle stopped dead and the words dried up.

'There's no question of adoption,' said Lennart. 'I have no intention of giving her up. Nobody will know we've got her. For those very reasons you've so eloquently expressed.'

Laila dropped the ladle. It bounced once, then lay there between them. Laila looked at Lennart, then at the ladle. When he made no move to pick it up, she squatted clumsily and took it in her arms as if it were the child they were discussing.

'You've lost your mind, Lennart,' she whispered. 'You've completely lost your mind.'

Lennart shrugged. 'Well, that's the way it is. You're just going to have to get used to the idea.'

Laila's mouth opened and closed. The ladle whisked around as if to disperse a horde of invisible demons. Just as she was on the point of uttering one of the sentences that were sticking in her throat, there was a knock on the door.

Lennart shot up from the table, shoved Laila out of the way and went into the living room, where he picked up the basket that held the sleeping child. The knock on the door was instantly recognisable. Jerry *just happened to be passing*.

With the basket in his hand Lennart went up to Laila and held up a rigid forefinger right in front of her nose. 'Not one word, do you hear me? Not a word.'

Laila's wide open eyes squinted a fraction as she shook her head. Lennart grabbed the baby things and threw them in the cupboard where they kept the cleaning stuff, then hurried over to the cellar steps. As he closed the door behind him he could hear Laila's limping footsteps in the hallway.

He crept down the stairs and tried to stop the basket tipping too much; he didn't want the child to wake up. He went past the boiler room and the utility room and opened the door of the guest room, Jerry's old room.

A wave of chilly dampness hit him. The guest room had not accommodated a single guest since Jerry moved out, and the only visitor to the room was Lennart himself, when he came down here once every six months to air it. There was a faint smell of mould from the bedding.

He put the basket down on the bed and switched on the radiator. The pipes gurgled as the hot water came gushing in. He sat for a moment with his hand on the radiator until he could feel it warming up; there was no need to bleed it. Then he tucked another blanket around the child.

The little face was still sunk in what he hoped was a deep sleep, and he refrained from stroking its cheek.

Sleep, little miracle, sleep.

He didn't dare leave Laila alone with Jerry; he hadn't the slightest faith in her ability to hold her tongue if Jerry asked some tricky question, so with fear in his heart he closed the door of the guest room, hoping that the child wouldn't wake up and start yelling or...singing. The notes he had heard would slice through anything.

Jerry was sitting at the kitchen table, shovelling down sandwiches. Laila sat opposite him, twisting her fingers around each other. When Jerry caught sight of Lennart he saluted and said, 'Hello there, Captain.'

Lennart walked over and closed the fridge door. A considerable proportion of the contents had been laid out on the table so that Jerry had a choice of fillings for his sandwich. He took a bite of one containing liver pâté, cheese and gherkins, nodded in Laila's direction and said, 'What the fuck's wrong with Mother? She looks completely out of it.'

Lennart couldn't bring himself to answer. Jerry licked gherkin juice off his stiff, chubby fingers. Once upon a time they had been slender and flexible, moving over the strings of a guitar like a bird's wings. Without looking at Jerry, Lennart said, 'We're a bit busy.'

Jerry grinned and started making a fresh sandwich. 'Busy with what? You two are never busy.'

A tube of fish paste was lying on the table in front of Lennart. Jerry had squeezed it in the middle, and Lennart began pointedly rolling up the bottom of the tube, pushing the paste towards the top. A slight headache had begun to burn around his temples.

Jerry polished off his sandwich in four bites, leaned back in his chair, locked his hands behind his head and gazed around the kitchen. 'So. You're a bit busy.'

Lennart took out his wallet. 'Do you need money?'

Jerry adopted an expression that indicated this was a completely new idea, and looked over at Laila. He noticed something and tilted his head. 'What's happened to your cheek, Mother? Did he hit you?'

Laila shook her head, but in such an unconvincing way that she might as well have said yes. Jerry nodded and scratched his stubble. Lennart stood there holding out his open wallet. The glowing points on either side of his head made contact and sent a thread of pain burning through his skull.

With a sudden jolt Jerry half-rose from the chair, heading towards Lennart, who instinctively recoiled. Jerry completed the movement at a more measured pace, and before Lennart had time to react the wallet was in Jerry's hands.

Jerry hummed to himself as he opened the notes compartment, seizing three hundred kronor between his thumb and forefinger with a vestige of his childhood dexterity before tossing the wallet back to Lennart. He said, 'That'll cost you, you know.' He went over to Laila and stroked her hair. 'This is my darling mother, after all. You can't just do whatever you like.'

His hand stopped on Laila's shoulder. As if he were expressing real tenderness, he grabbed Laila's hand and squeezed it. She took what she could get. Lennart watched, utterly revolted. How had these two monsters ended up as his family? Two fat self-pitying blobs who stuck to him like glue, dragging him down; how did that happen?

Jerry withdrew his hand and took a step towards Lennart, whose body automatically jerked backwards. Even if most of Jerry's hundred-kilo bulk came from kebabs rather than weights, he was still considerably stronger than Lennart, and he knew how to handle himself. No doubt about that.

'Jerry.'

Laila's voice was weak, pleading. The mother standing beside her disobedient son, saying *don't do that to the frogs, darling* and not lifting a finger. But Jerry stopped and said, 'Yes, Mother?'

'It's not what you think.'

'So?' Jerry turned to Laila and her eyes sought Lennart's. He shook his head briefly and angrily, leaving Laila trapped between a rock and a hard place. In her confusion she fell back on her usual escape route. Her body went limp and she stared down at the table, mumbling, 'I'm in so much pain, everything hurts.'

It was unlikely to have been Laila's intention, but the effect was exactly what Lennart had been hoping for: Jerry sighed and shook his head. He couldn't cope with hearing his mother going on and on about her stiff joints, the rheumatic twinges in her neck and the entire medical lexicon of side-effects from drugs she wasn't even taking. He lumbered out of the kitchen and Lennart's heart almost stopped when Jerry's shirt brushed over the giraffe's head on the worktop; Lennart had forgotten to hide it.

The giraffe rocked back and forth as Jerry went into the hallway and pulled on his biker boots. Lennart moved forward slightly so that his body was hiding the toy. Jerry looked up with a sarcastic smile.

'Coming to say goodbye? It's been a while.'

'Bye then, Jerry.'

'Yeah, yeah. I will be back, you know.'

Jerry slammed the door behind him. Lennart waited ten seconds, then hurried over and locked it. He heard Jerry's motorbike start up, then fade into the distance. He massaged his temples, rubbed his eyes and took a deep breath. Then he went back into the kitchen.

Laila was sitting exactly as he had left her, slumped at the table, picking at her blouse like a little girl. A stray sunbeam found its way in through the window and touched her hair; it shone for a brief moment with a golden glow. Against all expectation Lennart was gripped by a sudden tenderness. He saw her loneliness. Their loneliness.

Quietly he sat opposite her and took her hand across the table. A few seconds passed. The house was still after the natural disaster that was Jerry. But there had been another time. Another life. Lennart allowed himself to rest in his memories for a moment, thinking about how everything could have been different.

Laila straightened up a fraction. 'What are you thinking about?'

'Nothing. Just that we...maybe there's a chance.'

'Of what?'

'I don't know. Something.'

Laila withdrew her hand and started rubbing at a button on her blouse. 'Lennart. Whatever you say, we cannot keep that child. I'm going to ring social services, and we'll see what they have to say. What we need to do.'

Lennart put his head in his hands. Without raising his voice he said, 'Laila. If you so much as touch that telephone, I will kill you.'

Laila's lips twitched. 'You've said that before.'

'I meant it then. And I mean it now. If you'd...carried on with what you were doing, I would have done the same thing as I will do now if you make a call or speak to anyone. I will go down into the cellar and I will fetch the axe. Then I will come up here and hit you on the head with it until you are dead. I don't care what happens after that. It doesn't matter.'

The words flowed from his mouth like pearls. He was perfectly calm, utterly lucid, and he meant every word he said. It was a wonderful feeling, and his headache disappeared as if someone had pressed a button. The gauntlet had been thrown down, everything that needed saying had been said and there was nothing to add.

Life could begin again. Possibly.

6

Lennart and Laila.

It wasn't exactly a match made in heaven.

Perhaps some of you might remember 'Summer Rain' from 1969. It managed to get to number five in the Swedish chart, and it's probably on one of those compilation albums you can pick up in the supermarket for next to nothing.

When they first got together in 1965, and also started to work together musically, they simply called themselves Lennart & Laila, until they changed their name in 1972. They had a couple more songs that just nudged the bottom of the charts, enough to get them quite a few gigs, but they never really took off.

Then they got a new manager. He was twenty years younger than his predecessor, and the first piece of advice he gave them was to change their name. The old one sounded like a hokey downmarket version of Ike and Tina Turner, and the business of listing names had gone as far as it could go with Dave Dee, Dozy, Beaky, Mick and Titch. No; now it was all about something short and clever.

And so from 1972 onwards, Lennart and Laila went by the name of The Others. Lennart liked the feeling of coming from the outside, coming up from below, that was inherent in the name. Laila hated it and thought it was stupid. They didn't play the kind of music it suggested: they were more like The Lindberg Sisters than The Who, and they had no plans to smash up their acoustic guitars on stage.

But The Others it was, and it suited Lennart perfectly, because he wanted a fresh start. He had written a few songs that broke out of the old straitjacket with harmonies that put them somewhere between the Swedish chart stuff and 'Top of the Pops'. Something new—and what could signal a new direction more clearly than a new name? He shrugged off Lennart & Laila like an old raincoat and settled down to write their debut album.

By the spring of 1973, the album had been recorded and pressed. When Lennart held the first copy in his hands, he felt prouder than ever before. It was the first record he had made where he was happy with every one of the tracks.

The first single was 'Tell Me', a subtle hybrid of the classic Swedish dance band sound—saxophone, three chords—mixed with Beatles-style sections in a minor key, and a bridge that was almost like a folk song. It was a sure-fire Swedish chart hit, but so much more at the same time. Something for everyone.

At the beginning of May it was played on the radio for the first time, along with three other songs tipped to make the Swedish chart the following week: Thorleifs, Streaplers, Tropicos. And The Others. Lennart shed a few tears. It wasn't until he heard the song on the radio that he realised how good it really was.

A couple of days later he and Laila had a gig booked. The promoter had asked them to used their old name, because that was what people were familiar with. Lennart had no objections; he saw it as a farewell to old times. From Sunday onwards they would be singing a new song, in more ways than one.

So they left Jerry, who was seven years old at the time, with Laila's parents and drove the tour bus down to the park in Eskilstuna. It wasn't a major gig, just the two of them, Tropicos, and some local talent called Bert-Görans.

They had played with Tropicos on a couple of occasions in the past, and knew both Roland, the lead singer, and the rest of the lads in the band. There was a fair amount of back-slapping and congratulation aimed in Lennart's direction, because they all listened to the Swedish top twenty. Lennart managed to force out something positive about Tropicos' latest song, 'A Summer Without You', even though it sounded exactly the same as everything else. They didn't even write their own songs.

The evening went without a hitch. Lennart & Laila were even given the final spot, which meant that they had one up on Tropicos, so to speak, and they performed with considerable verve. Laila sang better than ever, perhaps because she knew it was a kind of swan song. Lennart had explained that they would never play these songs again, so as Laila tugged at the heartstrings with the final notes of 'Summer Rain' which ended their set, several members of the audience had tears in their eyes, and the applause was unusually enthusiastic.

Lennart had considered finishing off by mentioning that they would be called The Others from now on, and 'don't forget to listen in on Sunday', but in light of the applause it just seemed petty. He allowed Laila to have her swan song in peace.

Afterwards they had a few beers and a bit of a party. Lennart got talking to Göran, the guitarist with Bert-Görans, who also had greater musical ambitions than the rigid chart formula usually allowed. He expressed great admiration for Lennart's skilful interweaving of listener-friendly dance band tunes with what he called, 'more continental elements'. He was convinced this was the way forward, and they raised a glass to Lennart's future success.

When Lennart went to buy the next round, he couldn't find his wallet. He asked Göran to wait and hurried back to the other room, purring like a cat inside. He couldn't help it, there was something special about being praised by someone who actually knew what they were talking about. And Göran had proved himself to be a pretty good guitarist, so surely it was just possible that...

Lennart opened the door and his life was kicked in a completely different direction. He was looking Laila straight in the face as she stood there, bent over a table, her fingers spread wide. Behind her was Roland with his trousers around his ankles and his face turned up towards the ceiling as if he were suffering some kind of cramp.

Lennart had obviously disturbed them at a critical moment, because when Laila caught sight of him and launched herself across the table in a reflexive door-closing motion, Roland groaned as he was wrenched out of her. He grabbed hold of his cock, but couldn't manage to stop the ejaculation; the semen spurted, arching across the room to land on a make-up mirror. Lennart watched the sticky fluid work its way down towards a jar of fake tan which presumably belonged to Roland.

He looked at Laila. The fingers with the bright red nails still clutched the table, and a couple of strands of her hair had stuck to her cheeks. He looked at Roland and Roland looked...tired. As if he just wanted to lie down and go to sleep. His hand was still holding his stiff cock. It was bigger than Lennart's. Much bigger.

As Lennart slammed the door shut, all he could see in his mind's eye was Roland's cock. It followed him along the corridor, out into the car park, into the car. He switched on the windscreen wipers as if he were seeking some physical help to erase the image, but the cock forced its way through, violating him. It was that big.

He had never seen an erect penis other than his own. He had thought he was pretty much OK. Now he knew this wasn't the case. He tried to think what it might feel like to have a...a pole like that thrust inside you. It was difficult to imagine that it would be a pleasant experience, but Laila's face, in the brief second it took her to switch from enjoyment to terror, had told a different story. He had never seen that expression on her face. He didn't have the necessary tool to evoke it.

The wipers squeaked against the dry windscreen, and Lennart switched them off. The cock had gone, replaced by Laila's face. So pretty. So bloody pretty and so desirable. So ugly in its contorted ecstasy. He felt as if he were being ripped in two. He wanted to start the car and drive somewhere, lie down in a ditch with a bottle of whisky and die. Instead he just sat there, his arms locked around his stomach, rocking, and whimpering like a puppy.

After ten minutes the passenger door opened. Laila got in and sat down. She had tidied her hair. They sat next to one another in silence for a while. Lennart carried on rocking back and forth, but had stopped whimpering. Eventually Laila said, 'Can't you hit me or something?'

Lennart shook his head, and a sob escaped from his lips. Laila placed a hand on his knee. 'Please? Can't you just slap me a couple of times? It's OK.'

It was an ordinary Wednesday night and people were starting to leave the car park. Cheerful revellers strolled by. Someone spotted Laila in the car and waved. She waved back. Lennart glared at her hand, resting on his knee, then pushed it away. 'Has this happened before?'

'What do you mean? With Roland?'

An icy stalactite detached itself in the area between Lennart's chest and throat, tumbled down through the empty space in the centre of his body and shattered in his stomach. Something in her tone.

'With others?'

Laila folded her hands in her lap and sat in silence, watching a lone woman tottering along on too-high heels. Then she sighed and said, 'So don't you want to hit me, then?'

Lennart started the car.

The next three days were almost unbearable. They couldn't talk, so they kept busy. Lennart did little chores in the garden and Laila went running. Jerry went from one to the other, trying to lighten the atmosphere by telling Bellman stories, but all he got in response were sorrowful smiles.

Running was Laila's way of keeping fit, keeping slim and supple 'for you and the audience', as she had once said. The day after the gig Lennart was oiling the garden furniture as Laila passed him, wearing her blue windbreaker. He put the brush down and followed her with his gaze. The trousers and jacket were unnecessarily tight, and her long blonde hair was caught up in a pony-tail that bounced up and down on her back as she jogged along the village road.

He knew what this was all about. She was on her way to an assignation of some sort. A man was waiting for her in the bushes somewhere. In a little while she would meet him there and then they would be at it like rabbits. Or perhaps she just enjoyed running along in her tight clothes, making sure men were looking at her. Or perhaps it was both. She got them to look at her, then she ran into their houses and let them screw her, one after the other.

The oil splashed everywhere as Lennart slapped it onto the garden table with his brush. Back and forth, back and forth. In and out, in and out. The pictures flickered and excited, constricting his lungs and making it hard to breathe. He was going mad. That's the kind of thing people say, but it really did feel like that. His consciousness was standing on the threshold of a dark room. Inside there was oblivion, silence and—right in the corner—a little music box that played 'Auld Lang Syne'. He would sit in the darkness and turn the handle around and around, until he fell asleep forever.

But he kept oiling the table and when he finished the table he started on the chairs and when he finished the chairs Laila came home, red and sweaty from all the big cocks she had been riding. While she was stretching he secretly looked over her running clothes, searching for damp or dried-in stains. They were there if he wanted to see them, but he didn't want to see them, so instead he looked at the half-rotten porch step and decided to build a new one.

Sunday. The Swedish chart countdown.

Lennart woke up with butterflies in his stomach, which was a welcome change from the demons that had been tearing at his guts for the past few days. As he got out of bed he felt only ordinary honest-to-goodness nervousness. This was the day when The Others would step into the limelight. This was the day when he and Laila should have been sitting here holding hands, waiting expectantly for eleven o'clock when the countdown began.

That wasn't going to happen, so instead he set to work ripping up the old porch step. He struggled and wrenched with the crowbar until five to eleven, when Laila came out with the small battery-operated radio and sat down at the table next to him.

Apart from the utterly silent drive home from Eskilstuna, this was the first time since the incident that they had even sat near each other. Jerry was at a friend's birthday party, so there was no chance of him disturbing the moment. Lennart kept on working, while Laila sat with her hands on her knees, watching him. They heard the familiar theme tune, and a drop of sweat dripped from Lennart's armpit and ran down his side.

'Fingers crossed,' said Laila.

'Mmm,' said Lennart, attacking some nails so rusty the heads came off when he applied the crowbar.

'It's a wonderful song,' said Laila. 'I might not have told you properly, but it's a fantastic song.'

'Right,' said Lennart.

He couldn't help himself; Laila's words of praise did mean something to him after all. He couldn't quite see how they were going to move on, but at least they were sitting here waiting for their song. That had to mean something.

A couple of songs that were bubbling under were mentioned, then the presenter went through the chart. Number ten, nine, eight, seven, six. Lasse Berghagen, Hootenanny Singers and so on. Same old stuff. Lennart had heard them all dozens of times. Then it came. His heart started pounding wildly as he heard Kent Finell say, 'And at number five we have this week's only new entry…'

Lennart held his breath. The birds fell silent in the trees. The bees sat motionless on their flowers, waiting.

'"A Summer Without You" by Tropicos!'

The usual four notes that sounded just like any other song. Laila said, 'What a shame!' but Lennart didn't hear her. He stared at a rotten plank of wood and felt something inside him take on the same consistency as it shrivelled and died. Somewhere in the space outside him someone was singing:

> What do sunshine and warmth mean to me

When I know this will be a summer without you.

Roland. It was Roland who was singing. Tropicos. Number five. Highest new entry. Would keep on climbing. The Others. Nothing. Hadn't made the chart. No fresh start. It was sinking in.

Without you, what's a summer without you…

The world wasn't ready. All he could do was accept that fact. A calmness bordering on physical numbness came over Lennart. He glanced at Laila. Her eyes were closed as she listened to Roland's voice. The hint of a smile played on her lips.

She's listening to his voice and thinking about his cock.

Laila opened her eyes and blinked. But it was too late. He had seen. Suddenly he felt his arm jerk. The crowbar swung in a wide arc and landed on Laila's knee. She gasped and opened her mouth to scream.

It had just happened, he had had no control over the movement; he didn't feel he could be blamed for it at all. But then something changed. With Laila's squeal of pain and surprise, Lennart stood up and raised the crowbar again. This time he knew exactly what he was doing. This time he took aim.

He slammed the flat end of the crowbar down again, full force, on the same knee. There was a moist crunching sound and, as Lennart lowered the crowbar, blood began to trickle down Laila's shin and every scrap of colour left her face. She tried to get up, but her leg gave way beneath her and she collapsed at his feet, holding up her hands to defend herself and whispering, 'Please, please, no, no…'

Lennart looked at the bleeding knee; a considerable quantity of blood had gathered under the skin, and only a thin trickle was escaping where the skin had broken. He spun the crowbar around half a turn and brought it down once more with the sharp end.

This time things went well. The knee burst like a balloon filled with water, and the kneecap splintered to one side to release a cascade of blood, splashing all over Lennart's legs, the garden table, the demolished porch step.

Perhaps it was just as well that Laila stopped screaming and fainted at that point, otherwise Lennart might well have continued with the other knee. He had in fact realised what he was doing. He was putting an end to Laila's running. An end to staying slim 'for you and the audience' and all those men waiting in the bushes.

In order to make completely sure, he ought to smash the other knee as well. But as Lennart stood there looking down at his wife's inert body, the kneecap that was no more than a mass of cartilage, splintered bone and blood, he decided that was probably enough.

He would be proved right.

7

The room in the cellar had grown warmer and had reached a pleasant temperature, but the air was still damp, and the window up at ground level was covered in condensation. The girl was lying in her basket, gazing at the ceiling with big eyes. Lennart turned back the blankets and picked her up. She didn't make a sound, didn't react to the change in any way.

He held the giraffe before her eyes, moving it back and forth. She followed it for a second, then went on staring straight ahead. Presumably she wasn't blind. Lennart clicked his fingers loudly right next to her ear and her forehead wrinkled a fraction. Not deaf either. But she was so curiously...closed off.

What's happened to her?

He felt the girl was a little older than he had first thought, perhaps two months old. In two months a person can experience enough to instinctively formulate a strategy for survival. Perhaps the girl's strategy had been to make herself invisible. Not to be seen, not to be heard, not to make any demands.

Clearly the strategy hadn't worked. She had been dumped in the forest, and she would be lying there still if Lennart hadn't happened to be passing. He held her gently, looked into her bottomless eyes and talked to her.

'You're safe now, Little One. You don't have to be afraid. I'll look after you, Little One. When I heard you singing, it was as if...as if there was a chance. For me too. I've done bad things, you see, Little

One. Things I regret, things I wish I could undo. And yet I keep on doing them. Out of habit. Things have just turned out that way. Can't you sing for me, Little One? Can't you sing for me like you did before?'

Lennart cleared his throat and sang an A. The note bounced off the room's bare cement walls, and he could hear for himself that it wasn't absolutely pure. In the same way that you can't just pick up a pen and draw the picture you have in your head—unless you have a talent for that kind of thing—his voice couldn't produce the perfect pitch he could hear inside his head. But it was close enough.

The girl's mouth opened and Lennart held the note, moving so that his mouth was aligned with hers, sending his own imperfect note into her as he looked into her eyes. She began to tremble in his hands. No, not tremble. Vibrate. Something happened to the sound inside the room, and his note sounded different. He was running out of breath, and it was only when his own note began to fade out that he realised what had happened. The girl had responded with an A an octave lower. It ought to be impossible for a small child to produce such a low note, and the sound was slightly alarming. The girl was using her body like a sound box; she was like a purring cat, emitting a pure note in a register which should have been inaccessible to her.

When Lennart fell silent so did the girl, and her body stopped vibrating. He held her close and kissed her cheek as tears welled in his eyes. He whispered in her ear, 'I almost thought I'd imagined the whole thing, Little One. Now I know different. Are you hungry?'

He held her in front of him again. There was nothing in her face to indicate a desire for anything. He squeezed her chest tentatively. He just couldn't understand how she had been able to produce such a low note. The closest he could come up with was a purring cat, using its entire body as a sound box. But cats don't purr in sine waves.

You are a gift. You have been given to me.

Lennart checked the girl's nappy, put her back down and tucked her in. Then he went off to the storeroom to dig out Jerry's old cot.

8

For the first few days after Lennart came home with the baby, Laila waited for the knock on the door, the phone call, the uniformed men forcing their way into the house and asking questions before carting her off to a cell, possibly a padded one.

After a week she began to relax. On the few occasions when someone did ring, she still picked up the receiver cautiously, as if she were afraid of what was on the other end, but she was gradually beginning to accept that nobody was coming for the child.

Lennart spent a lot of time down in the cellar and, even though Laila was glad he had less energy to spare for stomping around in a bad mood, it still gnawed at her. She was constantly aware of the child's presence, and kept wondering what Lennart was actually doing. He had never been particularly fond of children.

Despite the fact that it hurt her knee—these days more metal parts than organic tissue—she made her way down the cellar steps now and again to see how the child was getting on. Lennart received her politely, while his body language made it clear that she was disturbing them.

She wasn't allowed to speak in the room. If she sat down, Lennart would place his forefinger on his lips and shush her as soon as she tried to say something. His explanation was that this time the child was not to be 'talked to pieces'.

Sometimes when she opened the door leading to the cellar she heard notes. Scales. Every time she just stood there, dumbstruck.

Lennart's tenor blending with another, higher voice, as clear as water, tinkling like glass. The child's voice. She had never heard anything like it, never heard *tell* of anything like it.

But still. Still.

It was a *child* they were dealing with here. A child shouldn't be lying in a cellar with scale exercises as its only source of stimulation.

Lennart still had quite a lot of work as a songwriter, and sometimes his presence was required in the studio when songs were being recorded. Such an occasion arose ten days after the child had ended up in their care.

Lennart usually thought it was fun to travel into Stockholm, to re-enter for a while the world that should have been his, but this time he was reluctant to go.

'You go,' said Laila. 'I'll take care of the girl.'

'I don't doubt that. The question is *how* you'll take care of her.'

Lennart was pacing around the kitchen with his leather jacket over his arm, the leather jacket that was reserved for trips of this kind; it was presumably intended as some kind of armour. Or else he needed to look tough, and found the jacket helped.

'What do you mean?'

'You'll talk. Talk and talk. I know you.'

'I'm not going to talk.'

'What are you going to do, then?'

Laila took the jacket and held it up so Lennart could put it on. 'I'm going to feed her and change her nappy and make sure she's all right.'

When Lennart had gone, Laila wandered around the house for a while doing little jobs, because she wanted to be certain he hadn't forgotten anything and wasn't coming back. After twenty minutes she opened the cellar door and went down the steps.

The girl was lying in Jerry's cot looking at a mobile of brightly coloured plastic animals. She was too pale and too thin. Too lifeless. No pink roses in her cheeks, no seeking, questing movements with her hands.

'Poor little soul,' said Laila. 'You don't have much fun, do you?' She picked the girl up and limped over to the storeroom. On the bottom shelf she found the box of winter clothes. She pulled out Jerry's first snowsuit and felt a lump in her throat as she dressed the child. A woolly hat with ear flaps completed the outfit.

'There we are, you poor little soul. Don't you look lovely now?'

She was snivelling as she made her way over to the cellar door and unlocked it. The little bundle in her arms brought back memories. Lennart could say what he liked, but she had loved Jerry. She had loved having a child to take care of, someone who needed her protection, someone who couldn't manage on their own. Perhaps it wasn't the best or most adult motivation, but she had done the best she could.

She opened the door and stepped out at the bottom of a flight of cement steps, taking in a deep breath of the chilly autumn air. The girl screwed up her face, and she opened her mouth as if to taste this new air. It seemed as if she were breathing a little more deeply. Laila crept up a few steps and peered out across the lawn.

Pull yourself together, Laila. You're crazy.

Their garden was secluded, and even if someone *did* catch a glimpse of the child or heard a cry, what did it matter? It wasn't as if the child had been kidnapped. It wasn't being hunted all over Sweden, she had checked the papers. Nothing about a missing baby. If Laila Cederström walked around her garden with a baby in her arms, people's natural reaction would be to come up with a reasonable explanation, not to hurl themselves at the nearest telephone.

Laila took the steps one at a time and went over to the lilac arbour in the furthest corner of the garden, then sat down on the bench with the child on her knee. It had been a wet, mild autumn, and the lilac leaves hadn't even begun to curl, let alone drop. They were sitting in a protective three-quarter circle of greenery, and Laila was able to relax.

Then she took the girl for a short walk around the sheltered parts of the garden, showing her the herb garden, the gooseberry bushes and the apples—yellow Astrakhans ripe for the picking. The girl's expression grew more lively the longer they stayed out, and her cheeks began to acquire a healthy pink glow.

When it started to drizzle, they went back to the house. Laila made up a bottle of formula and settled down in the armchair with the girl on her lap. The child slurped down the milk in just a few minutes, then fell asleep in Laila's arms.

Laila walked around the house with her for a while, just for the sheer pleasure of carrying the warm, relaxed little body. Then the telephone rang. Instinctively Laila clutched the child more closely. She looked at the telephone. It wasn't looking at her. It couldn't see her. She loosened her grip and the telephone rang again.

Agitated by the noise, she limped over to the cellar door and down to the girl's room as the telephone continued to ring up in the kitchen. It didn't stop ringing until she had tucked the child in and placed the giraffe next to her. Laila sat for a while, looking at the girl through the bars of the cot. Even when she was asleep there was something concentrated or watchful about her expression. Laila wished she could make it disappear.

Sleep well, little star.

The telephone rang again; it rang seven times before she managed to get back to the kitchen to pick it up. It was Lennart, and he wasn't happy.

'Where the hell have you been?'

'In the cellar.'

'Well, you can hear the phone down there, can't you?'

'I was feeding her.'

Lennart fell silent. That was obviously the correct answer. His voice was gentler as he asked, 'So did she take it?'

'She certainly did. A whole bottle.'

'And did she fall asleep then?'

'Yes. Straight away.'

Laila sat down on a chair and closed her eyes. *This is a perfectly normal conversation. A man and a woman are talking about a child. It happens all the time.* Her body felt so strangely light, as if in the short walk around the garden she had shed twenty kilos.

'So everything's all right then?' asked Lennart.

'Yes. Everything's fine.'

Laila could hear a door opening in the background at Lennart's end. The tone of his voice altered as he said, 'OK, good. I'll be a few hours, things are a bit tricky here.'

'No problem,' said Laila. A little smile curled around her lips. 'No problem at all.'

9

Lennart was very busy that autumn. He had to go into Stockholm at least once a week, and at home he spent a great deal of time at his keyboard. Lizzie Kanger, a singer who had had a minor breakthrough with the Eurovision Song Contest, was about to release a follow-up to her debut album, which had been panned. The record company had asked Lennart to 'tidy up' the songs that had already been written.

Lennart wrote new songs, retaining just enough phrases from the old crap for the contracted songwriter to accept the devastation of his original creation.

He knew exactly what he was letting himself in for. At the very first meeting with the record company they had played him a song he had been unable to avoid hearing on the radio all summer:

> Summer in the city, nineteen ninety,
> Do you remember me?

Some middle manager had switched off the DAT player and said, 'We were thinking of something along those lines.'

Lennart smiled and nodded, while his mind's eye conjured a desert with skeletons reaching out, screaming for help.

It would have been a terrible autumn if he hadn't had the time he spent with the girl to look forward to. Sitting there with her on his knee, her crystal clear voice responding to his practice scales, he felt he was in touch with something bigger. Not just bigger than his wretched keyboard fripperies, but bigger than life itself.

The music. She was *the music*. The real music.

Lennart had always believed that everyone was born with a musical talent. It was simply there. But what happened was that they were force-fed crap from an early age, and they got hooked. In the end they believed that the crap was all there was, that that was how it was supposed to sound. If they heard anything that wasn't crap, they thought it sounded weird, and switched to another radio station.

The girl was living proof that he was right. Of course, babies were not normally able to express the unspoilt music that existed inside them, but she could. He didn't want to believe that it was only by chance she had ended up with him. There had to be a purpose.

Another source of relief was that Laila seemed happier than she had been for some considerable time. Occasionally he even heard her humming to herself as she moved around the house. Mostly old pop songs, of course, but he actually like hearing her voice as he sat at his keyboard sweating over yet another three-chord tune he was trying to smarten up by inserting a surprising minor chord, even though it did feel like putting an evening jacket on a pig.

However, every rose has a thorn.

One evening when Lennart had been in the boiler room stoking up the fire for the last time and was on his way to the girl's room to get her ready for the night, he heard a sound. He stopped by the half-open door to the girl's room and listened. Very, very faintly he could hear the girl's voice as she lay in her cot...humming. When Lennart had been standing there for a while he began to pick out a melody he recognised, but was unable to place. Odd words that fitted the melody flickered through his mind.

Glances...something...eyes

Lennart refused to believe his ears. But it was impossible to deny it. The girl was lying there humming 'Strangers in the Night'. Lennart opened the door and walked in. The humming stopped abruptly.

He picked up the girl and looked into her unfathomable eyes, which never seemed to be looking into his, but at a point far beyond him. He realised what was going on. It wasn't actually 'Strangers in the Night' he had heard, but 'Tusen och en natt', Lasse Lönndahl's saccharine Swedish version of the same song. One of Laila's favourites.

This is how it happens.

The fact that it was totally unreasonable for a baby to be able to remember and reproduce a tune was something that didn't even cross Lennart's mind. The girl had already crossed so many boundaries when it came to music that he had grown used to it, but...

This is how it happens.

Crap has an astonishing ability to find its mark. It doesn't matter how carefully you try to enclose and protect. The crap seeps in through the gaps, through the cracks you have forgotten to fill. And then it takes over.

Lennart put the girl down on the straw mat, where she began clumsily hitting out at the colourful blocks Laila had put there. Lennart cleared his throat and began to sing quietly, 'O Värmland, thou art beautiful...' The girl took no notice of him; she simply carried on hitting the blocks until they were all out of reach.

10

It was a mild winter, and Laila was able to continue her outdoor excursions with the child well into December. At the beginning of January there was a cold snap with snow, and it was the snow rather than the cold that prevented her from going out when Lennart was away. She didn't want to leave any tracks.

Lennart had strictly forbidden her from having any contact whatsoever with the child, beyond what was absolutely necessary. She was not allowed to talk, or sing, or make any noise at all. The child was to live in a bubble of silence, apart from the singing practice which Lennart conducted with her. Laila had understood the aim of his project and thought it was completely insane, but since she was able to offer the child small oases of normality, she left him to it.

One afternoon she was sitting watching as the child played, or whatever it was she did. The girl had learned to grip things, and would sit there for ages with the same coloured block, picking it up and dropping it, picking it up and dropping it.

Laila tried to give her one of the soft toys she had brought out of storage. A little fox came bobbing along, 'Here comes Freddy Fox, sniff sniff sniff...but what's *this* he can smell?'

The girl was completely uninterested, and took no notice whatsoever of Freddy, even when he nudged her thigh with his nose. Instead she grabbed hold of her block once again, lifted it up to eye level and looked at it, dropped it, and watched carefully as it fell and rolled away. When it ended up out of reach, she simply waited until

Laila handed it back to her. Then she carried on picking it up and dropping it.

The next day when Lennart had shut himself in the studio, Laila called the childcare centre in Norrtälje.

'Erm, I have a question about...my child. She's almost six months old and I was just wondering about her behaviour.'

'How old is she exactly?'

Laila coughed and said, 'Five months. And three weeks. And I was wondering...she doesn't really react when...if you try to play with her, that sort of thing. She won't look, she just...she's got a block that she picks up and drops. And that's virtually all she does. Is that normal?'

'You say she doesn't react; if you touch her and try to attract her attention, how does she react then?'

'Not at all. She's only...how can I put this...she's only interested in inanimate objects. That's all she wants to do.'

'Well, it's difficult to make any kind of assessment over the telephone, but I would suggest that you bring her in so that we can have a look at her. Have you been here before?'

'No.'

'So which centre have you been attending, then?'

Laila's head was suddenly completely empty, and she said the first thing that came into her mind. 'Skövde.'

'Mmm. If I can just take her ID number, we'll see if we can—'

Laila slammed the phone down as if it had burnt her hand, then she sat and stared at it for thirty seconds before picking it up again. The dial tone. No voice was pursuing her, and she went through the conversation in her mind. The critical point was *but*.

It's difficult to make any kind of assessment over the telephone, but *I would suggest...*

Her fears were not groundless. That *but* meant something wasn't as it should be. Besides which, no doubt the staff at the childcare centre were very careful about what they said, so as not to frighten insecure parents.

When Lennart emerged from his home studio, Laila tried to raise the issue with him. Of course she didn't dare tell him she had made the phone call, so she had only her own vague observations to go on, which got her precisely nowhere. Lennart might possibly agree that the girl was unusually passive, but was that really a cause for complaint?

'Do you want her to be like Jerry? Getting up five or six times a night because he was lying there bawling his head off?'

It wasn't Lennart who had got up five or six times a night, but Laila didn't pursue that detail. Instead she said, 'I just wish we could get her checked out somehow.'

She saw the muscles in his jaw tense. She was approaching the danger zone. Lennart clasped his hands tightly together as if to prevent himself from doing something with them, and said, 'Laila. For the last time. If one single person finds out that we've got her, they will take her away from us. Stop thinking about all that, there's no chance. And besides...if it is what you think, if there is something wrong with her, what do you imagine they can do? Are they going to give her drugs? Put her in some kind of clinic? What is it you actually want?'

This final question was entirely rhetorical, and was actually a statement: *you are such a stupid bitch.* Lennart's hands were opening and closing, and Laila didn't say another word.

He had a point, anyway. What did she actually want? Did she want the child to have some kind of medical care? Drugs? No. All she really wanted, when she thought about it, was for someone who knew what they were talking about to look at the girl and tell her everything was all right. Or that it wasn't all right, but that the problem was called so-and-so, and there was nothing they could do. Just so she knew.

Two weeks later, Lennart went into the city for the final mix of the album. The snow had melted, but the temperature had dropped below freezing again and the garden was covered in ice in places; Laila wouldn't leave any footprints.

And the girl needed to get out.

The times when Laila dressed the girl for an outing were little special occasions. As she busied herself with the child's top, trousers, snowsuit and hat she felt a closeness to her that was otherwise missing. As she rolled up the tiny socks and put them on the child's equally tiny feet, she even allowed herself to formulate the thought: *I love you, Little One.*

It wasn't that she was indifferent to the child on a day-to-day basis, but there was never any response to the feelings she expressed. At best the child might explore Laila's face with her fingers, but she did it in the same way as she did everything else: methodically, almost scientifically. As if she were trying to understand how this particular object worked.

Perhaps that was why the business of dressing the child created a perception of mutual understanding. As Laila gently pushed the slender limbs into the snowsuit and slipped on her mittens, she was treating the girl like an object. Gently handling something that needed to be protected.

She carried the girl to the door and put her down on the step. The ice crunched beneath their feet as Laila held the girl's hands above her head so that she was half walking, half being carried up the steps.

The garden was covered in ice and lumps of frozen snow. Laila manoeuvred the girl towards the lilac arbour, its branches now bare of leaves. 'See this, Little One? This is ice.'

They hadn't got round to giving the girl a name. They had discussed the matter, but since she wasn't going to be christened and nobody had got in touch to demand a name, they hadn't come to a decision. Laila had heard Lennart say 'Little One' as well when he spoke to the girl on one occasion, and that was as far as they had got.

They sat for a while on the bench in the arbour. Laila gave the girl sticks and dry leaves to examine. Then they went for a little walk. The child's unsteady legs had difficulty with the conditions underfoot, and the cold made Laila's knee stiff, so they shuffled along a little bit at a time.

They were perhaps twenty metres from the house when Laila heard the sound of an engine. She had heard it often enough to recognise it. Jerry's motorbike.

She heaved the child up into her arms and staggered towards the cellar steps. She had managed ten metres when a sharp pain stabbed through her knee. She slipped on a patch of ice and fell forward. As she fell, she managed to twist to the side so that she landed on her shoulder instead of on top of the girl. Her head snapped downwards and hit the ice; everything went dark red before her eyes, and the girl slid out of her arms.

From inside the red veil she could hear the motorbike coming closer, and then the engine was switched off. The side stand clicked down and footsteps approached. A patch of light grew inside the redness and continued to grow until she could see the snow and the ice and the girl's blue woolly hat once more. Jerry's biker boots entered her field of vision and stopped.

'What the fuck are you doing, Mother? And who's that?'

II

Lennart was in the car on his way home. He wasn't dissatisfied, which was unusual. Normally he was more or less furious after a studio session or a meeting in Stockholm. But this time things had gone his way.

A new producer had come on board for the final phase of the album. When Lennart first saw the young lad ambling around the studio in his yellow shades, all hope had drained from his body. But surprise surprise, the new guy liked Lennart's stuff, called it 'updated Motown sound' and 'a fantastic vintage vibe'. He had picked up two tracks that had been recorded but weren't going to be included, and Lennart was now down as the composer of three of the tracks on the album. One of Lennart's songs was actually under consideration as the first single.

So Lennart didn't even pull a face when he saw Jerry's motorbike parked outside the house; not so much as a small sigh escaped him. He was temporarily wrapped in a protective cloak. He was a *composer*, and was above the trials of everyday life.

He and Laila had been married for twenty-five years, and had lived in the same house for almost as long. As soon as he closed the door behind him and began to undo his shoes, he could feel that something was different. Something had altered in the atmosphere of the house, but he didn't know what it was.

When he walked into the kitchen, he had his answer. Laila was sitting there. And Jerry. And on Jerry's knee sat the girl. Lennart stood in the doorway and the protective cloak fell around his feet. Laila looked at him with a pleading expression, while Jerry pretended to be unaware of his presence, grabbing the girl under the arms and lifting her above his head while saying, 'Toot, toot, toot.'

'Be careful,' said Lennart. 'She's not a toy.'

How much had Laila told him? Lennart waved at her and said, 'Laila, come here,' whereupon he turned on his heel and headed for the studio, where they could talk undisturbed. But Laila didn't follow him.

When he came back into the kitchen, Jerry said, 'Don't start, Dad. Sit down.'

Lennart walked over to Jerry and held out his arms for the child. Jerry didn't hand her over. 'Sit down, I said.'

'Give her to me.'

'No. Sit down.'

Lennart couldn't believe this was happening. 'Is this some kind of...hostage situation, or what?'

Jerry laid his cheek against the girl's. 'This is my little sister, for fuck's sake. Well, nearly. Can't I spend some time with her?'

Lennart perched on the very edge of the chair, ready to leap to his feet if Jerry tried anything. It was many years since Lennart had thought he had the slightest idea what went on inside Jerry's head. He was afraid of him, as we are afraid of everything unknown and therefore unpredictable.

The girl looked small and fragile as she sat there wrapped in Jerry's great big arms. All he had to do was squeeze, and she would crack like an egg. It was hard to bear, and Lennart tried to speak the only language he was sure Jerry understood.

'Jerry,' he said. 'You can have five hundred kronor if you give her to me.'

Jerry looked down at the floor, apparently considering the offer. Then he said, 'Do you think I'm going to hurt her or something? Is that really what you think of me?'

The offer of money had been a mistake. If Jerry realised how much the girl meant to Lennart, the situation could only get worse. So he picked up the newspaper and pretended to be interested in the US air-raids on Iraq without even glancing at the child.

After a while Jerry said, 'She's so bloody *quiet*. I mean, she doesn't make a sound.'

Lennart carefully folded the paper and rested his hands on it. 'Jerry. What do you want?'

Jerry got up, still holding the girl in his arms. 'Nothing in particular. How long were you intending to carry on like this?' He held the girl out to Lennart, but when Lennart reached up to take her, he pulled her away and gave her to Laila.

Lennart's fingers itched but he controlled himself. 'What do you mean?'

'Keeping her hidden like this. I mean, somebody's going to find out in the end. Somebody's bound to say something.'

Lennart managed to keep his tone indifferent as he asked, 'There's just one thing puzzling me. How did you find out we had her?' He glanced at Laila, whose lips were tightly clamped together.

Jerry shrugged his shoulders. 'Just glanced through the cellar window. And there she was. Anyway. I've been thinking.'

Lennart stopped listening. There was something wrong here. Why would Jerry decide to 'just glance' through the cellar window? And anyway, could you actually see the cot properly from the window?

Jerry's hand waved in front of his eyes. 'Are you listening to me?'

'No.'

'A computer. I want a computer.'

'What for?'

'You're always complaining that I'm not interested in anything,' said Jerry. 'Well, now I am. Computers. I want a computer. A Mac.'

It had indeed been a hostage situation; it was still a hostage situation even though Jerry had handed over the child.

'How much,' Lennart asked. 'How much does one of those cost?'

'It's a Classic I have in mind,' said Jerry. 'A Macintosh Classic. Ten thousand kronor, more or less.'

'And what do I get for that?'

Jerry snorted and punched Lennart on the shoulder. 'You know what I like about you sometimes, Dad? You cut to the chase. No pissing about.' Jerry rubbed the back of his neck and thought it over. Then he said, 'A year. Or six months. Roughly. Something like that.'

'And then?'

'And then we'll see.'

Lennart hid his face in his hands and rested his elbows on the kitchen table. At some point during Jerry's worst years, Lennart had wished his son dead. Now he was doing it again. But what use was that? He heard Laila's voice beside him.

'Well, it's good if Jerry has an interest. That's what I think.'

Lennart dug his nails into his scalp and said, 'Not a word. Not one word.' Then he raised his head and turned to Jerry. 'Would you like the *home delivery service* as well?'

'Yes, that would be nice. Cool. Thanks.'

Lennart's throat was so constricted with rage that he could barely manage a whisper. 'You're welcome.'

As Jerry moved towards the door, Laila got up and handed the child to Lennart without looking at him. She went over to Jerry, lowered her head and said quietly, 'Jerry, can't I come with you?'

Jerry frowned and he looked from Laila to Lennart. Then he seemed to realise what was going on, and said, 'I couldn't give a fuck what you two get up to, actually. But let's put it this way.' He turned to Lennart. 'If you so much as touch Mother...you can forget the kid. Got it?'

It wasn't only Lennart's throat that was constricted. Every muscle in his body had been twisted into ropes and pulled as tight as possible, until they started to tremble. Jerry took a step towards him. 'I'm asking you if you've got it. You leave Mother alone. One bruise, that's all it will take. Gone. OK?'

Lennart managed to move his head up and down in a stiff nod. The child moved uneasily in his arms. Jerry stroked the girl's cheek and said, 'Toot, toot, toot.'

Then he left. Laila didn't go with him.

12

Jerry was named after Jerry Lee Lewis.

For a few years it looked as though he too would go down a musical path, hopefully without the tragic consequences suffered by Jerry Lee. Under Lennart's supervision he started to practise on a little guitar when he was five years old. By the time he was seven he was already able to move through the basic chords with ease, and produce simple rhythms.

Lennart didn't quite see himself as a Leopold with a young Wolfgang to raise, but with some decent training Jerry could well become a competent musician, and that would do nicely.

Then came the business of the Swedish charts and 'Tell Me'.

Laila never revealed that Lennart was responsible for the demolition of her knee. She said she had fallen on a sharp stone and even when she was pressed she never changed her story. She spent ten days in hospital and underwent a series of operations.

When she came home, the atmosphere in the house had changed forever. Lennart showed no regret for what he had done; instead he started to regard Laila as some kind of not-quite-human being and treated her accordingly.

He started to hit her. Not much and not often, just when he felt she had stepped outside her not-quite-human boundaries. Laila had two choices: leave or put up with it.

The years passed and since Laila never did make a decision, it was made for her. Day by day, a new skin was painted onto her body until she became the person Lennart thought she was. Half a person. Cowed.

Jerry did his guitar practice without making any significant progress, but he plodded on. In the emotional chill that pervaded his home he became skinny and introverted, like a child who is cold all the time. The bullying started at junior school. Not much and not often, but enough to make sure he knew his limits, and to keep him well within those limits.

He had just turned twelve when he discovered David Bowie or, more accurately, he discovered 'The Rise and Fall of Ziggy Stardust and the Spiders from Mars'. And if he played that record until the needle started to wear the grooves away, he played 'Starman' until it wore a hole in the vinyl.

He didn't completely understand the words, but he understood the feeling and the atmosphere, and found the whole thing a great consolation. He also wanted to believe there was someone out there waiting, someone who could put everything right. Not God, but a starman with superpowers.

As the hormones began to kick in among his classmates, the bullying moved up a gear. Humiliating Jerry in front of the girls turned into a sport among the other boys. He went deeper into himself, and clung to his only secret: the fact that he could play the guitar.

'Space Oddity' replaced 'Starman' as his favourite song. He understood every single word, and identified completely with Major Tom, who decides to cut all ties with life on earth and floats away into infinite space.

Everything could have been different. It's frightening to think how apparently insignificant events can influence the direction of our lives. If Lennart hadn't forgotten his wallet, if Tropicos hadn't been competing for a place in the chart that same Sunday and so on. Something similar happened with Jerry.

His teacher had found out that he could play the guitar. She managed to persuade him to perform in front of the class during Fun

Time one Friday. Jerry already knew 'Space Oddity' perfectly, but from the Monday onwards he practised until his fingers ached.

On Thursday evening he played and sang to Lennart and Laila. Even though they didn't like David Bowie, they sat there dumbstruck. They'd had no idea. Both of them had tears in their eyes when he played the final chord. It was perhaps the best hour they'd spent together for several years.

Jerry found it hard to sleep that night. Fantasies that were all too appealing took over his mind. This would be his vindication. Just like in the films. He had the knack of hearing and seeing himself from the outside when he played, and he knew he performed the song brilliantly. Perhaps better than Bowie. His classmates would have no choice but to acknowledge that fact.

When the time came, Jerry took his guitar out of its case; he was perfectly calm. Regardless of what his classmates thought of the song, he would show them. He would show them that he could do something, and do it well. They might carry on treating him badly, but at least he would know that they knew.

He sat down on a chair next to the teacher's desk with the guitar resting on his knee, and gazed out over the room. Sceptical expressions, scornful smirks. He struck the first chord and began to sing, hitting the first note perfectly.

A crackling sound came from the school's internal loudspeaker system. Jerry stopped playing as a voice rang out. 'Good afternoon. This is the Principal speaking. Those pupils who wish to do so may go to the main hall and watch the television; Ingemar Stenmark will be making his second run in five minutes. We will then finish school for the day. Come on Sweden!'

There was the concerted sound of scraping and clattering as twenty-two chairs were pushed back and the whole class rose as one and raced to the hall to watch the Swedish hero celebrate yet another triumph.

In thirty seconds the classroom was empty, leaving Jerry alone with the teacher. She sighed and said, 'That was a shame, Jerry. But there'll be other times. Maybe we can do it next Friday instead?'

Jerry nodded and stayed in his seat as the teacher hurried off to join the Stenmark supporters in the hall. He didn't scream, he didn't cry, he didn't set fire to the school. He got up slowly, put his guitar back in its case and gave up.

If the Alpine Skiing World Cup had been another day, if Stenmark had done his run five minutes later, if the Principal hadn't been in such a good mood…

Everything could have been different.

Jerry didn't play the following Friday, nor any other Friday. He couldn't summon up the enthusiasm again. He knew his opportunity had slipped through his fingers. Stenmark won, by the way. As always.

Jerry's remaining years at junior school were spent in the special limbo reserved for the victim of low-grade bullying. It wasn't so bad that he refused to go to school, and he wasn't sufficiently ostracised to let him feel calm when he was there. He simply stuck it out.

He stopped playing the guitar and devoted his time to comics about superheroes, glam rock and model planes. Lennart tried to force him back to music, but Jerry had a strong will, at least when it came to negatives. He flatly refused. He had shoved the guitar under his bed, and there it stayed.

The signs started to announce themselves during his last term in Year 9. Jerry's body was changing. He grew five centimetres in just a few months, and everything began to bulk up. When school finished it was as if he had been released from a press, and his body blew out in every direction.

He had to eat more just to keep up with this hothouse growth, and became a frequent visitor at the pizzeria on the main square in Norrtälje. It was there he got to know Roy and Elvis. They were two years older than Jerry and had also, improbably enough, been named after music legends. Perhaps that influenced them to let Jerry become one of the gang. Elvis, Roy and Jerry. It sounded good.

In the autumn Jerry started at the grammar school, taking mainly technical subjects. Nobody from his old class was there and he was able to make a fresh start. He was a fairly big lad with something sly in his expression; it was probably best not to mess with him.

In October Roy and Elvis initiated him into their speciality: burgling holiday houses. They would head off on their mopeds to isolated cottages with feeble locks and ransack them for anything of value, mostly garden equipment and household items that Roy sold for next to nothing to a guy he knew in Stockholm.

Sometimes they found booze, and Jerry was happy to join in with the celebration after a successful outing. Roy had his own cottage with a TV and video player, where they could drink their haul undisturbed while enjoying films like *The Driller Killer, Maniac,* and *I Spit on Your Grave.* At first the graphic violence made Jerry feel slightly ill, but that soon passed.

He wasn't sick in the head. He didn't feel the slightest desire to do those kind of things, and he thought the debate about moral harm that was raging just then was ridiculous. But somehow the films captured how it *felt.* Once he had got used to it, he felt nothing but a great sense of calm as he watched Leatherface hang the girl up on the meat hook. It was right, somehow. That was how it was. Life and everything.

His final grades in Year 9 had been less than impressive, and he had only just got into grammar school. Things were going better now. Not despite but because of his leisure activities, he felt contented with life. His homework might possibly have suffered, but on the other hand he was able to concentrate when he was in school, because he didn't have to be on his guard all the time.

He finished the year with a much better grade than anyone could have hoped for. Lennart and Laila rewarded him with a computer, a ZX81 which absorbed a great deal of his attention in the weeks after he left school. A charming little story, all in all.

Everything could have been different.

At the beginning of July he met Roy and Elvis at the pizza place as usual. Elvis was a bit agitated. A friend of a friend had been to Amsterdam and brought back a decent lump of hash; he had given Elvis a little taster.

Well, you have to try these things. Later in the evening they sat down behind a tree in the local park and, with a fair amount of difficulty, rolled a joint; they passed it around, then did it again.

Jerry thought it was fantastic. He had heard that hash made you feel heavy and dull, but he felt completely on top of the world. It might possibly be a little bit more difficult to move his body than usual, but his mind! He could see everything so clearly, he knew exactly what was what.

Arms slung around each other, they strolled off towards Love Point where people usually gathered in the evenings. They were invincible, they were the Three Musketeers, they were the entire bloody history of rock and roll in one package.

There was some kind of party going on, a gang of people about their own age sitting around a bonfire. Someone was strumming away on a guitar. In walked Los Rockers making one hell of a racket! There was no messing about, people just had to make some room for them. Roy grabbed a bottle of wine to share with his compadres.

Jerry couldn't take his eyes off the guitar. It woke something in him. His fingers began to grope in thin air, remembering the wood, the strings, the frets. He could still do it. The guitar was longing for his fingers to release the music hidden inside it...

Someone spoke. A voice was tapping away at his consciousness, saying his name. With difficulty he dragged himself out of the guitar's hypnotic power, turned his head towards the voice and said, 'What?'

Two metres away sat Mats, known as Mats the Love Machine ever since he started driving around a couple of years earlier on a souped-up moped with an imitation leopard's tail dangling from the antenna. He had once pissed on Jerry in the showers. Among other things.

Mats leaned forward and said, 'I'm talking to you: wanna play, fat boy?'

It happened so fast. Everything had been moving in slow motion for a while and now somebody had pressed fast forward. Before Jerry had time to think, he had grabbed a lump of wood that was sticking out of the fire, walked over to Mats and smashed him across the face with the burning end.

Mats fell backwards with a scream and Jerry looked at the cooling, pointed piece of wood in his hand. He looked at Mats, writhing on the ground with his hands over his face. His mind started working again, his thoughts crystal clear. He could see exactly what the situation was. Mats was in fact a vampire. Simple as that.

Which meant there was only one thing for it. He grabbed the glowing stake with both hands and drove it into Mats' chest. Sparks flew, there was a hissing sound, and by the time Elvis and Roy got hold of Jerry, Mats had already started coughing up blood like the vampire he was. Or had been.

Events that had taken perhaps fifteen seconds would define Jerry's life for a long time to come. It involved police and lawyers, social services and youth services. Mats survived; he got away with the loss of an eye, a few shattered ribs and slight damage to one lung.

But something had gone wrong inside Jerry's head during the cannabis rush, and it refused to go back to normal. In that moment of clarity when he realised he had to free the world from a repulsive blood-sucker, an insight had taken root in his mind and refused to let go when the rush subsided.

There was a truth in what he had seen.

During a meeting with the family therapist, Laila explained what had really happened to her knee. The therapist regarded this as a possible breakthrough and a chance to move on, but for Jerry it merely provided further confirmation of what he already knew: the world was evil, people were evil, and there was no point in even trying.

When all the investigations and analyses were over, Jerry had slipped so far behind in his schoolwork that he couldn't go back. Didn't want to anyway. During his absence Elvis had passed his driving test, which opened up all kinds of new possibilities.

Freed from the burden of normality, Jerry let go of any semblance of ambition. The three of them moved on from summer cottages to bigger houses, and robbed a couple of petrol stations before they got caught. Jerry got a year in a youth offenders' institution, which only served to reinforce his view of the world.

When he came out, they started again. An old man was at home in one of the houses, and they knocked him down. When he started screaming abuse at them, they kicked him a few times until he shut his mouth. This played on Jerry's conscience for a time, but it passed. He was becoming hardened.

One day when he was shaving, he caught sight of himself and looked carefully. He examined his feelings, and realised he had crossed an important line. He could kill someone without it breaking him. If necessary. That was definitely progress.

His mother and father carried on with the usual shit, and he took no notice whatsoever. They didn't want him at home anymore, but he thought it worked very well; he liked having his room as a sort of hole to crawl back into from time to time. He didn't listen to a word they said in any case.

When Jerry was twenty, Elvis went out cruising in Norrtälje, high as a kite. He lost control of his Chevy on the hill leading down to the harbour, drove straight into the water and drowned. Nothing was the same after that.

The steam went out of Roy and Jerry. They felt obliged to burgle a couple of houses, and talked about trying some post offices, but it never happened. It was no fun anymore. They drifted apart, and since Jerry was spending more time at home, he was able to hear Lennart and Laila talking. When they organised an apartment for him through social services, he moved out.

He had a few bits and pieces stashed away which he sold so that he could buy a motorbike. He got a few dead-end jobs, but never stayed more than a couple of weeks. He built up a reasonable collection of splatter films on VHS.

That's how it was, and perhaps it couldn't have been any different.

13

In the spring the year after Lennart had found the girl, something very unusual happened. Laila received an offer. A group calling themselves DDT wanted Laila as their featured singer on a dance track. At first Laila thought it was a joke, and in a way she was right. The idea was to do a Swedish version of The KLF's monster hit 'Justified and Ancient', with Laila as Sweden's answer to Tammy Wynette, singing a couple of verses to a heavy dance beat.

Laila found out later that both Lill-Babs and Siw Malmkvist had been approached and turned it down. Perhaps other legendary Swedish chart-toppers had been asked too, before they ended up with the somewhat less legendary Laila.

She had no reputation to lose and no image to maintain, so she said yes. Anything to get out of the house.

The atmosphere had soured even more since the incident with Jerry. Lennart hardly spoke to her anymore, but at least he didn't hit her. It wasn't clear what Jerry had meant when he said Lennart could 'forget the kid' if his instructions weren't followed, but the threat certainly worked. Jerry got his computer and Laila was left in peace.

But it was as if a musty blanket had settled on things. The air in the rooms felt stale and close. Laila thought that a visitor who stepped through the door would only need one sniff to know: *There's something bad here. Something sick.*

But nobody came, apart from Jerry who called in from time to time to 'check things out'. Sometimes he insisted on holding the child, bouncing it up and down on his knee and saying, 'Toot, toot.' On these occasions Lennart stood there with clenched fists, waiting until Jerry had finished so he could carry the girl back down to the cellar.

Perhaps Laila experienced the child's shut-in existence as her own; sometimes she had to go out into the garden just to breathe. So she welcomed the chance to go into Stockholm and pretend to be a singer again, if only for a while.

The track was called 'Bearing Capacity: 0', and they explained to Laila that she would be singing a deliberate parody of The KLF's nonsense. She had no idea what it was about. 'We're walking on water underground, we're setting fire to the four words. Lead. Check. Bearing capacity zero' and so on.

Her voice held, the producer was happy, and Laila caught the bus back to Norrtälje without really understanding what she had done. But it had been fun. A new environment where everybody had been nice to her; that was a novelty for a start.

In April the girl's first tooth came through. Otherwise it was as if her development had come to a standstill. She made no attempt to crawl or shuffle along. She wasn't interested in hiding games, or peep-bo. She didn't imitate actions or movements; the only thing she reciprocated was sound: notes and melodies.

Sometimes Lennart took her out into the garden at night. On the odd occasion Laila was allowed to do it she would take the opportunity to whisper and talk to the girl as much as she could. She got nothing back—not a sound.

At the end of May, 'Bearing Capacity: 0' by DDT featuring Laila was released, and nothing happened. At first. Then something did happen, and then something else happened. In June it entered the *Tracks* chart, and climbed to number seven. People starting calling, wanting to interview Laila. She was given very specific instructions from DDT's record company on what to say about the lyrics. That was what she said.

The attention made Lennart nervous, but there was no need for him to worry. In a few weeks it was over. However, it did lead to a call from an agency wanting to book Lennart and Laila for a few gigs. Lennart decided they would try one as an experiment, in Norrtälje in August. It was a motor show for vintage car enthusiasts, a mixture of a family day out and a meeting for boy racers.

'So what are we going to do with the girl?' asked Laila.

'Well, it's only in Norrtälje. She'll be OK on her own for a couple of hours. It won't be a problem.'

It was a hot afternoon in the middle of July. They were sitting at the table outside drinking coffee. Perhaps it was the unexpected success or the fact that she had been able to get out and about a bit that gave Laila courage. A very simple question had been grinding away in her head for several months. Now she put it into words.

'Lennart. What's going to happen with the girl?'

'What do you mean?'

'Well, you must have thought about it. What's going to happen in the future. She's growing. She'll be walking soon. What are we going to do with her?'

It was as if a veil came down over Lennart's eyes and he moved a long way away, even though he was still sitting at the table fingering his coffee cup.

'She's not going to be part of all that,' he said. 'She's not going to be destroyed.'

'No. But…from a purely practical point of view? How's it going to work?'

Lennart folded his arms and looked at Laila as if from a great distance.

'I'm not going to say this again. So listen carefully. We are going to keep her here. We are not going to let her out. We are going to train her so that she adapts to that way of life. She won't be unhappy, because she won't have seen anything else.'

'But why, Lennart? Why?'

With exaggerated care, Lennart raised the cup to his lips, took a sip of the lukewarm coffee and placed the cup back on the saucer without making a sound.

'I do not want to hear these questions again. I will answer you now. But never again. Is that clear?'

Laila nodded. Even Lennart's voice had changed, as if a different version of him was speaking through his mouth. A person made from a heavier material, from his solid core. There was something compelling about the voice, and Laila sat there motionless, her eyes fixed on Lennart's lips as he said:

'Because she is not an ordinary child. She will never be an ordinary child. Or an ordinary person. She is white. Completely white. The only thing the world will do to her is to destroy her. I know this. I have seen inside her. People might regard it as a bad thing, keeping a child shut in. But it's the best thing for her. I'm sure of that. She is pure music. The world is a dissonance. She would go under. Instantly.'

'So it's for *her* sake? Are you sure?'

Lennart returned to the table. As if everything was pared away at once, his expression was suddenly fragile and hesitant. A lonely child in the forest. Laila couldn't remember when she had last seen that look, and it stabbed her in the heart.

Lennart said, 'And for mine. If she disappeared...I'd kill myself. She is the last. The last chance. There is nothing after her.'

They sat motionless. The needle in Laila's heart twisted around and around. A sparrow landed on the table, pecking at a few cake crumbs. Afterwards Laila would realise that they had been standing at a crossroads, and that a decision had been made. In silence, like all important decisions.

14

His parents hadn't said a word about the gig, but Jerry had seen the posters. He had been thinking of going to the motor show to meet up with some old friends but when he saw that Lennart and Laila would be playing, he changed his mind. There was something else he would much rather do.

The gig was due to start at two o'clock. At half past one Jerry jumped on his motorbike and rode over to the house. He reckoned that his parents would need a good half hour for the sound check and at least that to pack up and drive home, so he had a couple of hours on his own in the house. He calculated that they wouldn't have taken the kid with them.

The front door was no problem; he could have opened it with a credit card in his sleep, but he'd taken a screwdriver with him just to be on the safe side. It took him ten seconds to push back the old-fashioned catch and step into the hallway. Without taking off his boots he clattered down the cellar steps, shouting, 'Toot, toot!'

He gave a start when he walked into his old room. The child was standing upright in the cot with her hands resting on the frame, staring straight at him. There was something horrible about the way that kid looked at you, as if it could see straight through everything. But it was still just a kid in a red babygro with its nappy bulging out at the back. Not exactly something to be scared of.

Jerry had understood completely what this kid meant to his father. Forty times more than he himself had ever meant. It was quite upsetting. He didn't get it. What was so special about this little bastard that just stood there staring?

When Jerry seized the child under the arms and lifted it out of the cot, it just hung there limply; it didn't even kick its legs. Jerry poked it tentatively in the stomach and said, 'Toot, toot.' Not a smile, not even the hint of a frown. Jerry poked harder, really pushed this time. Nothing. It was as if he didn't exist, as if nothing he did or said could make an impression.

Playing hard to get, are you, you little bastard?

He laid the child down on the spare bed and pinched its arm, pinched hard. The soft baby skin was squeezed together and he could feel his fingers touching through the fabric and the skin. When nothing happened he moved on to the thighs, both thighs. Hard pinches that would have had any seven-year-old screaming the place down. The kid simply carried on staring straight through him without making a sound. Jerry had had enough. He was going to get some kind of fucking reaction.

He gave the child a resounding smack across the face. *Smack.* The little head jerked to the side and the cheek began to redden. But still not a peep out of her. Sweat broke out on Jerry's hairline, and a black lamp began to glow in his chest.

OK, maybe the little bastard was deaf and dumb and fuck knows what else, but it must surely have the capacity to feel *pain*? There ought to be tears, a grimace, something. Jerry's inability to make any impression on the child made him furious. He was going to get some kind of *response.*

He picked up the child, holding her at arm's length, and took a step away from the bed. 'If I drop you on the floor, you should bloody well feel that, shouldn't you? Don't you think?' He brought the child closer and said it again, so that it would understand. 'Do you hear me? I'm going to drop you on the floor.'

He never found out if he would have done it or not. As he uttered the last word, the child's hand shot out with reptilian speed and grabbed hold of his lower lip. Its fingers burrowed in, the little nails scraping against his gums. Then it pulled.

It hurt so much that tears sprang to Jerry's eyes. Whatever his intention may have been, the pain made him drop the child. It clung to his lip for less than a second, just long enough to tear it away from the gum slightly, blood seeping into his mouth.

The child fell onto the cement floor and landed on its bottom, where it lay looking up at Jerry as he pressed his hands to his mouth, whimpering. On the bedside table there was a sippy cup in the shape of an elephant, its ears forming the handles. Jerry took off the lid and spat. Blood and saliva mingled with the milk. He sat there spitting for a while until the worst had passed. Then he tore off a piece of a paper towel, rolled it up and pushed it under his lip like an upside-down plug of tobacco.

The kid was still lying on its back, looking at him. Jerry crouched down beside it. 'OK,' he said. 'No problem. So now we know.'

He picked up the girl, taking care to keep his face out of reach of her hands, and carefully placed her back in the cot. She was utterly calm; the only thing that had changed was that she now had a small amount of blood on the tips of the fingers on her left hand.

Jerry perched on the edge of the spare bed, his elbows resting on his knees. He looked carefully at her. Despite the fact that his lip was hurting, he couldn't hold back a big smile. He was positively beaming. Suddenly he grabbed hold of the bars and rattled the cot, shaking her to and fro.

'Fuck, sis!' he said. 'Sis! Bloody hell!'

The child didn't respond, but there was no denying it: he had a sister, sort of. He liked the little bastard. She was completely crazy. Nobody was going to mess with her. She was invincible, his sister.

Jerry was in the mood for a celebration, so he clattered back up the stairs and found a bottle of whisky and a glass, then went back down to the cellar, perched on the edge of the bed, half-filled his glass and clinked it against the bars of the cot.

'Cheers, sis!'

He took a big gulp and pulled a face as the alcohol penetrated through the paper towel and touched the wound. He spat the plug out onto the floor and rinsed his mouth clean with more whisky. Then he rested his chin on his hand and looked thoughtfully at the girl.

'Do you know what your name is?' he said. 'Theres, that's what. Like that Baader-Meinhof chick. Theres.' It was crystal clear, he could hear it as he uttered the name. 'Theres. That's it.'

He topped up his glass. The child pulled herself up into a sitting position, then to her feet. She was standing as she had been when he came into the room.

'What is it?' Jerry asked. 'Do you want to taste?'

He picked up a cloth and dipped it in the glass, then held out the damp corner to Theres, who didn't open her mouth. He pushed the edge of the cloth against her lips. 'This is what they used to do in the old days, you know. Open wide.'

Theres opened her mouth, and Jerry pushed the corner of the flannel in. The girl sucked at it, then lay down. She carried on sucking away at the cloth, never taking her eyes off Jerry.

'Cheers,' he said, emptying the glass.

After ten minutes and another glass, Jerry started to get restless. He looked around the room for something to do. A sudden inspiration made him look under the bed, and lo and behold!

He got down on his knees and pulled out the guitar case. It was covered in a layer of dust, and the lock had begun to rust after several damp winters, but there it was. He opened the case and took out the guitar, weighing it in his hands.

It's so bloody small.

When he thought back to his days as a guitarist, he remembered the guitar as a great big thing on his lap; his fingers had trouble stretching to the right frets. Now it was a toy in his hands, and he had no problem whatsoever getting his hand around the neck.

He tried an E minor, and it sounded bloody awful. He struck an experimental chord and started turning the tuner on the E-string—to begin with. There was something odd about the acoustics in the room.

When he plucked the string it sounded like a double note. He let the note fade away, and put his ear to the soundboard. The resonance sounded purer. He plucked the string again, leaning his head towards the body. He didn't have Lennart's ear; he could only hear notes in relation to one another, but surely the resonance sounded purer than the note itself?

Some kind of damage from the damp.

He straightened up so that he could reach the tuners, and saw that Theres had pulled herself up in the cot. He plucked the E-string again. This time he could hear where the purer note was coming from.

No, no, no.

Just for fun he tuned the E-string to the sound Theres was making, and moved on to the B-string. When he tuned that one to the sound she made, he was able to hear that the interval was absolutely perfect. He did the same thing with G, and so on. Tuning a guitar had never been so quick. He couldn't have done it better with an electronic tuner.

He took a swig straight out of the whisky bottle and looked at Theres, who was still standing up in her cot, her cheek bright red and her face expressionless.

'You're quite a piece of work, aren't you? So what do you think about this, then?'

He tried a C. Not the note, but the chord. C, E and G. Theres' clear voice responded; it was hard to tell where the guitar ended and she began. Jerry allowed the chord to die away. Her voice lingered for a couple of seconds before it too fell silent. Jerry took another swig from the bottle and nodded to himself.

'OK,' he said. 'Let's rock.' He stamped his foot to set the beat, struck C again and launched into the first line of 'Space Oddity'.

Beside him the girl joined in with pure, wordless notes. When he changed chords it took a second before she switched to the new note. Just as well. He would have been seriously spooked if she'd *known the song* on top of everything else. But she didn't. So he played it to her, with her. Then he moved on to 'Ashes to Ashes' so she could hear the whole story.

When Jerry had sung the last lines a few times with Theres, it was as if he woke from an enchantment. He looked around the room and realised there would be a hell of a fuss when his parents got home.

He put back the whisky and shoved the boozy cloth out of sight, gathered up the blood-stained plugs of paper and poured the contents of the cup down the sink in the laundry room. Finally he put the guitar back in its case. The room looked the same as it had when he arrived.

Theres was standing in her cot, looking at him. He leaned down and sniffed at her mouth: nothing. Almost a pity, really. It would have given Lennart and Laila something to think about if the kid had been standing there reeking of Famous Grouse when they got home.

'OK, sis. See ya.'

He left. After ten seconds he came back and took the guitar.

15

The gig wasn't quite the success the promoters had hoped for, but nor was it a fiasco. The majority of the audience consisted of fairly overweight men in denim jackets and women wearing too much make-up, all about the same age as Lennart and Laila. Only a small number of young people had turned up to see the singer behind 'Bearing Capacity: 0', which was just as well, because they didn't actually have permission to use the sampling on that song.

Lennart had programmed the synthesiser as best he could, but the audience got fairly watered down versions of their old hits or attempted hits. Not unexpectedly, they got the best response to 'Summer Rain'. Four drunks in leather waistcoats stood right at the front with their arms around each other and joined in the chorus, and the applause at the end was almost enough for an encore. But not quite.

A few people came up to talk to them, and a man with his gut protruding like a weapon under his T-shirt asked Laila for an autograph. Where would he like it? On his belly, of course. This turned into a bit of a trend, and another five men were inspired to ask for autographs on their bellies. Laila's strokes with the felt-tip became broader and broader, while Lennart stood next to her pretending to smile.

Then a shy, dried-up little man came over and expressed his admiration for the first and only record by The Others, and the whole thing turned into a very pleasant experience for Lennart too.

No, it wasn't a success, but Lennart and Laila still felt quite contented as they gathered up their cables and microphones and packed up the synth. There were people out there who remembered them. Not something they could build a comeback on, but a small consolation, if nothing else.

They had been away from home for at least half an hour longer than expected and the way Lennart drove, he would have lost his licence if he'd been caught by a speed trap. Without bothering to unpack the car he ran inside and down to the cellar to make sure everything was all right.

The child was lying motionless on her back, staring up at the ceiling. Lennart stood and looked at her for a few seconds, waiting for her to blink. When she didn't, he hurried over and grabbed her hand between the bars. The child wrinkled her nose. Lennart breathed a sigh of relief and pressed his lips against the little hand. Then he saw that there was blood on the fingertips.

He picked up the girl and changed her nappy, inspecting her body to see if she had scratched herself. He couldn't find anything except a few bruises on her thighs, and thought she must have bitten her tongue, or perhaps a new tooth had come through.

When he got back upstairs, the telephone rang. He got there ahead of Laila as she came hobbling in from the living room, and picked up the receiver.

'Lennart speaking.'

'Hi, it's Jerry.'

'Oh?'

Lennart quickly ran through in his mind what Jerry could possibly want now, and steeled himself. After a few seconds of silence on the other end, he said, 'So did you want something?'

'No. Just wanted to check if you were at home. Bye.'

The connection was broken and Lennart stood there with the phone in his hand, eyebrows raised. Laila looked at him anxiously.

'What did he want?'

Lennart replaced the receiver and shook his head. 'To check if we were at home. That's a new one.'

16

Two mud-smeared Indians slit open a man's stomach and ripped out his intestines to feast on them as Jerry slumped on the sofa, smoking a cigarette. He pressed stop; he couldn't even be bothered to fast forward to the bit where they hung the girl up on hooks through her breasts. He shuffled over to the video and ejected *Cannibal Ferox* before replacing it in the Italian cannibal section of the bookshelf.

He took out *Eaten Alive* and put it back, looked at the covers of *Cannibal Holocaust* and *Man from Deep River*, but he just wasn't in the mood. He'd seen every single film at least ten times, some more than twenty. He glanced at the jewel in his collection, the incomplete *Ilsa, She-Wolf of the SS*, which had at least made his stomach tingle the first few times he had seen it, but no.

A hole gaped inside him. He took a bottle of Russian beer out of the fridge, knocked the cap off on the edge of the sink and poured half of it down his throat to see if it helped. Not even slightly.

He went out onto the balcony and lit another cigarette, watching a few children with towels slung over their shoulders as they made their way home from a swimming excursion to Vigelsjö. Tanned, cheerful, slender, not a care in the world. Jerry sank down onto a stool and sighed; he took a deep drag and thought about how he was feeling.

A hole? Was it really a hole?

No, he was familiar with that feeling. An empty space that appeared, that you had to hurl things into, food, booze, films, excitement, until the echo stopped. This was different. This was as if something had appeared. Fear. It was white and shaped like a sphere, about the same size as a handball. It travelled around his body, unsettling him.

He wandered around the apartment and stopped at the guitar case, leaning against the wall in the hallway. Why the fuck had he brought the guitar home? The last thing he needed was a reminder of his fucking *childhood*. He stood there in front of the guitar, his head tilted to one side. In the distance, like a whisper through the water pipes, he heard the girl's voice. Theres' voice. Crystal clear, perfect.

He shuddered and carried the case into the living room, then took out the guitar. It had gone out of tune on the ride home, and it took four times as long to retune it without Theres and her voice next to him. When it sounded OK he tried a C7 just to see if his fingers still remembered. They did.

He messed about for a while, and at first his index finger wouldn't stretch to the barre chords, but soon that was fine too. Jerry rocked his upper body and got through Clapton's riff to 'I Shot the Sheriff' without any problem, then carried on strumming as he hummed the lyrics to himself.

Time passed, and without noticing how it had happened he was sitting there playing a sequence of chords he didn't recognise. He looked at his fingers, moving across the neck of the guitar by themselves, and went through the sequence again. It sounded good.

But what's the tune, for fuck's sake?

One more time, slower. He could hear echoes of both Bowie and The Doors, for God's sake; he sensed a melody behind the chords, but still couldn't place it. The Who? No. After running through the whole thing a couple of times more, he accepted the truth: the tune didn't exist. He'd just made it up.

He wrote down the sequence of chords on the back of an envelope. Verse, chorus. It needed a bridge of some kind. Jerry hummed the verse and tried out a few different things until he found a fully functioning transition, which he changed up before the final chorus. Not perfect, but it would have to do. Something he could work on.

Jerry leaned back on the sofa and exhaled. It had started to get dark outside the window. He looked at the guitar, at the envelope covered in scribbled chords and crossings out. He scratched the back of his neck.

So what was all that about?

At least three hours had passed since he took the guitar out of its case. No, not passed. Flown. His scalp was sticky with sweat and there was hardly any feeling in the fingertips of his left hand, which were red and swollen. It would soon pass, he knew that. A few days' practice, and the skin would harden.

17

Lennart turned down the handful of gigs they were offered during the autumn, and Laila wasn't exactly sorry. She had felt clumsy and rusty standing there on-stage at the motor show, and although she had enjoyed the attention, she wasn't dreaming of travelling all over the country signing autographs on the bellies of drunks. But what was her dream? Did she actually have one?

The Lizzie Kanger album which Lennart had worked on sold fairly well, and they got by on the royalties from that and the other projects Lennart had been involved in over the years. In theory, they could sit at home twiddling their thumbs while the money trickled in, just fast enough to cover the necessities. The house was paid for, and they had no major outgoings. Everything was set up for a slow, painless stroll down the road we all follow until the light's turned out.

Laila had been quite happy about that, and Lennart seemed to be grimly reconciled to the prospect. Until he found the child. Laila couldn't understand Lennart's febrile energy in relation to the child but in this as in most other things she just let him get on with it, because that was the easiest thing to do.

During the autumn and winter Lennart received more offers involving composition. Lizzie Kanger's little burst of success had sent ripples out across the water, and there was no lack of optimistic singers, both male and female, who wanted a similar pebble dropped into the stagnant pool of their career. A song, or just a catchy chorus—got anything up your sleeve, Lennart?

Lennart shut himself in the studio and plinked out phrases, adding bombastic synth riffs so that not even the tone deaf could fail to grasp the potential in the demos he sent out.

The girl had moved on to solids, and it was usually Laila who fed her—jars of baby food she gobbled with a surprisingly healthy appetite. And yet however much she ate, she remained unusually thin for a baby, which was puzzling, given how little exercise she had. Laila wished she had that metabolism.

As the autumn progressed the girl began to walk, but still she didn't say a word. The only sound that came out of her as she walked around the room was a low, soporific humming—melodies Laila had never heard. Sometimes Laila fell asleep as she sat on the spare bed watching her.

At some point the girl had found a piece of rope about twenty centimetres long with four knots in it, and she never let go of it. She chewed it, she stroked it, she rubbed it against her cheek and she clutched it in her hand when she was asleep.

As the weeks passed, the girl began to use her newly acquired ability to walk in a way that made Laila uneasy, although she didn't know why. The girl was *searching*. That was the only word for it.

With the piece of rope in her hand she moved around the room looking behind the cupboard, under the bed. She pulled out the drawers in the desk and closed them again. She took the cuddly toys she never bothered with out of their basket, looked in the basket. Then she went back to the desk, opened the drawers, looked under the bed and so on and so on, humming all the time.

That was all she did, by and large. Sometimes she would sit down on the floor and stroke the knots in her piece of rope, but after a while she was on her feet again, looking behind the cupboard. When Laila was feeding her, the girl's eyes never met hers. She continued to gaze around the room, as if she were still searching even when she wasn't on the move.

Laila would sit on the bed following the girl's progress around the room as a quiet horror began to whisper inside her. The longer she sat there watching the girl's purposeful search, the more convinced she became that there really was something to search for, and that the girl would *find* it any moment now. She couldn't imagine what it might be, and she wondered if the girl knew.

Winter dragged itself along. Dark afternoons and rain hammering on the cellar windows. By early spring, Laila had long given up trying to talk to the girl. Lennart's dictum had firmed of its own accord into law. The girl didn't speak, she hummed, and she didn't stop humming if someone spoke, even for a fraction of a second. In the end it seemed pointless to try. And after all, she hummed so beautifully.

Laila had started to leave the door of the girl's room open while she was sitting down there. It made no difference. When the girl got to the door she stopped as if an invisible barrier prevented her from continuing out into the rest of the cellar.

To give herself something to do, Laila had taken up knitting again. She had been sitting on the bed for an hour or so working on a new hat for the girl when something changed in the energy of the room.

Laila lowered her needles. The girl was standing with the tips of her toes pressed against the threshold, looking out into the cellar. Then she reached out through the door with one arm, as if to check that there really was a space on the other side. She took one step. Laila held her breath as the girl moved the other foot, then stood with her heels pressed against the other side of the threshold. The girl's head turned from left to right.

The humming faltered for a moment, as if she were hesitating. Then it changed character. A new melody, a new key. Laila's vision blurred, and she realised she was crying. Through her tears she saw the girl take an infinitely slow step back, saw the other foot follow until she was standing inside the room once more. She stood there motionless for a few seconds as the melody changed. Then she turned and walked back into the room, where she carried on searching as if nothing had happened.

What do you dream of, Laila? Do you have a dream?

Something had happened. Something had opened up inside Laila and pierced her torpor. She fumbled for the aperture and tried to see what lay behind. She couldn't see a thing.

Laila gathered up her knitting and fled from the room.

She had thought she was just going out for a drive. As if it were something perfectly natural. These days it was always Lennart who drove, because of her bad knee. But here she was, out on the road in the middle of the day, doing a hundred and ten on the twisting road to Rimbo.

It was only when she turned onto the forest track that she realised this was where she had been heading all the time. She stopped at the car park where the path leading into the forest began, and switched off the engine.

This was where Lennart had found the girl eighteen months ago. Laila got out of the car, pulling her coat around her to keep out the bitterly cold drizzle. The sky was overcast, and although it was midday it was gloomy among the trees. She took a couple of tentative steps and quelled the urge to shout. What would she be shouting for? What was she actually looking for? She was looking for the place. Then she would know.

Lennart's description hadn't been exact, but as far as Laila understood, it had been close to the track. She walked slowly across the damp tufts of grass and rotting leaves, searching for something that looked different. A chilly wind suffused with rain whistled between the tree trunks, making her shudder. Something white flickered on the periphery of her vision.

A broken branch was sticking out from the trunk of a pine tree, a fragment of a plastic bag hanging from it. Laila's gaze roamed over the ground. A couple of metres from the pine tree she spotted a hollow in the earth; a few leaves and twigs had blown into it. Laila pulled off the piece of plastic and lowered herself carefully next to the hollow until she was able to flop down into a sitting position. She scraped away the leaves and twigs.

Traces of earth that had been dug up were still visible around the hole. Laila squeezed the piece of plastic in her hand, released it, squeezed again. She examined it and found nothing but white plastic. She felt around in the hollow with her hand. Nothing.

This was where the girl came from. This was where she had lain. In this bag, in this hole. No other tracks led to this place, none led away from it. This was where it began.

What do you dream of, Laila?

She sat there for a long time with her hand in the hole, moving it back and forth as if she were searching for the remains of a residual warmth. Then she slumped, lowering her head. Icy drops of rain dripped down the back of her neck as she caressed the wet earth and whispered:

'Help me, Little One. Help me.'

18

Jerry also noticed the change in Theres' behaviour when he came to visit every few weeks, but it wasn't something that bothered him. Something about the way his sister kept searching gave him the impression she was looking for a way out, a way that did not lead through the door she had now started using as she examined the rest of the cellar. A loophole, so to speak. Such a thing didn't exist, he knew that better than most. But he let her carry on. They had other fish to fry.

A month or so after their Bowie session he had played her one of his own songs, running through the chord sequences that he had scribbled down on a piece of paper. He had thought the song was some kind of Britpop à la Suede, but when Theres added a melody line, it turned into more of a hybrid between Swedish folk music and the most mournful kind of country. No money, no love, and nowhere to go.

During the winter he withdrew his threat to reveal her existence to the outside world, but in return he insisted on being allowed to spend time alone with her now and again.

As soon as he had a couple of new songs in the bag he came to call. Shut himself in with Theres and hung a blanket over the window to stop Lennart spying on them. Then they got to work.

Without exception, the songs became significantly darker as they passed through the filter of Theres' voice. Or perhaps 'darker' was the wrong word. More serious. At any rate, Jerry was amazed at how good his songs were when he heard Theres sing them. When he was sitting on his own humming, they just sounded like ordinary songs.

There was no purpose in his writing apart from the fact that it made him feel better. As soon as he sat down with Theres and played an E-major seventh as the first chord—that was their little ritual—and Theres replied in her clear voice, it was as if something poured off him and out of him.

After that, when they started jamming and Theres elevated his simple ideas to genuine music, he was somewhere else for a few minutes, in a better place. Perhaps there was a loophole after all, a way of getting out. If only for a while.

19

Laila knew there had to be an end to it.

It had begun the day she came home after visiting the place where Lennart had found the girl. She had begun to search. First of all she had opened the wardrobe where they kept old records, and gone through them. Then she had searched the room where they stored clothes. Over the course of a few days she had opened every single box and drawer containing their old things. Then she started on all the nooks and crannies in the house.

When she finished she started searching in places where she had already looked. She might have been careless the first time. Missed something.

From time to time she came across an old forgotten toy or a souvenir from some holiday. She had stood for a long time, staring at a wooden man from Majorca that produced cigarettes from his mouth when you pressed his hat. She had completely forgotten about him, and tried to convince herself that *this is it*.

At the same time she knew it was a lie, and that what she was searching for didn't exist. And yet she kept on. In between times she went and sat downstairs with the girl, watching as she did the same thing. Laila felt as if she were on the way to crossing a boundary. At any moment she would hear a faint click inside her head, and then she really would be insane.

Things went so far that she began to long for that day. She would no longer have to take responsibility for her behaviour. Like the girl, she would have a bed, a room and food at set times. Nothing else.

But the exhaustion got there first. She began to spend her time sitting in the armchair in the living room, doing absolutely nothing. She no longer had the strength to search, to do a crossword, or even to think. Sometimes Lennart came and made derogatory remarks about her, but she barely heard him. She felt nothing but a vague sense of shame at what she had become.

One day when Lennart had gone to Stockholm and she had been sitting in the armchair for two hours, she did actually hear something like a *click*. A membrane burst, everything became clear and she made a decision. She sat up in the armchair, her eyes wide open.

She hadn't searched the garage. No. So now she was going to go into the garage and open a cupboard or pull out a drawer and the first thing she saw would be *it*. Irrespective of what it was, it would be the thing she had been looking for. She made the decision.

An eagerness and a sense of excitement she hadn't felt for a few months seized her as she hurried across the garden. The garage door was ajar, welcoming her, because Lennart had taken the car out. The sun poured down from a pale July sky. Laila pushed the door open further and stepped into the darkness.

On a bench lay some tools and things to do with the car, and beneath it a cabinet containing three drawers. Laila stood in front of the cabinet, slowly running her hand over the three drawers, like the host of Bingolotto when a lucky winner was about to choose his or her secret prize. What would it be? A holiday in the Maldives or a hundred kilos of coffee?

Laila said eeny, meeny, miny, mo in her head, and her index finger stopped at the middle drawer. She pulled it open.

It couldn't have been clearer. There was only one thing in the drawer. A brand new nylon rope, ten metres long. Laila took it out and weighed it in her hands.

So. Now she knew what she had to do. It felt right. It felt like a relief.

She lived through the following days as if she were on a high. Each daily task seemed like fun, or at least valuable, because she knew she was carrying it out for the last time. As she sat with the girl she felt sorry for her, searching fruitlessly. Laila's own search was over.

No more pain in her leg, no more embarrassment over her clumsy body, no more of the constant, nagging feeling that she wasn't good enough. It would all be over. Soon.

Lennart noticed the change in her and became gentler, almost kind. He was more tolerant than she was used to. But that was still what he was doing: tolerating her. She saw everything so clearly now. It would be a release for Lennart when he no longer had to drag her around with him. Nobody would shed any tears because she was gone. It was just a matter of getting it done.

That was a problem. She wasn't afraid of dying, but however ridiculous it might sound, she was afraid of hanging herself—because it would hurt, and because it was ugly somehow.

Then again, she wouldn't actually need to use the rope. The rope was just a guide; the result was the important thing. After a little thought she decided how she wanted to do it, and the only thing that remained was to wait for the right opportunity.

It was almost a month before it came along. At the beginning of August it rained heavily for a week, followed by several days of beautiful hot weather. Perfect conditions for ceps in the forest. Lennart set off to forage, and for once he went on his bike.

Laila made a jokey comment about how it would be interesting to see what he came home with this time. Lennart was very confused when she leaned forward as he got on his bike, kissed him on the cheek and said goodbye.

Before he turned the corner he glanced back over his shoulder. She was waving. Then she went inside and fetched the vacuum cleaner hose.

She felt perfectly calm as she disconnected the hose from the cleaner and found a roll of packing tape. A tingle of expectation in her chest, that was all.

She didn't bother saying goodbye to the girl. If there was anyone who couldn't care less whether she lived or died, it was the girl. They had spent a lot of time together but there had never been any real contact. The girl lived in her own world, and there was no room for anyone else.

What about Jerry? Well yes, Jerry would definitely be upset, and she couldn't imagine how it would affect his relationship with Lennart. Nor did she care. It had taken quite some time, but she had managed to reach the level of ruthlessness necessary to take her own life.

She closed the garage door and locked it from the inside, then switched on the fluorescent light. She wouldn't have minded a more flattering light, but there was nothing she could do about that.

The vacuum cleaner hose fitted so perfectly over the exhaust that there was no need for any tape. She pulled the hose around the car and clamped it firmly in the partly-open back window. Then she got into the driver's seat and closed the door.

So. That's it then.

The car key was attached to a keyring with a plastic Snoopy on it. In the absence of an alternative, she kissed the little dog on the nose, said goodbye, put the key in the ignition and turned it. The car started.

And the stereo. She had forgotten that some quirk made it impossible to turn off the radio when the ignition was on, so as the exhaust fumes poured in through the window, filling the interior of the car with a fug, she was forced to listen to some stand-up comic telling a story about some hysterically funny incident at a pub in Västerås. Laila closed her eyes and tried to do the same with her ears.

It only took a minute or so before a drowsiness and a slight feeling of nausea overcame her. Her eyelids were a hundred times heavier than usual and located somewhere beyond her body where she was unable to open them. Everything was going exactly as she'd hoped, and oblivion was creeping closer. Far away she heard the comic finishing his story in that way that tells you it's time to laugh, then he put a record on. Laila was going to die to the sound of some contemporary pop hit, and it didn't matter. She heard the measured beat of a trumpet, the sound of a triumphant marching drum, and then a voice she recognised:

> Hello, Söderboys, here's your good old Annie...

Julia Caesar. Belting out 'Annie from Amerrrica', which had been a hit for her at the age of eighty-two.

> I left my love, I left my ma, I went away
> I set sail for the land of the YOO-ESS-AY!

Laila knew what was coming; her body tensed, her eyelids flickered and she clenched her jaw as Julia Caesar went for it: a scream that came from the toes up and made the speakers rattle. 'YOONIGHTED STATES OF AMERRRICA!'

Laila forced her eyes open. The car was full of poisonous fog, and her muscles had been replaced with lead. From the radio Julia Caesar was still working her improbably powerful old lady's voice.

Laila coughed. She managed to free her arms, and rubbed her eyes. A lump in her stomach was trying to force its way up into her throat.

What the fuck. What the FUCK.

Julia Caesar. Eighty-two years old. Standing at the microphone singing this absolute nonsense with such enthusiasm, for fuck's sake. She'd seen her on TV. The grey, wavy hair, the old, heavy body, the arms flung wide and the glint in her eye as she roared out her ridiculous song.

No more. Laila managed to move her numb left arm so that it landed on the door handle. She pulled and the door opened. She hurled herself sideways and slithered out onto the garage floor. As she crawled towards the door the floor was swaying, side to side, and she might well have collapsed if the regular beat of the music hadn't driven her on.

YOONIGHTED STATES OF AMERRRICA!

She'd forgotten how many verses the song had. She had to get out before it finished. This might be the last verse. But as her fingers went into spasm fumbling with the key, Julia Caesar took pity on her and set off again.

There's plenty of things in Sweden
Both in the good old days and today
That come from the YOO-ESS-AY!

Laila managed to turn the key, pressed down the handle and fell out into the summer. She lay on her back on the concrete in front of the garage, glowering up at the sky. While waves of nausea flooded her body, she saw the green leaves on the lime tree fluttering against the clear blue as white cotton clouds drifted by.

She heard an eager scrabbling and rustling, then a squirrel came scampering down the trunk; he stopped and listened to the music coming from the garage, then disappeared around the other side of the tree as the song faded out.

Yes, there's something about old Sweden
That's certainly more than all right...

Laila had managed to recoup just enough strength to push the garage door with her foot, so that it closed on the further adventures of the comedian. Then she just lay there breathing, breathing.

After ten minutes she was able to sit up. After another ten minutes she managed to go back into the garage and turn off the engine. She pulled the hose off the exhaust pipe and left all the doors open. As she walked over to the house with the hose dangling behind her like a tame snake, something occurred to her.

She had misinterpreted the signs. It wasn't the last thing she should have gone for. It was the first. The first place she had searched was the wardrobe containing their record collection. Something had told her to look there first. She remembered very clearly that she had actually seen 'Annie from Amerrrica' among all the singles and 78s.

She hadn't given it a thought. But she did now.

In spite of everything, there was a consolation to be found, something that never let her down. Something that was so close to her she hadn't been able to see it. The music. The songs. The records. Julia Caesar's song didn't have a message, but her performance did, and it was very simple: *Don't give up.*

Laila threw the hose into the cleaning cupboard and went to the wardrobe to look for 'You Are a Spring Breeze in April' by Svante Thuresson. She would listen to that. Then she would listen to something else.

20

Towards the end of October Lennart began to feel that it was becoming unendurable. He had nothing against classic hits from the Swedish charts but for God's sake—within reason! From morning to night it was Siw Malmkvist, Lasse Lönndahl and Mona Wessman.

Laila might at least have shown some kind of discrimination and worked her way, for example, through Peter Himmelstrand's many superior compositions, but no. She played whatever she fancied, whatever she happened to find in their extensive record collection. You might get an hour's relief with Thorstein Bergman, but immediately afterwards Tova Carson would be chirruping away at some clumsily translated German pop. Lennart would sit in the kitchen being lulled into a state of restfulness by 'Last Night I Had the Strangest Dream', only to be driven to flight by 'Skip to My Lou'.

Only one thing stopped him snapping off the arm and hurling the damned record player through the window: Laila was happy. It was a long time since Lennart had had anything against Laila being happy; but it was also a long time since he had had enough love or energy to try to *make* her happy. Now she was taking care of it herself.

It wasn't really a bubbling happiness, more a constant spiritual smile that meant she would prepare decent meals or do some cleaning, for example—during breaks in the music. So all he could do was grit his teeth as Anita Lindblom took a deep breath and bellowed 'Thaaaat's life' for the third time that day. It had to be worth it.

In any case, Lennart had started to spend a lot of time down in the cellar, where the pounding beat of Swedish pop could be heard only as a distant changing of the guard. The girl's musical education ought to be expanded, so Lennart bought a portable CD player and started to play classical music to her.

The very first thing he played was one of his personal favourites: Beethoven's Spring Sonata in F-major for Violin and Piano. He had decided to start simply with piano and violin sonatas, then move on to string quartets and finally full symphonies. Introduce the instruments one at a time, so to speak.

He would long remember how the girl reacted. She was standing in her cot as usual, sucking on the piece of rope with four knots in it, when Lennart pressed play.

The girl stiffened during the enchanting violin theme and soft piano accompaniment that introduce the first movement. When the roles were reversed and the piano, carefree as a spring brook, repeated the theme, the girl began to sway as she stared into space, her expression halfway between ecstasy and fear.

After forty seconds she frowned as if she sensed that something was about to happen. As the violin built up to the piano's powerful descent, then emphasised it with a coarser stroke, the girl's face contracted and she shook her head, her fingers tightly clutching the frame of the cot.

The piece grew calm once more, the violin became gentle and compliant, but the girl listened with suspicion in her face as if she sensed that the harsher elements were still lurking beneath the surface. As the violin became more agitated and the piano grew excited in the background, she began to shake and jerk back and forth in the cot, her face contorting as if she were in pain.

Lennart jumped up and switched off the CD.

'What is it, Little One?'

The girl wasn't looking at him, she never did. Instead she fixed her gaze on the CD player as she shook the bars of the cot. Lennart had never seen anyone react to music like that. It was as if the strings were stroking every nerve ending within her, or a hammer was hitting every single one. The music went right into her.

Lennart switched to one of the cello sonatas. The girl was less agitated by the cello's softer tone, even when the tempo grew faster. When they reached the short Adagio in the Sonata in A-major, she joined in with the melody for the first time.

After experimenting for a few days, it was clear that it was always the adagio sections that appealed to the girl most. Allegro passages made her anxious, and a scherzo could plunge her into despair. Lennart programmed the CD so that it played only the adagio sections. Then he sat down on the bed and watched, listening, as she added her voice, a third instrument, to the sonatas.

At first he was happy. He felt he was resting within the very genesis of music. Then he went upstairs and at a stroke found himself in the outer reaches of the nadir of Swedish pop music. Well, that was fine. He was in a state of harmony.

But all good things come to an end.

As the days turned to weeks and Beethoven gave way to Schubert and Mozart, Lennart sat in his musical sanctuary staring at his fingers. There was something wrong with them. He tried picking the girl up to feel her weight and warmth, but it didn't help. He put her back in the cot.

He couldn't have her on the floor when the music was playing. She would go over to the CD player and start examining it in quite a destructive way. She would beat the speakers with her small fists, or try to pick the whole thing up as if she were trying to shake something out of it.

At first Lennart had interpreted her behaviour as a sign that she didn't like the music after all, but on the one occasion when he let her continue until she managed to destroy the player, he realised what she was after. She was searching for the music, for where it came from. She wanted to get inside the machine and find what was playing. Since this was impossible to explain to her, Lennart simply bought a new player and made sure she couldn't get at it.

After putting the girl back in her cot, Lennart walked around the room studying his fingers. They looked white and shiny to him, like piano keys. He placed them on an invisible keyboard and pretended to play along with the Mozart sonata emerging from the speakers. No. It wasn't playing he missed, he had played enough. He opened and closed his hands. They felt so strangely *empty*. Something was missing, they needed something to do.

He went out into the cellar and switched on the light above the workbench. Various tools hung neatly from their hooks. Screws, nails and fittings were tidily sorted in compartments on a shelf. He had never been what you might call a handyman, but he liked the tools themselves. They were so definitive. Each tool intended and made for a specific purpose, an extension of the human arm. Lennart picked up the drill and weighed it in his hand. It felt good. When he pressed the button, nothing happened. Run down. He rooted out the charger and inserted the battery. He picked up one or two chisels, tested the weight of the hammer.

What about making something?

Laila had made stuffed cabbage leaves, and the house was blissfully silent. When they had finished eating and Lennart was loading the dishwasher, he said quite casually, 'I was just wondering if there was anything we needed? Anything I could make?'

'Like what?'

'I don't know. That's why I'm asking.'

'What do you mean by make?'

'Make. You know, make. Put pieces of wood together so they turn into something. Make.'

'What do you want to do that for?'

Lennart sighed and rinsed the remains of the sauce from his plate before putting it in the dishwasher. Why had he even bothered to ask? He poured powder into the compartment and slammed the door shut with unnecessary force.

Laila had been following his activities with her chin resting on her hand. As he picked up the dishcloth and began wiping the table, she said, 'A shoe rack.'

Lennart stopped making circular movements over the wax cloth and visualised their hall floor. There were only four pairs of shoes. They each had a pair of outdoor shoes and a pair of clogs. Their Wellingtons were in the cellar.

'Yes,' he said. 'I could do that.'

'Then we could put our wellies there too,' said Laila.

'Yes. Good idea.'

He looked at Laila. She had lost a few kilos in recent months. Presumably this had something to do with the fact that he no longer found chocolate wrappers all over the house. She had stopped comfort eating.

It must have been something to do with the light, bouncing off the wax cloth and illuminating her face from a side angle. For a brief moment, Lennart thought Laila was pretty. The distance between his hand and her face was only half a metre, and he watched his hand slowly rise from the table and caress her cheek.

Then he grabbed the dishcloth and scrubbed at a dried-on patch of lingonberry jam with such force that the wax cloth slid to one side. He rinsed out the cloth, draped it over the tap and said, 'All right, a shoe rack.'

Over the next few weeks Lennart made a shoe rack, two towel rails and a key cupboard. When he couldn't come up with anything else they needed, he moved on to bird boxes.

Sometimes as he stood there surrounded by the smell of freshly sawn wood, listening to the sound of some Schubert quartet from the girl's room, he felt perfectly contented. Step by step, everything had moved in the right direction. The sharp, hard edges of his existence had been rounded off with both grade one and two sandpaper, and he could run his hand over life without getting splinters in his fingers.

He put on the ear protectors and started up the jigsaw to cut out the windows and doors in the facade of a nesting box representing their own house. It was a tricky job that required concentration, and when he switched the saw off and removed the ear protectors five minutes later, sweat was pouring down his forehead.

The silence after the angry buzzing of the saw was pleasant, but wasn't it a bit *too* quiet? He couldn't hear any music from the girl's room, nor any humming. He put down the tools and went to investigate.

The girl had climbed out of her cot. While he was sawing, unable to hear anything, she must have fetched a hammer behind his back, then gone back and started on the CD player. Through a combination of hitting and wrenching she had managed to open up the front of both speakers and rip out the cones. She was now sitting on the floor scratching at them with her fingers, tugging at the wires as she shook her head.

He went over and tried to take the broken pieces off her, but she refused to let them go. She shook them and bit them.

'Give those to me,' he said. 'You might cut yourself.'

The girl stared at him, her eyes narrowed. Then she said, with absolute clarity, 'Music.'

Lennart was so stunned he gave up the tug-of-war and simply stared at her. It was the first word he had heard her say. He lowered his head to her level and asked, 'What did you say?'

'Music,' the girl repeated, making a noise somewhere between a growl and a whimper as she banged the speaker cone on the floor.

Lennart got down on his knees beside her and said, 'The music isn't there.'

The girl stopped banging and looked at him. *Looked* at him. Gazed into his eyes for a few seconds. Lennart took this as an encouragement, and tried to explain more clearly.

'Music is everywhere,' he said. 'Inside you. Inside me. When we sing, when we play.' He pointed at the ruined CD player. 'That's only a machine.'

He had forgotten his resolution not to talk to the girl. It didn't matter. Both Laila and Jerry had talked to her, so that project had had it. He pointed at the CD player again. 'Do you understand? A machine. It's people who make music.'

He took out the CD, a cheap Naxos edition of Schubert's Second String Quartet. He pushed his forefinger through the hole and held it up in front of the girl. 'The music is pressed onto this.'

The girl didn't react to his words, but she was staring at the CD with big eyes. She tilted her head to one side, wrinkling her nose. Lennart turned the disc around to see what she was looking at. And saw himself.

Of course.

As far as he was aware, the girl had never seen a mirror before. He turned the shiny surface towards her once again and said, 'That's you, Little One. That's you.'

The girl stared at the disc on his finger as if she were under a spell, and whispered, 'Little One…' as a trail of saliva dribbled from the corner of her mouth. She crawled closer without breaking eye contact with her reflection. She reached out her hands for the disc and Lennart let her take it. Only then did he notice that she had dropped the piece of rope with the knots in it; it was lying on the floor behind her, chewed and stroked to death. She only had eyes for the CD.

When Lennart lifted her up and put her back in the cot, she clung firmly to the disc with both hands as she gazed down into the silvery pool of light, completely unreachable. But still Lennart rested his head on the frame of the cot and said, 'But the music isn't there, Little One. It's here.' He placed his forefinger on her heart. 'And here.' On her temple.

21

Jerry didn't get around to visiting his parents until the spring. He was actually busy with a little business enterprise.

He had been working in the billiard hall in Norrtälje for a couple of years, cash in hand, stepping in as and when required. One evening when he was in the café washing coffee cups, an old acquaintance came in. Ingemar. They chatted for a while and when Jerry offered him a contraband Russian beer from the secret stash, Ingemar raised his eyebrows. 'Have you got fags as well?'

Jerry said he hadn't, and that the Russian beer was really only for regular customers, but he hardly thought Ingemar had turned into the kind of bloke who'd go running to the cops, had he?

'No, no,' said Ingemar, opening the beer with his lighter. 'Quite the reverse. What if I said eighty kronor a carton? Interested?'

'Are we talking about that Polish crap made from straw and newspaper?'

'No, no, Marlboro. I don't honestly know if it's some kind of pirate factory or what, but they taste the same. Here. Try one.'

Ingemar held out a packet and Jerry examined it. It didn't have a registration mark or stamp, but apart from that it looked like an ordinary packet of cigarettes. He shook one out and lit it. No difference whatsoever.

Ingemar was a truck driver these days, working mostly in the Baltic states. He had a contact in Estonia who sold cheap cigarettes if you didn't ask too many questions. He looked around the room;

two of the billiard tables were busy and three people were sitting at a table smoking. 'Shouldn't be a problem to shift say fifty cartons a month here. Add on a bit for yourself and you're laughing.'

Jerry thought it over. A hundred and twenty kronor was a good price for a carton of fags. That would mean a profit of two thousand a month.

'OK,' he said. 'Let's do it. When can you deliver?'

Ingemar grinned. 'Right now. I've got the car outside.'

Ingemar didn't have his truck parked outside the billiard hall, just an ordinary car. He looked around and unlocked the boot. Two black plastic sacks took up half the space. He showed Jerry the cartons, bundled in packs of five.

'Four thou,' he said. 'As agreed.'

'But I haven't got that kind of money on me, you know that.'

'Next time. This will give you a bit of start-up capital.'

They carried the sacks down to the room where the rubbish was stored, and shook hands as they agreed to meet in a month's time.

That same evening Jerry managed to shift eight cartons, which made it easier to fasten the remainder to the back of his motorbike under cover of darkness and drive home. In future he would ask Ingemar to deliver direct to his door.

He stacked the forty-two cartons in four neat piles in the corner of the living room, then sat down in the armchair and contemplated them, hands folded over his stomach. *So there you go,* he thought. *All of a sudden you're an entrepreneur.* To show he was taking the whole thing seriously, he emptied his wallet and put Ingemar's six hundred and forty kronor in an envelope.

He sat there rustling the remaining three hundred and twenty. He usually worked a six-hour shift at the hall, earning fifty kronor an hour. If it went on like this, his hourly rate had suddenly more than doubled.

A hundred kronor. After tax, so to speak. Top job, to say the least. Executive or something.

The fifty cartons disappeared, and the following month Ingemar got his money and delivered the next batch to Jerry's apartment. It was tempting to expand the operation, but Jerry realised he ought to be careful, selling only to people he trusted. Mustn't get greedy. That was when things went down the pan.

His role as deputy supplier commanded a modicum of respect from those around him. He could hang out in the billiard hall even when he wasn't working, and people were more inclined to talk to him than they had been. He bumped into people in town, that kind of thing. The satisfaction he'd been getting from the time he spent with Theres no longer felt so vital.

However, at the beginning of March he packed up his guitar, strapped it to his motorbike and started the bike first kick. He had seriously begun to consider buying a new one, with an electric starter. It was a possibility these days.

The house was still there, looking exactly as it had when he went round four months earlier. But something had changed. It took a while before Jerry was able to put his finger on it, but as he sat at the kitchen table drinking coffee with Lennart and Laila, picking up a biscuit from the plate, he saw it with sudden clarity.

He was sitting at the kitchen table drinking coffee and eating biscuits with his parents.

It had just sort of happened, quite naturally. As if it was normal. No suspicion about his visit, no implied criticism and none of the simmering discontent between his parents that could erupt into a caustic remark at any moment. It was just coffee, home-made biscuits and a nice cosy chat. Jerry looked from Lennart to Laila; they were both dunking macaroons in their coffee. 'What the fuck is going on with you two?'

Laila looked at him. 'What are you talking about?'

Jerry waved at the table. 'For fuck's sake, you're sitting here like...I don't know...something out of *Neighbours*. As if everything in the garden was rosy. What's going on?'

Lennart shrugged his shoulders. 'Is there a problem?'

'No, there's no problem. That's what's so bloody spooky. Have you joined a cult or something?' Jerry just didn't get it. He gobbled a couple more biscuits, said thank you and went down into the cellar.

The cot was gone, and Theres was sleeping in his old bed these days. She wasn't wearing a nappy, so presumably she had learned how to use the toilet in the cellar. A home-made cupboard had appeared, with a fretwork front. Jerry could just see a CD player behind the fretwork. Theres was standing in the middle of the floor, not moving a muscle. She was holding a CD in one hand.

She had grown into a very pretty little girl. Her pale blonde hair had begun to curl around her face, framing her enormous blue eyes and making her look like an angel, nothing more or less.

Jerry was very taken with the sight of her, and sat down on the floor in front of her without speaking. Her eyes were fixed on his lips. After perhaps ten seconds, she took a step forward, hit him hard across the mouth and said, 'Talkie!'

Jerry almost fell over backwards, but managed to support himself with one arm. A reflex action made him give Theres a slap that was hard enough to knock her over. 'What the fuck are you doing, you little bastard!'

Theres got to her feet, went over to the bed and crawled up onto it. She sat facing the wall, her back to him, and started humming something. Jerry felt at his mouth. No blood.

'Now then sis,' he said. 'We're not starting all that again, are we?'

Her shoulders hunched and she bent her neck as if she were embarrassed. Jerry's heart softened and he said to her back, 'Oh, let's forget it. It doesn't matter.'

He crept over to her and realised it wasn't that she was ashamed. She had simply bent her head so that she could see her reflection in the CD. Jerry reached out to take it. 'Let's see what you've got there.'

Theres pulled the disc away and *growled.* There was no other word for the sound that rose from her throat. Jerry laughed and withdrew his hand. 'OK, OK. I won't take it. I get it. It's fine, sis.'

He sat quietly beside her for a while, looking at her as she looked at herself. Without turning her head, Theres eventually said, 'Talkie.'

'But I am talking. What do you want me to say? Sorry, or what? Are you cross because I haven't been around? Is that it? OK, I'm sorry.'

'Tarrie talkie. Singie.'

Jerry frowned. Then he understood. He took out the guitar and played a C. Theres turned and looked at his fingers as he played C again. Her arm shot out. She whacked him on the hand with the CD, and let out a single note.

Jerry controlled himself and didn't hit back. A red welt was beginning to appear on the back of his right hand. Theres sang the note again, and raised the CD for a fresh attack.

'OK, OK,' Jerry said. 'Calm down. Here you go.' He played E-major seventh, and the disc was lowered. 'I forgot. Sorry.'

As he hadn't got around to writing anything new, Jerry just sat strumming for a while, playing a few appropriate chords as Theres improvised a melody. The tunes that began to emerge sounded at least as good as the one he had laboriously written down in advance.

He muted the strings with his hand and looked around the room. Her meagre little world. The CD player, the bed, the jars of baby food.

Is this it? Is this the way it's going to be?

He was roused from his pondering by a pain in his right hand. Theres had stabbed at him again.

'Tarrie talkie!'

Jerry rubbed the back of his hand. 'For fuck's sake, do you think I'm a machine or something?' He knocked on the body of the guitar. 'The tarrie will talkie when I want it to talkie, OK?'

Theres leaned forward and gently stroked the neck of the guitar, whispering, 'Tarrie? Tarrie?' She laid her ear against the strings and for a moment Jerry thought the guitar was going to reply. He too lowered his head towards the fretboard.

From the corner of his eye he just caught sight of the CD heading straight for his cheek, and jerked his head away. The edge of the disc hit the wood of the guitar and made a small notch. Theres opened her eyes wide and screamed, 'Tarrie! Poor tarrie!' She reached out to the guitar as if to comfort it and as tears welled in her eyes, Jerry got to his feet.

'Listen sis, no offence, but there's something wrong inside your head. No question.'

22

What had happened? What kind of sect had Lennart and Laila joined?

Just the usual one, the two-member sect that diligent married couples are inducted into, if they're lucky. The sect with the motto: *We only have each other.* Lennart couldn't say exactly how he had reached this point, but one day he found himself standing in front of the microwave warming pastries as he waited for Laila to get home from Norrtälje. As he watched the pastries slowly spinning around on the plate, he realised that he missed Laila. That he was looking forward to her coming home so they could have a cup of coffee and a warm pastry. That it would be nice.

It might sound simplistic, but if something can be expressed simply, then why not express it simply?

Lennart was beginning to appreciate what he had.

It wasn't a matter of falling in love with Laila all over again, of forgetting the past and starting afresh. That only happens in the magazines. But he was beginning to look at his life with different eyes. Instead of grinding his teeth over everything he had missed out on, he was actually looking at what he had.

He had his health, a decent house, work he enjoyed and which brought him a certain amount of recognition. A wife who had stuck with him all these years and who had his best interests at heart, in spite of everything. A son who at least wasn't a drug addict.

And on top of all that he had been chosen as the guardian of the gift down in the cellar. It was impossible to fit the girl into the usual scheme of things; she was a freak of nature, and a considerable responsibility. But the simple fact of bearing a responsibility can be something that gives meaning to life.

So not a bad life, all in all. Maybe not the stuff of a tribute journal or a framed obituary, but perfectly *acceptable.* Fine. Perfectly OK.

He still couldn't say that Laila looked good exactly, but sometimes, in a certain light...She had lost at least ten kilos in recent months, and a couple of times when they were lying in bed about to go to sleep, he had been turned on by the warmth of her body, her skin, and they had done what man and wife tend to do. This led to more ease and intimacy, and that meant his opinion of her changed a little more, and so on.

When the girl was five years old, Lennart and Laila were celebrating their wedding anniversary. Yes, celebrating. There was wine with dinner and more wine afterwards, as they sat looking at old photo albums and listening to Abba. Suddenly the girl was standing in the middle of the living room floor. She had come up the stairs from the cellar by herself for the first time. Her eyes swept around the room and did not pause when they reached Lennart and Laila. She sat down on the floor by the fire and started stroking the head of a stone troll she found there.

Lennart and Laila were happy and slightly tipsy. Without even thinking about it they picked the girl up and settled her between them on the sofa. She wouldn't let go of the stone troll, but clamped it firmly between her thighs so that she could keep running her hand over it.

'Hole in Your Soul' faded away, and the introductory piano notes of 'Thank You for the Music' floated out across the room.

I'm nothing special, in fact I'm a bit of a bore...

Laila sang along. Even if she couldn't quite get Agnetha's clarity—or her high notes—it sounded pretty good. She was accompanied by the girl, who picked up the melody instinctively, adding her own voice a fraction of a second after Abba's voices reached her ears.

Lennart got a lump in his throat. When the chorus came around he just couldn't help joining in too:

> So I say thank you for the music, the songs I'm singing
> Thanks for all the joy they're bringing...

They were singing about the thing that united them. They swayed together on the sofa, and the girl swayed along with them. When the song came to an end amid the sound of crackling, both Lennart and Laila had tears in their eyes, and their heads almost collided as they both leaned down at the same time to kiss the girl on the top of her head.

It was a lovely evening.

The girl had started leaving her room. It was remarkable that it had taken so long, but now the day had come when she wanted to expand her world.

Her development was slow in every other area too, except music. Her toilet training had taken a long time, she was awkward and clumsy when she moved and she had the eating habits of a small child. She still refused to eat anything except jars of baby food, and Lennart had to travel to shopping centres a long way from home to stock up on Semper and Findus without arousing suspicion. She had a tendency to become attached to inanimate objects rather than living things, and her use of language was developing very slowly. She seemed to understand everything that was said to her, but spoke only in sentences of three or four words in which she referred to herself as 'Little One'.

'Little One more food.' 'Little One have it.' 'Away.'

The exception was lyrics. Given the girl's limited vocabulary, it was astonishing to hear her sitting there singing, in perfectly pronounced English, a song she had heard. 'Singing' is perhaps the wrong word. She *reproduced* the song. The day after the wedding anniversary, for example, she wandered around the cellar singing with Agnetha Fältskog's particular diction, and she knew almost all the words.

After that evening Lennart relaxed his restrictions, and Laila was allowed to share her taste in music with the girl. Schubert and Beethoven were joined on the CD player by Stikkan Anderson and Peter Himmelstrand.

But the problem Lennart had refused to face was now a fact. They couldn't let the girl show herself outside the house. One possibility was to lock her in, but that wasn't really an option. So what were they going to do?

'Lennart,' said Laila a couple of days later when they were out in the garden hanging up yet another bird box, 'we have to accept that it's over now.'

Lennart was right at the top of the ladder, and dropped the bird box he was hanging up. He clung to the tree and leaned his forehead against the trunk. Then he came down, sat on the third rung and looked Laila in the eye.

'Can you imagine it?' he said. 'Handing her over and never seeing her again?'

Laila thought about it, tried to imagine it. The absence. The cellar empty, the jars of baby food gone, the girl's voice never to be heard again. No. She didn't want that.

'Don't you think we'd be allowed to adopt her, then? I mean, regardless of how it all started, we're the ones she's used to now. They'd have to take that into account, surely.'

'For a start, I'm not sure they'd be so understanding, and secondly...' He took Laila's hand and squeezed it. 'I mean we know, don't we? There's something wrong with her. Seriously wrong. They'd put her in an institution. A place where they wouldn't even appreciate what we value about her. They'd just see her as...damaged.'

'But what are we going to do, Lennart? Sooner or later she's going to walk out of the front door, and then we'll have even less chance of keeping her. What are we going to do?'

'I don't know, Laila. I don't know.'

It was what Laila had said about the front door that gave Lennart the idea. The problem could be expressed very simply: the girl could not be allowed to go out the front door. Their house was quite sheltered and there was very little risk that anyone would see her through the window. The only person who came to visit was Jerry.

However, if she went out through the door, she could carry on up the drive. Out onto the road. Into the forest, into town. To other people who would set in motion the machinery that would take her away from them.

Lennart came up with the solution. He didn't know if it would work, but it was the only thing he could think of. Without mentioning it to Laila, he made up a story. When it was ready, he told the girl his story.

It went like this: the world was a place populated by big people. People like Lennart, Laila and Jerry. Once upon a time there had been little people as well. People like the girl. Like Little One. But the big people had killed all the little people.

When Lennart saw that the girl didn't understand the word 'kill', he changed it to 'eaten up'. Like food. The big people had eaten up all the little people.

At that point in the story the girl did something extremely unusual. She asked a question. With her gaze firmly fixed on the wall, she asked him, 'Why?'

Lennart hadn't exactly polished his story, and had to come up with an answer very quickly. He said it depended on what was in your head. Almost all people had hatred and hunger in their heads. Then there were people like Lennart, Laila and Jerry who had love in their heads.

The girl tasted the word she had sung so many times, but never actually spoken, 'Love'.

'Yes,' said Lennart. 'And when you have love in your head, you want to love and take care of the little people, you don't want to eat them up.' He carried on telling her about all the big people he had seen sneaking around the garden, hunting for a little person to eat. Things were so bad that if the girl went outside, she probably wouldn't even manage to get through one song before a big person grabbed her and ate her up.

The girl looked anxiously over towards the window, and Lennart stroked her back reassuringly.

'There's no danger as long as you stay indoors. Do you understand? You have to stay in the house. You mustn't stand looking out of the window, and you must *never, ever* go out through the big door. Do you understand, Little One?'

The girl had crawled up into the very corner of the bed and was still looking over at the window with an anxious expression. Lennart began to wonder if he had succeeded *too* well with his story. He took her bare feet in his hands and caressed them with his thumb.

'We'll protect you, Little One. There's no need to be afraid. Nothing is going to happen to you.'

When he left the girl's room a little while later, Lennart forgave himself for his horrible story. Partly because it was necessary, and partly because there was a grain of truth in it. He was convinced that the world out there *would* eat her up, if not quite as brutally as he had suggested.

However much Lennart might have forgiven himself, his story had a powerful effect on the girl. She no longer dared to leave her room, and insisted on the window being covered so that the big people wouldn't catch sight of her. One day when Laila came into the room, the girl was sitting with a Mora knife she had fetched from the tool cupboard and was making threatening gestures towards the blanket hanging over the window.

Laila didn't understand what had happened, but from odd words the girl said she began to piece things together, and eventually she pinned Lennart down: What had he actually said?

Lennart told her about his story, but left out the worst bits. In the end Laila agreed not to correct the girl's view of the world. She didn't like what Lennart had done, but since she was unable to come up with a better idea, the girl could go on living with her misconceptions.

Lennart also had his doubts about whether it had been a wise move. The incident with the Mora knife was only the beginning. When Lennart locked it away, she fetched a chisel, a screwdriver, a saw. She placed the tools around her on the bed like an arsenal of weapons at the ready for when the Big People arrived. When Lennart tried to take them away, she let out a single, heart-rending scream.

He had to be a little more cunning. He swapped the most dangerous tools one at a time for less dangerous items. The saw for a hammer, the chisel for a file. They were hardly suitable toys, but the girl never hurt herself. She just wanted the tools as a kind of magic circle, a spell surrounding her as she sat on the bed.

If she moved to the floor, she took the tools with her and arranged them neatly around her. They had become her new friends; she sang to them, whispered to them and patted them. She was never calmer than when she was lying curled up inside her circle with a Mozart adagio on the CD player. Sometimes she would fall asleep like that. After one slip-up, Lennart learned that he must always move the tools with her when he put her to bed, otherwise she woke up screaming.

Time passed, and the girl's fear moderated to anxiety which in turn moderated to watchfulness. The quantity of tools was reduced. One day when Lennart had left the drill out, he came into the girl's room to find her sitting with it on her knee, talking quietly to it. From time to time she would press the button and the drill would buzz in response, whereupon the conversation would continue.

It became her new favourite, and Lennart let her keep it, because she allowed him to remove all the rest. It enabled her to move about more as well. She was once again brave enough to set off on small journeys of discovery, but always with the drill in her hand.

Lennart had to smile as he watched her sneaking around the cellar with the tool at the ready, as alert as the sheriff waiting for the black hats to ride into town. She couldn't sleep unless she was clutching the drill.

The girl had reached the age of seven by the time she showed an interest in the drill's normal function. Each day she came one step closer to Lennart as he stood at the workbench in the cellar. She didn't protest when he picked her up and sat her on the bench; instead she clutched the drill to her chest and watched what he was doing.

He had just finished yet another nesting box, and showed it to the girl. She had been staring intently at it while he was working, but looked away when he held it up in front of her. That was normal.

Lennart picked up the new drill he had bought after he let the girl keep the old one. Just for fun he revved the motor a couple of times, pretending that his drill wanted to talk to hers. She wasn't interested.

He had a size 10 bit in the chuck, and Lennart finished off the box as he usually did. 'Right, now we're going to drill the entrance hole. This is where the birds will go in and out. Cheep, cheep. Birds.'

The girl watched as Lennart drilled out the hole, then sat staring at it as if she were waiting for something. When Lennart lifted her down from the bench, she growled and walloped him across the shoulder with her drill. He put her back and she leaned close to the hole, whispering, 'Cheep, cheep,' as she continued to stare at it.

A feeling of sorrow plummeted through Lennart's stomach. He decided to make an exception.

Early next morning he took the girl out into the hallway. When he opened the front door, her eyes widened. She struggled to free herself from his grip, and filled her lungs with air ready to scream. Lennart just had time to say, 'Ssh! SSH! They can hear us!'

The girl's mouth snapped shut and her little body began to shake as Lennart cautiously opened the door and pretended to peer out into the garden. 'Quiet,' he said. 'Careful. Not a sound.'

He bundled the girl out through the door, but had to pick her up in order to get her to the nearest tree where there was a nesting box. Her body was clenched, as hard as ice.

It was a May morning, and the birdsong was cascading through the shrubs and trees. Lennart lifted the girl's head towards the box, which was exactly the same as the one he had made the previous evening.

Suddenly her mouth opened and she relaxed in his arms. A robin emerged from the hole and sat there for a moment looking around with rapid, jerky movements before it flew away. The girl followed it with her eyes and a dribble of saliva ran down her chin.

Lennart had no idea how she might interpret what she had just seen. Did she think drilling holes made the birds appear, or disappear, or did she in fact understand perfectly?

He put her down on the ground and said, 'The birds live in there, they fly around—'

But he had hardly begun the sentence before she raced back to the house and slammed the front door behind her.

23

By February 2000 greed had got its claws into Jerry after all, and it was all Apple's fault. The Power Mac G4 with the 500 MHz processor was finally due for release after the initial hassle with Motorola, and was going to cost around thirty thousand kronor. So far, so good. He had the money, he'd started to save a year ago when he picked up the first rumours.

But then there was Cinema Display. Along with the release of the new G4 there was to be a 22-inch flat screen with the best definition and the slickest design ever. And that would cost around thirty thousand as well.

The dumpy iMac on Jerry's computer desk suddenly felt like something from the stone age. He'd started messing around with Cubase 4 for writing songs, but it was so slow. He wanted to upgrade to 4.1, he wanted to run it through the 500 processor and he wanted to see it on that big, flat screen.

It became an obsession. Jerry imagined that when he had that silver chassis standing underneath his desk and that stylish screen with its transparent frame sitting on top, everything would be *perfect*. There would be nothing more to strive for. He longed for that computer as a believer longs for redemption. When it was his, when it was all in place, he would feel a peace and purity that would wipe every trace of dirt from his life.

But to achieve this state of bliss some fancy footwork would be required. He had to sell more cigarettes. He had already doubled his order with Ingemar in December, and in January he took one hundred and fifty cartons, and also put the price up by ten kronor from the previous month.

The demand from his regular customers couldn't meet Jerry's supply, however gallantly they puffed away. Mats, who ran the billiard hall, had discovered Jerry's activities, and he now dealt from home. He asked his regulars to spread the word among their connections that there were cheap fags available at Jerry's address.

The connections duly turned up, and soon their connections came as well. By February Jerry had managed to scrape together twelve thousand kronor in addition to the thirty thousand he already had, and placed another big order with Ingemar.

A week or so later he had a visitor at the billiard hall. A guy of his own age came in—shaved head, tribal tattoo snaking up his neck beneath the biker jacket—and leaned on the bar. He looked Jerry in the eye and informed him that his business activities would cease immediately.

Jerry pretended he didn't understand; he wondered aloud what the visitor's problem with the billiard hall was, and explained that he wasn't actually the owner. If he wanted it shut down, he would have to speak to Mats. The guy didn't even crack a smile; he just said that Jerry had been warned, and if he carried on, things could get very nasty.

Jerry's hands were shaking slightly when the man left, but he wasn't really scared. He'd heard about a gang who had got together in the offenders' institution in Norrtälje; they called themselves Bröderna Djup after the singing group, which was an incredibly stupid name for a criminal organisation, and was one reason why Jerry didn't take the threat seriously. Besides which, there was nothing to suggest that this guy really did belong to some kind of gang. He was probably a free agent like Jerry himself, but with a slightly harder attitude.

Jerry was a bit more careful about checking the spy hole in the door before he opened it, but he kept on selling his cigarettes. No slap-head pumped up on steroids was going to come between him and his Cinema Display, his heart's desire.

He had only fifty cartons left of the latest delivery when his life was once again kicked in a new direction. One evening at the beginning of March, the doorbell rang. Jerry got up from the infinitely slow download of a web manual on creating homepages and went to look through the spy hole.

Outside stood a friend of a friend whose name he didn't know, but who had bought from him a couple of times before. He opened the door. As soon as he saw the expression on the man's face close up, he realised something was wrong. From behind his back the man produced a long metal shoehorn and despite the fact that Jerry didn't understand what the danger actually was, he moved to shut the door. Too late. The shoehorn had been shoved into the opening and it was impossible to close the door.

Then he heard running footsteps on the stairs, and seconds later they were in. The man with the shoehorn whispered, 'Sorry, no choice,' and took off.

There were three of them: the guy who had been in the billiard hall and two more who at first glance were barely distinguishable from him. Same shaved heads, same jackets.

They took the sacks of cigarettes. They forced Jerry to show them where he kept his money, and took that as well. Then they took Jerry. Calmly and politely they led him down the stairs to a waiting car. Jerry was numb with fear, and it didn't even occur to him to scream. Half-slumped in their arms he noticed they had a Volvo 740. A real hick's car. However, the reason for it soon became apparent. The car was equipped with a tow bar.

They drove Jerry down to the gravelled car park next to the Lommar swimming pool. Beneath the sign that announced *Sweden's second-longest water slide*, they threw him on the ground and handcuffed his feet together. Then they ran a chain from the handcuffs to the tow bar. When they put on 'We Live in the Country' by Bröderna Djup at full volume, Jerry shat himself.

The guy from the billiard hall wrinkled his nose as he became aware of the smell. He pointed at Jerry's soiled backside and said, 'I take it that means you get it now.' He waved his hand in a circular movement over the dark, deserted car park. 'I warned you, fat boy. We're going for a little drive. There's going to be blood and shit all over the gravel, but look on the bright side. You're bound to lose a few kilos.'

From inside the car, Bröderna Djup were squealing and grunting as they imitated all the animals they were going to buy when they had sold their possessions. Jerry wept and whispered, 'Please, please, no. You can have anything you want.'

The guy smirked. 'Like what? You've got fuck all. We've just taken everything.'

Jerry was about to vomit with fear, and tried to form his lips around the words that would promise them all his savings, all his... everything. Before he had the chance, the guy taped his mouth shut and said, 'We don't want to wake the neighbours, now do we?' Then he got in the car and revved the engine, dousing Jerry in a cloud of exhaust fumes.

He was dragged across the gravel and his shirt ripped, baring his back to the sharp stones. He plunged into a vortex of imagining the skin, the muscles being ripped from his body until his naked skeleton was screaming against the ground. He wanted to lose consciousness, he wanted to die quickly, he wanted...

He didn't even notice when the car stopped, ten metres from where it had started. All three of them climbed out, stood around him and pissed on him. Then they unhooked him from the tow bar. He heard a voice in his ear, 'Next time it'll be the full treatment, OK?'

Doors slammed shut and gravel sprayed over his face as the car shot away. He lay there staring up at the night sky and the bright winter stars. His back was burning, and he was breathing heavily and unevenly through his nose.

It took ten minutes before he managed to get up and rip the tape from his mouth. His feet were still fastened together, and he stank of piss and shit. Shuffling and hopping, he made his way towards the lights and the apartment blocks, barely noticing when he fell and cut his cheek open on a sharp stone. Something inside him had broken beyond repair.

24

When Jerry hadn't been in touch for a month, Laila began to get worried. Although there had been periods before when they went for months without hearing from him, they usually spoke every couple of weeks or so. But Jerry didn't ring, and when Laila rang him there was no reply.

She might have investigated the matter more closely, she might even have broken the taboo and gone to visit Jerry—if she hadn't had a new project that took up so much of her time and her attention.

She had started teaching the girl to read.

She still couldn't imagine what the future might look like. The girl was around eight years old now, she would probably be nine soon, and what was going to happen when she got older? When she reached puberty, when she became a teenager, when she became...an adult? Would she and Lennart be sitting here as pensioners with a grown woman in the cellar, a woman who had never set foot outside the door?

It didn't bear thinking about, so Laila took one day at a time. She had created a compensatory fantasy in which the girl was a refugee threatened with deportation, and that was why they were keeping her hidden. She had read about such cases in the local newspaper, and the fantasy fitted in well with the unpleasant story Lennart had served up to the girl. A hostile world was out to get her, and if she showed herself she would be sent away, perhaps even killed. Like Anne Frank. It made Laila feel much better.

Since the girl was disinclined to speak, it was no easy matter to teach her the alphabet, to get her to repeat and imitate the sounds that corresponded with the letters. To begin with it was downright impossible. For example, Laila wrote 'A' on a piece of paper and said the letter out loud. The girl wouldn't look at the paper, didn't make a sound.

Laila tried with other letters, other ways of writing them or illustrating them. She drew pictures of objects the girl would recognise, wrote their names in big letters, said them out loud. The girl showed no interest whatsoever; she simply sat there playing with her drill, or arranging nails in dead straight lines without even acknowledging Laila's existence.

When Laila eventually came up with the solution, she could have kicked herself for her stupidity. It was just so obvious. She *sang* the letters. The girl imitated her. Laila held the piece of paper with the letter on it in front of her face so that the girl wouldn't look away, and sang 'Aaa' as if the letter itself was singing. When she swiftly lowered the paper she could see that the girl had looked, before her eyes slid away. She carried on with the rest of the vowels in the same way.

It took several weeks, but eventually it happened. The girl began to associate the symbol with the sound. When Laila held up the piece of paper with U on it on front of her face, there was silence for a little while as the girl waited for the note. When it didn't come she supplied it herself, a humming but perfectly clear 'Uuuu...'

Lennart was in the middle of one of his studio periods again, but listened to Laila's stories of the girl's progress and made encouraging comments and suggestions. For example, when Laila explained that she was having a problem with the consonants, he suggested that she should use lyrics the girl already knew, isolating individual words and getting the girl to sing them.

Laila decided on the Swedish version of 'Strangers in the Night' by Lasse Lönndahl, as Lasse had a tendency to extend the vowels, but still enunciated the consonants clearly, which made it easier to sing individual words.

Tusen och en natt, låg jag allena
Drömmande och matt...

Laila began with the word 'en', extending the word as she held the piece of paper with the word on it in front of her. 'Eeennn...eeennn...' She had to repeat it over and over again, and go through the song many times with sudden interruptions and much scribbling on the paper, but eventually the girl was singing from the same hymn sheet, so to speak.

As they approached the summer, Laila could hold up a piece of paper with the word '*tusen*' or '*natt*' on it, and the girl would sing what was written there.

Laila had rung and rung, she had even gone to Jerry's apartment, struggled up the stairs and rung the bell. No one had opened the door, but when Laila peered through the letterbox she could see that there was no post or junk mail on the floor. Jerry was still around somewhere. She had shouted through the letterbox, but there was no response.

And then one day in early June, there he was standing on the porch steps. Laila hardly recognised him; it was a stranger she invited to sit down at the kitchen table. When Lennart emerged from the studio he reacted the same way, and seemed on the point of asking who he was.

If Laila had lost maybe ten kilos by watching what she ate since the winter, Jerry had lost three times as much in less time. There were bags under his eyes, and a few grey hairs had come in at his temples. A badly healed scar ran across his right cheek. The air of self-evident authority with which he had commanded a room was gone. He had begun to look like Lennart.

They sat in silence for a while. Then Laila asked, 'What's happened to you, love?'

A shadow of his former ironic smile passed over Jerry's lips. 'You might well ask. I'm on a disability pension, for a start.'

'A disability pension? But you're only thirty-three!'

Jerry shrugged his shoulders. 'I managed to convince them.'

'Of what?'

'That I can't work. That I'm finished. That I can't be around people.'

Laila reached across the table to stroke Jerry's arm, but he moved it away. She said, 'But why, love?'

Jerry scratched the scar, pale beneath the stubble, looked her in the eye and said, 'Because I hate them. Because I can't cope with seeing them. Because I'm scared of them. Will that do?'

Jerry got up from the table and when Laila tried to stop him, he pulled away from her. He picked up the guitar he had left in the hallway and went down to the cellar.

25

It was a kind of homecoming. When he caught the familiar smell of wood, smoke, soap powder and general cellar aroma, it took him straight back to his childhood. He felt like an empty shell; he accepted the sensory awareness gratefully because it made him feel as if he contained something after all.

He had thought things would go all right with Lennart and Laila, but he could hardly bear to look at them either. Behind every face was another face, behind every sentence uttered, dark motives lurked. Yes, he had paranoid delusions. He'd even got a piece of paper to prove it.

The girl was waiting for him in the dimly lit room. Straight back, arms down by her sides and a drill in her hand. Jerry sat down on the bed and opened the guitar case.

'Hi there, sis. Did you miss me?'

The girl didn't reply. Jerry relaxed slightly. He played E-major seventh, and the girl picked up the note. A few more chords, an improvised sequence and the girl sang a melody. Jerry breathed a long sigh. The girl was standing in the darkness over by the CD player; he could only see her outline.

'Bloody hell, sis,' he said. 'At least I can hang out with you.'

He put down the guitar and went over to the window to remove the blanket. When he lifted one corner, the girl whacked him on the thigh with the drill and screamed, 'No!'

Jerry jerked backwards and let go of the blanket, which fell down. 'What the fuck are you doing—'

He broke off. The girl was curled up in the corner, holding the drill in front of her as she peered up at the window. Jerry crouched down in front of her. 'What's the matter? You're crazier than me, for fuck's sake. Are you scared of the window?'

'Big,' said the girl. 'Dangerous outside. Want to eat up Little One.'

'What are you talking about? Are there big people out there who want to eat you up?'

'Yes.'

Jerry nodded. 'You're not wrong there, sis. That's the right attitude to have. I only wish I'd realised it earlier. So why do they want to do that, then?'

'Hate in head.'

Jerry had an idea of what was going on here. He had been wondering how the hell Lennart and Laila were going to keep the girl indoors. Evidently they had come up with a solution.

'So what about me, then? Why don't I want to eat you up?'

'Love in head.'

'Love in...Are you saying I love you, kind of?'

The girl didn't reply. A shadow flickered across the wall as, out in the garden, Lennart or Laila walked past. The girl jumped and curled up in a tighter ball. When Jerry hung the blanket up again, she relaxed and said, 'Play. Sing.'

They jammed for a while. Jerry played songs in a minor key, and the girl made them even gloomier with her clear, flowing loops, transforming them from simple melodies into a lament on the whole of life and the human race. For a good fifteen minutes Jerry didn't feel afraid at all. He could have gone on much longer if his increasingly robust efforts hadn't broken one of the guitar strings.

His back was covered in sweat as he put the guitar back in its case and clicked the lock shut. 'You know what?' he said, without looking at Theres. 'However fucking crazy you might be, you're right. If I love anyone, it's you.'

26

After that, Jerry's visits became more regular again. It grieved Laila that he couldn't really be bothered with her and Lennart anymore, but she took solace from the fact that spending time with the girl seemed to be doing Jerry good. The dark cloud that hung over him had always dispersed a little when he came up from the cellar.

Laila carried on teaching the girl. In time she was able to read words in both upper and lower case letters that had nothing to do with a song, although she did read with a strange, musical diction. It was time for the next step: teaching the girl to make the letters herself. To write.

This turned out to be an even harder labyrinth to negotiate. The girl could hold a pen, but flatly refused to draw the letters Laila wrote on a pad. When Laila tried to guide her hand, the girl growled or yelled out some swear word she had presumably picked up from Jerry. It might have been funny hearing her scream 'Bloody hell!' or 'For fuck's sake!' if the words hadn't been spewed out with such aggression, frequently accompanied by a blow as Laila tried to hold onto her hand. Laila abandoned that approach.

She tried drawing the letters with crayons, she tried letting the girl scratch them with the nails she had grown so fond of lately, but nothing worked. The nineteen steps leading down to the cellar seemed more and more depressing as the winter drew in, and her leg started to ache even more. She was not getting through; and Lennart didn't have any helpful suggestions.

The girl's new interest was hammering nails into pieces of wood. She would keep at it until there was no more space, and the piece of wood split from the amount of nails crammed into it. As Christmas approached Lennart taught her to crack nuts with the hammer: that too became an obsession.

And that was literally how the problem was cracked as well. One afternoon Laila was watching the girl as she sat on the floor, filled with grim concentration, smashing nuts on a chopping board. The arm moving up and down, the carefully judged blow, the monotonous motion. Tock, tock, tock.

An idea came into her head, and after all there was nothing to lose. In the store cupboard Laila found Lennart's old portable Halda typewriter. She carried it in and placed it on the floor next to the chopping board. The girl looked at it for a while from different angles, then raised the hammer to deliver a blow, but Laila managed to snatch the machine away just in time.

Although it would turn out to be a good idea, it took almost a year before Laila's efforts really came to fruition. Every key was a new obstacle to surmount, but by the time the girl was ten years old she had learned every sound that corresponded with a symbol that corresponded with a key, and she began to put together simple words.

Jerry's visits tended to cause backsliding. The girl withdrew and didn't want to do the exercises, but Laila was patient and didn't mention it to Lennart. If the girl could bring Jerry a bit of happiness, it was worth the delay.

Besides which, Laila didn't really know why she was doing this. What pleasure would the girl gain from being able to read and write? Would she ever participate in a society that required these skills?

Sometimes Laila grew tired of the tough, tedious, drawn-out project. Then she would put on a record, Bibi Johns or Mona Wessman, and sing for a while with the girl. It felt like a kind of togetherness, and gave her new strength to carry on.

27

Jerry didn't like leaving his apartment, and conducted most of his contact with the outside world via the internet. His pension didn't cover much more than food, rent and his internet connection. In the autumn of 2001 he came across something called Partypoker. Jerry was a moderately good player and began betting quite carefully, winning as much as he lost.

Six months later the number of players had increased significantly thanks to a couple of spots on cable TV and some articles in the press. New players started up who weren't particularly good, and he found he could bring home a small profit. Not huge sums, but welcome additions to his meagre allocation from the state.

One evening he got into a game with a guy who called himself Bizznizz, and who played like an idiot. Jerry thought it had to be a ploy to drive up the stakes. However, he carried on. After a couple of hours it seemed to him to be perfectly obvious when the guy was bluffing and when he was seriously betting on his hand. By that stage Jerry had won just over a hundred dollars.

In the next hand Jerry held three tens, refusing to drop out as the stakes were pushed up, and in the end only he and Bizznizz were left in, with the pot at nine hundred dollars. Jerry thought the guy might be bluffing on a putative full house, but at the same time he realised with a sinking feeling that this could well be the hand Bizznizz had been laying the groundwork for. And yet Jerry still couldn't drop out.

He raised with his last three hundred; despair clutched his heart with its cold fingers as Bizznizz declined to fold, and went for the showdown. It was three weeks until pension day, and Jerry would have nothing left to live on.

He didn't understand what he was seeing when the other guy's cards came up. There was a moment of disconnect as his eyes flicked between the open cards and Bizznizz's cards. It looked as if the idiot only had a pair of threes!

Only when the money came rattling into his account did he realise it wasn't a misunderstanding. The idiot had sat there bluffing with a low pair, and then been stupid enough to go for the *showdown*! Jerry had won something in the region of five thousand kronor from Mr Bizznizz.

He didn't play any more that night. The game had given him an important insight. There were any number of total idiots out there playing on the net. Idiots with money. All he had to do was find them, and make sure he ended up at the same table.

Jerry began by methodically scanning every website, blog and discussion forum that had anything to do with poker. He gathered information. After a couple of weeks he had a fairly clear picture of the kind of people who played on the net, at least in Sweden. It was true that most used different aliases and usernames when they played and when they were in a discussion, but some were so attached to their names that they couldn't help using them even when money was involved.

Jerry's stroke of genius was to start secretly reading forums for people who were likely to have a knack for earning money quickly and easily. Stockbrokers and the IT crowd. He even looked at some of the forums on *Dagens Industri*, the Swedish equivalent of the *Financial Times*. A discussion page for property owners in Danderyd proved useless; he combed through page after page on renovations and cheap tradesmen without finding what he was looking for, but a page for owners of Abyssinians—a fashionable and expensive breed of cat—turned out to be pure gold.

He was actually looking for any mention of internet poker.

Someone who had recently come into money, for example, had entered the forum to ask for advice on their newly acquired Abyssinian. The cat was so lively, shredding the Svenskt Tenn designer curtains—what could he do? The cat owner might get into conversation with another owner, and poker would be mentioned in passing.

That was the key: in passing. These nouveau riche types thought it was fun to mention *in passing* how much they had spent on a bottle of wine or a suit, or the fact that they had *just thrown away thirty thousand in a game of online poker the other night* in spite of the fact that they were such bad players, ha ha, but not to worry, they were sitting on a hundred and twenty thousand IBM B-portfolio options, say no more.

That kind of comment. Made in passing.

It was a time-consuming and tedious task. Often Jerry would find a perfect candidate, but then never see that person on the poker site. Either he was no longer playing, or he was using a different handle.

But he compiled a list, and as time went by one of these rich or slightly less rich idiots would turn up at the table. Then it was time to join the game.

There was no ideology behind it. No Robin Hood fantasies on Jerry's part. On the contrary. Since the opportunities to skin rich people were so rare, he also gathered information on ordinary players, gambling addicts and poor people. The main thing was that they played badly.

To tell the truth, it gave him even more satisfaction to fleece someone he knew to have problems. He found Wheelsonfire on a forum for caravan owners, complaining that he couldn't afford a new fridge for his caravan—did anyone know where he could find a second-hand one? The fact that he was a bad poker player was mentioned in a different context.

When Wheelsonfire popped up on Partypoker and Jerry managed to take four thousand off him, he felt a deep, sincere and malicious pleasure. *No new fridge for you, wanker. You can sit there roasting on your campsite while your food rots.*

His fear of other people and his unease around them grew neither better nor worse. But his contempt increased. As did his income. A year or so after he had begun playing and gathering information, he was bringing in eight to ten thousand a month, as a general rule, money that the tax office hadn't yet realised they should be enquiring about.

He sat there in his little apartment in Norrtälje, dipping his virtual fingers in the global river of money. He played for five or six hours a day, and regardless of whether he won or lost, he was never gripped by greed. It didn't matter to him. The important thing was that he had a little power base where he could sit and let his lash whistle across the backs of all those world-wide idiots. He could flog them hard and almost hear them whimper. Sometimes he even felt something that resembled happiness.

28

When the girl was about twelve years old, she became listless. Nothing seemed to reach her anymore. Day in and day out she sat on her bed staring at the wall, doing nothing. She didn't sing, she didn't talk, she barely moved, and she had to be fed baby food from the jar with a spoon; that was still the only thing she would eat.

It became quite frightening after a while, and Lennart and Laila began to have serious discussions about whether they should give her up and let the professionals take care of her. Drive somewhere no one knew them and just leave her at a hospital, then drive away without saying anything. But it felt too cold, too terrible not to know what might become of her. So they waited.

After all, everything seemed to have gone so well. The girl had learned to write using the typewriter, she could form whole words and sentences. She spent a long time typing out every single word from an old copy of the local paper. Articles, adverts, the speech bubbles in the cartoon strips, the TV guide. It took her almost four months to type out the entire newspaper onto sixty pages of A4.

It was when this project was almost finished that something happened. Laila saw the first sign when she went down to the cellar one morning and found the girl staring into the washing machine; she closed the door, then looked inside the tumble drier. Then the laundry basket.

'What are you looking for?' Laila asked, but as usual the girl ignored her.

Another day Laila stood silently by the workshop door watching the girl opening drawers and looking in cupboards just as she had done when she was little, just as Laila had done.

The girl had grown to be beautiful with her curly golden hair, and there was something deeply upsetting about seeing this lovely creature wandering around and around like a swan in a cramped cage, searching for something that didn't exist. The dark, gloomy cellar, the rattling as she pulled out yet another drawer of random tools, while her golden hair cascaded over her shoulders.

Laila tapped on the door frame with the crutch she had started to use to help her get down the stairs, and the girl immediately stopped searching, went to her room and sat on the bed. Laila sat down beside her.

'Little One? What is it you want?'

The girl didn't answer.

A week or so later, Laila had gone down to the cellar one evening to get a pair of gloves from the storeroom. She stood in the doorway of the girl's room, watching her as she slept. With her hair spread over the pillow, her arms resting straight down by her sides, she looked like a very beautiful corpse. Laila shuddered.

Then she caught sight of the typewriter. There was a blank piece of paper in it, a pale glow in the reflection of the cellar light. No. Not blank. There was something written on it. After checking that the girl really was asleep, Laila went into the room and carefully pulled out the sheet of paper.

The girl's writing ability also seemed to have deteriorated. There was just one line, without any punctuation. It was the first thing Laila had seen that the girl had come up with for herself. It said:

'Where love how love colour feels how it is where'

Laila read the line several times, then her gaze slid over to the bed. The girl's eyes were open, shining faintly as she lay there looking at Laila. She sat down on the edge of the bed with the piece of paper in her hand.

'Love,' she said. 'Is it love you're searching for, Little One?'

But the girl had closed her eyes again, and didn't answer.

29

One morning in the middle of October, when Lennart was in the garage putting the winter tyres on the car, Laila sat in the living room feeling despondent and restless at the same time. She tried playing a Lill-Babs song to cheer herself up, but it didn't help.

There was a knot of anxiety in her stomach, an ominous feeling. She walked up and down the room, leaning on her crutch, but the feeling wouldn't go. As if something had happened just now, something she ought to know about. Suddenly she got the idea it was something to do with the girl. As she limped towards the cellar, she became more and more convinced that she was right. Their poor foundling had taken the step from apathy to the final separation that is death.

She felt she should hurry. Perhaps it wasn't too late.

She didn't ground the crutch properly on the fifth step, and it slid away when she put her weight on it. She fell head first down the stairs, and when her head met the edge between the wall and the staircase, she heard rather than felt something crack in the back of her neck.

Steps. She could hear footsteps. Back and forth. Light, tiptoeing steps. Her entire back was a blue flame of pain, and she couldn't move her head, couldn't feel her fingers. She opened her eyes. The girl was standing next to her.

'Little One,' Laila wheezed. 'Little One, help me. I think I've... had it.'

The girl looked her in the eye. Studied her. Looked her in the eye. Never before had the girl looked her in the eye for so long. She leaned down and looked even deeper, as if she were searching for something in or behind Laila's eyes. The girl's eyes enveloped Laila like two dark blue wells, and for a brief moment the pain disappeared.

In her confusion Laila thought: *She can heal. She can make me whole. She's an angel.*

Laila opened her trembling lips, 'I'm here. Help me.'

The girl straightened up and said, 'Can't see it. Can't see it.'

A shape that shouldn't have been there flickered on the edge of Laila's field of vision. A hammer. The girl was holding a hammer in her hand. Laila tried to scream. She could only manage a whimper.

'No,' she whispered. 'What are you going to do what are you—'

'Quiet,' said the girl. 'Open look.'

Then she struck Laila's temple with the hammer. Once, twice, three times. Laila was no longer able to feel anything, her sight went and she was blind. Her hearing seemed to be drifting around the room, however, and she could hear the girl grunt in annoyance, footsteps walking away.

Laila no longer had any idea what was up or down, she was floating in a vacuum and only her hearing was keeping her alive, a fine thread that had come to breaking point.

She heard a clinking sound as the girl put something down on the floor. Her hearing guessed that it was nails, perhaps five of them. Then she felt something. A sharp point against her skin, someone took a deep breath and the last thing her hearing perceived was a harsh metallic clang and a crunching, cracking sound as her skull split open beneath the point of the nail.

Then there was silence as the process of opening up the skull continued.

One hour later Lennart came down to the cellar. He didn't even have time to scream.

30

In some ways Jerry was lucky that day, because he unconsciously established an alibi for himself. The wide-ranging police investigation that was to follow would probably have focused more closely on Jerry if he hadn't decided on that particular day that he'd had enough of sitting around indoors, and spent several hours at the bowling alley.

He didn't know anybody there, he just sat at a table and drank several cups of coffee, ate a couple of sandwiches and read the papers, distractedly watching the semi-useless players as they went after their strikes and spares. After that he went to the Co-op Forum store and spent half an hour hanging out in the media department, where he bought a few DVDs. At the cheap supermarket he stocked up, out of habit, on cans of ravioli and instant noodles. An impulse led him to Jysk, where he wandered around for a while and eventually bought a new pillow.

He couldn't have arranged things better if it had been planned. A whole day when his activities could be confirmed by the staff in the bowling alley, checkout assistants and his printed receipts. This would actually end up being the police's only grounds for suspicion: the fact that his alibi was almost *too* watertight for a recluse like Jerry. But they couldn't really arrest him for that.

He went home and had a beer, then rang Lennart and Laila. No one answered, but it was possible to trace the call later, extending his documented afternoon activities by a further half hour. By that stage the bodies of his parents had grown so cold since the morning that he couldn't possibly have been the perpetrator.

He then had his final unplanned stroke of genius. He got on his motorbike and went to visit his sister.

There was some suspicion that he knew about body temperature, knew they had to be reported dead before too long had elapsed if the time of death were to be fixed within the period for which he had an alibi.

Needless to say, no such thoughts were in Jerry's mind as he drove out to his parents' house through the darkness. There were no thoughts in his mind at all. It was good to be out on the bike. The forward movement of his body replaced the circular movement of his thoughts, going round and round inside his head.

He drove right up to the porch steps, noticing that the light wasn't on in the kitchen. However, he could just see a glimmer of light behind the blanket at the cellar window. He went up the steps and knocked. No one came. He tried the handle, and found that the door wasn't locked.

'Hello?' he shouted as he walked into the hallway, but there was no answer. 'Anyone home?'

He hung his leather jacket on Lennart's homemade coat rack, which in his opinion was a bit kitsch, and took a stroll around the house. He couldn't understand it. Since the occasion many years ago when he and Theres had checked out Bowie, he didn't think his parents had ever left her alone.

Have they taken her with them?

But the garage door was shut, which meant the car was still inside. Without giving the matter any more thought, he went and turned on the cellar stair light. He stopped with his hand on the switch and listened. The door was ajar, and he could hear some kind of motor coming from down below. He pulled the door open.

He managed five steps before he collapsed on the stairs, before his brain registered what his eyes were seeing. His windpipe contracted and it was impossible to breathe.

Lennart and Laila, what ought to be Lennart and Laila judging by their clothes, were lying next to one another at the bottom of the staircase. The whole floor was covered in blood. Strewn around in the blood were a number of different tools. Hammers, saws, chisels.

Their heads were mush. Pieces of skull with short or long clumps of hair still attached lay scattered all over the floor, lumps of brain matter were stuck to the walls, and all that was left above Lennart's shoulders was a piece of spine sticking up with a grubby bit of skull still attached. The rest of his head lay crushed and spread all over the floor and the walls.

Theres was kneeling in the blood next to what remained of Laila's head, which was slightly more than in the case of Lennart. In her hand she held her drill; the battery was so run down that the bit was hardly rotating at all. With the last scrap of power left in the machine she was busy boring her way in behind Laila's ear. A little pearl earring in Laila's earlobe vibrated as the drill laboriously worked its way through the bone. Theres struggled and tugged, changed the direction of the drill and managed to pull it out, wiped the blood from her eyes and reached for the saw.

Jerry was on the point of passing out through lack of oxygen, and he managed to draw a panting breath. Theres turned her head in the direction of the sound, looked at his feet. A strange calm descended over Jerry. He was not afraid, and even though what he was seeing was obviously horrific, it was just like a picture, something to register: *what I am seeing is horrific.*

Somewhere deep inside he had sensed that things would end up like this, one way or another. That it would all end badly. Now it had happened, and even if it couldn't have been any worse, at least it had happened. There was nothing to add. This was just how the world was. Nothing new, even if the details were disgusting.

'Theres,' he said, his voice almost steady. 'Sis. What the fuck have you done? Why have you done this?'

Theres lowered the saw and her eyes slid from Laila to Lennart, over the bits of their heads strewn all around her.

'Love,' she said. 'Not there.'

THE OTHER GIRL

I

She was born on November 8, 1992, one of the last babies delivered in the maternity unit at Österyd. The unit was in the process of being moved to the central location in Rimsta, and they had already started packing. Only one midwife and a trainee were on duty.

Fortunately it was an easy delivery. Maria Svensson was admitted at 14:42. One hour and twenty minutes later, the child was born. The father, Göran Svensson, waited outside the room as usual. That's what he had done when their other two children were born, and that's what he did this time. As he waited he flicked through a few copies of a magazine, *Året Runt*.

Just after four o'clock the midwife emerged and informed him that he had been blessed with a perfect daughter. Göran abandoned the article on breeding rabbits he had been reading and went in to see his wife.

As he walked into the room he made the mistake of looking around. A number of bloodstained compresses had been tossed aside into a metal dish, and Göran was hit by a wave of nausea before he managed to look away. The combination of a sterile environment and bodily fluids revolted him. That was why he could never be present at a birth.

He pulled himself together and went over to kiss his wife's sweaty brow. The child was lying on her chest, a wrinkled red lump. It was incomprehensible that it would turn into a person. He ran his finger over the child's damp head. He knew what was expected of him.

'Did it go OK?' he asked.

'Yes,' said Maria. 'But I think I'm going to need a few stitches.'

Göran nodded and looked out of the window. It was almost completely dark outside, wet snowflakes licking the glass. He was a father of three now. Two boys and a girl. He knew Maria had wanted a girl, and it didn't make any difference to him. So everything had turned out for the best. His eyes followed a trickle of liquid running down the window pane.

A life begins.

A child had been born on this day. His child. The only thing he wished for now was a little more happiness. Sometimes he would pray to God for this very thing: *give me a greater capacity to feel happiness.* But his prayer was rarely answered.

A miracle had taken place in this room, just a few minutes ago. He knew that. But he couldn't make himself *feel* it. The trickle of liquid reached the bottom of the window and Göran turned back to his wife, smiling. What he felt was a faint satisfaction, a certain sense of relief. It was done. It was over for this time.

'Teresa, then,' he said. 'Happy with that?'

Maria nodded. 'Yes, Teresa.'

It had been decided long ago. Tomas if it was a boy, Teresa if it was a girl. Good names. Reliable names. Arvid, Olof and Teresa. Their little trio. He stroked Maria's cheek and started to cry without knowing why. Because of the image of the wet snow against the window of a warmly lit room where a child had been born. Because there was a secret he would never be part of.

When the nurse came in to do Maria's stitches, he left the room.

2

Teresa was fourteen months old when she started daycare. Lollo, the childminder, had five other children to look after and Teresa was the youngest. It was a problem-free induction. After only four days Maria was able to leave her daughter for the whole day and go back to work full-time at Österyd Pets.

Göran had been forced to start work at the state-run liquor outlet in Rimsta when the Österyd branch closed down. The most noticeable change was that it took him half an hour longer to get to and from work every morning and afternoon, so he was rarely able to pick the children up from the childminder, which he missed.

However, he had managed to negotiate one early shift each week, on a Wednesday, and he usually made sure he at least picked Teresa up. Despite the fact that it was Maria who had most wanted a girl, Teresa turned more to her father, and he couldn't deny that he felt something special for her.

The boys were lively, as boys ought to be. Teresa was significantly quieter and more secretive, and Göran appreciated that. She was the child who was most like him. Her first word was 'Daddy' and her second was 'no', stated very firmly: 'No!'

Do you want this? No!

Can I help you with...? No!

Can Daddy borrow the crayon? No!

She fetched things for herself, she handed things over when she felt like it, but she rarely allowed herself to be influenced by the questions or expectations of others. Göran liked that. She had a will of her own, small as she was.

Sometimes at work he had to bite his tongue to stop himself coming out with the first word that sprang to mind these days.

'Could you fetch a pallet of beer, Göran?'

'No!'

...which was not what he said, of course. But he would have liked to.

At this stage Arvid was five and Olof seven. They weren't particularly interested in their little sister, but they put up with her. Teresa didn't make much noise except when someone tried to get her to do something she didn't want to do. Then it was No! and No! again, until she very occasionally had a complete temper tantrum. She had a limit, and when she was pushed beyond that limit, she was horrendous.

Her favourite soft toy was a little green snake they had bought at Kolmården; she called it Bambam. One day when Teresa was eighteen months old, Arvid started teasing her, trying to take the snake off her by pulling its tail.

Teresa clung to the snake's head and said, 'Avvi, no!', but Arvid carried on pulling. Teresa resisted with all her might and ended up tipping over forwards as she clutched the head and screamed, 'Avvi, no-no!' Arvid gave the snake a tug and it flew out of Teresa's hands as she lay on the floor shaking with rage.

Arvid waved the snake in front of her face, but when she didn't even reach out to try and take it, he got bored and threw it back to her. She cradled the snake in her arms, whispering, 'Bambam...' with tears in her voice.

So far, so good. Arvid forgot about his sister and started rummaging around under the bed for a bucket of Lego. But with a grudge-bearing capacity unusual in such a small child, Teresa hauled herself to her feet and toddled over to the shelf by her bed, where she picked up a glass snowdome with an angel inside.

A blizzard whirled up around the angel as Teresa went over to

Arvid and waited by his side until he sat up. Then she slammed it against his head. The globe broke and cut open both Teresa's hand and Arvid's temple. When Maria heard the screams and came running into the room, she found Arvid lying in a pool of water, blood and bits of plastic, yelling along with Teresa, whose hand was bleeding quite badly.

Arvid's summary of the incident was, 'I took her snake and she hit me over the head.' He omitted the detail that at least a minute had passed between the two events. Perhaps he had forgotten, perhaps he didn't see it as being of any significance.

3

By the time Teresa turned four, it was obvious that it was Daddy who mattered. Not that she distanced herself from Maria, but it was Göran she turned to in all essential matters. With the boys, the situation was reversed. For example it was Maria who drove them to football training. No actual decision had ever been taken, it was just the way things were.

Maria wanted to *do* things, while Göran was perfectly happy to sit quietly with Teresa while she was drawing or pottering about. If she asked a question he answered her, if she wanted help with something he helped her, but without making a fuss about it.

Her favourite activity was making necklaces with plastic beads. Göran had acquired every plastic bead in the toy shop in Rimsta, in every imaginable shape and colour, and had even got the assistant to go down to the storeroom and dig out some boxes they had taken off display. Teresa had an entire shelf stocked with at least sixty little plastic containers into which she had sorted the beads according to a system only she understood. Sometimes she would spend days altering the system.

The beads were threaded onto coloured wool or fishing line, and after patient instruction Teresa had learned to tie the knots herself. It was a constant production line; the only problem was the product.

Maria's parents had been given theirs. Göran's parents had been given theirs. Family and friends and relatives of friends had been given theirs. Anyone who might possibly deserve a necklace made of plastic beads had been given one. Or two. Göran's father was the only one who wore his. Probably to annoy Göran's mother more than anything.

But it would have taken a family of biblical proportions to generate a demand to meet the supply. Teresa made at least three necklaces a day. Göran had put up lots of tacks above her bed to hang the necklaces on. The wall was now more or less full.

One Wednesday afternoon in the middle of October, Göran picked his daughter up from the childminder as usual. She got out her beads and thread as usual and put them on the kitchen table, and Göran sat opposite her with his usual evening paper. Concentrating hard, Teresa tied a stop-knot at one end of a length of fishing line. Then she made a selection from among her containers, and started threading.

When Göran had finished looking for news about the EU decision on Sweden's state monopoly on alcohol sales and found nothing but more misery from Hallandsås, he lowered the paper and looked at his daughter. She seemed to have decided on a necklace in red, yellow and blue. Using her fingers as tweezers, she skilfully picked up one bead at a time, threading them onto the line as she breathed audibly through her nose.

'Sweetheart?'

'Mm?'

'Couldn't you make something other than necklaces with your beads? It's just that you've got such a lot.'

'I want a lot.'

'But what for?'

Teresa stopped dead, a bright yellow bead between her fingers. She looked at Göran with a frown. 'I collect them.'

She held his gaze, as if she were challenging him to question her. His eyes flickered down to the newspaper, open at a picture of some lake somewhere. Pollution. Dead fish. Local population up in arms.

'Daddy?' Teresa was studying the yellow bead, her eyes narrowed. 'Why do things *exist*?'

'What do you mean?'

Teresa's eyebrows moved even closer together, and she looked as if she were in pain. She took a few breaths through her nose as she always did when she was concentrating. Eventually she said, 'Well, if this bead didn't exist, I wouldn't be holding it.'

'No.'

'And if I didn't exist, then nobody would be holding this bead.'

'No.'

Göran sat there as if he had been hypnotised, staring at the bright yellow dot between his daughter's fingers. The grey October day outside the window had gone. Only the yellow dot existed, and Göran felt as if something was pressing against his eardrums, like when you're sinking towards the bottom of the swimming pool.

Teresa shook her head. 'Why is it like that?' Her gaze swept over the containers on the table, their multi-coloured contents. 'I mean, all these beads might not exist and there might not be anybody to make necklaces with them.'

'But the beads do exist. And so do you. That's just the way things are.'

Teresa put the yellow bead back in its container and crossed her arms tightly over her chest as she continued to look at the kaleidoscope of coloured dots in front of her. Gently Göran asked, 'Have you all been talking about this at Lollo's?'

Teresa shook her head.

'So what made you think about it, then?'

Teresa didn't reply, but stared at her array of beads with an expression that could best be described as furious. Göran leaned forward with his chin resting on his hand so that he was closer to her level, and said, 'There is actually one person who hasn't had a necklace; do you know who that is?' Teresa didn't react, but Göran gave her the answer anyway, 'It's me. I've never had a necklace.'

Teresa bent her head so that her nose was pointing at the floor, and her voice broke as she said, 'You can have them all if you want.'

Göran got up from his chair. 'But sweetheart…'

He knelt down next to his daughter's chair and she fell into his arms, rested her forehead on his collarbone and wept. Göran stroked her head and said, 'Sssh...' but Teresa just carried on weeping.

When Göran said, 'Couldn't you make me a necklace? I'd like a yellow one. All yellow,' she banged her forehead against his collarbone so hard that it hurt both of them, and kept on weeping.

4

Since Teresa had been born late in the year, she started school before she turned seven. She could already read simple books and add up and take away, so the schoolwork itself wasn't a problem. At the first parents' evening Göran and Maria heard a great deal of praise for their daughter, who approached every task with diligence and great seriousness.

Nor did gymnastics or practical subjects pose any difficulties for her. She found it easy to understand instructions, and her fine motor skills were very good. She was always well-behaved.

The teacher closed her file. 'So…all in all I think we can say things have gone very well indeed. She's a…serious little girl, Teresa.'

Göran had reached for his jacket and started to put it on, but Maria thought she picked up a change of tone in the teacher's last remark, and asked her to elaborate. What did she mean, serious?

The teacher smiled as if to smooth things over. 'Well, as a teacher I couldn't wish for a better pupil, but…she doesn't play.'

'You mean…she's not with the other children?'

'No, no. When they're given things to do, she has no problem working with others. But, how can I put this, she doesn't like to use her imagination. Play. Make things up. As I said, she's…serious. Extremely serious.'

What Göran had accepted long ago, Maria now perceived as a warning bell. Since she herself was a sociable person, she found it difficult to see her daughter as a serious-minded lone wolf. For Maria, loneliness was not to do with inclination or choice; no, loneliness was a failure. She had a number of hobby horses, but the most important was: 'People are made to be together.'

Göran was not about to contradict her, particularly as he thought she was right, theoretically. He was popular at work as a conscientious and reliable person, but he wished he took greater real pleasure in the company of others.

The work at the liquor outlet suited him down to the ground. A customer came up with their numbered ticket, you exchanged a few words and dealt with their purchase. You might perhaps chat for thirty seconds or so if there weren't too many people waiting. He looked smart in his green waistcoat and shirt, he was polite and knowledgeable about the stock, he was *service minded.* He met a lot of people, but in small doses—it was perfect for him.

Maria, on the other hand, was pally with lots of her customers. Practically every day she came home with long stories the customers had told her, and several dog and cat owners had become her friends. She was invited to more parties and weddings and so on than she could ever manage to attend.

Göran would suffer agonies for several days in advance if there was to be some kind of social tasting night at work. If it hadn't been for his purely professional interest in, for example, new wines from Languedoc, he would probably have declined. As far as he was concerned, it would have been better if they'd just sent small samples by post.

As a consequence, they interpreted the information from the parents' evening differently. Göran was pleased that things were going so well for Teresa at school, while Maria was worried that things were so difficult for Teresa at school. Every day she started quizzing Teresa about what she had done during break times, who she had played with, who she had talked to. It got to the point where Göran started hoping Teresa would lie, make up some friends and games just to satisfy Maria. But making things up just wasn't in her nature.

Arvid and Olof were always having friends round. Some of these friends had younger brothers and sisters, and Maria would occasionally ring the parents and explain the situation, begging them to send a small sibling along for Teresa as part of the package. In Göran's opinion, Teresa handled things as well as she could. She would show the visitor her things, suggest games they might play and try in her own way to make the best of their forced proximity.

His heart swelled a little with pride as he watched his daughter take responsibility for a situation not of her making, and contracted with pain when he saw how badly things went. Teresa would meticulously set out the game and explain the rules while the other child looked anxiously around, wanting to go to the toilet. It would end in silence with a small sibling tugging at its big brother's sleeve and asking to go home.

In the spring Göran was made manager of his store. Rudolf retired and recommended Göran in glowing terms. He was already in charge of ordering and product selection, and was responsible for much of the contact with suppliers.

He had to go for an interview, and felt it went reasonably well. Later he was told that he had been given the job due to his extensive knowledge, despite some reservations about his suitability for the managerial role itself. He understood perfectly.

From a purely practical point of view it meant an extra twelve thousand kronor a month, more responsibility and longer working days. He was no longer able to finish early on Wednesdays. He and Maria took the bold step of securing a loan to renovate the kitchen, and for the first time in their lives they were able to buy a brand new car.

By May Göran had already begun to wish he could step down from the post he had taken up in March, but once an upward movement has begun, it takes a great deal of determination to break it. Göran did not have that determination. He gritted his teeth and stuck with it, worked harder. His daring decision to carry a wider selection of wines in Tetra-paks was a success, and sales increased.

In June he led a team-building weekend at a conference centre, and when he came home he was so worn out that he slept for fourteen hours.

It pained him that he had less time to spare for Teresa. He did his best to be there for her and the boys when he came home exhausted, but something had slipped away from him and he didn't have the strength to work out how to get it back.

Teresa had taken over her brothers' Lego since they lost interest in it. Maria had kept all the instructions, and Teresa spent a lot of time putting together all the different models as she listened to a tape of Allan Edwall reading Winnie-the-Pooh, over and over again.

Sometimes Göran would come in and just sit down in the armchair in her room to watch her, to listen to the clicks as the Lego pieces fitted into one another and Allan Edwall's dark, gentle voice. He would feel close to her for a while, until he fell asleep.

5

In the October of Teresa's second year in school there was to be a fancy dress disco at Hallowe'en. There would be soft drinks and sweets, and prizes for the best costumes. Maria had managed to miss the whole thing, and it wasn't until she got home at five o'clock that she spotted the piece of paper saying the disco would start at six.

Göran was busy stocktaking and probably wouldn't be home until late evening, so with every scrap of her positive determination Maria sat Teresa down on a chair in the kitchen and asked her what she wanted to be.

'I don't want to be anything,' Teresa replied.

'At the fancy dress disco, I mean,' said Maria. 'What do you want to dress up as?'

'I don't want to dress up.'

'But we've got loads of stuff. You can dress up as anything you like—a ghost or a monster, whatever.'

Teresa shook her head and got up to go to her room. Maria stepped in front of her and made her sit down again.

'Sweetheart. Everybody else will be dressed up. You don't want to be the only one who isn't dressed up, do you?'

'Yes.'

Maria massaged her temples. It wasn't because she found this difficult. It was because she found it totally absurd. She couldn't think of *one* good reason why a person wouldn't dress up when they were going to a fancy dress disco. However, she controlled herself and did something she perhaps did all too rarely. She asked a question.

'OK. Can you tell me *why* you don't want to dress up?'

'I just don't.'

'But *why*? You can dress up as somebody else.'

'I don't want to be somebody else.'

'But it's fancy dress. If you don't dress up, you can't go.'

'I won't go, then.'

Teresa's attitude was as crystal clear as it was untenable. Maria couldn't accept it. Teresa would end up being odd if she was allowed to follow every whim. Since Teresa wasn't old enough to have an overview of the consequences of her actions, it really came down to a question of upbringing, of taking responsibility as a parent.

'Right,' said Maria. 'This is what's going to happen. You *are* going to the disco and you *are* going to dress up. The matter is not up for discussion. There's only one thing I need to know: what do you want to dress up as?'

Teresa looked her mother in the eye and said, 'A banana.'

If Maria had had a different sense of humour, she might have laughed at her daughter's obviously defiant answer, then hunted out everything yellow she could lay her hands on. However, she didn't have that particular sense of humour. Instead she nodded grimly and said, 'OK. If that's the way you want it, I'll decide for you. Stay there.'

It is possible that we inherit certain characteristics from our parents. If this is the case, it was her sense of order that Teresa had inherited from her mother. In the clothes storeroom was a big box labelled 'Fancy Dress', since neither Arvid nor Olof had anything against getting dressed up—quite the opposite, in fact. After a few minutes Maria was back in the kitchen with black and red make-up, a black cape and a pair of plastic fangs.

'You can be a vampire,' she said. 'Do you know what a vampire is?'

Teresa nodded, and Maria took this as a sign of approval.

When Göran got home at eight o'clock, Maria asked him to pick Teresa up from the disco. He turned around in the hallway and went mechanically back to the car. This week had almost finished him, and the world felt like a piece of flat stage scenery as he drove towards the school.

Music was pounding from the gym, and a few children in costume were charging around outside the entrance. Göran blinked and rubbed his eyes. He couldn't do it. He just didn't have the strength to walk into that pulsating grotto of excited little bodies and well-meaning parents.

He wanted to go home. He knew he couldn't. With an effort he hauled his soul to its feet from its slumped, sideways position and walked towards the entrance, smiling and nodding at the parents who had been kind enough to organise this inferno.

Multi-coloured lights flashed across the darkened room. Sweets and popcorn were scattered all over the floor, and infants dressed as monsters were running around chasing one another while Markoolio sang that song about heading for the mountains to drink and screw. Göran peered into the darkness, trying to spot his daughter so that he could take her home.

He had to walk around before he found her sitting on a chair by the wall. She had thick black kohl all around her eyes, and her mouth looked oddly swollen. From the corners of her mouth ran painted-on trickles of dried blood. Her hands were resting on her knees.

'Hi, sweetheart. Shall we go home?'

Teresa looked up. Her eyes shone bright within their frame of black. She got up and Göran held out his hand. She didn't take it, but followed him out to the car.

It was a relief to close the car door. The sound was muted and they were alone. He glanced at Teresa, sitting in the passenger seat staring straight ahead, and asked, 'So did you have a good time?'

Teresa didn't reply. He started the car and pulled out of the school car park. When they were driving along the road, he asked, 'Did you get any sweets?'

Teresa mumbled something in reply.

'What did you say?'

Teresa mumbled something again, and Göran turned to look at her. 'What's that in your mouth?'

Teresa parted her lips and showed her fangs. A cold shudder ran down Göran's spine. For a brief moment he thought she looked genuinely horrible. Then he said, 'I think you could take those out now, sweetheart. So I can hear what you say.'

Teresa removed the teeth and sat there with them in her hand, but she still didn't say anything. Göran tried again.

'Did you get any sweets?' Teresa nodded and the best follow-up Göran's weary brain could come up with was, 'Were they nice?'

'I couldn't eat them.'

'Why not?'

Teresa held out the fangs. Göran felt a stab of pain in his chest. A dot of sorrow grew and grew, pressing against his ribs. 'But sweetheart, you could have taken them out. So you could eat your sweets.'

Teresa shook her head and said nothing more until they had parked on the drive at home. When Göran had switched off the engine and they were sitting in the darkness she said, 'I told Mum I didn't want to go. I *told* her.'

6

The Svensson family lived in a new house on what had been agricultural land before it was carved up. A narrow strip of conifers and deciduous trees separated them from their nextdoor neighbour. Among the trees were two big rocks, or rather boulders, lying side by side in such a way that a cave a few metres square was formed at their base. The autumn before Teresa turned ten, she had begun to spend more and more of her free time there.

One day at the end of September when Teresa was sitting in her secret room setting out an exhibition of different-coloured autumn leaves, something blocked the light from the entrance. A boy of her own age was standing there.

'Hi,' said the boy.

'Hi,' said Teresa, glancing up briefly before returning to her leaves. The boy stayed where he was without speaking, and Teresa wished he would go. He didn't look the way people usually looked. He was wearing a blue shirt, buttoned right up to the neck. Teresa tried to concentrate on the leaves, but it was difficult with someone standing there watching her.

'How old are you?' asked the boy.

'Ten,' said Teresa. 'In a month. And a week.'

'It was my tenth birthday two weeks ago,' said the boy. 'I'm seven weeks older than you.'

Teresa shrugged her shoulders. Boys always had to boast. Sorting out the leaves, which had absorbed her completely only a moment ago, suddenly seemed childish. She scraped them into a heap but couldn't leave while the boy was standing there blocking the opening. He looked around and said with a certain amount of gloom in his voice, 'I live here now.'

'Oh, where?'

The boy nodded in the direction of the house on the other side of the trees. 'There. We moved in yesterday. I think this is our garden. But you can use it if you want.'

'I don't think it's up to you to decide.'

The boy looked down at the ground, took a deep breath and let out the air in a long sigh. Then he shook his head. 'No. It's not up to me to decide.'

Teresa didn't understand what kind of boy this was. At first he had seemed boastful, and now he was standing there looking as if somebody was about to hit him. 'What's your name?' she asked.

'Johannes.'

Teresa thought that was quite a safe name. Not like Micke or Kenny. She got up and Johannes moved so that she could get out. They stood facing one another. Johannes swirled the leaves around with his toe. He was wearing a pair of trainers that looked almost new. Teresa said, 'Aren't you going to ask what my name is?'

'What's your name?'

'Teresa. I live here too. There.' She pointed at her house. Johannes looked at the house, then carried on poking at the leaves with his foot. Teresa wanted to go home, but in some strange way she felt as if she ought to look after Johannes. There was something about that shirt that looked so uncomfortable. She asked, 'Shall we do something?'

Johannes nodded without making any suggestions, so Teresa went on, 'So what shall we do, then? What do you usually do?'

Johannes shrugged his shoulders. 'Not much.'

'Do you like board games?'

'Yes.'

'Can you play Chinese checkers?'

'Yes. I'm really good at it.'

'How good?'

'I usually win.'

'So do I. When I play my dad.'

'I usually win when I play my mum.'

Teresa went inside and fetched the game. When she came back Johannes had crawled into the cave and was sitting there waiting for her. She didn't like him sitting there. That was her place. But she remembered her father saying that those rocks were actually on the neighbour's property, just as Johannes had said. So she couldn't really chuck him out. But she could move him.

'That's my place,' she said.

'So where shall I sit?'

Teresa pointed to the back wall of the cave. 'There.'

When Johannes got up, Teresa saw that he had been sitting on her pile of leaves. He scooped them up in his arms and tipped them out in his designated place, then gathered them together and patted them down before sitting on them. Teresa was still annoyed with him for moving into her cave, so to tease him she said, 'Are you frightened of getting your trousers dirty?'

'Yes.'

The direct answer disarmed her and she couldn't come up with anything else to say, so she put the board on the ground and sat down opposite Johannes. In silence they picked up the plastic counters and placed them on their spots. Then Johannes said, 'You can start because you're the smallest.'

A wave of heat spread over the tips of Teresa's ears, and she snapped, 'You can start because it's my game.'

Johannes shook his head. 'You can start because you're a girl.'

Teresa's ears were positively on fire by now, and she was on the point of getting up and walking out. But then she would have to leave the game behind, so instead she said, 'You can start because you're much more stupid than me!'

Johannes looked at her open-mouthed. Then he did something unexpected. He started to giggle. Teresa glared at him. Johannes giggled for a while, then he became totally serious and made his first move. She couldn't work him out.

Johannes won the first game and Teresa agreed to start the next game, since he had started last time because he was more stupid than her. She lost again. Johannes played in a strange way, as if he were thinking everything out well in advance.

She didn't really want to play any more, but Johannes said, 'Just one more time, winner takes all.'

They played one more game and Teresa won, but she had the distinct feeling that Johannes had lost on purpose. It was getting dark, and Teresa gathered up the game. She said, 'Bye then,' and left Johannes sitting in the cave.

7

A few weeks later they were inseparable, and who would have expected anything else? Johannes was a strange boy, but Teresa was old enough to see herself from the outside, and realised she was pretty strange too. She tried to fit in with her classmates as best she could, but it never really worked.

She wasn't bullied, she wasn't exactly excluded, but she wasn't *part* of it all. She wasn't *there*. She knew all the skipping games as well as anyone else and had the courage to swing higher than any girl in her class, but it was all the talk in between. The chatter, the gestures. She just couldn't do it, and became stiff and odd when she tried to imitate the others. So she gave up.

The only person in the class who actively sought her out was Mimmi, but she wore secondhand clothes and didn't wash her hair and wasn't all there, because her mother was a junkie. Teresa rebuffed her kindly. When that didn't work, she rebuffed her somewhat less kindly.

Johannes was odd in a more normal way. It was as if he had a shell of bad oddness, but if you just scraped away a little bit, a better kind of oddness emerged. Teresa knew he attended the Waldorf school in Rimsta, and that was all she knew. They never talked about school. Jennifer in Teresa's class said the Waldorf kids were crazy and just made stuff out of clay.

Like Teresa, Johannes liked learning things. He read a lot of books, mostly about war and birds. Sometimes they would talk about something, wonder about something, and the next day Johannes would have looked it up and come back with the answer, telling her for example that only certain female ants became queens, most were soldiers or workers.

They often hung out among the trees and made up various games and competitions. Who could throw pine cones most accurately (Johannes), who could run fastest (Teresa), or who could name the most animals starting with the same letter (usually Johannes). What they didn't do was play games involving imagination, or anything that might dirty Johannes' clothes. This meant they spent quite a lot of time talking instead.

Once when Johannes didn't turn up as usual in the afternoon, Teresa went to his house and rang the doorbell. His mother opened the door. She was small and slender and looked scared. Her eyes were enormous, and twitched as if she wanted to blink but couldn't. When Teresa asked about Johannes, his mother said he would probably be home any minute—would she like to come in and wait?

No, she wouldn't. She could see through the doorway that it was dark inside, and it smelled extremely clean. This was such a contrast with her own house that it felt uncomfortable. She went and sat on the garden wall instead.

After no more than ten minutes a black, shiny car turned into the drive. It made almost no sound. The car stopped a few metres from Teresa, the driver's door opened and a man wearing a suit and tie stepped out. He was short but broad-shouldered, and looked like a cartoon character. His face was so clean and clear that it could have been a drawing.

The man smiled at Teresa, showing his white teeth. Even his smile looked as if it had been drawn. He said, 'Would you mind not sitting on the wall, please?' and Teresa jumped down at once. The man took a few steps towards her, held out his hand and said, 'And you are...?'

Teresa took his hand, which was warm and dry, said, 'Teresa,' and before she even realised how it had happened she had bobbed a curtsey, something she never normally did. Her knees just bent by themselves. The man held onto her hand and said, 'You're a friend of Johannes, I gather?'

Teresa stole a glance at Johannes, who had got out of the car and was standing by the bonnet looking slightly wary. She nodded. The man let go of her hand and said, 'Well, in that case I'd better not hold you up. Off you go and play.'

The man turned and walked towards the house, while Teresa and Johannes stood motionless, as if they had been turned to stone. It was only when the front door had closed that Johannes left his place by the bonnet and came over.

'My father,' he said in an apologetic tone of voice. 'What are you doing here?'

'Waiting for you.'

'Did you ring the doorbell?'

'Yes.'

Johannes looked over towards the house and pulled a face. 'You shouldn't do that, my mother gets so...don't do it again.'

'No. I won't.'

Johannes hunched his shoulders and gave a long sigh, something he did from time to time that made him seem several years older. Then he said, 'Shall we do something?'

Something had happened that made Teresa able to say what she said next. It was cold outside and therefore it was a perfectly natural thing to say, it was just that she'd never said it before. She said, 'We could go back to my house.'

8

Over the winter they met up mostly at Teresa's house when they weren't outdoors. Arvid and Olof teased her at first and said, 'Kissy kissy' and 'Where's your boyfriend?' but soon gave up when neither Teresa nor Johannes took any notice.

Mostly they played board games. Monopoly, Othello, Battleships and Yahtzee. They tried chess a couple of times, but Johannes was so unbelievably good there was no point. Ten moves, and it was checkmate for Teresa.

'It's only because I know what to do,' Johannes said modestly. 'Dad taught me. I'd rather play something else.'

When the weather improved they went back to meeting up outdoors, and spending time in the cave. Johannes had started reading the Harry Potter books, and lent the first one to Teresa. She didn't like it. She couldn't believe the story. She did feel a bit sorry for the boy who had such a difficult time, but when that giant turned up on his flying motorbike, she stopped reading. Things like that just didn't happen.

'But it's just pretend,' said Johannes. 'It's made up.'

'But why would you want to read about it?'

'Because it's cool.'

'I don't think it's cool at all.'

Johannes got cross and started rummaging around in the box of stones they'd collected. 'Well, what about that Robinson Crusoe you like so much? That's made up as well.'

'It is not!'

'It is so! That never really happened, I read it in the National Encyclopaedia.'

Back to the National Encyclopaedia. As soon as they needed proof of something, Johannes was there with his National Encyclopaedia. He'd explained that it was a whole lot of thick books with absolutely everything in them. Teresa had begun to wonder if this National Encyclopaedia really existed. At any rate, she'd never seen it.

'We-ell,' said Teresa. 'At least it *could* have happened. That business with owls bringing the post can't have happened.'

'Why not—haven't you heard of pigeon post?'

'And flying motorbikes? And magic umbrellas? Are they in your encyclopaedia too?'

Johannes folded his arms tightly across his chest and glowered at the ground. Teresa was extremely pleased with herself. It was usually Johannes who fixed things so that you were left with no possible answer. Now she'd done it. She pulled the box of stones towards her and started arranging them in order of size, humming as she worked.

After a while she heard a strange noise. Like a frog, or the sound you make when you've got something stuck in your throat. She looked up and saw that Johannes' shoulders were moving up and down. Was he laughing? She tried to come up with something caustic to say, but then she realised he was crying, and the corrosion trickled away.

He was crying in his own way. An almost mechanical 'uh-uh-uh' was coming out of his mouth as his shoulders kept time, bobbing up and down. He would have looked like someone *pretending* to cry, very badly, if it hadn't been for the tears pouring down his cheeks. Teresa didn't know what to do. She would have liked to say something kind to Johannes, but nothing occurred to her, so she just sat there facing him as he jolted out his grief over something she didn't understand.

Johannes took a deep breath and wiped his face with the sleeve of his jacket. Then he said, 'Can we pretend something?'

Teresa's body felt soft. If it would make Johannes feel better to pretend, then she could certainly give it a go, so she said, 'Like what?'

'Can we pretend we're dead?'

'How do we do that?'

'We just lie down. And pretend we don't exist. Or we can pretend it's a funeral.'

Johannes lay down and stretched out. For once he didn't seem to mind about his clothes. Teresa lay down next to him and looked up at the angular ceiling of the cave. They lay like that for a while. Teresa tried to think about nothing and discovered that it wasn't too difficult.

Eventually Johannes said, 'Now we're dead.'

'Yes,' said Teresa.

'We're lying in a grave together, and everyone has gone home.'

'How can we talk, then? If we're dead?'

'The dead can talk to one another.'

'I don't believe that.'

'We're pretending.'

'OK.'

Teresa looked up at the grey stone ceiling and tried to imagine it was earth. It was impossible. Then she tried to imagine it was a grave like the Vikings had, where they put stones over the corpse. That was easier. She was dead and she was lying beneath a mound of stones. It was rather nice.

'We are the dead,' said Johannes.

'Yes.'

'Nobody is going to come knocking, nobody is going to ask us to do anything.'

'No.'

'Everyone has forgotten us.'

The faint sounds from outside faded away as Teresa drifted into a dense bubble of silence. She had been worried about her lost gym shorts, she had been worried about the darkness under her bed, but now she was no longer worried. It was so simple, being dead. She became completely calm. She might have dropped off to sleep for a moment when she heard Johannes' voice as if from far away.

'Teresa?'

'Yes.'

'When we grow up—shall we get married?'

'Yes. Although I don't think we can say that now. Not when we're dead.'

'No. But later. We'll get married. And then we'll die at the same time. And lie in a grave together.'

'Yes. Good.'

9

In the autumn when Teresa was in Year 5, the class was given the task of writing about their summer. Teresa devoted most of the space available to a description of the family's trip to Skara Sommarland, although it had only lasted three days and she hadn't enjoyed herself at all. In the last couple of lines she mentioned that she had also been swimming, cycling, and played board games. The things she had done with Johannes, the things that had taken up most of the rest of the holiday. She didn't mention his name.

Of course the rest of the class knew that she and Johannes were friends; it was unavoidable in a small place. But Johannes was nothing to boast about. He wore short-sleeved shirts, beautifully ironed; when he wore shorts he pulled his socks up too high, and he became stiff and awkward as soon as they bumped into other children their own age. The fact that he had a bicycle with twenty-four gears didn't help at all in the circumstances.

So she avoided mentioning Johannes. During the summer she had had to put up with a great deal of teasing, not to mention sneering, when she was seen with him. She didn't want to hear the sniggering or vomiting noises from her classmates if her essay about the summer was read out.

On one level, therefore, you could say that Teresa's account of the summer was untruthful. On another level, it wasn't. She merely avoided mentioning details that might show her in an unfavourable light; remodelled the facts where necessary.

She knew it was normal and right to visit Skara Sommarland and describe the feeling of her stomach dropping away on the highest water slide, even though she hadn't been on it. She knew it was OK to complain a bit about how cramped the chalets were, but not to say how tired she was of her father, who never had the energy to join in *anything*.

And yet her account was not a lie. She had had a lovely summer holiday, but she didn't want to write about what had made it so enjoyable. So everything she had written was true, it was just that it had happened in a different way.

For Christmas that year Johannes was given a Playstation 2, which changed a lot of things. By unspoken agreement they had already abandoned the cave during the summer. Too childish. When the autumn came it was as if they were looking for a new direction, a new way of being together.

Once the gossip about Teresa and Johannes started to circulate around the village, her brothers started to be nastier to Johannes, which meant that her home was no longer the sanctuary it had been. She didn't like being in his house; there was something about the atmosphere that made her uncomfortable, almost afraid.

For a while they did a lot of cycling, riding around the lanes and exploring dilapidated barns and old gravel pits, or visiting the sheep grazing in a field a couple of kilometres away. Sometimes they cycled into Österyd, and it was on one of these excursions that they ended up in the library. Despite the fact that it was a small place, Österyd had a decent library with various sections, secluded reading areas and a couple of chess boards.

It soon started to get dark earlier and earlier, and for a while they cycled to the library straight after school and played draughts on the chess board, since Johannes wasn't quite such an expert in that game, or read books and talked quietly.

Things might well have gone on like that if Johannes hadn't been given the Playstation for Christmas. By the spring Teresa was forced to spend some time at his house in spite of everything if she wanted to be with him.

The shiny black leather sofas and the glass table. Johannes' mother, sneaking in with juice and biscuits. A tough guy by the name of Max Payne, shooting people dead on the TV screen. Johannes' fingers, flying over the buttons and control sticks. And the cold. It was cold in the house. Teresa had to have a blanket over her as she sat beside Johannes, following his progress through New York's underworld.

Johannes bought a game called Tekken 4 and an extra handset. They played against one another. Little Japanese girls and cartoon monsters. Teresa was not without talent; she knew exactly what to do and sometimes won. But she only enjoyed it for a short time. Johannes could carry on for hours.

When Teresa was leaving, Johannes' mother would often come rushing in with a hand-held vacuum cleaner to hoover up the biscuit crumbs before Teresa had even got through the door. She would walk the two hundred metres to her own house, and sometimes she felt as if she wanted to cry. But she didn't cry.

One day in May, at four o'clock in the afternoon, Teresa was standing in her garden with no idea what to do. Her bike was directly in front of her, leaning against the wall of the garage; the path leading to Johannes' house was on her left, the drive leading up to the main road was on her right, and her own house was behind her. She didn't want to go in any of those directions.

She stood there on the lawn, arms dangling at her sides, and the only directions that held any appeal were up and down. To sink down into the earth, or fly up among the clouds. Both routes were closed to her. She wished she was an animal, she wished she was someone else. She wished she had the ability to pretend.

She must have stood like that for five minutes, motionless. As she stood there a very clear thought formed in her mind and crystallised into words. She repeated them to herself over and over again.

I have nowhere to go. I have nowhere to go.

She swayed on her feet. She considered allowing herself to fall forward with her arms held at her sides to see if the ground would open up. She knew it wouldn't, so she didn't do it. Instead she turned her body to the left and forced her legs to move. She left the path to Johannes' house and went and sat in the cave. She looked at the rough walls, tried to remember when she and Johannes had had their collections of various objects in there. It just made her feel sad.

I have nowhere to go.

The words refused to leave her, they went round and round and wouldn't let her think about anything else. Enveloped in the words she went back to the house, kicked off her shoes in the hallway, went to her room and closed the door behind her. She took out an empty notebook she had been given as a present for her eleventh birthday, and wrote the words right at the top of the first page:

> I have nowhere to go.

Immediately more words appeared in her mind, and she wrote those down too:

> There is no road.

She sucked her pen and looked at the words. She was able to think again, and tried to find a sentence that fitted with the other two. In the end she chose:

> And yet I must go.

She put down the pen and silently read through what she had written. Then she read it out loud.

> I have nowhere to go.
> There is no road.
> And yet I must go.

It sounded good. It almost sounded like a real poem. Somehow everything seemed easier when she had written it down. As if it wasn't about her anymore. Or rather it was about her, but in a better way. As if she was part of something big when she stood there not knowing what to do.

She flicked through the notebook. It was a lovely book, with a leather cover and at least eighty empty, cream-coloured pages. Her stomach flipped as she thought of those pages being filled. With her words, her sentences. After sucking her pen for a while she wrote:

> There must be someone else.

Then she carried on with that thought until she reached the bottom of the page. She turned over and carried on writing.

10

The summer between years 5 and 6 was different from the previous one. Teresa had begun to develop breasts, and tufts of downy hair were visible in Johannes' armpits. If they cycled to a remote spot to swim they were embarrassed when they had to change in front of one another, and Teresa hated that. It was so unnecessary.

One day when they were drying off in the sun on a rock by the lake, Teresa wrapped her arms around her legs, drew her knees up to her chin and said, 'Johannes. Are you in love with me?'

Johannes opened his eyes wide and looked at her as if she had asked in all seriousness whether he came from Saturn. He answered very firmly: 'No!'

'Good. Because I'm not in love with you either. So why are things so strange between us?'

Teresa had been afraid that Johannes would dismiss the question, say that he didn't know what she meant, but instead his eyes narrowed in concentration. He looked out across the water and shook his head. 'I don't know.'

Teresa looked at his pale, slender body with its prominent knees and elbows, his sharp chin and high forehead. His full, girlish lips. No. He wasn't her type of boy. Against her better judgment she thought those hairy, slightly loose-limbed boys were the most attractive.

She asked, 'Do you want to kiss me?'

'Not really.'

'But will you do it anyway?'

Johannes turned to look at her. He scrutinised her face searching for signs that she might be making fun of him, but found none. 'Why?'

Teresa shrugged her shoulders. She looked at his soft, rounded lips and felt a tingle in her stomach. She really wasn't the slightest bit in love with him, but she wanted to know what those lips felt like.

Johannes gave an embarrassed smile, and he shrugged too. Then he leaned forward and placed his lips on hers. The tingle in Teresa's stomach grew stronger. Their lips were as dry and warm as the crust on a freshly baked loaf of bread. Then she felt his tongue between her teeth and pulled her head back.

'What are you doing!'

He couldn't look her in the eye, and his cheeks flushed deep red. 'You said you wanted us to kiss.'

'Yes, but not like *that*.'

'But that's what you do.'

'When you're in love, yes, but I mean we're not in love, are we?'

Johannes curled up into a ball just as Teresa had done and muttered, 'Sorry.'

Teresa also started to blush, but mostly because she realised she had been stupid. She was about to place her hand on Johannes' shoulder, but gave him a playful punch instead. 'Doesn't matter. It was my fault. OK?'

'You said you wanted us to kiss.'

'Listen, can we just forget this now?'

Johannes looked up from his cocoon. 'What do you mean?'

'This whole thing. Can we forget about it now?'

Presumably Johannes understood what she meant. All of it. The whole boy-girl thing. He said, 'I suppose so.'

Teresa rolled her eyes. *I suppose so.* Oh well. Johannes really wasn't her type. As if she had a type. Two steps and a jump and she was in the water. She dipped her head beneath the surface and felt rather than heard the muted splash as Johannes followed her.

In October, Johannes' father disappeared. One day he came home and said that he had met someone else, that it had been going on for a long time, and that he now intended to start a new life and *have a bit of fun at last.* He packed two suitcases, got in his car and drove off.

This was what Johannes told Teresa the following day as they went for a walk to see if the sheep were still there. Johannes walked along with his hands pushed deep in his pockets, staring straight ahead as he talked. When he had finished, Teresa asked, 'Is it hard?'

Johannes stopped and looked at his shoes. 'It would be hard,' he said, 'if he came back.' He looked up and smiled even more unpleasantly than the man in the GB ice cream ads. 'It would be absolutely fucking fantastic if he could just bloody well stay away. If he never came back.'

Teresa almost recoiled. It was rare for Johannes to swear; she hadn't really thought he knew any swear words. Now he'd used two in the same sentence. An almost nasty expression played around his mouth and eyes as something scrolled through his mind.

The sheep were still there, and Johannes and Teresa walked out into the field, running their fingers through the wool. Johannes was distant, answering Teresa's questions in monosyllables.

A wolf had recently been spotted in the area, and as Teresa moved among the woolly bodies she tried to imagine herself as that wolf. The muscles that could bring death, the powerful jaws. The field a bloodbath after she had passed through. All the sweet little sheep lying among their own innards.

Why do they do that? Why do they kill everything they see?

Johannes was lost in his own thoughts, Teresa in hers. They parted without deciding when to meet up again.

Teresa went home and looked up wolves on the internet. They kill because the flight response of the prey triggers the hunting response of the wolf. If all the sheep stood still after the first one had been killed, they'd survive.

She clicked on the next link, went on reading. Each fact led to fresh questions, and after a couple of hours she knew more about wolves than any other animal. There was something fascinating about the fact that this mythical creature still existed in Sweden, albeit in small numbers. Terrifying. And promising.

11

The day before she was due to go back to school after the Christmas holiday, Teresa was standing in front of the mirror in the bathroom. She hated her appearance. Her cheeks were too round and her eyes were too small, she had a slightly upturned nose, and all in all it made her look like a pig.

She wished someone could tell her what to do. Should she pluck her eyebrows, use a kohl pencil, should she bleach her hair? If someone could guarantee that it would help, she'd do it. But she didn't think it would help. She'd look like a tarted-up pig instead of just a pig, and that would be worse. She could already hear the taunts.

But the worst thing was something that had happened over the last few months. Over the waistband of her knickers hung folds of pale, flabby skin. She had started to get fat. The bathroom scales showed fifty-eight kilos, only four kilos more than in September, but they had settled in the wrong places.

She probably had the largest breasts in the class but instead of showing them off with a push-up bra and tight tops as some of the girls did, she just wanted to hide them, squash them down. All they did was make her feel even more clumsy and disgusting.

Teresa looked herself in the eye in the mirror and made a decision. She wasn't going to sit around feeling sorry for herself. She was going to do something about it. She found a facial scrub among her mother's things and rubbed it over her face until the skin was red, then rinsed it off and dried herself. The greasy sheen on her cheeks had disappeared for the moment.

She dug out her hooded top and jogging pants and put on her trainers. She would take up running. Four days a week, at least. Yes. That would suit her. Running alone along the roads, torturing herself. She would become a wolf, a lone wolf, strong and swift as she raced past people's homes. The wolf would eat up the pig with a huff and a puff.

Her cheeks were still burning from the facial scrub and her determination as she ran out from her drive. After two hundred metres the cold air started to make her chest hurt. She gritted her teeth and staggered on.

When she had covered another two hundred metres the pain in her chest was so bad she wanted to stop, but then she heard a moped chugging along behind her and forced herself to go on; she didn't want anyone to see her give up.

The moped caught up with her. In the saddle sat Stefan, who was in Year 8, and behind him Jenny, who was in Teresa's class. Jenny never missed an opportunity to relay what Stefan said and what Stefan did, just to emphasise the fact that they were very much an item.

Stefan slowed down and puttered alongside Teresa.

'Faster! Faster!' he yelled.

Teresa forced a smile and carried on at the same speed, moving so slowly that Stefan had to use his feet to balance the moped and stop it falling over. Her chest was about to explode.

Above the chugging of the engine Jenny shouted, 'Move your backside!' and leaned over to smack Teresa's bottom. The shift in weight distribution made the moped wobble, and Teresa had to step onto the verge, where she slipped on the frosty grass. She managed to avoid falling by running down into the ditch.

The moped accelerated and shot off up the road, Jenny's white-blonde hair flying out behind her, as clear as the rump of a fleeing deer. Teresa stood panting in the ditch, her hands on her hips. She felt as if she were dying. Her windpipe was constricted, her lungs were aching and she was embarrassed, embarrassed, embarrassed.

After catching her breath for a couple of minutes she went back the way she had come. As she sat in the hallway taking off her trainers, Göran came down the stairs.

'Hi sweetheart. What have you been doing?'

'Nothing.'

'Have you been out jogging?'

'No.'

Teresa walked past him and went into the kitchen, where she took three cinnamon buns out of the freezer and put them in the microwave. Göran lingered in the doorway. He cleared his throat a couple of times as if he were gathering himself, then asked, 'How are things?'

Teresa stared at the buns, slowly rotating in the microwave. 'Fine.'

'Fine? I don't think you look as if things are fine.'

'No. Well. They are.'

Teresa mixed a glass of O'Boy chocolate milk and when the microwave pinged she took out the three buns, put them on a plate, pushed past Göran, placed the glass and the plate on the coffee table in the living room and switched on the television. The Discovery Channel was showing a documentary about elephants.

Göran came and sat down next to her. Since he had stepped down from his managerial role and become an ordinary assistant again, the dark rings under his eyes had faded and he had become more available as a father. The problem was that nobody was interested in his availability anymore. Teresa couldn't say exactly when it had happened, but at some point she had stopped talking to her father about anything important.

But still. When they had been sitting there for a while, and had learned that elephants can express emotions in a similar way to humans, and that they drink approximately two hundred litres of water a day, there was a kind of quiet companionship between them. Teresa ate her buns and drank her O'Boy. It felt good.

She turned to her father to start a conversation in spite of everything by asking how things were with *him*. But Göran had fallen asleep. He was lying there with his mouth half-open, gurgling as he breathed. When a drop of saliva appeared at the corner of his mouth, Teresa turned away and concentrated on the elephants.

The program had moved on to explaining how elephants had been used as executioners and killing machines in large parts of Asia. Crushing heads, crunching bones with their trunks. Human emotions. Yeah, right.

12

In February a For Sale sign appeared by the roadside, and it was pointing to Johannes' house. Teresa hadn't seen much of him lately, and the sign came as a surprise to her. She hadn't been round to his house since his father moved out, but when she saw the sign she went over and rang the bell.

Johannes opened the door. When he saw her his face lit up and he gave her a quick hug. 'Teresa! Good to see you! Come in!'

She only had to take one step into the hallway to see how much the house had changed. Shoes and boots that used to be arranged on a shoe rack as if they were standing to attention were now lying around all over the place. When she took off her jacket she could feel that the house was several degrees warmer than it used to be.

In the living room Johannes' games were strewn all over the coffee table with a half-empty packet of crisps next to them. Johannes slumped down on the sofa and offered her the packet; Teresa took a couple of crisps and sat down on the armchair.

Johannes spotted a box and grinned. 'Shall we have a game of Tekken? Just for fun?'

Teresa shrugged her shoulders and Johannes slithered off the sofa to insert the game. Only now, seeing Johannes in this altered environment, did Teresa notice how much *he* had changed. His clothes hung loosely, his movements were casual and his smile had been freed from a pressure that said there was nothing to smile about. He just smiled.

'Where's your mum?' she asked.

'Some Spanish course, I think. Or dancing, I don't know.'

Teresa tried to picture this. It was almost impossible. But if she needed final proof, she got it when her gaze fell on the hand-held vacuum cleaner that Johannes' mother had used so assiduously in the past. It was covered in a thin layer of dust.

Johannes chucked her a handset and she manoeuvred adroitly through the menus and chose Kuma, the bear in the red T-shirt. To her surprise Johannes chose Lee Chaolan, who resembled a well-groomed male model more than anything. He used to go for Julia Chang, the woman with the unbreakable glasses.

As the intro began to play, Teresa pressed pause.

'Johannes,' she said. 'Are you moving house?'

Johannes pushed back his hair, which he had allowed to grow. 'Yes. Dad's frittered away his money somehow, and now he wants half the house.'

'What do you mean, half the house?'

'Mum has to buy him out if we want to stay here, and she can't do that.'

'So where are you going to live?'

'Dunno. In an apartment, maybe. In Österyd. I mean, I'll be starting Year 7 there anyway, so...what about you?'

'What do you mean?'

'Where will you be going to high school?'

'Österyd, I suppose.'

'Great. We'll see each other there, then. Maybe we'll be in the same class.'

'Yes...'

Teresa didn't want to be in the same class as Johannes, and his nonchalant attitude almost made her want to cry. She wished she could go somewhere far, far away where no one knew her, and start all over again. With...yes, with Johannes. But it was too soon for that. And it was already too late.

'Teresa?'

'Yes?'

'Are we playing, or what?'

She pressed the start button and the fight began. Kuma lumbered into the arena. Lee made his moves. Suddenly Teresa felt it was absolutely essential for her to *win*. With a frenzy that was unusual for her, her fingers flew over the buttons as she tried to achieve the combos she could still remember.

But it was no use. Without disturbing one hair in his perfectly groomed fringe, Lee threw Kuma around all over the place, kicked him and beat him until he lay flat out in his red T-shirt, with his nose pointing skywards.

Teresa's cheeks burned and she just wanted to scream. This was totally unreal. In reality the bear would have torn the model to pieces, ripped his head from his body. The floor would have been covered in blood.

13

Johannes moved house in the middle of May. Teresa stood in the window of the box room on the second floor munching on a piece of crispbread with peanut butter as she watched the last removal van disappear down the drive. A fly was dancing against the glass, and the gritty paste in Teresa's mouth became difficult to swallow. Then it was over. Somewhere in the house Maria was shouting for Teresa to come and try on her graduation dress.

The dress that had fitted perfectly in the middle of May didn't fit quite so well in the middle of June. Teresa stood right at the back along with the rest of Year 6, miming the words to the traditional songs, *Den blomstertid nu kommer* and *Barfotavisan*. She saw the youngest children racing around or hopping impatiently on the spot. The summer was almost here.

Arvid and Olof had their end-of-year assemblies later in the week and Göran had to work, so Teresa's family was represented by Maria, along with Göran's parents Ingrid and Johan. There wasn't much conversation afterwards as they sat on a blanket behind the football field having their picnic. Johan sat fingering the necklace made of plastic beads which he still wore, and Ingrid handed over a gift voucher for five hundred kronor.

It was a beautiful day, perfect for the end of the school year. Wispy clouds drifted across a picture postcard blue sky, and children's laughter rang out in the warm air. Teresa sat cross-legged on the blanket and realised she was really happy. When Ingrid placed a hand on her knee and said, 'Just think, you've got the whole glorious summer ahead of you,' she answered in all honesty, 'Yes, it'll be lovely.'

She would never fully understand what happened the following day.

She and Johannes had agreed over the phone that she would come over to his new apartment. When she stepped out into the garden at ten o'clock in the morning, she was filled with something light and happy. It was another lovely day, and it would be nice to cycle the four kilometres to Österyd. The seventy days of the summer holiday lay before her like empty, brightly coloured boxes, just waiting to be filled.

She had been given a new bike for her twelfth birthday just over six months earlier. Three gears—she didn't want any more than that. She checked that the tyres were well pumped up before she jumped on and set off along the gravel track.

The stones crunched beneath the wheels and the breeze fanned her face as she sped along. She had to cycle a kilometre along the gravel track before she came out on the main road leading to Österyd. When a bird chirruped in a tree close by, she clearly formulated the thought: *I am a child on the first day of my summer holiday. I am cycling along a fine gravel track.*

She looked up and saw the track snaking away between the fields. She stopped pedalling and just coasted along. *I am a child and the summer holiday has just…*

Something changed.

At first she thought it was a storm cloud that had drifted over and blocked the sun, the feeling was so strong. But the sky was virtually cloudless, and the sun was pouring down its light over the world.

So how come she suddenly thought the gravel track stretching out ahead of her disappeared into darkness in the distance? After all, she knew this stretch very well. Two hundred metres along the flat, then up a hill, then the field where the sheep were, then a gentle slope down to the main road. But that wasn't what she could see now. She could see a track leading towards the great unknown, surrounded by vast expanses upon which her feet had never walked.

She had thought that the world consisted of a number of different places, and the roads between them. That was all that existed, her little planet. It was as if she had been swimming around in a little creek, and now she had suddenly been dropped in the middle of the sea, with no land in sight in any direction. She couldn't get her breath, she gripped the handlebars tightly and braked. She rubbed her eyes.

There's something wrong with my eyes. I can't see properly.

She got off her bike and looked back in the direction she had come from. The track snaked off in the same way and disappeared behind a grove of elder trees. She no longer believed that her house was at the end of the track. Everything had been erased or was being erased behind her, and the contours were blurred.

Fear clutched at her heart. She was a small person cast out into the universe, and she knew nothing about anything.

Stop it. What are you doing?

The fear ebbed slightly. Perhaps she could talk herself round. She tried. It worked to a certain extent, but she couldn't shake off the feeling that everything behind her had been erased. She hauled herself back onto her bike and cycled home. The house was still there.

She rang Johannes and told him she'd had a puncture. The experience remained in her body. It wasn't that she was afraid of leaving her own garden, it was just that she did so less and less often.

One Saturday Johannes came over to her house on his bike, although they hadn't made any arrangements. He was wearing a pair of crumpled shorts that reached down to his knees, and a yellow T-shirt that emphasised his tan. Teresa felt almost shy as they hugged.

He had been to Majorca for a week with his mother, he explained as Teresa got out crispbread and peanut butter. His mother had met some guy who lived in Norrköping, and she had gone off to spend the weekend with him, so Johannes was as free as a bird. Maybe he could stay over?

Teresa wasn't prepared for this disruption of her normal routine, so she replied evasively that she would have to check with her parents. As they sat opposite one another at the kitchen table, she felt for the first time that she didn't know what to say to Johannes. It was as if he came from another world. The world outside her garden.

The situation was saved by Olof who came in to make himself a sandwich; after a while he and Johannes were deep in a discussion about Runescape. When Olof went to the toilet, Johannes asked, 'Do you fancy going for a swim?'

'I haven't got a swimsuit.'

'Well, we can always go skinny dipping.'

Teresa would gladly have given every last krona of her savings to avoid what happened next: a blush began to spread across her whole face, and she stared down at the floor. She heard Johannes snort.

'Oh, come on. We sorted all that out, didn't we?'

'Well yes, but...'

That kiss. Teresa had thought Johannes wouldn't remember it, but obviously he did, and that made her even more embarrassed. She wanted to slither out of her skin and dissolve into a puddle. Just to have something to do, she took out another piece of crispbread. The knife scraped loudly as she spread the peanut butter right to the very edges with exaggerated care. She took a bite and the crunch was deafening. Johannes looked at her and she looked out of the window.

When Olof came back and asked Johannes if he fancied a game of Runescape, Johannes glanced at Teresa and she shrugged. They sat down at the computer in the living room and Teresa watched as they took it in turns to kill off monsters and evil wizards.

She never got around to asking Maria and Göran if Johannes could stay over. He had dinner with them, chatting mainly with Arvid and Olof. After dinner he went out and got on his bike. Teresa followed him to say goodbye.

When he had rung the bell and set off, it was as if something occurred to him. He swung around and pulled up next to Teresa, his feet on the ground to balance the bike.

'Teresa?'

'What?'

'We are friends, aren't we? Even if things are a bit different, sort of.'

'What do you mean?'

Johannes swirled his foot around in the gravel in a way that she remembered from when he was little.

'Just...I don't know. I mean, things aren't the same anymore. But we can still be friends, can't we?'

'Is that what you want?'

Johannes frowned and considered the question. Then he looked Teresa in the eye and said very seriously, 'Yes. That's what I want.'

'Then we're friends.'

'But is that what you want?'

'Yes. That's what I want.'

Johannes nodded several times. Then he gave a big smile and said, 'Good,' leaned forward and kissed Teresa on the cheek. He pushed down the pedals and disappeared down the drive, waving over his shoulder.

Teresa stood there with her arms dangling and watched him disappear along the gravel track. She saw the track dissolve in that same mist, she saw Johannes cycling along the track. In a minute he would be swallowed up by it, and there was nothing she could do.

14

Normally the members of the family lived in separate little worlds, but that summer they surrounded Teresa more closely. At first she thought it was because Johannes had moved away. Or perhaps it was his absence that made her notice her family's presence.

Whatever the reason, Arvid and Olof started to ask if she wanted to join in when they were playing computer games. Maria tried to get her to come along when it was time to go shopping, and Göran was usually available for a game of cards. She began to suspect there had been a secret family meeting, and a decision had been made: *everybody must play with Teresa.*

At first she accepted it. She played and surfed the net with Olof and Arvid, she helped Maria in the kitchen and she played Cheat and Old Maid with Göran until they knew each other's strategies so well they had to double and triple bluff to get anywhere.

But after a couple of weeks she began to feel there was something rather strained in their efforts, as if they were staff at a summer camp she was visiting.

One morning when she was standing in front of the mirror pulling her cheeks back to see what she would look like if she was Chinese and not fat, she saw something else instead. She let go of her cheeks and examined her face.

She had brown hair and thick, brown eyebrows. Her nose was small and slightly upturned, her lips were thin. The rest of the family also had brown hair and brown eyes, but in a lighter shade. They had fuller lips, and their noses were straighter and more slender than Teresa's. She couldn't see any resemblance between them.

It struck her with absolute certainty: *I'm adopted.*

The thought didn't upset her; quite the reverse. It explained a great deal. She didn't belong, it was that simple.

Something inside her told her it wasn't true. She had seen the announcement of her birth that had appeared in the newspaper, she had seen her christening photo. Something else told her these things were fake. Her heart told her this, stubbornly pounding the new message into her blood: *you don't belong here.*

In the middle of July, Arvid and Olof were going to a football camp. Maria and Göran had taken the opportunity to book a weekend away with Silja Line, along with Teresa. Now Teresa said she didn't want to go. They tried to persuade her, but behind their pleading she thought she could hear an undertone of relief. The idea of getting away from the changeling for a couple of days. She thought they deserved it. They were nice people really, both of them. She had realised this now she didn't belong to them anymore.

They left her with a supply of ready-cooked meals, and Maria wrote completely unnecessary little notes for her about how various things worked, but Teresa just let her carry on. Eventually they got in the car and drove off, waving furiously to Teresa as she stood on the porch. She went inside and closed the door behind her.

Silence.

And silence.

She crept through the hallway. Silence.

It wasn't the first time she had been home alone, but the silence took on a completely different weight when she knew she was going to be on her own for forty hours. Göran and Maria would be home the following evening. The thought that the house was now hers was exciting and a little bit frightening. She could do whatever she wanted without the risk of anyone coming home and catching her.

She had no plans. The only thing she had thought about, or rather heard in her mind, was this very silence. The fact that every sound in the house would come from her. She tried not to make any noise at all as she padded into the kitchen.

Humming and buzzing. The fridge, humming quietly; the flies buzzing hysterically as they banged against the kitchen window. Teresa stopped and stared at them. There must have been ten flies dancing across the window pane, hurling their bodies against the hard glass in their quest for a gap, a way out. All Teresa had to do was lift the catch and open the window.

But the flies belonged to her now, just as everything in the house belonged to her. She folded her arms and looked at her flies. Then she sat down on a chair and looked at her flies. Waited. Sometimes a fly left the window and took a turn around the kitchen, but it was soon back, banging against the glass.

The fridge gave a rattle and stopped humming. The flies carried on buzzing. The faint thuds as they gathered themselves and made another onslaught on the glass, a fleeting higher note from one individual fly, like a disappointed question before it once again fell back into the collective note that filled Teresa's head.

She sat there as if she were nailed to the chair, her auditory perception hypnotised by the humming and buzzing, just as the TV screen's white hiss can draw the eye if you're not careful. She was erased and recreated.

With a sudden movement she got up from the chair and went to the bathroom to fetch her mother's hairspray. She found a box of matches in a kitchen drawer. She carefully folded the curtains back from the window until she had two clear rectangles of glass with the helpless little bodies flying around.

She struck a match and held it in front of hairspray's nozzle, pressed the button. A cone of fire spurted towards the window, sweeping across the flies. She took her finger off the button. Four flies dropped onto the windowsill, their wings seared off. She pulled up her chair and sat down to study them.

One of the flies had lost only one wing and was spinning around on the spot like a propeller; it managed to get to the edge and fell on the floor. Teresa stamped on it. Of the remaining three, two were walking around like clumsy beetles, and one was lying on its back waving its legs in the air. Teresa pressed her thumb down on that one until it stopped waving its legs. When she had finished looking at the other two, she squashed them with the matchbox.

Two more sprays, and she had cleared the window. She rearranged the curtains and swept the corpses into her hand, threw them in the bin. Then she made herself a peanut butter sandwich. As she was eating, another fly appeared and started banging against the window. She left it alone.

She felt quite still inside, apart from a slight feeling of shame in her stomach which was not dissimilar to vertigo. She quite liked it. It was something to hold onto.

As she was putting the hairspray back she caught sight of her mother's make-up. She made an attempt. Mascara and kohl around her eyes, concealer on the pimples on her cheeks, pink lipstick. She had no idea what to do with blusher, so she finished off by teasing up her hair with spray.

It looked bloody awful. The concealer, which should have brought about a straightforward improvement, was the wrong shade and showed up as dark patches on her pale skin. Apart from that, she looked like an ugly girl with colour on her face. She quickly got undressed and took a shower, scrubbing her face with soap several times.

She pressed the shower head against her pubes. It felt quite nice. She tried rubbing herself with her index finger, but felt nothing. She had watched *Sex and the City* a few times and realised it was possible to do things to yourself. But it didn't work for her. Maybe she was doing it wrong.

She squatted down and rested her head in her hands as the warm water flowed over her back. She tried to cry. Only dry sobs emerged. She visualised how sorry for herself she was, and had almost succeeded when she decided she'd had enough, and turned the thermostat until the water was ice-cold. She let the cold water pour over her until her face was stiff and her skin covered in goose-pimples. Then she turned off the shower, dried herself and got dressed.

When she came out of the bathroom the house was just as silent, but her chilled body now felt like a crystal in the silence, an element of clarity in the still fuzziness. She went and sat at the computer, launched Google and typed in 'poems'.

The result surprised her. It had just been an idea, because her head felt so clean and pure. She would read poems. But the top results were pages where people who weren't poets had posted stuff they had written. She opened a page called poetry.now.

She read one poem, then another. She found a girl called Andrea, fifteen years old, whose poems she liked; she did a search using her name and found several more examples of her work. They were called 'Loneliness', 'Is it just me?' and 'Black angel'.

Teresa read on, open-mouthed. *She* could have written those poems. They were about her. Andrea was a couple of years older than her and lived in Västerås, and yet they were almost exactly the same. She clicked on another page and discovered Malin from Stockholm, sixteen years old, who had written a poem called 'The Bubble', in which she described how she lived inside a bubble whose walls were impossible to break down.

That was exactly how it was. Teresa felt the same, but hadn't found those particular words. Nobody else could see the bubble, but she was shut inside it all the time. Malin had put it into words.

Teresa scrolled down and saw that some people had left comments about the poem, saying it was really good and well written and that they felt the same. A shiver ran through Teresa's body and she felt as if she had a fever. She clicked on the box that said 'leave a comment' and was asked to log in.

She got up and walked around the living room, then went into Göran and Maria's bedroom, where she lay down on the bed and stared up at the ceiling. Then she rolled herself in the duvet and curled up, whimpering like a puppy.

I'm too small.

Almost everyone writing on poetry.now was a girl. The youngest she had found was Matilda, fourteen years old. Teresa thought her poem, 'Tears', was childish. And she was twelve, almost thirteen. She tossed and turned in the bed until she started sweating and relaxed. All these other girls who were older than her but felt the same, where were they? What did they look like?

She got out of bed and a feeling of restlessness she couldn't pin down drove her all over the house. When she got to the bathroom she picked up the hairspray. The box of matches was still on the kitchen table. Five flies had appeared since she was last here. She brought them all down with one circular spraying movement. She looked at them as they crawled around on the windowsill.

In her mother's sewing box she found a pack of pins. She nailed the flies to the windowsill, one by one. They remained alive, waving their little legs. The feeling of shame in her stomach grew until she could almost see it, touch it. A sticky, orange jellyfish floating just beneath her ribcage.

She took a deep breath and tried to get rid of the jellyfish. It didn't go away, but it shrank. She took another deep breath. The jellyfish disappeared. She looked at the skewered flies.

That's how simple it is, she thought. *It isn't you who makes the decisions. It's me.*

She fetched a small wooden chopping board and transferred the flies. One of them who had tiny bits of wing still attached to its body buzzed feebly when she picked it up, impaled on the pin, but fell silent when it was secured to its new base. She took the board into the living room and placed it next to the computer.

She spent a while sorting out an email address, which was a requirement for creating an account at poetry.now. When the registration page for Hotmail asked for her date of birth, she made herself three years older than she was, just to be on the safe side. She gave the same date when she registered with poetry.now.

From time to time she looked at the flies. They were all still alive.

She would have liked to know what kind of food she could give them so they would stay alive. But who knows what flies eat?

Using her grandfather's surname and her own middle name, she became Josefin Lindström from Rimsta, fifteen years old. She was in.

She couldn't get to sleep that night. After tossing and turning for a couple of hours, she got up and put on her dressing gown. The house felt even more silent and mysterious with the darkness outside the window. She crept cautiously down the stairs.

As she approached the living room, she started to feel afraid. She had the feeling there was a creature in there. A huge, insect-like creature with slime dripping from its jaws, just waiting to grab her. She took a deep breath, and another. Then she switched on the light.

Nothing. The chopping board was where she had left it, next to the computer. She padded over and looked. All the flies had stopped moving. She pulled out a pin and removed the fly. It was dead. It had suffered during its final hours of life, but now it was dead.

Teresa stuck the pin in her arm. A drop of blood welled up. She licked it off. Then she went and fetched a small cushion and lay down on the floor with the cushion under her head. She closed her eyes and pretended she was dead.

After a few minutes she had fallen asleep.

15

Österyd usually had two classes in each year group at high school level, and the policy was to move children on from juniors to high school. Many children came in at that stage from village schools, and the aim was to break up the structure so that the new arrivals would find it easier to fit in.

Teresa's class was joined by a strikingly pretty girl from Synninge called Agnes; Mikael, who from day one looked and behaved like a fight just waiting to happen, plus a number of others with less outstanding characteristics. Johannes ended up in the parallel class.

Everyone checked each other out, testing the waters, and Teresa did her best not to draw attention to herself in any way. After a few weeks she had established herself in the role of the quiet girl who minded her own business, but without appearing to be some kind of idiot who needed to be taught a lesson.

She carried on using Arvid and Olof's computer when it was available, and on her thirteenth birthday she was allowed to take it over when her brothers bought a new one with a more powerful processor. The first thing she did with the computer that now belonged to her was to set a password. When she was asked to type in her password twice, she chose *gravel pit* for no real reason.

When she logged on to poetry.now, she found a new poem written by a thirteen-year-old girl called Bim. Nothing good could come of a name like that, but to Teresa's surprise she really liked the poem, which was called 'Evil':

where I am no one can be
inside the brain lies thinking
porridge is not good
talk misleads
the name does not mean me
the moon is my father

It was incomprehensible in a way that appealed to Teresa. Concrete and vaguely unpleasant. Entirely to her taste. Besides which it was nice to find someone of her own age who wrote like that.

Under the guise of her alter ego Josefin she wrote a comment praising the poem, and said she hoped Bim would write more. When she had sent the comment it occurred to her that Bim could have done exactly the same as her, but the opposite way round. She might be a much older girl, or even a boy.

She scrolled through several new poems without finding anything else she liked. Then she did what she hadn't dared to do while the computer didn't belong to her. She opened a blank Word document so that she could write a contribution of her own for poetry.now. Not one of the old poems in her exercise book, but something completely new. Something current.

The cursor flashed, exhorting her to key in the first word. She sat with her fingers resting on the keys. Nothing came to her. She wrote 'I am sitting here' and deleted it immediately. She wrote 'talk misleads' and stared at the two words for a long time. Then she deleted them.

She went and lay on her bed, buried her face in the pillow, folded the sides of the pillow over her ears and pressed hard. Everything was suddenly dark and silent, and patterns made of golden threads danced on the inside of her eyelids. The threads turned and twisted to form the word 'everyone'. Suddenly a whole sentence was flashing at her.

Everyone is actually called something else.

She lay there breathing heavily, waiting for more. Nothing came, so with her hair plastered to her forehead with sweat she sat down at the computer and wrote, 'Everyone is actually called something else.'

She didn't understand what it meant, but it was true. Not only on the poetry forum, but everywhere. Inside every person there is another person. She wrote that down too. With a sudden burst of daring she put down the two words from Bim and added to them. Then she rounded it off with a final line.

She pushed back her chair and looked at the words she had written.

> Everyone is actually called something else
> Inside every person there is another person
> Talk misleads and behind the words are other words
> We can be seen only when it is dark
> We can be heard only when there is silence

Before she had time to change her mind, she copied the poem into 'make a contribution' on poetry.now. She didn't know whether the poem was any good, but it looked like a real poem, and what she had written was true.

She sat with her fingers on the keys and there was absolute silence inside her head. Nothing more came.

How do you actually do this?

The following day she went straight to the library after school. There were three shelves of poetry, comprising perhaps two hundred books. She had no idea where to start. Under 'new arrivals' was a book called *Pitbull Terrier*. It had a red cover showing a black monster dog, and was written by somebody called Kristian Lundberg. Teresa took it off the shelf and read the first lines of the first poem:

> Poems about
> the month of April are all banal
> We spit on poems like that
> Poems like that are as predictable as death

Teresa sat down in an armchair and carried on reading. She hadn't thought poems in books could look like this. There was a lot she didn't understand, of course, but there were almost no difficult words and a lot of the pictures were very easy to get her head around. She particularly liked 'the tide of death is rising'.

After an hour she had read the whole book, and had a slight headache. She looked along the shelf and found two more collections by Kristian Lundberg. After glancing around she pushed them into her school bag along with *Pitbull Terrier* and cycled home.

When she logged onto poetry.now she saw that someone had left a comment about her poem. Bim.

'good poem i am also other though i hear when there is sound write about porridge'

Teresa read these few words over and over again. 'i am also other' could mean that Bim, like Teresa, was a different person from the one she was pretending to be on the forum. Or perhaps the whole thing meant something else, just like her own poem.

There was, however, no doubt about one thing: those first two words. It was the first positive comment anyone had made about something she had written.

When she had finished staring at Bim's words, she noticed that it actually said 'Comments (2)' below the poem. She scrolled down and found another reaction, this time from Caroline, aged seventeen. It said, 'A completely incomprehensible poem about nothing. Get a life.'

Teresa stopped breathing. Her eyes prickled and the tears began to well. She clamped her hands together. Then she got up, fetched a hand towel and rubbed her eyes so hard that her eyelids swelled up. She scrunched up the towel and breathed into it, slowly and deeply.

She sat down at the computer again, went into Hotmail and got herself a new address, then created a new account at poetry.now. This time she was Sara from Stockholm, eighteen years old. She searched for Caroline, and found that she had written a number of poems. Most were about unhappiness in love. Boys who had betrayed her. The comments were very positive. Sara from Stockholm was of a different opinion. She said, 'I have read several of your poems about unhappiness in love and it seems to me that you don't really deserve anything else. You are a vile, self-obsessed person no one could ever love.'

She could hardly breathe as she pressed send. Then she lay down on her bed and took out one of the poetry collections she had stolen from the library. It was called *He Who Does Not Speak Is Dead.*

It seemed to be completely unopened. Nobody had read it before her.

The following day Teresa became acquainted with the term 'troll'. She had thought no one would react to Sara's comments. She was wrong. Caroline seemed to have a lot of fans on poetry.now, and eight people had commented on her comment, a couple of them at some length.

Every single comment, whether long or short, made it clear that Sara was a very bad person who had no feelings—*you come up with something better, then.* And so on. In two of the replies she was called a 'troll', and realised it was some kind of term. She looked it up and found that 'troll' came from *trolling*: dragging a baited hook through a shoal of fish and waiting for them to bite. Translated to internet forums: posting unpleasant or stupid comments just to get a reaction. A person who does this is a troll.

Teresa crossed her arms tightly over her chest and looked out of the window. She felt happy and peaceful. Lots of girls had read what she'd written and felt compelled to express their point of view. Because she was a troll.

I am a troll.

It suited her perfectly. She lived in the world of humans even though she had been swapped in her cradle, and really belonged to the dark, wild forest. A troll.

16

During the winter and the spring she was a regular visitor to the library, reading her way methodically through the poetry section. When she got home, trolling took up a considerable amount of her time. She created several different aliases on various forums. She was Jeanette, aged fourteen and Linda, twenty-two. On a forum dealing with anorexia and bulimia she was My, aged seventeen, and received over thirty-five replies to her contribution in which she stated that all anorexics should be force fed and then have their mouths taped shut so they couldn't run off and throw up.

By chance she ended up on a forum for people who enjoyed renovating old houses. For this she created Johan, twenty-eight, who absolutely loved vandalising, even burning down, houses like that. On a site for those who considered themselves environmentally friendly Tomas, forty-two, wrote about how much he adored his 4x4, and campaigned for a reduction in the tax on petrol.

But she tended to stick to forums like Lunarstorm, where young girls discussed their problems. Their indignant little comments would make her shudder with pleasure, and as time went by she discovered an even more effective weapon than cynicism, namely irony.

On a forum about animal rights, containing despairing accounts of cruelty towards the dear little furry creatures, Elvira, fifteen, wrote about an experiment in Japan where they had poked out the eyes of eight hundred baby rabbits just to see if it affected their hearing, then set fire to them to see if the little blind screaming bunnies could find their way out of a labyrinth. Elvira got over forty replies, quivering with rage over the cruelty of man.

The only exception was the wolves. On a forum where the rights of wolves were discussed, her alias Josefin maintained a more reasonable tone, and put forward Teresa's own views. She needed at least *one* place where she could be herself, or almost herself.

Trolling gave her a key insight: you don't need much energy to provoke a powerful reaction, as long as you use that energy in the right way. Something as simple as a broken plastic fork stuck in the lock of a classroom door could lead to a circus lasting at least half an hour, involving the caretaker, a locksmith, teachers and relocated lessons, and it only took five seconds to do.

How long did it take to put a drawing pin on a chair, and how much chaos did that cause? It was just like on the internet: all it took was a few clicks, a few words in the right place and in seconds there were twenty people busy expending far more time and energy on responding than it had taken her to write the comment in the first place.

Teresa might not have looked like much to the rest of the world, but through her alter egos and her well-planned little tricks she, the troll, took up more of other people's time and thoughts than pretty Agnes, for example, could ever hope to do.

Everybody loved Agnes, and Teresa just couldn't work her out. She was so bloody nice. All the pretty girls Teresa had known had been full of themselves, stupid, and obsessed with their appearance. Not Agnes. She was nice to everybody, worked hard in school and didn't seem to care at all about how she looked.

If she had her hair in plaits she looked cute, if she wore it loose she looked pretty, and if she tied a scarf around her head she was as beautiful as a movie star, but without seeming to notice. Teresa ought to have hated Agnes, but she just couldn't bring herself to do it.

One afternoon when Teresa was standing by the poetry section in the library flicking through some newly arrived collections, she heard a discreet 'Hi' behind her. She turned around and was met by a breath of fresh air mixed with the scent of flowers, emanating from Agnes.

Teresa said, 'Hi,' and felt a blush spread over her cheeks. As if she were about to sit an exam and hadn't done a stroke of work. She stood there like a lump, saying nothing. Agnes seemed uncomfortable too, shifting her weight from one foot to the other. Then she pointed to the shelf behind Teresa. 'I was just going to...'

Teresa moved to one side and surreptitiously watched Agnes, who was glancing over the thin spines of the books. When she was apparently unable to find what she was looking for, she began to move slowly along the rows, reading every single title.

'Were you looking for anything in particular?' asked Teresa.

'Yes,' said Agnes. 'It said on the computer that they had several books by Kristian Lundberg, but I can't find them.'

'Do *you* read Kristian Lundberg?'

'Why?'

'No, I just...nothing.'

'Do you?'

'I might have read the odd thing.'

Agnes carried on peering at the section where the books should have been, and pulled out a volume of Kristina Lugn's collected poems instead. She flicked aimlessly through it and said, 'It was Mum who said I ought to look at that Lundberg guy. But I don't know, I mean he's not much fun, is he?'

'No, well, not like Kristina Lugn anyway.'

Agnes shook her head and smiled the smile that could probably bring down trees. 'I think she's good, because her poems are like really really sad and really really funny at the same time.'

All Teresa could come up with was, 'Right.' She didn't understand what somebody like Agnes could get out of Kristina Lugn's splenetic humour. But she crouched down and pulled out *Close to the Eye*, Anders Bodegård's translation of poems by Wislawa Szymborska. She held it out to Agnes and said, 'Try this. It's quite funny too.'

Agnes opened the book at random and started to read a poem. It took Teresa a few seconds to realise she was standing there holding her breath. She exhaled silently and slowly as she contemplated Agnes, whose plaits lay on either side of the book, framing the picture and creating an image that could have been used in advertising to promote literacy.

Agnes giggled, closed the book and looked at the front and the back. 'She won the Nobel Prize, didn't she?'

'Yes.'

Agnes gazed at the shelves full of poetry, and sighed. 'Do you read a lot?'

'Quite a lot.'

'I don't really know where to start.'

Teresa pointed at the book in Agnes' hand. 'Start with that one, then.'

Now it was just the two of them, Teresa was beginning to suspect that Agnes wasn't quite so clever as she appeared to be in school. Agnes probably needed clear directives and the chance to go over things if her intelligence was going to shine.

Agnes fingered the Szymborska book, mumbled, 'Cool, thanks,' and went over to the issue desk. Teresa pretended to be reading Kristina Lugn, but secretly watched Agnes as she handed over the book Teresa had recommended, then got it back. Teresa had the unusual sense of being on home ground. She had read at least forty of the books on the shelves behind her, and they carried her like a silent cheer squad.

She could easily have made a fool of Agnes, with the home crowd behind her, but she hadn't done it.

The encounter in the library didn't make Teresa and Agnes friends—far from it. But it created a kind of secret mutual understanding. A week before the summer holidays Agnes told Teresa during the lunch break that she had now read everything by Szymborska. She wondered if Teresa had listened to Bright Eyes? Teresa said she hadn't, and the next day Agnes brought in a CD of *Lifted* that she'd burned.

That was all it was. And perhaps that's all there could be with

Agnes. Even though she was popular, there was a kind of remoteness about her, a sense of distance between her and those around her which had nothing to do with superciliousness. It was as if she arrived in every moment three seconds after it had happened, and you never saw her sitting whispering with another girl, their heads close together. She wasn't really *there*. It was impossible to say whether this was down to absent-mindedness, insecurity or something else. Teresa often found herself secretly studying Agnes. It didn't make her any the wiser.

To Teresa's amazement, not only did she like Bright Eyes—or Conor Oberst, as she discovered he was actually called—she thought he was absolutely brilliant. That fragile voice and those dark, well-written lyrics.

For the first time in her life she bought a CD, even though she already had the copy Agnes had burned for her. Bright Eyes was the first artist she thought deserved that respect. He became her constant companion during the long summer holiday.

17

It must have happened during the summer. At any rate it was a done deal when Teresa started Year 8 in the autumn. Agnes and Johannes were an item. She didn't know how it had happened, but she saw them kissing in the playground before they went off to their respective classes for registration.

The sight created such a storm inside her that her analytical ability went haywire. She couldn't work out how she felt, or why. Therefore she took the picture of the two of them, screwed it up and tried to toss it into a dark corner right at the back of her head where she wouldn't have to deal with it.

It didn't go too well. That same evening she was lying on her bed listening to Bright Eyes. The song said it was the first day of his life, that he was glad he hadn't died before he met someone, and Teresa felt hot tears of fury spring to her eyes.

She plugged the MP3 player into her computer and deleted every single Bright Eyes track. Then she deleted the entire playlist. Unfortunately she had also bought every one of his CDs. She gathered them up, went down to the cellar and placed them on the chopping block. Only then did she realise how ridiculous her behaviour was, and lowered the axe.

I'm not going to give them the satisfaction.

Bright Eyes was not Agnes' property. He couldn't be, since Agnes probably didn't understand a single word of the lyrics. What could those lines of alienation, of nonchalant despair, possibly mean to

Agnes? Nothing. They were just cool words. Cool words to listen to with Johannes, curled up together in Agnes' bed…

Teresa put down the axe, went up to her room and replaced the CDs in the rack.

She sat down at the computer. On the Friends discussion forum for victims of bullying she wrote a long contribution in defence of school massacres. Which weapons could be used in Sweden, where it was so difficult to get hold of firearms. She was expecting lots of replies.

Unfortunately her contribution was removed before anyone had time to respond, so instead she used a different alias and wrote a real tear-jerker about the terrible bullying she had been subjected to, notes with horrible things written on them stapled to her body. They didn't dare remove that, and she got lots and lots of sympathy which didn't touch her at all.

As the autumn swept in with falling leaves and chilly afternoons, it was clear that Agnes and Johannes were serious about their relationship. Teresa had never thought otherwise.

They were always together at break and lunchtime, and had to put up with a certain amount of envious teasing, which they ignored completely. After a while the scornful comments dried up, and soon the two of them were an institution, a fact that simply had to be accepted.

Teresa remained neutral. Johannes said hello to her in the corridor and sometimes they chatted for a while, with or without Agnes. Eventually Teresa found she had done the same as everyone else, at least on one level: she had accepted the situation. It was kind of completely natural for those two to be together. You only had to look at them to see that it was as if they were made for each other.

On another level it made you want to throw up. But then again, that was a different story.

It eventually got to the point where an outside observer might regard Johannes, Agnes and Teresa as a little trio. Not in the way that Johannes and Agnes were a *couple*, but Teresa was the *third* person who was seen around them, who talked to them more than anyone else.

In her loneliness Teresa came up with ideas like poking herself in the eye with a hand blender or banging her head against a wall until it split open.

At the end of September, something happened that was to change a lot of things.

Teresa's family were all caught up in different activities and interests; they often ate at different times, all living in a world of their own under the same roof. There was only one thing that brought them all together, and that was *Idol*. Arvid and Olof started watching first, and one by one the rest of the family were drawn into the talent show's enchanted circle.

Perhaps it was a subconscious emergency measure. Without *Idol* the family would probably never have sat down together, could maybe even have been described as dysfunctional, in need of help. But now there was *Idol*, and in the absence of anything else it had turned into a little family occasion, with tasty snacks and lively conversation of a kind that never happened in their everyday existence.

It was on *Idol* that Teresa saw Tora for the first time. Tora Larsson from Stockholm. Even her audition was an unusual story. Boys and girls would come in and sing like broken cement mixers, then be absolutely furious with the judges when they didn't get any further. Or they sang well, and were ecstatic when they found out they'd got through.

Tora was different. Small and thin, with long blonde hair, she walked into the studio and fixed her eyes on a point above the judges' heads. She said. 'My name is Tora Larsson. I am going to sing.'

The judges laughed indulgently and one of them said, 'And are you going to sing something special for us?'

Tora shook her head, and the judges pulled faces as if they felt sorry for a very small child. 'So what's the name of the song you're going to sing?'

'I don't know.'

The judges looked at each other and seemed to be on the point of asking someone to come and remove the girl. Then she began to sing. Teresa recognised the song, but couldn't place it.

> A thousand and one nights I lay alone,
> Alone and dreaming
> Dreaming of a friend
> A friend like you...

The usual thing was for the optimistic contestants to sing a contemporary song, hoping that a little of the stardust from the original artists would rub off on them. Not Tora. Unless Teresa was very much mistaken, this song was way past its sell-by date.

But the voice, the voice. And the way she sang. Teresa sat motionless on the sofa, and it was as if that voice went straight through her breastbone. Tora Larsson didn't make any gestures, didn't try to play any kind of part. She simply sang, and it moved Teresa even though she didn't understand why. Even the judges sat there lit up like candles for the minute or so she was singing. Then the voice fell silent, and they came to and looked at each other.

'You're definitely through,' said one of them. 'You have a voice like...I don't know how to describe it. If certain artists could kill for that voice, we'd have a bloodbath here. You're through, one hundred per cent. But you *must* learn to engage with the audience.'

Tora nodded briefly and walked towards the door. Not the slightest expression of joy, not a word of thanks. She didn't even look the judges in the eye. One of them clearly still felt the need to justify their existence, and before Tora opened the door he called out: 'And next time try to choose a song that's more of a challenge. A more difficult song.'

Tora half-turned, and Teresa just managed to catch a glimpse of a totally alien expression on her face. A hint of a grimace, suggesting that she had just been stabbed in the back and was about to unsheathe her claws. Then she turned away and walked out.

The family on the sofa started arguing; they were all agreed that the girl had a fantastic voice, but she hadn't given much in the way of a performance, blah blah blah. Teresa didn't listen and didn't join in. Tora had done the most brilliant audition she had ever seen on *Idol*, because she didn't seem to give a toss about any of it, even though she was clearly the best. That was the way to do it. Teresa had already chosen her winner.

On the way up to her room that night she was humming to herself:

> Alone and dreaming
> Dreaming of a friend
> A friend like you...

THE GIRL WITH GOLDEN HAIR

I

When Jerry looked back on his life, he could clearly distinguish a number of points where it had changed direction, always for the worse. The most extreme change of course had occurred that afternoon in October 2005 when he found his parents massacred on the cellar floor. It was still unclear to what extent the shift this had brought about was positive or negative.

He had sat on the stairs for a long time, considering the situation. Theres continued dissecting Lennart and Laila with the tools she had to hand until he asked her to stop, because the noise was making it difficult to think. When she moved towards him he told her to stay where she was, and Theres flopped down on her bottom in the pool of blood on the floor.

He assumed a lot of people would have panicked, started screaming or throwing up or something along those lines. The scene in front of him was the most disgusting thing you could imagine. But perhaps there was a positive side-effect from watching all those films showing extreme violence after all. He'd seen most things—much worse than what Theres had done, in fact. For example, she wasn't actually *eating* his parents.

Or perhaps he was just numb, incapable of taking in the situation on any other level apart from a scene in a film in which he was now required to participate. The problem was that he hadn't been given a script, and hadn't a clue what to do.

He realised he would have to phone the police, and went through the information he had assimilated from dozens of films and true crime series. He knew he had an alibi that could be checked, but that this alibi was getting weaker by the minute. He didn't know how long Lennart and Laila had been dead, but Theres must have been working for quite some time to make such a comprehensive mess of them.

Of course the simplest thing would be to ring the police and explain exactly what had happened. He would probably get into trouble because he had known about Theres' existence but hadn't reported it, he might get a year inside, but that would be it. Lennart and Laila would be buried and Theres would end up in the loony bin. End of story.

No. No. That was no good at all. He did *not* want that to happen. It was the bit about Theres and the loony bin that really stuck in his throat. However crazy she was—and we're talking seriously crazy here—he didn't want to see her sitting in some cell picking at her nails for the rest of her life. So he just had think of something, and fast.

After pondering for a while he had a useless plan that was the best he could come up with.

'Theres?' he said. The girl didn't look at him, but she did turn her head in his direction. 'I think you'd better…' He broke off, rephrased what he was going to say. 'Go and change your clothes.'

The girl didn't react. He didn't want to go over to her, didn't want to get too close to the scene of the crime where he might be *contaminated*, to use the technical term, or leave traces behind. In a louder voice he said, 'Go to your room. Put on some clean clothes. Now.'

The girl stood up, leaving a trail of blood behind her as she walked through the cellar. Jerry went upstairs and gathered together a sleeping bag, a loaf of bread, a tube of caviar and a torch. He went outside and around the house, then down the cellar steps and in through the other door.

Being careful not to step in any of the bloodstains, he went to Theres' room and found her sitting on the bed and staring at the wall. She had changed into a clean velour tracksuit but her blonde hair was caked with dried blood and her hands, face and feet were covered in almost-black, coagulated clumps. For the first time since the whole thing had started, Jerry felt his stomach turn over. Seeing the remains of his parents stuck to Theres' skin was somehow more unpleasant than the sight of their bodies.

'Come on,' he said. 'We're going.'

'Where?'

'Out. You have to hide.'

Theres shook her head. 'Not out.'

Jerry closed his eyes. In the midst of the chaos Theres had created, he had managed to forget that she had more problems with her view of the world than the obvious ones. He had to work from her perceptions.

'The big people are coming,' he said. 'They're coming here. Soon. You have to get away.'

The girl hunched her shoulders as if she was trying to protect herself from a blow. 'The big people?'

'Yes. They know you're here.'

In a single movement the girl got up from the bed and grabbed hold of a small axe that was lying on the floor. It showed signs of recent use. She moved towards Jerry.

'Stop!' he said. Theres stopped. 'What are you thinking of doing with that axe?'

Theres raised and lowered the axe. 'The big people.'

Jerry moved back a step to make sure he was out of range, and said, 'OK. OK. I'm going to ask you a question now, and I want an honest answer.' Jerry snorted at his own stupidity. Had he ever heard Theres lie? No. He didn't believe she was even capable of lying. And yet it was a question he needed her to answer. He pointed at the axe.

'Are you intending to hit me with that?'

Theres shook her head.

'Are you intending to hit me or stab me or...chop me up in any way?'

Another shake of the head. Sussing out the reason why Theres regarded him differently from his parents could wait for a later conversation. Right now all Jerry needed to know was that being around her didn't mean he was in mortal danger. To be on the safe side, he added, 'Good. Because if you do anything to me, the big people will come and get you. Straight away. Bang, get it? You are not to *touch* me, is that clear?'

Theres nodded, and Jerry realised that what he had just said was true, basically. He told Theres to put on some shoes, and made sure he kept his eye on her as they left the room.

When he opened the outside door Theres stood there as if she was glued to the floor, refusing to move and staring out into the darkness with big eyes. Enticing her, exhorting her to move forward didn't help, so instead he pretended to listen hard, then whispered with simulated fear, 'Come on, sis! They're coming, they're coming! I can hear their machines!'

At last Theres unglued her feet from the floor, and Jerry had to move out of the way as she rushed towards the doorway with the axe firmly clutched to her chest. She carried on up the garden, looking to right and left, adrenaline-fuelled panic in every movement. Jerry made the most of the opportunity and fled towards the forest with her.

Jerry had a childhood memory of an opening among the trees about five hundred metres into the forest, and he managed to find it with the help of the torch. The branches of a huge oak hung down over the glade, and the ground was covered in dry leaves. He pulled out the sleeping bag, unzipped it and showed Theres how to crawl inside. Then he gave her the torch, the bread and the caviar.

'OK sis,' he said. 'You've caused a hell of a problem, and I don't think we're going to be able to fix this. But you're to stay here, OK? I'll come back as soon as I can. Do you understand?'

Theres shook her head violently, and glanced anxiously around the glade where the fir trees stood in dark ranks. 'Not go.'

'Yes,' said Jerry. 'I have to. Otherwise we've had it. If I don't go...

The big people will come and take both of us if I don't go. I have to go back and fool them. That's just the way it is.'

Theres wrapped her arms around her knees and curled up into a ball. Jerry crouched down and tried to catch her eye, but without success. He picked up the torch and shone it on her. She was shivering, as if she was terribly cold.

It was always going to end up like this.

What he didn't understand was why he had regarded the whole situation as *normal* for such a long time. Why he had got used to the fact that his parents had a girl in the cellar, a girl who was now thirteen years old and didn't know a thing about the world. Why this had become perfectly natural.

And now he was stuck with the consequences. A trembling girl he was going to have to leave alone in the forest, his parents chopped up into little bits back at home. He could have put a stop to it all long ago. And yet he had to carry on now, because there was nothing else he could do. He got up. Theres grabbed at his trouser leg.

'Sorry,' he said. 'I have to. They'll come for us otherwise. Both of us. I'll be back as soon as I can.' He pointed at the sleeping bag. 'Keep warm.'

Theres mumbled, 'The big people are dangerous. You'll be dead.'

Jerry couldn't help smiling. 'I'll be fine. I'll be back.' He didn't dare delay any longer, so without any further words of farewell he turned and left Theres in the glade.

Behind him Theres held out the axe, as if she were offering it to him. For protection. But Jerry had already disappeared in the darkness, and for the first time since she was found, the girl was alone in the vast outdoors.

Five minutes after he got back in the house, Jerry called the police. Five minutes which he used for something he hadn't yet had the opportunity to do. To grieve. With his head drooping he stood motionless in the middle of the hallway as a lump formed in his stomach. He let it grow, tasting its colour and weight.

Without moving a muscle, in the middle of the hallway in his childhood home. All the times he had taken off his shoes in this hallway, the shoes getting bigger and bigger. The aroma of cooking from the kitchen, or bread baking. Happy or sad, coming home from nursery or school. Never again. Never again in this house, never again with his parents.

The lump rose and fell inside him. He gave himself five minutes to take his leave of everything. He stood completely still. He didn't cry. After five minutes he went to the telephone in the kitchen, rang the emergency number and explained that he had just got home and found his mother and father brutally murdered. He didn't recognise his own voice.

Then he sat down on a chair in the kitchen. While he waited for the police, he tried to work out how he ought to behave. What he would *say* wasn't difficult. He had found them on the floor of the cellar, end of story, he didn't know anymore. He'd gone into shock and it had been twenty minutes before he called the police.

It was the strange voice he had heard coming out of his mouth that worried him. *How* should he talk, *how* should he behave? He calmed himself down with the thought that there was probably no set pattern. Double murders were unlikely to be an everyday occurrence for the Norrtälje police, so they would have nothing to compare with, nothing to make his behaviour appear suspicious.

However, he did get up from his chair and go outside to wait. A normal person wouldn't want to sit in the house where his parents lay murdered.

Would they?

He knew nothing, and could only hope that whoever was on their way knew nothing either.

As he had expected he immediately became the prime suspect and was taken into custody. He was interrogated in minute detail over what had happened when he found his mother and father, and what he had done during the course of the day.

He had hoped he would be released after a few hours, but that didn't happen. The bodies had to be removed and the forensic pathologists had to do their job, and the information he had given had to be checked. Jerry spent the night on a bunk bed in a cell, where grief over his parents and anxiety over Theres kept him wide awake.

In the middle of the night he was brought up for further questioning with regard to the fact that they had found traces of someone living in the cellar. Clothes, jars of baby food, spoons with comparatively recent remains of food on them. What did he know about this? He knew nothing. He didn't visit his parents all that often, and had no idea what they got up to.

Since he had been expecting these questions, and suspected there would be fingerprints, he admitted that he had been in his old room a few times. But he hadn't seen any signs of anyone else living there, not a thing. This was something new to him, a complete bloody mystery, in fact. Who did they think had been living there?

He was taken back to his cell to pick more foam out of his mattress, and towards morning he was released without a world of explanation. He was asked to stay in the Norrtälje area.

After a bus ride and a short hitch-hike he was back in the garden. There was no sign of activity from the outside, but blue and white tape was fastened across the front door. Jerry looked over his shoulder to make sure no one was following him. It felt as if someone was, but it might just as easily be a ghost created by his exhausted brain.

He didn't dare to believe he had got off so lightly. Presumably the police had checked his alibi and gathered evidence that made him an unlikely murderer, but he had so much valuable information that he kind of thought it ought to *show*. That they'd be back to drag it out of him.

He got on his motorbike and started the engine. As he rode out onto the gravel track that would take him to the glade from the opposite direction, he decided that, with the greatest respect, he didn't give a damn about any of it. They would just have to carry on as best they could. The only thing that mattered now was Theres.

Why this was the case he had no idea. He hated people. The police officers who had questioned him during the night had been arseholes to a man, and his only pleasure had been in comprehensively fooling them. He wasn't really mourning his parents, but his childhood. He no longer had any friends. But Theres.

Theres?

No. He couldn't get his head round it. It was just something he had to do. She was kind of the only person he didn't feel the slightest scrap of hatred or contempt for. Perhaps it was that simple.

He propped the motorbike against a tree in the forest, waited for five minutes to be on the safe side, just to make sure no one was following him. Then he set off.

It took him over half an hour to find the glade because he was coming from the wrong direction, and when he did find it he was met by the very thing he had feared: nothing. The glade was empty. Only the dry leaves, scattered over the ground or blown into piles. He rubbed his eyes.

What the fuck happens now?

The forest was not large. Sooner or later Theres would reach a track, someone would see her, someone would…it was impossible to work through all the links in the chain. Just one cold fact remained. They were fucked, big time.

Jerry looked around and caught sight of something blue on the edge of the forest. The unopened tube of Kalles Caviar had been thrown a couple of metres in among the trees. Next to it lay the bag containing the sliced loaf, also unopened. Only the sleeping bag and the torch were missing. Perhaps she had taken them with her.

Before long the shit would really hit the fan. But for the time being he was here in this silent glade in the middle of the forest, where no bastard had any questions or accusations to throw at him. He took the bread and the tube of caviar and sat down on the ground in the middle of the glade, squeezed a generous amount of caviar on a slice of bread, slapped another slice on top and tucked in.

He closed his eyes and chewed. His body felt doughy after a night in the cells, and the sticky mess he was swallowing didn't help. He dreamed of just sitting there, disintegrating, rotting away and turning into the formless mass he felt like. Becoming one with nature in the silent stillness.

Then came the hiccup. He had swallowed too quickly.

He hiccupped and hiccupped, and couldn't stop. Then came the sobs, competing with the hiccups to make his body jerk as he sat there. So much for his quiet absorption into the earth. He put his head between his knees. Suddenly he threw caution to the winds, flung his head back and yelled, 'THERES! THEERRREESS!'

The bellow stopped both the sobbing and the hiccupping. Without any real hope he listened for an answer. None came. However, there was a rustling sound among the leaves a couple of metres from where he was sitting. His mouth hanging open, he saw a hand shoot up out of the ground. The only thing his tired brain could come up with was the poster for some zombie film, and his instinctive reaction was to shuffle backwards half a metre.

Then his brain made the right connections and he crawled forward to help Theres out. She wasn't just covered in leaves. With the help of the axe she had hacked away and dug herself a hole, crawled into it wrapped in the sleeping bag, then scooped earth and leaves over her until she was invisible.

Jerry dug away a considerable amount of earth with his hands until his sister lay exposed in her blue cocoon. He wondered what she would have done if he'd been kept in custody for a week. Would she just have stayed in her hole? Maybe she would. He unzipped the sleeping bag and helped her to crawl out. She was still clutching the axe.

'You're just too fucking much, you are,' he said.

Theres looked around carefully, examining the trees as if they might attack her at any moment, and asked, 'Big people gone?'

'Yes,' said Jerry. 'They've gone now. All gone.'

2

During the next few weeks Jerry was constantly afraid that the apartment would be searched. He didn't know how the police operated in cases like these, but in the TV series he'd seen, house searches happened all the time. If the police knocked on the door and wanted to search the place, they were fucked. There was nowhere to hide Theres.

But nobody knocked on the door; nobody rang the bell. The only thing that happened was that Jerry was called in for questioning again. When he got home Theres was still there, and the apartment appeared to be untouched. Perhaps it wasn't like the TV after all.

Many people that Jerry had never seen before came to Lennart and Laila's funeral, drawn no doubt by curiosity thanks to all the articles in the press. 'Bestial murder of Swedish chart toppers.' Lennart and Laila should have seen the headlines. In spite of everything, they had ended their career as chart toppers.

It was only when the funeral was over that Jerry began to come down to earth, gather his thoughts and try to look clearly at the situation. Up to that point his mind had been constantly fixed on the murder, and he had gone to the computer several times a day to Google news and comments relating to his parents.

Theres didn't make much noise. When he tried to ask her why she had done what she had done, she refused to talk about it, but it did seem as if she realised that what she had done had hurt Jerry;

perhaps she was even ashamed of herself.

Jerry had no idea what actually went on inside her head, and he was scared of her. He put away every knife, tool and sharp object in a locked cupboard. At night he made up a bed for her on the sofa in the living room and double deadlocked the front door so she couldn't get out. Then he locked the door of his own room. He still found it difficult to drop off because he was afraid she would manage to get in while he was asleep and vulnerable. She was his sister, and she was a total stranger.

She never made any demands; in fact, she rarely spoke at all. She spent most of her time sitting at the desk, aimlessly tapping the computer keyboard or simply staring at the wall. It would probably have been more trouble looking after a hamster. More trouble, but less worry. A hamster didn't have the ability to turn into a wild lion with no warning.

Theres caused him practical problems in only one respect, and that was her food. She refused to eat anything other than jars of baby food. That would have been fine, except that every single person in Norrtälje seemed to know the man whose parents had been murdered. It might have been his imagination, but Jerry had the feeling people were looking at him everywhere he went.

He didn't dare go into the local supermarkets and put twenty jars of baby food through the checkout. Someone might start to put two and two together. He tried to solve the problem by buying a couple of jars here and there, but Theres got through at least ten jars a day, and it was too time-consuming to spread his purchases like that.

He considered buying in bulk over the internet, but gave up on that idea. His name had been mentioned all over the place, and a hundred jars of baby food on his account, a box with his name on the address label might also raise eyebrows somewhere.

He tried to get Theres to eat something different, he tried to explain the problem to her, but that did no good. When he stopped buying baby food to see what would happen, she stopped eating. He thought hunger would eventually make her see sense, but after four days she hadn't eaten anything, and it was starting to show in her face. He was forced to capitulate and set off on a long expedition to stock up on pureed chicken casserole and meatballs.

At some point in the middle of all this, Jerry began to seriously despair. The locked doors, the difficult shopping expeditions, the constant fear. The way Theres had come to dominate his existence without saying or doing anything. *Why the hell had he got into all this?*

He realised he was going to have to hand her over sooner or later. A great big anonymous basket on the steps of the youth psychiatric service. Then he would be free to live his own life again. Without fear or anxiety.

But for the time being, the food problem had to be solved. Jerry took the only course of action he could think of and rang Ingemar. They hadn't been in touch since Jerry had explained that he was finished with the cigarette business after the incident with Bröderna Djup. When Jerry asked if he was still in a position to get hold of just about anything, Ingemar was up for it straight away.

'As long as we're not talking about drugs...shoot. What do you need?'

'Baby food. Can you get hold of baby food?'

It was a point of honour to Ingemar that he never asked about the goods he supplied, but from the silence that followed Jerry's question, it was clear that his principles were being severely tested. However, the only thing he eventually said was: 'You mean that stuff in jars? Stewed meat, that kind of crap?'

'Yes.'

'And how many do you want?'

'A hundred, maybe.'

'Jars? I'm not exactly going to make a fortune on this, you know.'

'I'm offering you the retail price. Eleven kronor a jar.'

'Twelve?'

And so it was agreed. When Jerry hung up, he felt as if a weight had been lifted from his shoulders. He had made a decision. When the hundred jars were gone, he would hand over Theres. It was a nice even number and it felt right. Another two weeks, approximately.

Ingemar turned up with the jars and Jerry paid him. When Ingemar asked if he would be needing any more, Jerry said no. Then he carried in the two boxes himself. The labels on the jars were in some kind of East European language, and each one contained something that was presumably meat stew. Theres didn't seem to care, she shovelled down the contents with the same joyless single-mindedness she always displayed when she was eating.

Since the keyboard was one of the few things that seemed to interest her, Jerry had started teaching her to use the internet, and that evening they had something resembling a pleasant interlude together as they sat side by side at the computer, and Jerry demonstrated how to get onto different sites and forums, how to set up an email account and so on. Perhaps it was because he had set a definite end date for their relationship that he felt more relaxed.

During the night Theres became ill. As Jerry lay there trying to get to sleep, he heard a long drawn-out whimpering from the living room. He hesitated before getting up and unlocking the bedroom door, as always alert to any changes in Theres that might suggest a shift in her mood.

He didn't need to worry. Theres was hardly in a state to harm anyone. The room stank, and when Jerry switched on the light he saw Theres flat out on the sofa, her face greenish-white. She had thrown up all over the floor, and one hand was waving feebly.

'What the fuck, sis…'

Jerry fetched cloths and a mop, cleaned the floor and gave Theres a bucket to throw up in. As he headed back to his room, Theres whimpered behind his back. He stopped, sighed, and sat down in the armchair. When he had been sitting there for a while, something struck him.

He picked up one of the jars of baby food, unscrewed the lid and sniffed at the contents. He wrinkled his nose. Not that baby food normally smelled good, but surely it shouldn't smell like *this*, for fuck's sake? Behind the smell of stale meat there was an undertone of...acetone. Something suffocating, fermented. He turned the jar around to look for the sell-by date, but it had been rubbed out until it was illegible.

Theres was writhing as her stomach contracted with cramp, emitting a damp croaking noise. Sweat poured down her face and a trickle of dark green bile seeped out between her lips and stuck to her chin. Her head drooped helplessly over the edge of the sofa.

Jerry ran into the kitchen and fetched a towel and a bowl of water. He wiped Theres' face, dabbing her forehead with the cool water. Her skin was hot and her eyes shone like marbles. She was shivering, and a new kind of fear nudged its way into Jerry's body.

'Listen, sis, you can't be this sick. You just can't, you hear me?'

He couldn't take her to hospital. She had no patient number or ID card or anything, and he might as well go straight to the police station and turn himself in. Of course he could just dump her there, but then again someone might see him, and in any case he couldn't put her on the back of his motorbike in this fucking state and how was he supposed to...

Theres' transparent gaze fixed on his and she whispered, 'Jerry...' before her body contracted in a series of fresh cramps, twisting the damp sheets around her thin legs. Jerry stroked her head and said, 'It'll be OK, sis, it'll be OK. You've just got a bit of a bad stomach, nothing serious.' Presumably he was trying to convince himself.

He fetched her a drink of water. Five minutes later she brought it back up. He changed her bedclothes, which were soaked through and stinking. Two hours later they were just as wet. He got her to swallow an Ibuprofen tablet, which came straight back up. He chewed his nails until his fingertips hurt, and didn't know what to do.

Towards six o'clock the dawn began to breathe on the windows and found an exhausted Jerry slumped in the armchair next to Theres, staring blankly at her skinny body as it lay on the sofa curled up into a question mark. Her breathing was jerky and shallow and her voice was so weak Jerry could barely hear her when she said, 'Little One bad. Made them dead. Mum and Dad. Little One soon dead now. That's good.'

Jerry sat up and rubbed his eyes with the damp hand towel he had changed several times during the night. He leaned closer to Theres. 'Don't talk like that. You didn't kill them because you're bad. I don't know why you did it, but it's nothing to do with being bad, I do know that. Why do you say you're bad?'

'You're sad. Because Mum and Dad got dead. Little One bad.'

Jerry cleared his throat and adopted a firmer tone of voice: 'Right. Stop calling yourself Little One, stop saying you're bad, and stop calling them Mum and Dad. Pack it in.'

Theres was once more gazing into emptiness. When she said, 'Little One soon be dead', Jerry's anger flared up. He placed his hand over her head and squeezed her temples between his thumb and middle finger.

'Stop it!' he said. 'It's *I will soon be dead.* I! And you're not going to die. You can fucking forget that. I'm looking after you. If you die I'll kill you.'

Theres frowned and did something he had never seen before. She *smiled.* 'You can't do that. When you're dead you're dead.'

Jerry rolled his eyes. 'It was a joke, stupid.'

The subtle lightening of the atmosphere in the room came to a sudden stop: 'Mum and Dad got dead. Then. Little One got them.'

Despite the fact that Theres was obviously no threat, Jerry backed away from her slightly. 'What the hell are you talking about, and stop saying Little One, what do you mean you *got them*?'

'I got them. They're mine now.'

'They are not yours! They're not even your parents, will you stop talking like that!'

Theres closed her eyes and her mouth and rolled over so that she was lying with her back to Jerry. Her narrow chest rose and fell jerkily as she breathed. Jerry leaned back in the armchair and sat there listening to her breathing; he tried to get to sleep, but without success.

He asked the question straight out: 'Why did you do it?' But there was no answer.

Perhaps it was the lack of sleep combined with being shut in the apartment, but during the course of the morning Jerry got more and more irritated. He had known for a long, long time that there was something seriously wrong with Theres, and that she could hardly be held responsible for her actions. However, he still couldn't cope with her lack of emotion when it came to what she had done. *I got them.*

That's probably something you might come out with if you've bagged a couple of ducks with a shotgun. Not when you've killed two people—who just happened to be Jerry's parents, regardless of what he thought of them. *I got them.*

Theres seemed to have improved after her dreadful night. She was still pale and couldn't even keep a sip of water down, but she sat up on the sofa with a couple of pillows behind her, flicking through an illustrated Winnie-the-Pooh book Jerry had had when he was little. In his confused state Jerry thought she looked shamelessly *smug* as she sat there. *I got them.*

Jerry stood by the unit housing all his videos with his arms folded, looking at her as she studied the nice, brightly coloured pictures without the slightest concern for all the grief she had caused. Without considering what he was doing he selected *Cannibal Holocaust* and said cheerfully, 'Shall we watch a film?'

Without looking up from the book, Theres asked, 'What's a film?'

You'll see, thought Jerry, inserting the tape in the video player. If he did have a thought in his head it was something to do with getting Theres to realise that killing wasn't just tra-la-la and *I got them*, but a seriously unpleasant business.

The film began, and people were chopped up and slaughtered with screams and tears, internal organs were removed and bodily fluids spurted. Jerry noticed that what had happened to his parents had made him more sensitive, and he no longer took any pleasure in the images. From time to time he glanced at Theres, who was sitting on the sofa watching the bloodbath, her face completely expressionless.

When the film was over he asked her, 'What did you think? Lots of people died, didn't they? Pretty gruesome.'

Theres shook her head. 'They weren't really dead.'

Jerry had always thought *Cannibal Holocaust* was one of the better splatter films. It felt and looked real. Since Theres was totally unfamiliar with the phenomenon of film, he had thought she would see it as a pure documentary, which fitted in with his somewhat unclear aim.

'What do you mean?' he said, stretching the truth. 'Of course they were really dead. You could see that, couldn't you? I mean, they got hacked to pieces.'

'Yes,' said Theres. 'But they weren't dead.'

'How do you know that?'

'No smoke.'

Jerry had prepared a number of responses to possible objections in order to get her to understand at last, but this was so unexpected that all he could say was, 'What?'

'There was no smoke. When they smashed the heads.'

'What are you talking about? There's never any smoke.'

'Yes. There's a little bit of smoke. Red.'

Theres had approximately the same expression on her face as when Jerry had said, 'If you die I'll kill you.' She looked suspiciously amused, as if she knew that Jerry was teasing her, and would soon admit it. Then he realised what she was talking about.

'You mean blood,' he said. 'There was loads of blood, all the time.'

'No,' said Theres. 'Stop it, Jerry. You know.'

'No, I don't know. It just so happens that I've never killed anyone, so I don't know.'

'Why have you never killed anyone?'

Jerry didn't really know how he had expected Theres to react to the film. With tears, perhaps, or screams, or a refusal to watch, or fascination and lots of questions. This hadn't been among the possible alternatives.

Acidly he said, 'I don't know, I suppose the opportunity never came up.'

Theres nodded, her expression serious. Then she said, as if she was explaining something to a slightly backward child, 'Blood comes later. First smoke. Just a bit. Red. But then it's gone. You can't find any more. But you get that little bit. That's love. I think.'

There was something about the way she spoke. With the monotonous, soporific voice of someone reading out the stock market prices, she listed dry facts that brooked no contradiction, and for a moment Jerry started to believe that what she said was the truth. Then a minute or so passed in silence, and the spell was broken. Jerry looked at Theres. Beads of sweat had started to break out along her hairline. He plumped up her pillows and shook the blanket, told her to lie down and rest. When she was settled he perched on the edge of the sofa.

'Sis,' he said. 'I've asked you this before, but now I'm asking you again. Just say all that stuff about smoke and so on when somebody dies is true. And say I've got it inside me as well. Are you thinking of trying to take it?'

Theres shook her head and Jerry asked the obvious follow-up question. 'Why not?'

Theres' eyes grew misty and she blinked a few times, but Jerry couldn't let her fall asleep until he had an answer. He shook her shoulder gently and she said, 'I don't know. It says stop.'

Her eyes closed and Jerry had to be content with her answer. He went and lay down to try and sleep off the worst of the woolly mess inside his head, but sleep wouldn't come. After half an hour he got up, took a cold shower and went out to buy some baby rice.

She has to eat something, after all.

On the stairs he met his neighbour, Hirsfeldt—an elderly man whose neat clothes were in sharp contrast with his face, which was strongly marked by his fondness for alcohol. He peered at Jerry in the harsh morning light as it bounced off the concrete. 'Has somebody moved in with you?' he asked.

Jerry's stomach went cold. 'No. Why do you ask?'

'But I can hear them,' said Hirsfeldt. 'You can hear everything in this building. I can hear somebody throwing up like a sick calf, and it's not you.'

'It's a friend—she's not very well, so I'm letting her stay with me for a few days.'

'That's very kind of you,' said Hirsfeldt in a tone which implied that he didn't believe a word Jerry said. Then he tipped his exaggeratedly elegant hat. 'My condolences on your loss, by the way. A terrible business.'

'Yes. Thank you,' said Jerry, hurrying off down the stairs. When he had covered two flights he looked up through the gap between the landings and thought he could see a tiny bit of Hirsfeldt's coat by his door. As if he were standing there listening.

Jerry gave up the idea of walking to the big supermarket, and quickly headed for the local shop. He didn't dare leave Theres alone for too long. What if she woke up and did something while bloody Hirsfeldt was sniffing around the letterbox? Why couldn't people just mind their own business?

He'd planned on buying ordinary baby rice, but they'd run out, so he had to buy Semper's organic baby rice, one year and up. When he put the box on the conveyor belt, the checkout girl gave him an odd smile. He'd seen her several times before, she'd seen him, and she was bound to know who he was. If it hadn't been for the incident with Hirsfeldt he wouldn't have been particularly bothered, but now he felt like a hunted animal as he hurried home with the baby rice in a plastic bag.

Theres was still asleep, and Jerry flopped down in the armchair to catch his breath. When she woke up he put the TV on very loud to drown out any possible suspicious noises. He couldn't stop himself from going over to the window a couple of times to peer down at the street.

The day passed against the backdrop of repeats and ad breaks on TV4. Theres lay on the sofa, following everything with dull eyes. He tried feeding her a couple of spoonfuls of baby rice. Then he sat on the armchair, hugging his knees and waiting anxiously for the poor attempt at nutrition to come back up again. When it didn't, he was absurdly pleased and gave her a little more. She'd had enough then, but at least she didn't throw it up.

The incidents with Hirsfeldt and the checkout girl had brought things to a head. Jerry could no longer amble along pretending everything would be fine. Unfortunately, he was much too tired to be able to come up with any kind of strategy. He fed Theres a few spoonfuls of baby rice from time to time, was pleased when she kept it down, wiped her sweating brow and sat with her as fresh cramps racked her body from time to time.

For Jerry, the hours that passed in their little bubble were dominated by two strong impressions. The first was claustrophobia. The room felt smaller than usual, the walls were closing in around him and outside the walls were watchful eyes. He shrank into himself, compressed down to a stock cube whose sole function was to feed and care for Theres.

However, the claustrophobia was balanced by a new discovery: the joy of caring for another person. It was deeply satisfying to support Theres' head with his hand as he brought the spoon to her lips, then watched her swallow and keep down the food he had given her. He got a warm feeling in his chest when she sighed with relief as he wiped her hot face with a cool, damp towel.

Or maybe it wasn't quite such a pretty picture. Maybe it was all about power, the fact that she was completely dependent on him. No one had ever depended on him for survival, but Theres was very clearly in that position now.

Nobody even knew she existed. He could press a pillow over her face and nobody would say a word.

But did he do that? No, not Jerry. He made her baby rice and moistened towels and changed sheets. He was there for her, looking after her. He had such power over her that he didn't even need to exert it. Jerry was a terrific guy, for a change.

Idol started at eight o'clock. When some girl pitched up and started melodramatically wailing, 'Didn't we almost have it all', Theres lay on the sofa and sang along in a weak voice. Jerry's eyes grew moist, no thanks to the girl on the screen.

'Bloody hell, sis,' he said. 'You could do a much better job than her. You can sing the crap out of the lot of them.'

Later in the evening Theres took a turn for the worse. The cramps were coming more frequently, and when Jerry took her temperature the thermometer showed 40.3. By midnight she was too weak even to lift her head to vomit, so Jerry had to sit by her, poised with a towel. He might have fainted with exhaustion if the fear hadn't kept him awake.

He dragged his mattress into the living room and lay down on the floor beside her. He no longer cared if Hirsfeldt called the cops or if the checkout girl was spying on him from the bushes, he just didn't want Theres to die. He'd never seen anyone this ill. If Ingemar showed his snout in Norrtälje again, Jerry would knock it down his throat.

He might just have dropped off for a moment when he heard Theres whisper, 'Toilet.'

He carried her to the bathroom, then sat in front of her holding onto her shoulders to stop her falling off the toilet. She was so hot his palms were covered in sweat. It was impossible to understand how her little body could produce so much heat. Her head was drooping, and suddenly she gave up the last vestige of resistance and went limp.

'Sis? Sis? Theres!'

He lifted her head. Her eyes had rolled back so that the whites were showing, and a dribble of saliva trickled from her motionless lips. He put his ear close to her mouth and could hear the faintest sound of breathing, a puff of desert heat against his ear. He picked her up and carried her back to the sofa, bathed her with cloths soaked in cool water, then lay down beside her and took her hand.

'Sis? Sis? Don't die. Please. I won't hand you over. I'll look after you, do you hear me? I'll sort it out somehow, but don't die. Do you hear me?'

Jerry curled up on his mattress without letting go of her hand; he lay there staring at her mouth in the semi-darkness, because only her lips moving from time to time indicated that she was still alive. Jerry fixed his gaze on them and realised something he should have grasped long ago: *Don't die. You're all I've got.*

Perhaps five minutes had passed, or it might have been an hour. Perhaps he was asleep and dreaming, or perhaps he was awake and really did see what he saw. If he was dreaming, then he dreamed that he was lying on a mattress next to Theres holding her warm, lifeless hand when her mouth opened a couple of centimetres. A first he was pleased, because it was the clearest sign of life for a couple of hours. Then he saw the thin curl of red smoke beginning to emerge from her lips.

Panic hammered a nail into his chest and he leapt to his feet. Crazed with exhaustion and fear, he grabbed the damp towel and threw it over her mouth, over her face, to stop the smoke escaping. He pressed the fabric against her lips, shaking his head dementedly.

It's not like this, this isn't what happens, this isn't happening.

A few seconds passed and he expected to see the red smoke begin to seep through the fabric. Then he realised what he was doing. He ripped away the towel and placed his ear to her mouth. He couldn't hear or feel anything, and he banged his temples with both hands until brass bells started reverberating in the back of his head.

I've killed her. I've killed her. I've suffocated her.

Theres opened her eyes and Jerry screamed and staggered backwards, knocking over the coffee table which went crashing to the ground. She held her hand out to him. Jerry took a couple of deep breaths and regained control of himself. He took her hand and whispered, 'I thought you'd died. Just now.'

Theres closed her eyes and said, 'I was dead. Then I wasn't dead.'

Someone knocked on the wall. Hirsfeldt was awake.

During the night the fever began to abate, and by morning her temperature was down to 38 degrees. Theres was able to drink water, and even managed a little of the apricot puree left in the fridge. She sat up in bed and managed to hold the spoon herself. Jerry had slept for a couple hours, and felt so relieved he had to express it in some way. When he stroked her cheek she didn't look at him, didn't give the slightest hint of a smile. But nor did she move her head away.

An hour or so later Jerry was sitting at the computer searching for property to rent.

3

After a couple of days spent exchanging emails and making phone calls, Jerry gave Theres detailed instructions on what she could and couldn't do during his absence, then set off for Stockholm to check out an apartment in Svedmyra.

It was a three-room apartment, 82 square metres, in an area that turned out to be so quiet and peaceful that you could have heard a pin drop on one of the many glassed-in balconies.

Jerry plodded slowly from the subway station and tried to get a feel for the place. It felt...finished. Maybe things had happened here once upon a time, maybe young lads in caps had run around feeling trendy among the three-storey brick buildings, but that was long ago. The lads had hung up their caps, and had their feet up with the cat and the TV these days.

When Jerry had checked out the discussion pages on different areas, there was one expression that had come up a few times, presumably posted by older people: *running up and down the stairs.* They complained that there was always somebody running up and down the stairs. Jerry had a feeling that Svedmyra was a place where there wasn't a great deal of running up and down stairs. Enough said.

The apartment was on the top floor, and wasn't much to get excited about. Two bedrooms with a view of some pine trees, a large bathroom with a washing machine and a living room with a kitchen area. The contract was one hundred and forty thousand kronor, and the black market agent had assured Jerry that the last person he'd heard of who got an apartment here through legal channels had been on the housing list for twelve years.

The minor and major criminals Jerry had come into contact with over the years would usually have been easy to pick in a line-up, but the agent looked so smart and trustworthy that Jerry became quite suspicious. Suit, neatly combed hair; ingratiating teeth.

If the agent had been a wide boy in a track suit and a gold chain, Jerry would have found it easier to cough up the fifty thousand he had brought with him for the deposit. In the circumstances, however, he refused to pay more than twenty-five. The agent went on at length about the fake contracts that had to be sorted out, the papers that had to be signed and so on, but Jerry stood his ground.

He took another walk round the apartment as the agent laid it on with a trowel, getting more and more annoyed. Jerry saw how he could have his computer desk next to the broadband outlet there, put the bed there, which room Theres would have and so on. He liked the place. When the agent said he wasn't prepared to do a deal unless Jerry paid a deposit of at least forty thousand, Jerry said he wasn't prepared to move from twenty-five, but that he would pay an extra ten on top once the whole thing had gone through. One hundred and fifty thousand in total.

Twenty-five one-thousand-kronor notes changed hands, and they shook on it.

Sitting on the subway and then on the bus to Norrtälje, Jerry was quite pleased with himself. If he'd been conned, then it wasn't the end of the world. He had a good three hundred thousand tucked away from his internet poker.

But he hadn't been conned. A week later he was able to collect the keys, sign the contract and hand over the rest of the money for the apartment where he would be living with his daughter, according to the official version.

The move itself was a problem. Jerry didn't have all that many possessions, but there were a number of things he couldn't carry down the stairs by himself. The bed, the sofa, the bookcases. Among other things. There was no one he could ask for help, and even if Theres could have carried one end, he didn't dare let her be seen like that in Norrtälje.

He would have to use removalists.

On the designated day he explained to Theres that a couple of men would be coming to help them move their things to Stockholm. She was terrified, her eyes darting all over the apartment in the quest for a place to hide. Jerry coaxed her into the bathroom, where she locked herself in.

Quarter of an hour later the doorbell rang, and outside stood two lads who made Jerry shrink on the spot. Now he understood the name of their company, Twin Transport. Two identical lads aged about twenty-five wearing overalls towered above him. Both were over two metres tall. Jerry's hand disappeared inside a huge paw as they said hello.

They emptied the bedroom and kitchen in no time, and Jerry soon abandoned any attempt to help when he realised this was a smooth ballroom dance, with furniture and boxes as props, and he was only getting in the way. The only thing he insisted on carrying down himself was the computer. He had recently upgraded to the latest Mac, and he wanted to make sure the box containing the computer didn't get squashed.

The huge removal van was no more than a third full and only the sofa in the living room remained, as Jerry carefully placed the box next to the bookcase and made sure it was safe. The twins stood watching him with their arms folded, smiling indulgently. Jerry followed them up the stairs. As they were approaching his floor he heard a door close; presumably Hirsfeldt, being nosey until the last possible moment.

Mats (or it might have been Martin) stopped in the doorway and said, 'Hello?' When Jerry caught up with them he saw through the gap between their backs that Theres had emerged from the bathroom for some reason, and was standing in the hallway, her fists clenched by her sides, staring wide-eyed at the twins.

The big people, Jerry thought. If Theres had strange ideas about adults, the sight of the twins was unlikely to help much.

Jerry said quietly, 'My daughter. She's a bit...different.'

As if to confirm his statement Theres began slowly backing away into the living room. When the twins cheerfully moved towards her, she held her hands up in front of her for protection as she continued to walk backwards.

'Theres,' said Jerry, who couldn't get past the massive backs, 'Theres, they're not dangerous. They're helping us.'

Theres moved into the almost empty living room. She cast a panic-stricken glance at the balcony door, and for a moment he thought she was going to throw herself out.

'Theres. What a lovely name,' said one of the twins, distracting her sufficiently to stop her making a dash for the balcony door before that particular escape route was blocked. Instead, like the very small child she resembled at that moment, she threw herself on the sofa and pulled the blanket over her head.

Mats and Martin looked at one another, grinned and said, 'OK, kid—here we go.' Before Jerry could stop them they each picked up one end of the sofa. Incapable of coming up with a better solution, he dashed out onto the landing and positioned himself so that he was blocking the view from the spy hole in Hirsfeldt's door as Mats and Martin carried the sofa downstairs. He didn't dare to imagine what Theres must be feeling as she lay there quivering under her blanket, unceremoniously carted out of her safe haven.

When the twins had placed the sofa in the van and Jerry had managed to persuade them to stop trying to coax Theres out, he sat down beside her and whispered, 'Sis? Sis? Everything's fine. I'm here and they're not dangerous, I promise.' He fumbled under the blanket and found her hand, squeezed it. A gesture that would have been unthinkable just a week ago.

When the twins had brought down the last of the boxes and were ready to set off, Theres refused to leave her cocoon. Jerry tried to get up, but she squeezed his hand harder and hissed, 'Don't go. Don't go.'

Jerry weighed up the situation, then asked the twins: 'Is it OK if we ride with you? In the back?' The twins shrugged and said well, it was against the rules really, but… Jerry seized the moment and said they could add an extra couple of hours to the invoice. It had been cheaper than he expected anyway, because the twins had worked so fast.

He dug out another blanket and wrapped himself in it, then found the torch in one of the boxes. When the doors closed and he switched on the torch, he thought it wasn't such a bad idea after all. They could avoid the midnight taxi ride Jerry had been planning to get Theres out of Norrtälje without the risk of being spotted by anyone he knew.

When Jerry was young, he had had the usual fantasies about leaving Norrtälje and returning many years later to great acclaim, giving major interviews to the local press. He'd given all that up long ago, and resigned himself to becoming quietly embalmed in his desolate apartment.

Even though he was now travelling in a dark removal van like a thief in the night, at least he had finally escaped. Good or bad? Difficult to say, but as the van bumped along and Jerry tried to visualise the places they were passing, he felt a small stirring of excitement. He was on his way. At last.

When they had been on the road for about quarter of an hour, Theres poked her head out. She looked around the dark interior, and Jerry swept the beam of the torch around to show her no dangers were lurking. She said something and Jerry had to lean closer to hear her over the roar of the engine. 'What did you say?'

'The big people,' said Theres. 'When are the big people going to make Little One dead?'

'Listen, sis…' Jerry moved closer to her, but Theres retreated into the far corner of the sofa. When Jerry shone the light on her he saw that she was at least as terrified as she had been up in the apartment. He switched off the torch to avoid dazzling her, and spoke into the darkness.

'Sis, this whole business with the big people—it's all just made up. It's not true. It was just some crap Dad made up because...because he didn't want you to run away.'

'You're lying. The big people have hate in their heads. You said it too.'

'Yes, but that was just so that you'd...forget it. But nobody's going to kill you. You don't need to be scared.'

They sat in silence in the darkness for a long time. The sound of the engine was soporific, and Jerry might have fallen asleep if he hadn't started to feel really cold. He wrapped the blanket more tightly around him and stared at a thin strip of light along the bottom of the doors. The feeling of being on the way had been replaced by a sense that he was being *transported*, like a piece of furniture or a pig, and his good mood evaporated. When they had travelled so far that he could tell from the sound of the engine that they were driving along a street with buildings on either side, Theres said, 'Are the big people nice?'

'No,' said Jerry. 'That's going a bit far. That's not what I said. Most of them are nasty bastards, if they get the chance. I'm just telling you they're not going to kill you. Or hurt you.'

Jerry added silently: *unless they've got something to gain from it.*

When the doors opened Jerry was blinded by the white winter light. Theres had crawled back under her blanket, and Martin and Mats were waiting outside with their arms folded.

'It's the third floor, isn't it?' said one of the twins, pointing at Theres. 'I think you'd better try and get the girl to go up with you. It was a bit of fun once, but...'

Jerry asked them to back off a little and leaned over Theres, whispering where he thought her ear might be, 'Come on, sis. Everything's fine. I'll hold your hand.' A few seconds passed and Jerry had begun to consider carrying Theres wrapped in the blanket, when a hand emerged. He took it and gently folded back the blanket, then led her out of the van.

She walked with her head bent, as if she expected a devastating blow to the back of her neck at any moment. When it didn't come, she stole a quick glance at the twins. They waved in unison with exactly the same expression on their faces, like something out of a cartoon. Jerry wondered if they lived together as well.

He held his head high as they walked towards the door, because there was no longer anything to hide, and he didn't want it to look as if there might be. There were always watchful eyes. Here comes a father with his daughter to take over their new apartment, nothing odd about that. Theres, however, was playing her role very badly, and her fingers were squeezing his hand like pincers.

She relaxed slightly once they were inside the small lift, and looked around in confusion when they came out onto the landing; she couldn't understand how they had got there. Jerry unlocked the door of their apartment and left it open, then led Theres to her new room.

'This is where you're going to live,' he said. As Theres looked suspiciously around the completely empty room, he added, 'With furniture, and stuff, of course. We'll have to buy a bed and...'

Theres went and sat on the floor in the corner, drew her knees up to her chin and looked as if she wasn't entirely displeased with the current state of the room. Jerry heard a bang and a muffled curse from the stairs and said, 'Listen, they're bringing the furniture up now, so...'

Theres hugged herself even more tightly and stayed where she was, unassailable. A minute or two later the twins came lumbering in with the sofa, and Jerry asked them to put it in Theres' room. She would have to sleep on it until he managed to get a bed. The girl followed the movements of the two big men with her eyes wide open, her fingers constantly intertwining. The twins seemed to have accepted that they couldn't make any contact with Theres, and placed things in her room in silence.

Each time they came in Theres slackened the grip around her knees a fraction, and by the time they brought in the last two little boxes containing her clothes, she was on her feet.

'So,' said Mats, or Martin, looking around the apartment where the paltry furnishings echoed in the emptiness. He seemed to be searching for something positive to say, but had no success. Instead he finished off with, 'There we are, then.'

'Yes,' said Jerry. 'There we are.'

4

A couple of days after they had moved into the apartment, Theres started her first period. Jerry was sitting at the computer trying to make a bit of money in a poker game when Theres came out of her room and said, 'How did it get to be open?'

Jerry was so preoccupied with the game that he didn't look away from the screen as he asked, 'How did what get to be open?'

Theres came and stood next to him and said, 'It's coming out. Who did it?'

Jerry gave a start when he saw her. Then he understood. Her knickers and T-shirt were spattered with red, and blood had trickled down her left leg, all the way to the ankle. Theres wasn't afraid, just puzzled as she stood there staring at her sticky fingers.

Jerry folded in the poker game, something he'd been intending to do anyway, and logged out of Partypoker. He scratched his head, not knowing where to start. Despite the fact that he had decided what the official version of his relationship with Theres was going to be, this was the first time he actually *felt* like a single dad.

'Well...' said Jerry. 'This is something that happens. It's going to happen every month. You're going to bleed like this. From now on.'

'Why?'

'To be perfectly honest...I don't have much of an idea. But it's because you're growing up. It happens to all girls as they grow up. They bleed for a few days each month.'

Theres carried on looking at her fingers, her eyes sliding over her stained clothes and striped legs. Then she frowned and asked, 'What am I?'

'What do you mean? You're a girl—is that what you mean?'

'More.'

'You're about thirteen years old, you're...I don't know what you are. You'll have to work that out for yourself.'

Theres nodded and went back to her room. Jerry stayed where he was for a while, thinking he was completely useless. That was how things were with Theres. She accepted everything you said to her, as long as it wasn't contradicted by something she'd been told in the past. When he went into her room she was sitting quite happily on the floor looking through a pile of CDs as she bled onto the rug underneath her.

'Sis,' said Jerry. 'I have to go and buy a couple of things. You go and have a shower, and then...' Jerry found a blank sheet of paper, wrote the word 'menstruation' on it and gave it to Theres.

'That's what it's called. When you bleed like that. Look it up on the net while I'm out. When you've had a shower.'

Jerry pulled on his jacket and hurried out. The problem of Theres and her periods had never even crossed his mind. He had never thought of her as a young woman, or even a girl, really. She was too different to be anything other than simply herself. Neuter. But now it had happened.

He knew a bit more about the phenomenon than he had told Theres, but not a great deal. During his wild years he had managed to get laid a few times, but he'd never lived with anyone. Never followed a girl's or a woman's daily routine. Except Laila's, of course, and she hadn't been comfortable talking about that sort of thing.

Besides which, it was so difficult to explain things to Theres because her view of the world was so fucked up. To put it briefly, she thought people were out to get one another. Jerry agreed with her up to a point—man is a wolf to his fellow man and so on—but her version was more violent and concrete, and above all it was the big people who were after the little people so that they could kill them and exploit them.

It was true that the twins' friendliness had caused some confusion in her conviction, and a couple of times she had ventured out onto the balcony to look at the people down below, but her basic attitude was one of deep suspicion. As far as Jerry was concerned that was a perfectly acceptable attitude, but she needed to loosen up a bit if she was going to be able to live among other people.

In the local shop Jerry read the packets of panty liners and tampons very carefully, but was none the wiser. On top of everything else, the damned things came in different *sizes*. He had to try and imagine what Theres might be like down there. This evoked a modicum of excitement which made him uncomfortable, and he grabbed a small and a medium of each kind.

A man of his own age was sitting at the checkout, and as he passed the boxes over the reader, Jerry said, 'My daughter. It's her first period.' The man nodded sympathetically and asked if Jerry was on his own. Yes, he was. And what about Mum? Well, she'd cleared off. To Sundsvall, of all places. Didn't want anything to do with her daughter. Very sad, that kind of thing. Yes, very sad indeed.

Jerry was quite pleased with himself as he left the shop. That was all sorted, then. People did have a tendency to stand around gossiping in local shops. The man on the checkout seemed happy to chat, and if anybody asked, Jerry had given a reasonable account of himself and Theres. Job done.

When he got home, Theres was sitting at the computer with wet hair. 'How's it going?' he asked.

'It's English,' said Theres. 'I don't understand.'

'Oh, for fuck's sake,' said Jerry. 'Shift.'

Theres got up, and of course she had bled all over her clothes on his desk chair. Jerry took out a box of tampons and a box of panty liners, and gave them to her. 'Here. These things will stop you bleeding. Well no, they won't stop you bleeding, but they're like a kind of bandage. A plaster. Understand?'

Theres turned the box over and shook her head. Jerry opened the box of tampons and found a number of hard, compressed cotton cylinders and a plastic tube. He sat down in the armchair and read the instructions until he had worked out what to do.

Why the fuck did girls have periods? What was actually the point? The instructions didn't contain any answers to that particular question, just the practical matters. His cheeks were on fire as he explained to Theres how to insert the tube then push out the cylinder with the string attached. When she pulled down her knickers to do as he'd told her, he turned away and said, 'Go and do it in the bathroom.'

Theres obeyed, and Jerry flopped down in the armchair. He felt dirty. This wasn't a new experience, but he didn't want to feel dirty in this particular way. Theres had begun to develop breasts and she was a pretty girl—beautiful, in fact. She was completely in his power, and an entire scenario flickered through his brain for a few seconds until he gritted his teeth and forcibly ejected the unwanted images.

She was his sister, and he was no fucking incestuous paedophile, end of story! She had that problem girls get, and it was no more complicated than him having a nosebleed once a month, for example. A bit of cotton wool up his nose, and that was that. The fact that he felt so uncomfortable and had to look away didn't mean he was a psycho with a filthy mind.

Sorted. When Theres shouted from the bathroom a little while later to say that she couldn't manage, he went in and helped her to insert the tampon, made sure the string was in the right place, and explained to her that she would have to change it a couple of times a day, and she could bloody well do that herself. Then he washed his hands.

5

Perhaps it had something to do with her menstruation and perhaps not, but Theres was changing. From time to time she opened up her shell a little and peered at the outside world. She had started to take a serious interest in the internet, and when Jerry wasn't using the computer she often sat there clicking through articles on Wikipedia, mainly about different animals.

One day when Jerry was reading the paper in the living room, Theres asked, 'What's this?'

Jerry looked at the screen and saw that Theres—presumably by following various links—had ended up on a website called poetry.now. There was a poem about cats on the screen.

'It's poetry,' said Jerry. 'Poems. You write like that when it's a poem, I think. Do you think it's good?'

'I don't know. What's good?'

'How the fuck should I know? It doesn't seem as if it has to rhyme these days, anyway. Write something yourself, then you can see if anybody says anything.'

'How shall I write?'

Jerry clicked through to another poem that he thought seemed very disjointed, and appeared to be about not knowing what you want to be. He waved at the screen. 'You just write like this, kind of. A few sentences here and there. Hang on, we'll set you up an account.' Jerry keyed in a made-up name and linked it to her email account. Why had they set up an email account for her anyway—who the hell was she going to write to? Oh well, at least it was useful now. 'All you have to do now is choose a username and press enter, then you can write whatever you want.'

Jerry went back to his armchair and the evening paper, while Theres sat with her fingers resting motionless on the keys. After a while she asked, 'What's my name?'

'Theres. You know that.'

'When did I get Theres?'

'You mean the name?' Jerry thought about it, and realised he had come up with it years ago, but had used it so often it had become completely natural. He didn't see any harm in telling her the truth. 'You got it from me.'

'Who is Theres?'

'Well, you are.'

'Before.'

Jerry sensed they were approaching the tangled thicket that was Theres' view of humanity, and he hadn't the strength to hack his way through right now, so he said, 'You just have to come up with a username, not your own name. Write Bim or Bom or something,' whereupon he went back to his newspaper.

He heard the keys tapping away, and five minutes later Theres said, 'What do I do?'

Jerry got up and looked at the screen. Under the username Bim she had actually written a poem:

> where I am no one can be
> inside the brain lies thinking
> porridge is not good
> talk misleads
> the name does not mean me
> the moon is my father

'The moon is my father,' said Jerry. 'What do you mean by that?'

'He watches when I'm asleep,' said Theres. 'My father.'

The moon often shone in through her bedroom window at the

time when she was going to bed. She might have got the bit about how fathers behave from something she'd read.

'Of course,' said Jerry. 'Good poem. Send it.'

He showed her how to click send. Then she sat with her hands resting on her lap, staring at the screen, until Jerry asked her what she was waiting for.

'Someone to say something,' she said.

'It might take a while, you know. Check again tomorrow.'

Theres got up and went out onto the balcony. Jerry watched her as she stood there touching her face, running her fingers over it as she gazed down at the street.

The following day there was a positive comment about the poem from somebody called Josefin. Jerry showed her how to reply to comments, and how to make comments of her own. When Theres had been clicking away and writing for a while, she asked, 'Are they people?'

'Who?'

'The ones who are writing.'

'What else would they be?'

'I don't know. Are they little people?'

'Most of them are, I suppose. Young, anyway.'

When Jerry had been showing Theres how to use the poetry site, he had noticed that almost all the users were girls between fourteen and twenty, with only the odd boy or older person. Without any planning he seemed to have given Theres an opportunity to take a step closer to the world and people her own age.

She sat at the computer for several hours, so quiet and with such intense concentration that Jerry didn't want to interrupt and tell her that he needed to work. When she had read through all the poems on the website, she said, 'They're sad.'

'Who? The people who write the poems?'

'Yes. They're sad. They don't know what to do. They cry. It's a shame.'

'Yes, I suppose it is.'

Theres furrowed her brow in concentration. She looked at the computer, at her hands. Then she got up and went out onto the balcony for a while. When she came in, she asked, 'Where are they?'

'The girls? All over the place. One might be in the building opposite, another might be in Gothenburg. A long, long way away.'

Jerry had been sitting in the apartment all day, and twilight was beginning to fall outside. He had a sudden inspiration. 'Shall we go out and look?' he said. 'See if we can spot any of them?'

Theres stiffened. Then she nodded.

During the days and weeks that followed, Theres ventured further and further from the apartment. At first she wanted to hide as soon as she caught sight of an adult, but gradually she accepted that the big people's hunger was at rest on weekdays, and that they were not about to fall on her.

Children didn't interest her, because she seemed to think they belonged to a different, non-threatening species. No, it was mostly people of her own age she was searching for. She wanted to see what they were doing, what they looked like, what they were saying. More than once Jerry had to extricate her from embarrassing situations where she was simply sitting and staring at someone, or was very obviously eavesdropping on a conversation.

She began to speak more like a normal teenager, and Jerry bought her clothes that looked like what her contemporaries were wearing. The only thing he couldn't sort out was her hair. He tried taking her to the hairdresser, but as soon as the woman picked up the scissors Theres started screaming, and refused to stay in her chair. Nothing could convince her it wasn't dangerous.

Apart from her hair, which Jerry trimmed with the kitchen scissors, you could have taken her for just about anybody if it hadn't been for that constantly distant, evasive look in her eyes. So Jerry wasn't fooled. He knew that in actual fact he hadn't a clue what was going on inside her head. Not a clue.

A more ambitious or restless person than Jerry would probably have got fed up with the way they lived, but as the days slipped into one another and the sun rose and fell over the square in Svedmyra, Jerry discovered that he was quite content with his existence.

He went back to his childhood home to pick up a few things he wanted to keep, then got a firm in to clear the house. He put it in the hands of an estate agent; the history of the house meant they had to drop the asking price, which was already low, but when the bills were paid and the commission deducted, there was still a couple of hundred thousand left over for Jerry, enough for at least a year or two without any financial worries.

He played Civilisation and Lord of the Rings online, chatted with other players, checked out films with or without Theres, and went for walks. They spent a few evenings sitting together looking through his VHS tapes of videos from different artists: Bowie, U2, Sinéad O'Connor.

Theres was particularly taken with Sinéad; over and over again she begged Jerry to rewind the tape so that she could join in with 'Nothing Compares 2 U'. After those evenings Jerry rummaged through some of the boxes that hadn't been unpacked yet and found his old bits of paper with chord sequences scribbled on them, songs they used to sing when Theres was little.

As winter turned to spring Jerry started playing the guitar again and they worked their way through the songs, adding lyrics that Theres suggested here and there, writing new ones. For fun Jerry bought a microphone so that they could record the songs on Garageband and play about with them afterwards.

Jerry had no ambitions when it came to music, but it was a sin and a shame that a voice like Theres' would never reach a wider audience. Despite the fact that they hardly had any lyrics, the songs Theres recorded on Garageband were better than most things Jerry heard on the radio.

He couldn't shake off the feeling. That it was all such a fucking... waste.

6

You can plan for things, work towards them for years, and yet they never materialise. Or you just happen to be in the right place at the right moment, and everything falls into place. If you want to believe in something like Fate, she's a capricious character. Sometimes she stands there blocking the doorway you were born to pass through, and sometimes she takes you by the hand and leads you through the minute you poke your nose out. And the stars gaze down and keep their counsel.

One day at the beginning of May when Jerry came out of the shop, there was a wallet lying on the low wall by the bike stand. He sat down beside it and glanced around, pretending to be catching his breath. None of the people enjoying the spring sunshine was looking in his direction. He slipped the wallet into his pocket.

When he got home he investigated his find and was disappointed. He had been hoping for a few hundred-kronor notes, perhaps some interesting cards and a furious owner who would have to spend the whole afternoon ringing around and cancelling them.

But the wallet belonged to a young girl, sixteen years old according to her ID card, and contained only a few bits of paper with telephone numbers on them, two twenty-kronor notes and a Nordea bank card. Perhaps that would have been the end of the matter—Jerry might even have gone down and put the wallet back, if he hadn't found a piece of paper in one of the side pockets.

'IDOL 2006' it said at the top in white letters on a blue background. It was a flyer with the time and place of the auditions for this year's program. Grand Hotel, May 14.

Jerry looked at the ID card. Presumably the girl—Angelika Tora Larsson—had dreams of stardom.

Jerry was still inclined to give the wallet a chance to be reunited with its owner. Then he spotted the small print right at the bottom of the flyer: 'Minimum age 16 years. Bring ID and completed application form'.

And Fate stepped aside and opened the door.

'Sis? How would you like to be on that program we saw? You remember, the one where people were singing?'

Theres was sitting at the computer reading an article about tigers. She nodded without taking her eyes off the screen.

'No, seriously,' said Jerry. 'Would you like to do that? There'll probably be loads of people.'

'You'll come too.'

'Yes, absolutely. Of course I will. But it would be cool to sing in a place where people could hear just how good you are, wouldn't it? I mean, it's kind of a waste just singing in here with me, don't you think?'

Theres didn't answer, and Jerry realised he was actually talking to himself; she had already given him her answer. Jerry held out Angelika's ID card. 'What do you think? Does this girl look like you?'

'I don't know.'

Jerry scrutinised the photograph. It had presumably been taken a couple of years ago, because the girl hardly looked like a teenager. She wasn't exactly like Theres apart from the long, fair hair, but he didn't think they'd check that carefully. After all, she wasn't exactly trying to get into a political summit meeting.

He continued the train of thought. ID number, name. Check, TV. It probably wasn't a particularly good idea, all things considered. He had got carried away by the possibility. But it was too dangerous, anything could happen. Oh well. He would keep the ID card; you never knew when it might come in handy.

Theres got up from the computer and said, 'Come on, then.'

'Come where?'

'We're going now. To the TV program.'

Jerry smiled. 'It's not for ten days, sis, and I don't think...We need to give this some thought.'

He thought. And thought. He downloaded the application form just for fun, and filled it in; he checked out where the Grand Hotel was, just to amuse himself. Just to see if it was possible, he sat down with a pin and a drafting pen and changed a one in Angelika's date of birth to a four. And just to finish what he had started, he rubbed the card around in the gravel a little bit just to make it look scruffy, so that the change would be less noticeable.

Since they had nothing else to do, he and Theres practised a couple of songs that sounded good when she sang them a cappella. Theres wanted to sing 'A Thousand and One Nights', which Jerry didn't think was a good idea. But then it didn't really matter, because she wasn't going to the auditions anyway.

Of course it would be good if Theres could get out and meet some people of her own age, and obviously it was almost criminal that more people didn't have the chance to be touched by her voice, and no doubt there was some kind of desire for revenge within Jerry, *listen to this, you bastards,* but regardless of who these bastards might be, they could be dangerous in the long run.

He kept thinking like that, and he was still thinking like that at eight o'clock on the morning of May 14 when they took the subway to Kungsträdgården just so that they could stroll over to the Grand Hotel and check things out. They walked along Nybrokajen holding hands. Theres asked about everything she saw, and Jerry hardly knew the answer to any of it. He felt lost in the middle of Stockholm.

Up to now only his thoughts had been opposing the whole thing, while his feelings and impulses had kept driving them forward. Now at last his feelings began to catch up. He wasn't in control of the situation at all. When they had passed Berzelii Park and turned into Stallgatan, Jerry stopped, let go of Theres' hand and said, 'No. No. I don't think we should do this, sis. We're fine as we are, aren't we? This is only going to cause trouble.'

Theres looked around. Boys and girls of her own age, alone or in groups, with or without parents, were walking past them. Without looking in Jerry's direction, she simply followed them.

Jerry was on the point of shouting 'Sis!' after her, but stopped himself just in time, dashed after her and said, 'Tora. We're going home now.'

Theres shook her head and kept on walking. Without Jerry noticing exactly when it happened, the disparate groups became a crowd, and they were at the back of a queue that was more than a hundred metres long, with people joining on behind them. Jerry tugged gently at Theres' hand but she stood there open mouthed, gazing at all the girls who were slightly older than her, and refused to move.

Jerry realised he wasn't going to get her away without causing a scene, and it was impossible to know what she might do if he started behaving in an unexpected way. He had said they were going to come to the auditions. They had come. Now they were here. Theres was behaving according to what had been said so, with sweat pouring down his back, Jerry joined the queue and whispered, 'Just remember your name's Tora. If anyone asks. Tora Larsson. Your name is Tora Larsson, OK?'

Theres shook her head. 'That's not my name.'

Jerry realised his mistake, and rephrased. 'No, that's right. But if anyone asks what your name is, you have to answer Tora Larsson.'

'Yes.'

'And if anyone asks how old you are, what do you say?'

'Sixteen.'

'OK. OK.'

Although it wasn't OK at all. Jerry felt as if everyone was looking at him; he felt like a deviant, he felt threatened as he stood there in the middle of the pack of girls. Most of them were probably between sixteen and twenty. Further away stood a couple of groups of boys and a few older girls, but the majority were just a couple of years older than Theres, and only a few of them had an adult with them.

The opposite was true of Theres. He had never seen her so calm when she was among other people, and presumably she was calm for the same reason that Jerry was overcome with a mild feeling of panic as he stood there surrounded by the aroma of hairspray, lip gloss and chewing gum. She was with her own kind. Jerry wasn't.

After an hour the queue began to shuffle forwards, and after another two hours they had reached the registration desk. Jerry clenched his fists in his trouser pockets as Theres handed over her application form and ID card. His heart almost stopped as the woman dealing with the registration looked from the form to the card, back to the form.

'Do you use your middle name?' she asked. Theres didn't answer. 'Hello,' said the woman. 'I'm talking to you.' Jerry saw that Theres had begun to draw back her lips, and he heard a faint growling. He quickly stepped in.

'Yes,' he said. 'She uses her middle name. It was her grandmother's name.'

The woman ignored him and fixed her gaze on Theres. 'Listen to me. What's your name?'

'Tora,' said Theres. 'My name is Tora Larsson.'

'There you go,' said the woman, writing the name next to a number. 'That wasn't so difficult, was it? We don't want to have the wrong name down for you if you go and win, now do we?' Her tone implied that Theres winning was just about as likely as Bruce Springsteen releasing a disco album, but Theres was given a number to pin on her sweater.

Then all they could do was wait. The wannabes sat scattered about or crowded together in a vast room below street level. From time to time groups of four were called into one of the four rooms on the next floor up, where an initial audition was held, and some were then filtered through to meet the real judges a couple of days later.

Jerry sat down with Theres in a corner behind a gigantic plastic yucca. As Theres gazed around Jerry sat with his head between his knees, grinding his teeth at his own stupidity. When he eventually looked up he saw Theres slowly wandering among the groups of young people, studying them as if they were pictures at an exhibition. That was relatively normal. It was OK. After all, this was one of the reasons they were here, wasn't it?

Calm down, Jerry. It's fine. Everything's cool.

After quarter of an hour, Theres came back and sat down next to him.

'They're scared,' she said.

'Who?' said Jerry. 'The ones who are going to audition?'

'All the little girls and all the little boys,' said Theres. 'They're scared of the big people.'

'I should think they're just nervous, mostly.'

'They're nervous because they're scared. I don't get it.'

Jerry smiled, in spite of everything. The new expressions Theres had learned still sounded strange coming out of her mouth. 'What don't you get?' he asked.

'Why they're scared. There are lots of us. There aren't lots of big people here.'

'No,' said Jerry. 'That's one way of looking at it, I suppose.'

A little way off sat a girl who actually looked even younger than Theres, and Jerry wondered if any of the others were here under false pretences. The girl was rubbing her scalp compulsively, and suddenly started shaking and sobbing. Theres got up and went over to her, crouching down by her feet.

Jerry didn't hear what they said, but after a while the girl stopped crying and nodded bravely. She took Theres' hand and gave it a brief pat. Theres allowed it to happen. Then she came back to sit with Jerry.

'What was that all about?' he asked.

'I can't tell you,' she said, staring straight ahead. Jerry had never seen her like this. A heavy, solemn calm emanated from her, so strong that Jerry unconsciously moved slightly closer, drawn to her so that she would soothe his own anxiety. Her back was straight and she was utterly still, with an impassive expression on her face that suggested she had seen through the whole thing, that the ghost was nothing but smoke and mirrors.

A little while later it was an older girl with teased black hair who broke down, dragging her friend down with her until they were both sitting there sobbing as the mascara smeared their cheeks. Theres went over and sat with them.

The result was not as immediate this time, but Jerry could see how quickly the two girls accepted Theres and listened to what she said. One of them laughed out loud and shook her head, as if Theres had said something absurd but uplifting. When she noticed that Theres wasn't smiling, she stopped laughing and leaned closer to listen.

And so it went on. There were no more breakdowns among those who were waiting, but from time to time a boy or girl came back from one of the rooms upstairs and obviously hadn't got the reception he or she expected. The boys were usually furious, and Theres took no notice of them, but sometimes there was a girl with tears running down her cheeks, and Theres was there to console her. Or whatever it was she was doing.

Some ignored her, others became slightly aggressive when this stranger tried to make contact in their darkest hour, but several moved close to Theres and sat down with her to talk. Sometimes it ended with a hug which Theres accepted without reciprocating, sometimes she was given a piece of paper or a card. A name or phone number, presumably.

Towards three o'clock a woman with a headset and a clipboard came in and called out Theres' number, along with three others.

Theres, deep in conversation with a red-haired girl who had practically had to be carried down the stairs from the audition room, didn't react. Jerry ran over and told her it was her turn now. Theres stood up and said goodbye to the red-haired girl, who whispered, 'Good luck,' in a voice thick with tears.

'Do you want me to come with you?' asked Jerry.

'There's no need,' said Theres, and headed for the stairs. Jerry watched her go into a room on the next floor along with clipboard-woman, and his heart clenched. Something had changed irrevocably today. He didn't know if this was a good thing or a bad thing. As usual.

Three minutes later, Theres emerged. Some of the girls she had talked to had waited, presumably to see how she got on, and she was immediately surrounded by seven eager, questioning faces.

Theres' expression was unreadable. She looked exactly the same as when she walked in. The only thing that told Jerry how things had gone was a brief nod, then seven cheering voices.

THE OTHER GIRL

I

The experience with Tora Larsson's song had shaken Teresa. She was boiling inside and needed to let off steam. As soon as she got to her room that evening, she logged on to Lunarstorm to see how the discussion was going. *Idol* was always a hot topic.

She thought she had been struck by spontaneous dyslexia. It took a while for her to grasp that it did actually say what she thought it said. Tora Larsson was the most written about of that evening's contestants, and most people thought she was terrible, or worse. They said she had no presence, no star quality. They said her clothes were ugly and her haircut was even uglier. They said the song she sang was crap. The only thing nobody complained about was her voice, but everything else about her appearance was scrutinised and deemed to be dire, stupid, meaningless and boring.

Teresa had always conducted herself sensibly in chat rooms and on discussion forums. Apart from the wolf forum, she was a calculating troll who dragged her baited hook where it would have the greatest effect, only to watch with an ironic smile as the little fish made their pathetic attempts to bite. But now she saw red. She was so agitated that her fingers would hardly obey her as she logged in with her alter ego Josefin, and started to write her reply.

She tried to remain calm, in spite of everything. She wrote that Tora Larsson had the most fantastic voice that had ever been heard on *Idol*, and that what others called a lack of star quality was just Tora being herself. That it was nice to see somebody who wasn't trying to be Britney or Christina. She said she was convinced that Tora Larsson could sing just about anything, because she was singing from who she was, not who she was pretending to be.

It didn't really cover everything Teresa felt, but it was impossible to put the most important things into words so it would have to do. She clicked on send. The answers came quickly. One or two people who agreed with her plucked up the courage to crawl out into the open and give her tentative support, but the majority simply jeered. You'd have to be a complete loser to like such a reject. Tora was totally out of place; she wouldn't get a single vote, and so on.

It was a relief for Teresa to let herself go. She hadn't felt comfortable writing calmly about what she really felt. Now she gave free rein to everything that was boiling and fermenting inside her.

Her joy in finding exactly the right phrase came to the fore as she wrote about the detractors' vacant heads, how they had been force fed so much plastic pop music that their brains short circuited when they actually saw a real person; she suggested they get up from in front of the computer and go kneel before the shrine to Elin Lanto which they no doubt had in their bedroom, next to their signed *Idol* poster of Kaj Kindvall.

Less-gifted barbs came back at her, and Teresa was in her element. Sometimes she got hesitant support from the sidelines, someone who squeaked, 'Hi, Josefin. You're right', fanning the flames. A few dropped out of the mudslinging and new participants joined in. However, those who supported her stayed on.

At one o'clock in the morning, Teresa wrote, 'Good night', and logged out. Her head was buzzing, but the pressure she had felt was gone. When she went to bed the image of Tora Larsson remained in her mind's eye for a long time before she managed to fall asleep.

The following day there was a lot of talk in school, but Teresa didn't join in the discussions. Somewhere inside she knew you can't convince people that something is fantastic if they don't already think it is. Her behaviour on the net was just a way of letting off steam, not a serious attempt to recruit support.

Besides which, there was a key difference in school. The general opinion was the same as it had been on the net: that Tora Larsson was useless and didn't have a cat in hell's chance. This view was put forward by the loud, popular girls whose opinions always got airtime, along with the small number of boys who cared enough. From a purely statistical point of view there must have been some people who thought differently, but in the real world they didn't even have the courage to squeak. They either agreed or stayed out of the discussions.

A girl called Celia from 9a stood up in the dining room and did a horrible imitation of Tora. With a blank expression and her mouth half-open she burbled, 'A thousand and one nights, does anyone know where I left my tights' to general sniggering. Teresa flushed with anger, but said nothing. She couldn't work out what it was about Tora Larsson that had touched her heart, but it was something, and she acted on it. She felt like a faithful warrior as she squeezed superglue into the keyhole of Celia's locker during the lunch break.

Teresa's nails got shorter and shorter as she chewed them through the different stages of the final audition. The judges were unimpressed by Tora Larsson's stage presence, and it sounded as if they were always on the point of sending her home. But her voice triumphed in the end. Maybe they were only playing to the gallery, but the judges seemed almost reluctant to give her a place in the final twenty whose fate would be decided by the viewers. It was as if they wished they could ignore her voice. But it was more than perfect, it was magical, and it couldn't be dismissed.

Teresa could relax, temporarily at least. Now it was up to her and all the others who *understood* to make sure Tora Larsson stayed in the competition so that they could see more of her.

The following week was 'agony week' on *Idol.* Twenty competitors would be reduced to eleven. Agony was the word, said Bull. Tora Larsson was to sing in the first semi-final, and as the evening approached Teresa was so anxious she didn't know what to do with herself.

She knew it was ridiculous to invest so much emotion in a fucking *Idol* contestant, but she couldn't help it. She had watched Tora's performance several times on the net, and the effect it had that first time was still there.

As the family settled down noisily in front of the TV as usual, Teresa was sitting inside a bubble. She didn't want to hear the others' small talk, and above all she didn't want to hear their opinions. If they said anything negative about Tora, Teresa might well explode. When Tora walked onto the stage, Teresa dug her nails into the palms of her hands and sat there, taut as a piano string.

A few months had passed since the filming of the auditions, but Tora hadn't changed much. Some stylist on the program had presumably had a go at her hair and clothes, but the general impression of a person from another, less broken world remained intact.

Appropriately enough, Tora sang 'Life on Mars', and it was doubtful if Teresa so much as blinked during her performance. One thing had changed, actually. Tora completely ignored the audience in the studio, but she did look into the camera from time to time. Every time Teresa met that gaze, a shock went through her.

A small affair, the lyrics said; but it wasn't a small affair to Teresa. She thought it was the best performance she had ever seen on *Idol*. When it was over she said she wasn't feeling very well, and left the family in the living room. She felt absolutely fantastic, but for one thing she didn't want to hear what the others had to say; for another, she obviously needed to hit the phone.

Since she didn't want to run out of credit on her mobile, she went and sat in her parents' bedroom and rang the number for Tora over and over again until her index and middle fingers were sore. Then she went back to the TV in time for the announcement of the results. Tora had got through. Of course.

She spent the evening defending Tora on various internet forums. There were a few more supporters, but there was still a huge preponderance of people who thought Tora was more or less useless. Presumably those who did like Tora liked her so much they had helped her get through by ringing over and over again.

2

Teresa saw things differently these days. Ever since she had started reading about wolves, she had fantasised about herself in wolf form. The teeth, the agility, the danger. Lone wolf. She was the lone wolf, slinking around the residential areas and terrifying the anxious little people who immediately rang the local paper.

But at school she had begun to observe and recognise the other aspect of man as wolf: the pack mentality. The social game, the pecking order. She was so intensely absorbed by Tora that her opinion became a litmus paper showing the composition and content of those around her.

She saw. Saw how it was permissible for an alpha female like Celia to establish what the group should think. When she yelped you had no choice but to flatten your ears and laugh, whimper, act submissively. Otherwise the snap of the teeth might come. A derogatory comment about your new trousers? Everyone immediately realised they were the ugliest trousers they'd ever seen.

The boys stood around pushing each other, physically or verbally. Who got to deal out the insults, and to whom; and who was that person in turn permitted to joke with before the pack showed its displeasure by turning away?

Among wolves, the rank order was more or less established at the cub stage, but since classes in school had been rearranged over the years, this was more like the second life-stage of the wolf, when hierarchies were established: the onset of sexual maturity.

Teresa saw clearly for the first time how this conflict was played out in the corridors, in the playground, in the dining room. Day after day. And it frightened her. The lone wolf may be a romantic idea, but in practice it's an animal that is destined to die.

The clusters at break time, the dress codes, the taste in music and the in-jokes that bound the packs together. Teresa would have been perfectly happy to have been left off the text message lists, not to be included in the gossip, not to be invited to parties if only she had been left in peace.

But that was no longer the case. True, she had never actually rolled over and showed them her throat, so she was never *actually* bullied, but she was poked and prodded. An amusing comment in the showers about her fat thighs, some boy who pulled a face as she walked past. An anonymous text: 'Shave your armpits before somebody throws up'.

Nothing more than that, but it was quite enough.

She was competing in an endless series of *Idol* that she could never win. The best she could do was lose with dignity.

It was time for the first weekly final in the TV competition. Eleven contestants would be reduced to ten, and the theme was Eighties. Teresa hadn't read the TV papers and had no idea what she was going to see. When the program started, she discovered that Tora would be appearing in fifth spot.

She regarded the four who came before Tora as filler. Arvid and Olof sat there headbanging ironically when one of the boys did 'Poison', doing a particularly bad hard-man act. A chubby girl sang 'The Greatest Love of All' so hard she almost burst a blood vessel; Maria thought it was 'lovely'.

Then came Tora. Teresa crawled into a tunnel, with only the television visible at the other end. Everything else was extinguished—literally as well. Only a single spotlight fell on the stage where Tora Larsson stood, wearing a black dress that merged with the background so that almost the only thing you could see was her face. She looked straight into the camera and sang.

Teresa stopped breathing.

'Nothing Compares 2 U'. The words told the familiar desolate story. The camera angle changed, but Tora continued to gaze into the close-up camera, and soon the angle shifted back again. Tora's face filled the screen. She was looking straight at Teresa, who only remembered to breathe when her chest started hurting.

The song continued, and it wasn't a question of liking or not liking it. Teresa was bewitched; transported. She was no longer in her living room, surrounded by her family. She was with Tora, she was inside her eyes, inside her head. They gazed into one another and dissolved, melted into one.

Towards the end of the song a few tears trickled down from Tora's eyes, and it was only when the last note had faded away that Teresa realised her cheeks were also wet.

'Sweetheart, what is it?' asked a voice from a long way off. Teresa returned to the living room and saw her mother's face close to her own. She dashed away the tears and waved crossly. She wanted to hear what the judges had to say.

They weren't particularly impressed. While there was no denying that Tora had an incredible voice, this wasn't *Stars in Their Eyes*. Contestants were expected to bring something of their own to the competition, and this had been nothing more than a straight copy of the original, blah blah blah. Teresa couldn't understand what they meant, but realised that, bewilderingly, Tora was in danger. The pack was growling.

Tora listened to the negative comments with the same indifference and self-possession as she had shown when positive comments were made. No gratitude, no distress. She just waited until they had finished, then left the stage. She was replaced by a pastel-coloured bouncy ball singing 'Girls Just Wanna Have Fun'.

Teresa sat through the rest of the songs with a fateful note quivering through her bones. When the lines opened for voting she got up without a word and went into her parents' bedroom. She had just reached for the phone to start calling when Maria came in and sat down on the bed.

'Are you all right, sweetheart?' she asked. 'Are you upset about something?'

Through gritted teeth Teresa said, 'No, Mum. I'm not upset. I just want to be on my own.'

Maria settled down more comfortably, and Teresa just wanted to scream. Maria tilted her head on one side. 'Tell me. What is it? I can see there's something wrong. Why were you crying earlier on?'

Teresa could no longer contain herself. Her voice was trembling with anger, the telephone was glowing just in the corner of her field of vision, and she spat out, 'Why do you have to start caring right *now*? I just want to be left in peace, can't you understand that?'

'Now that's not fair. You know perfectly well I always...'

Teresa had had enough. She got up, ran to her room, got out her mobile and started ringing. She only had enough credit for three calls.

Ten minutes later she went back downstairs to sit with the others, and the very thing she feared had happened. Tora Larsson was voted out. The very best artist she had ever seen hadn't received enough votes to stay in the competition.

She didn't know how many people rang in, and it was probably totally irrational, but at that moment she was convinced that her missing votes had made the difference. The twenty or so calls she could have made would have saved Tora. She would still have been in the competition if only Maria had left her alone.

3

Teresa had the weekend to calm down. She didn't look at any of the discussion forums on the Friday; she didn't want to see the gloating comments. On Saturday she started to come to her senses again. It was over. She had got far too involved, but now it was finished.

She had no intention of watching *Idol* again, but for God's sake—it was only a girl standing there singing, nothing more. Tora Larsson. A girl who was a couple of years older and blessed with a fantastic singing voice, was that really something to get so worked up about? No. And yes.

They were as different as two people of the same age from the same country can be, and yet there was something about Tora that made Teresa feel as if she *recognised herself.* In spite of their dissimilarity, it was Teresa standing there in front of the threatening audience, the blasé judges. It was Teresa who had a wall around her heart, and yet at the same time held it in her hands, the blood seeping between her fingers. The silent scream, the suppressed panic.

It is impossible to say why we love something or someone. We can come up with reasons if we have to, but the important part happens in the dark, beyond our control. We just know when it is there. And when it goes away.

Perhaps it would be accurate to say that Teresa was grieving, as we might grieve for a friend who has moved abroad or even further away, to the other side. She would never see Tora Larsson again, never experience that intoxicating recognition of a twin soul. Never meet those eyes again.

Despite the fact that Teresa was often alone, she rarely felt lonely. But this weekend she did. An empty space had appeared and it followed her like a white shadow wherever she went. She wandered aimlessly around the garden listening to Bright Eyes, sat for a while curled up in the cave that had been her and Johannes' secret place.

She listened to the words of the song: a lover you don't have to love. She stood for some time looking at the house where Johannes used to live. Swings had been put up in the garden, there were plastic toys in lots of different colours strewn around. A couple of trees had been chopped down. Bright Eyes sang in her ear in his cracked voice, and she felt as if everything was slipping away from her. As if she was fourteen years old, and it was already too late.

Seized by a sudden impulse she went indoors and started searching through her wardrobe. She would start wearing colourful clothes! She always wore black, white, grey. Now she was hunting for trousers, T-shirts, blouses or cardigans in different colours. From now on she was going to look like a rainbow!

She gave up when the only things she could find that satisfied her sudden whim were either too short because she'd outgrown them, or too tight for her disgusting fat legs and round belly. In the end she grabbed a yellow woolly hat, crammed it on her head and lay down on the bed on her stomach to read Kristian Lundberg's latest collection, *Job*.

> I dreamt about her She was standing beside my
> bed, pale grey like ash, whispering in my
> ear—'Do not be afraid, do not be afraid!'

The constant hovering emptiness made her restless, unable to concentrate. She pressed the palms of her hands to her ears and mumbled, 'Nobody likes me, everybody hates me, think I'll go and eat some worms...' over and over again until she was sweaty and felt revolting in her woolly hat. Then she went down to the kitchen and made herself some sandwiches.

And so the weekend passed.

Nothing special happened in school, nothing special happened anywhere. Johannes and Agnes had got themselves matching necklaces, blue stones that meant happiness to some native American tribe or something. They asked if Teresa wanted to go with them to a gig where some local bands were playing the following weekend, but Teresa said no. She couldn't help liking them, but she couldn't cope with their company for any length of time. They were just too cheerful.

One afternoon as Teresa was getting on her bike to cycle home, she heard Jenny say to Caroline that it looks disgusting when fat people ride bikes; the saddle disappears up their arse like some weird variation on anal sex. Teresa wept for a while as she pedalled home, then spent the rest of the journey fantasising about someone raping Jenny with a red-hot iron spike.

That evening she sat at her computer and considered doing a little bit of trolling on Lunarstorm, but it had somehow lost its charm since she had felt genuine hatred and gone into battle on Tora's behalf. Instead she joined the discussion forum on wolves. A few sightings in Värmland, someone whose chickens had been eaten (but that could just as easily have been a pine marten), someone drawing comparisons with wild boar, claiming they were a much greater threat. The thread thinned out and trailed off into a recipe for how to cook wild boar.

A new thread on how the very existence of a wolf somewhere in the vicinity paradoxically brings a feeling of security in these times when so much of our environment is being destroyed. This wild, beautiful and admittedly dangerous creature is still out there. Teresa rested her chin on her hand and scrolled down. She suddenly stiffened.

She had glimpsed the name 'Tora Larsson' in one post. She read it more carefully. 'MyrraC' was making a comparison between the wolf and Tora Larsson from *Idol*. Saying it was the same thing. Fear of the unknown. If something didn't behave in an approved, predictable way it was rejected, thrown out, irrespective of how beautiful or natural it might be.

Teresa thought the comparison was a bit lame, but still. The contribution had been posted just a couple of minutes earlier, and judging by MyrraC's profile she seemed to be about fifteen or sixteen. Teresa wrote a reply and said that she felt the same, the whole thing was just so tragic.

Myrra was online, and a reply came through just a minute or so later. After they had exchanged a couple of messages Myrra asked if she could have Josefin's email address so they didn't have to use the wolf forum to talk about this.

After some hesitation Teresa gave her address, with the comment: 'The name does not mean me.' Only when she had clicked on send did she remember where she had got the line from. She looked through her old documents until she found the poem she had written as a reply that time.

> Everyone is actually called something else
> Inside every person there is another person
> Talk misleads and behind the words are other words
> We can be seen only when it is dark
> We can be heard only when there is silence

Was it only a year since she had written that? It felt like much longer. And yet she discovered that she liked it, and wasn't ashamed of it. It wasn't too bad for a thirteen-year-old.

She pulled on her yellow woolly hat and felt slightly more cheerful. In an attack of nostalgia she went and fetched the box containing all her plastic beads. Carefully she took out all the little jars, with a lump in her throat as she thought about that little girl who would sit for hours, sorting them according to different systems. For old times' sake she started to thread a necklace. She used the very smallest beads, and discovered that her fingers were clumsier than they used to be. It was an incredibly fiddly task, but a sense of loyalty to her younger self drove her to continue until she had finished it.

You can go to hell she thought, without directing the comment at anyone in particular, and fastened the necklace around her neck with some difficulty. Then she checked her messages. There was indeed something from MyrraC, but also a message that had been sent ten minutes earlier from sereht@hotmail.com. It sounded vaguely like some form of spam or virus and she was about to delete it, but double-clicked by mistake and the message opened.

> hi i remember the poem thank you for saying nice things about when i sing i remember your poem too inside every person there is another person thats true my name was bim then you can write to me i like wolves too

Teresa read the words over and over again, trying to puzzle out what the message said. So the person who had written it was the person who had called herself 'Bim' on poetry.now, and who had written the poem Teresa had quoted on the spur of the moment when she gave out her address. She had used the alias 'Josefin' on poetry.now too, which was why she had been recognised.

So far so good. That kind of thing could happen when threads crossed in the mesh that was the internet. But why was the message so oddly written, and what did Bim or Sereht mean by 'saying nice things about when i sing'? Teresa understood perfectly well what it implied, but it seemed too far-fetched. She wrote a reply ignoring the strange bits and asked whether Bim had carried on writing poems; she herself hadn't.

Then she sat at the computer and waited, refreshing her Inbox every couple of minutes. Ten minutes later a reply arrived.

> when im called bim i write some poems when im called tora i sing when im called theres i dont do anything but im also called wolf and i bite and little one who stays in

> her room because the big people want to eat her up whats your name

Teresa believed.

She believed that this Theres was the same person as Tora Larsson. If Theres had written, 'Hi! My name's really Tora Larsson. Glad you liked me on *Idol*', Teresa would have been sceptical. But this fitted. The other-worldly creature she had followed on TV ought to talk like this, write like this. And she was writing to *her*. Teresa clutched at her chest with both hands. Her heart was pounding as if she had just finished a route march, and her cheeks flushed bright red. Her fingers were sweaty, slipping on the keys as she began to write a reply.

Calm down, Teresa. It's not that amazing.

She deleted what she had written and stood up. The clock on her bedside table was showing quarter past twelve. When she went to the bathroom, the rest of the house was dark and silent. She took a long shower, then turned off the hot water and stood under the running, ice-cold water for a long time. Then she got dressed, put on the yellow woolly hat and sat down at the computer again. During her absence Theres had sent another message.

> whats your name my name is theres most of the time you are small arent you and not big writing with a different name and fooling me because then you mustnt write you can only write if youre the same as you say you are if you are write now because im going to sleep soon

Teresa's fingers were cool and dry now. They flew over the keys with ease as she wrote:

> Hi Theres.
>
> My real name is Teresa, almost the same as yours, and I'm 14 years old. You're 16, aren't you? I really meant what I wrote on the wolf forum. I thought you were way better than everyone else on *Idol*, and it feels really weird

> to be sitting here writing to you, I almost feel a little bit scared. I'm sure you have a much more exciting life than me, and I don't really know what to write about. I've always liked wolves and I know quite a lot about them. I listen to Bright Eyes a lot, and I read poetry sometimes. What do you do when you're not singing?

Teresa couldn't bring herself to check the message to see if it was embarrassing or crap. She just sent it. After five minutes a reply arrived.

> i am fourteen years old like you so we are almost the same with the same name but i dont know where to put full stops and things when you write you can teach me i dont do anything exciting and you mustnt be scared im the one who should be scared i hardly do anything but now im going to sleep and tomorrow we will write more

They were the same age and they had almost the same name. Theres and Teresa. It was perfect.

BOTH THE GIRLS

I

Max Hansen.

If that name means anything to you, then either you're interested in old Danish films, or you're in the music industry. The Hansens came from Denmark, and when their only son was born in 1959, they named him Max after the actor who appeared in the first film they saw together in the cinema, *Beautiful Helena.*

It would be quite interesting to investigate Max Hansen's early years, to try and work out how such a person is formed, but that lies outside the scope of this narrative. It is enough to report that the family moved to Stockholm when Max was two years old, that he grew up as a Swede, and that he makes his entrance into this story forty-five years after that move.

In his twenties Max tried his hand at a musical career as the singer with the glam rock band Campbell Soup, but the only thing this led to was that he got to know the more successful band Ultrabunny and through a series of decisions and coincidences, ended up as their manager.

When Ultrabunny dissolved due to the songwriter's crippling writer's block, Max looked around for another band to help along the way. He had a winning attitude, a firm handshake, and a particular talent for making himself look much more important than he was. After a couple of years he had a small stable of fairly successful acts.

It was the middle of the 1980s, and Café Opera was the playground of choice for anyone who was someone or wanted to be someone in the music industry. Max wasn't at the top of the tree, but he made sure he invited the right people, hung out in the right company and made useful contacts. If an up and coming songwriter needed something to shove up his nose, Max wasn't slow to share, and when some well-known band made their noisy entrance, a bottle of chilled champagne would sometimes arrive at their table. Who's it from? Max Hansen, over there. Come and sit yourself down buddy, what did you say your name was? Spread the name around, spread the name.

The girls they let in solely because of their looks swarmed the tables, pretending to be unimpressed. Max focused on the ones with the wrong brand of handbag and the slightly desperate look. Chatted for a while, made sure he said hi to a couple of faces they would recognise from TV; that was usually all it took. Home to his two-room apartment on Regeringsgatan and wham, bam, thank you ma'am, breakfast not included. His all-time record was thirty in one month, but to make that he'd had to trawl Riche on the nights when Café Opera was dead.

And so it went on. Max had a highly developed sense of hierarchy, which was both a blessing—because it told him what his position should be within a group—and a curse, because it informed him implacably that he had got stuck two tiers below the top level.

If it had been just *one* tier, his artists would probably have stuck with him even if they got their big break, and would then have hauled him up with them. As it stood, if things started to go too well they left him when their contracts ran out.

He was fortunate enough to sign a completely unknown band, Stormfront, on a five-year contract that was dubiously advantageous for him; he then saw them break through after only a year. This made him plenty of money, but also led to a whole lot of bad feeling. The band bad-mouthed him constantly and called him a parasite: what should have been his great success turned out to be the beginning of his decline.

A few years after Stormfront had left him, pissing on his hall carpet by way of a farewell gift, the situation was completely reversed.

The only young artists he had any chance with were those who *hadn't* heard of him. Or those who knew exactly who he was, but were desperate. He still had his contacts, in spite of everything.

By the end of the nineties there was a saying in the industry that summed up the situation perfectly: 'Max Hansen—the last chance'. There were still songwriters, producers and record companies he could turn to if there was anything brewing, but they were down at the lower end of the scale, and the good times were over.

One thing remained unchanged: his taste for young girls. Since it was no longer enough to say hi to the right people in order to make an impression (and since the right people no longer said hi back), he had to bring in the heavy artillery to get the tender young flesh into his bed: the half promises.

Times had changed. In the mid-eighties, the dream of fame had been just that—an unattainable dream for most people. But now, thanks to the reality TV explosion, Lisa from Skellefteå and Mugge from Sundbyberg could suddenly believe, in all seriousness, that they were rising stars, that something big was just around the corner, and they grabbed at every opportunity.

Max hung out in the Spy Bar, keeping an eye out for anyone whose star had noticeably begun to fade. Those who had done the suburban clubs and shopping malls, and who now had only the odd gig with a backing track in a small-town pizza joint to keep the dream alive. Then he struck.

In this context his nickname, 'Last chance' was no liability. The girls in question were usually painfully aware that their moment had passed, even when they kept up a good front. 'Last chance' at least meant there *was* a chance, and that was what Max told them.

Untapped potential, a good stylist, a songwriter I know who's worked with the Backstreet Boys, this guy at the record company who's looking for someone exactly like you, contacts in Asia, they absolutely love Swedish girls over there.

Sometimes it worked, sometimes it bombed. In November 1999 Max recorded his first shag-free month since he was twenty. He got a hair transplant to restore his fringe, had a few wrinkles ironed off his upper lip and considered his situation.

It wasn't that he actually scammed the girls. He did give them a few numbers to call, occasionally set up the odd meeting. With a girl from *Big Brother* he even managed to get her song listed as 'bubbling under' on *Tracks*, plus a few gigs in shopping malls. OK, so his promises were dubious, but these were hard times.

He decided to change tactics. Trawling in Spy Bar had become more and more difficult, and he decided to go back to basics. He started turning up at the public end-of-term concerts at music schools, and he kept an eye on the young girls who sang on TV, then got in touch.

Sometimes he would manage to get one of them into a manufactured group for a tour in Japan, or fix a couple of appearances at games fairs where they needed a Lara Croft. He recorded videos of girls dancing in their underwear, and he made the position clear: they could put out or push off, and yes, he was intending to film it.

One evening when he was sitting on his sofa half-drunk, jerking off to a DVD of a girl he had taped a couple of days earlier dancing clumsily to 'Oops, I Did It Again', he realised he had reached some kind of rock bottom, and that he hadn't the slightest desire to do anything about it. Then he came and fell asleep.

That was the situation when Max Hansen switched on the television at the end of September 2006 to watch 'agony week' on *Idol*. Every single boy and girl he saw on the program had some measure of talent, and he thought he could predict the ones who would get through, and how things would go for them after that. He was really after those who were voted off.

An incredibly pretty and innocent girl from Simrishamn piqued his appetite, but he suspected she was one of the ones where all contact had to go via the parents. However, he did make a note of her name as a possibility for business rather than penetration.

Then came Tora Larsson with 'Life on Mars', arousing something in him that was usually fast asleep: his curiosity. He couldn't work her out. He had been in the business for such a long time, and was musical enough to recognise a matchless voice when he heard it, but the girl herself? And her performance? What was all that about? Was it fantastic, or utter crap?

For once he had *no idea* how things would go for her, even though her voice echoed in his head long after she had stopped singing. She was pretty as a picture and at the same time ice-cold, in a way that was both repellent and arousing.

Tora got through, and the following day Max got hold of her contact details through an acquaintance at TV4. An address, nothing more. He printed out his standard letter with some modifications, but decided to wait and see how things went before sending it. Presumably she would have received a number of offers.

He watched the program when Tora sang 'Nothing Compares 2 U'. He was pleased when she went out, because that increased his chances. If he had ever seen an uncut diamond, he was looking at one right now. She had the voice and the appearance going for her, more than most in fact, but there was a hell of a lot missing if she wanted to have a successful career and become really popular.

And who would polish this diamond if not Max Hansen? Filled with inspiration, he dispensed with his standard letter and put together a new one, in which he went through her current qualities and defects, explained how he could help her, and outlined the opportunities that were open to her.

As usual he exaggerated a fair amount, but there was still a significant level of truth in what he wrote. He managed to convince himself that he just wanted to take her under his wing and help this fragile plant to grow, and so on. He almost got tears in his eyes; it was only the discovery that he had got an erection while he was writing that brought him back to reality.

He went straight down to the post box to send the letter. By the time he got back to the apartment, a part of him was already waiting anxiously for a reply.

He wanted this. Oh, how he wanted this.

2

The *Idol* adventure had been quite taxing for both Jerry and Theres, although in very different ways. It had changed them, and it had changed their relationship. Jerry had been forced to bring out aspects of himself that he didn't know existed, and he had seen elements of Theres that were completely new to him.

It had begun at the very first audition. On the subway he had asked her what she had actually said to console all those weeping girls, and Theres had replied, 'Words.'

'I get that. But what kind of words?'

'Normal words. The way things are.'

That was all he could get out of her, and his curiosity would eventually be satisfied by something that happened.

Theres sailed through the various stages of the *Idol* auditions in the spring and summer as if it was something completely natural, while Jerry became more and more exhausted. He hadn't realised there was so *much* of it. He thought you just turned up, sang for the judges, were either accepted or not accepted, and then you were ready for the program.

But that wasn't how it worked. After the preliminary audition at the Grand Hotel, Theres was asked to come back three days later with the same number, the same clothes and the same hairstyle to avoid any continuity problems; she had then sung for the main judging panel, got through and been congratulated by a small group of girls.

There had been breakdowns and streaky mascara on that occasion too, and once again Theres had stepped in; bending her head close to the distressed contestant, whispering words that Jerry strained, unsuccessfully, to hear. Theres was given more bits of paper with telephone numbers on them, and made not the slightest attempt to ring them.

But there was more. A month or so later there was the *final audition* at Oscar's Theatre, and Jerry had to put up with hours and days of waiting while Theres sang solo or in various groups. Every day he hoped she would be eliminated so that it would all be over, every day she got through. There was sweat and suffering and kids singing in every corner and cameras filming and it was hell on earth.

When Theres had finally been filtered through as one of the twenty lucky contestants who would return for the live shows in the autumn, Jerry felt undiluted relief. Not because she had got through, but because it was finally over. For now. He would worry about the autumn when the time came.

One very hot day in the middle of July, when the heat between the three-storey buildings was enough to make your skin hurt, Jerry finally found out what it was that Theres did.

They had gone into the local shop to choose an ice cream each, when they heard raised voices from the direction of the freezer. Then the owner appeared, marching towards the storeroom and dragging a girl of about thirteen by the arm.

From a few monosyllabic exchanges Jerry realised that the girl had been stealing, and she was now being called to account. The owner was squeezing the girl's forearm hard with one hand, and she was sobbing, 'No, look, I'm really sorry, I won't...'

Like anything unexpected that has some element of violence, it created a kind of physical numbness in the observer, and Jerry stood there with his arms dangling as he watched the owner push open the doors leading to the storeroom and drag the girl along with him.

He thought the owner was basically a nice guy who just wanted to make a point, rather than reporting the incident to the police. A good telling-off, and that would be the end of the matter. That was his interpretation. Theres' interpretation was different.

When Jerry emerged from his temporary paralysis, he caught sight of Theres. She had gone over to the shelf containing kitchen items, picked up a carving knife and ripped off the packaging. She was now heading for the storeroom with great determination, holding the knife at waist level.

'Sis? Sis!'

He ran after her and grabbed her by the shoulder. Theres raised the knife and turned to face him. Her eyes were empty, her face a grimacing mask. Instinctively Jerry let go of her shoulder and held up his hands in self-defence. Theres seemed to be on the point of stabbing at him, but stopped. He could hear a low growl coming from her throat.

Incredibly, Jerry had enough presence of mind to see that there was a question in her expression, her posture: *Why are you getting in my way? You have one minute to explain.*

'You're wrong,' Jerry said. It was the quickest thing he could come up with to give himself a little bit of breathing space. 'You're wrong. You're doing the wrong thing.'

'Little girl will be dead,' said Theres. 'The big person will kill her. Not wrong.'

Jerry made a huge effort to speak in clear sentences that Theres would hopefully be able to grasp as truths. 'You are wrong. He is not going to kill her. He is not going to harm her. He is going to say… words to her. Some harsh words. Then she will be allowed to leave.'

Theres lowered the knife a fraction. 'How do you know?'

'You have to trust me.' Jerry pointed at the storeroom doors. 'In a couple of minutes she'll come out. She won't be harmed. I promise.'

The knife returned to waist level as Theres stared fixedly at the doors, keeping watch. Jerry looked around the shop. Fortunately there were no other customers, but someone could come in at any moment.

'Theres? Could you give me the knife?'

Theres shook her head. 'If the little girl doesn't come, the big person will be dead.'

Jerry scratched the back of his head hard. His scalp was damp and more sweat was breaking through. He got the dizzying feeling that his and Theres' day-to-day existence was no more than a matter of tripping along across suspension bridges. There was actually an abyss between them, a chasm so deep that he couldn't even see the bottom. It had just become visible for a moment.

'OK,' said Jerry. 'But if...*when* the little girl comes out, will you give me the knife then?'

Theres nodded.

They waited. A minute passed. Two. No other customers came into the shop. Jerry stood next to Theres, staring at the closed double doors. When another minute had passed, an irrational fear began to grow in his breast. That Theres was right. That a murder or rape was being committed right now in the storeroom. He glanced at Theres. Her face was hard, closed. The girl needed to come out *now*, otherwise something terrible was going to happen.

And then she appeared. The doors opened and the owner saw Jerry, nodded in greeting and gestured at the tear-stained creature meekly trailing behind him.

'Sometimes you just have to make a stand, don't you?'

Jerry nodded and took a step to one side so that he was standing at an angle that hid the knife from the owner's view. The girl headed for the exit, and the owner called after her, 'You're welcome to come in again. But no more of that kind of thing.'

The girl shook her bowed head, and Theres followed her. Jerry let her go, because she no longer had the knife in her hand. He glanced sideways and saw that it was lying on top of the ice cream freezer.

The owner was talking about how it was essential to tackle this kind of thing from the start rather than simply letting these kids carry on, because they would end up paying for it later. Jerry nodded and made noises to indicate agreement as he manoeuvred the knife into his hand behind his back. When the owner turned away, he hid it among the packets of crisps. Then he left.

Theres and the girl were sitting side by side on the wall outside the shop. The girl was curled up into a weeping bundle, and the scene looked familiar. This time Jerry was going to find out what it was all about. The girls were sitting with their heads close together, taking no notice of him, so he crept around them until he was standing on the pavement behind the wall.

As he moved into position he could hear Theres' voice like a rhythmic mumble, rising and falling as if she were singing a lullaby. When he got closer, he could hear what she was saying.

'You mustn't be afraid.'

'No.'

'You mustn't get upset.'

'No.'

'You are little. They are big. They do bad things. They will be dead. They are angry because they will be dead. You are little. You will not be dead.'

'What do you mean?'

'You will live forever. You are not in pain. You do not hurt anyone. You have a lovely song inside your head. They have ugly words. You are soft. They are hard. They want your life. Do not give your life to them. Do not give them tears. Do not be afraid.'

Her voice had a hypnotic quality that made Jerry start to sway back and forth where he stood. He too was touched by the message. *Do not be afraid, do not be afraid.* The fear he had felt in the shop was washed away, like words written on the shore. He had never heard Theres' voice like this. It was caressing, inviting, healing. It was the voice of a mother comforting her child, it was the voice of a doctor telling the patient that everything will be fine, and it was the voice of the person who takes your hand in the darkness and leads you out.

Despite the fact that the voice wasn't even speaking directly to Jerry, he swayed along with its rhythm and believed the simple truth it revealed: There was nothing to be afraid of.

As he swayed he lost his balance and moved his foot to straighten up. Theres heard it, and turned around. For a second she gazed into his eyes, looking at him like a stranger. Then her eyes slid away and she stood up. The other girl got up too. She was holding her head high now, relieved. Jerry shook himself as if to wake himself from a dream he didn't really want to leave.

On the way home Theres said in her normal voice, 'You mustn't lie. You're not to lie.'

'What?' said Jerry. 'I haven't lied. Everything turned out just the way I said.'

Theres shook her head. 'You said the little girl wouldn't be harmed. She was harmed. The big person harmed her. What you said was wrong.'

Yes, thought Jerry. *Bloody good job, too.*

During the late summer they would still sit jamming with the guitar sometimes, writing outlines of songs, but something had changed between them. After the incident in the shop Jerry had the feeling that he had unequivocally been moved into the category 'big people', and could therefore no longer be trusted. That it was only statistics that made Theres accept his presence: he hadn't tried to kill her yet, and therefore was probably unlikely to do so in the future.

He thanked his lucky stars that she couldn't remember how their acquaintance had started. He really had been trying to hurt her then. Perhaps she did remember somehow, and it was lying there beneath the surface, smouldering away as a lingering suspicion of evil intentions. But he had been a different person then. Or had he? Do we ever really become a different person?

Perhaps not. But people change. When Jerry looked back at his youth, he could hardly grasp what kind of person had broken into summer cottages and run wild. He seemed like the bad guy in some obscure old film.

It was when he sat on the cellar steps in his childhood home looking at the remains of his parents smeared all over the floor that he had taken the step. No. It was just after that. When he had decided to protect and care for the person who had murdered them. He could have made a very different choice. But at that critical moment he took a step in an unexpected direction and set off along a new road. Since then he had continued on that road, and it was taking him further and further away from his former self. It was just visible, far far away, and soon it would have to start sending postcards if it wanted to communicate with him.

3

Two months before Max Hansen sat down to write his message to Theres, she got a letter from TV4 congratulating her on a successful audition, and inviting her to present herself at Studio 2 in Hammarbyhamnen for sound check and make-up five hours before the program was to be recorded. There was also a new contract which involved signing over all her rights to everything.

Jerry couldn't work out what idiotic impulse had made him set this particular ball rolling. The papers and the contract made it clear that he had no control whatsoever, that TV4's machinery had both him and Theres firmly in its grasp. They were no longer the ones rolling the ball; the ball was rolling along with them inside it.

He might have been able to hide the papers and forget the whole thing if it hadn't been for the fact that Theres was expecting them to arrive. Some girl at the auditions who had got through last year but fallen at the last hurdle had explained the whole thing to her. Theres knew exactly what was going on, and knew the date even before the papers arrived. There was nothing he could do.

Besides which, he felt the same as he had when it came to the auditions. However nervous Jerry was about the whole thing, a part of him was curious to see how things might go. The ball again. Something has been set in motion, and must be allowed to complete that movement.

They practised 'Life on Mars' and when the day of the recording arrived Jerry gave Theres precise instructions. The incident in the shop haunted him, and he was pushed to the very limit of his patience as he explained to Theres over and over again that whatever happened, she was not allowed to harm the big people.

'What if they want to make me dead?'

'They won't do that. I promise.'

'But if they do?'

'They won't. They won't do you any harm at all.'

'But they'll want to. They always want to.'

And so on and so on. The time when they would need to leave was drawing closer and closer, and Jerry still wasn't sure he had got anywhere. He turned to the last inducement he could come up with: 'OK. Bugger all that. But listen to me. I'll be furious if you do anything. Furious and upset.'

'Why?'

'Because...because it'll cause all kinds of problems.'

Theres was quiet for a little while. Then she said, 'You want to protect the big people.'

'Think that if you want. But actually, I just want to protect you. And myself.'

Jerry had to use all his powers of persuasion to get his own pass at TV4, but after all it wasn't exactly unknown for *Idol* contestants to want someone with them to provide support. He promised to stay in the background and not disrupt the preparations for the recording.

He went and sat right by the edge of the stage as Theres tested microphones and sang to the backing tape that had been prepared for her. As usual her voice gave him goosebumps, and all activity in the studio seemed to stop completely during the three minutes the song lasted.

Then Theres was given instructions on how to behave with regard to the cameras, and Jerry started chewing his nails when he saw her body stiffen as a choreographer gently took her by the shoulders to move her into the right position. Jerry was on the point of leaping out of his seat to explain the choreographer's instructions, but the young man—who in Jerry's opinion was almost certainly gay—was so soft and flexible in the way he moved that Theres never seemed to perceive him as a real threat.

Jerry couldn't hear what was said, but he could see that Theres was listening to the instructions, looking at the cameras and into the cameras. When she sang the song again, she moved her body and her eyes in a way that suggested she had embraced the choreography, at least to a certain extent.

It was time for lunch, and when Theres quietly accepted that she couldn't sit among the rest of the contestants eating baby food, Jerry began to relax slightly. She was adapting to the situation in spite of everything, and perhaps it was all going to work out.

After lunch a woman came along, cast a critical eye over what Theres was wearing, then disappeared and came back with a shimmering silver number which she ordered Theres to put on in the changing room. This too went well. The woman had picked up on the title of the song and found something that was a cross between a spacesuit and a ball gown. It didn't particularly suit Theres. She wasn't bothered in the slightest.

One hour before the recording they were told to go along to make-up. After being directed up various flights of stairs and along corridors, they came to a large room with eight empty hairdresser's chairs. A young woman with seriously teased blonde hair was sitting reading a magazine, while a big black woman of about Jerry's age was sweeping underneath the chairs.

The blonde woman stood up as they came in, welcomed Theres without looking at her and held out her hand. When Theres made no move to take it, Jerry shook it instead. Her hand was cold and slender, and she had lots of bracelets around her wrists. She was wearing a very low-cut top that emphasised a pair of unnaturally globular breasts; Jerry assumed he ought to find her attractive, but he didn't.

Theres sat down in the chair and when Jerry went and stood next to her, the woman pointed to an ordinary chair at the far end of the room and said, 'It would be fantastic if you could go and sit over there.' When Jerry hesitated, she said, 'Or outside would be brilliant too.'

Jerry lumbered over to the chair and perched on the edge. He had a bad feeling, and he wanted to be ready. The woman slipped a black hairdresser's cape around Theres' shoulders as she sat staring at her own reflection. Silence. The only sound was the whisper of the broom across the floor.

Jerry glanced towards the sound. The woman who was cleaning had a broad, dark brown face and coal-black curly hair caught up in a bun at the back of her neck. She must have weighed ninety kilos, and everything about her was big and round and soft; you might have thought she had been put there purely as an effective contrast to the make-up girl's blonde rigidity.

The cleaner seemed to become aware that he was looking at her; she turned towards him and fired off a smile that was impossible to resist. Jerry felt like an idiot as the corners of his mouth curled upwards without any help from him, and he had to stare at the floor. Then he caught sight of himself in a mirror, and the smile died away.

Not much to write home about.

He looked like a superannuated teenager. He had made a special effort for the occasion and combed his hair back and up into some kind of rockabilly style, and with the bushy sideburns he could never quite bring himself to shave off, he looked like an Elvis well past his prime. His puffy face, the dark circles under his eyes, the nose that seemed to get bigger every year. The fact that someone had given this face a smile was a major event.

He saw a flash of silver in the mirror, then everything happened very quickly. The make-up girl had obviously decided that Theres' face didn't need any major input, and instead had turned her attention to her hair. It was long, blonde, and slightly wavy.

When Jerry saw the flash of silver, the make-up girl had already grabbed hold of Theres' hair with one hand, and in the other she was holding a pair of scissors that flashed for a second before she moved them down towards the girl's neck. If Jerry had seen what was going to happen, he could have prevented it. But his attention had wavered for a short while, and now it was too late.

Theres growled and hurled herself to one side, which made the chair spin around with some speed. The footrest hit the make-up girl's shins. She gasped with pain and fell backwards. In a second Theres was out of the chair and on her, snatching the scissors out of her hand.

It all happened so fast. Jerry had barely got out of his chair by the time Theres raised the scissors in order to stab the make-up girl in the face. Fortunately there was someone quicker than him. As Theres raised her arm, a dark hand grabbed hold of her wrist. With a single movement the cleaner lifted Theres and plonked her back in the chair as she said, 'Hey girl! You mad or something?'

She took the scissors off Theres and threw them back on the make-up table. Then she stood there with her hands on Theres' shoulders as Jerry hurried over. The expression on Theres' face was something completely new. There was fear, but also sheer amazement. Her jaw had dropped and her blue eyes were wide open.

'Thanks,' Jerry said to the cleaner. 'I mean...thank you very much.'

'That's OK,' the cleaner said with a strong American accent. 'What's the girl's problem?' She squeezed Theres' shoulders. 'Hey there! What's your problem? You seem pretty nervous!' Theres didn't move; she simply stared in the mirror at the creature towering behind her.

The make-up girl got up from the floor, her legs trembling.

'What the fuck...' she said. 'This is crazy, I don't have to put up with this.' She had started to cry, and the streaky mascara gave her a ghost-like appearance. She pointed at Theres and sobbed, 'She's off her head, she shouldn't be here, she shouldn't be anywhere, she needs locking up...'

She staggered out, presumably to report to a higher authority. The cleaner spun the chair around so that Theres was facing her, and tried without success to catch her eye.

'Hey girl,' said the cleaner. 'You're so pretty. You shouldn't be so angry. Come on, let's get you looking even better.'

She lifted up Theres' hair, and Theres allowed it to happen. She plugged in the curling tongs and started to wind strands of hair around it; Theres simply kept on staring. After a couple of minutes Theres turned her head in Jerry's direction and asked the question that explained her incomprehensible acceptance of the fact that someone was touching her. She asked, 'Is that a human being?'

Jerry blushed and started stammering out an answer, but the cleaner just laughed and said, 'Where have you been for the last hundred years, girl?' as she carried on doing Theres' hair.

'I'm really sorry,' said Jerry. 'She's not really used to...being out like this.'

'You must live in a weird place—where do you live?'

'Err, Svedmyra.'

'Svedmyra? Is that the name of the place? Don't you have any black folk in Svedmyra?'

'I think it's mostly...old Swedes.'

The cleaner shook her head and started rubbing mousse into Theres' scalp. Jerry was inexpressibly grateful for her intervention and would have liked to inform Theres that yes, this was a human being, and probably a good one. But if the prerequisite for her tolerance was that she regarded the cleaner as something else, then it would be best if things continued as they were.

Naturally Theres had seen black people before, but Jerry hadn't realised how she regarded them, because she had never asked. Perhaps the cleaner's strong accent also contributed to the fact that Theres saw her as some kind of alien creature.

'Excuse me,' said Jerry, 'but what's your name?'

The cleaner wiped the mousse on her overall and held out her hand. 'Paris.' She pronounced it *perris.* 'And you?'

'Jerry. Is that...perris as in the city?'

'Yes. My sister's called Venice.'

Jerry tried to come up with some witticism about whether they had a brother called London, but it just sounded stupid, and before he managed to think of something else to say, the make-up girl was back with a man trailing behind her.

The man had a pass on a cord around his neck. He was in his thirties, and looked as if he hadn't slept for a week. When the girl started going on about what had happened, his eyebrows went up and the outer corners of his eyes went down in an expression that said: *Here we go again*. Presumably a complaint from the make-up girl wasn't a unique occurrence.

He listened without interest for thirty seconds, then glanced over at Paris who was busy making Theres' eyebrows a little darker in order to bring out her blue eyes. He shrugged and said, 'Yeah, yeah. But everything seems to be back on track now,' at which point he turned and walked out.

The make-up girl followed him, and Jerry heard her say, 'That's actually *my* job!' to which the reply was, 'Evidently not.'

Paris gently swept a powder brush over Theres' face, and once again Jerry was amazed when Theres closed her eyes, as if she was enjoying it. Paris lowered her voice, 'In America we have a saying: *Go fuck yourself.*' She nodded in the direction of the door. 'That woman. The number of times I've wanted to...how would you say it in Swedish?'

Jerry thought for a moment, then said, '*Stick och brinn.*'

'*Stick och brinn.* Like...fuck off and burn?'

'Yeah,' said Jerry. 'Fuck off and burn. *Stick och brinn.*'

Paris undid the cape and removed it. She said, '*Stick och brinn*,' gave Theres a big smile and said, 'Not you, honey. You did good. Maybe next time you should just relax a little.'

She picked up the broom which she had dropped in the midst of all the tumult, and carried on with her work. Theres stood there looking at herself in the mirror. In her silver dress she looked like something from a sci-fi film, a wondrously beautiful creature sent to Earth to ensnare and seduce mankind. Or to be ensnared and seduced.

Jerry cleared his throat, went over to Paris and held out his hand. 'Thank you very much,' he said. 'I don't really know what to say.'

Paris looked at his hand without taking it. 'You could do something instead.'

'Sorry?'

'Dinner would be nice,' said Paris, her concentration fixed on the movement of the brush across the floor.

'Dinner?' Jerry understood each individual word she said, but what they implied was so unimaginable that his brain couldn't make a sentence out of them.

Paris sighed and stopped brushing. 'Yes, dinner. You take me out to dinner. Sometime. Someplace. Don't you do that in Sweden?'

'Oh yes, absolutely. Yes,' said Jerry. 'Absolutely. I'd be delighted. Any time. Or anywhere. Or...shall I...have you got a phone number?'

With a kohl pencil Paris wrote her phone number on a tissue, and Jerry tucked it in his wallet as if it were a claim certificate for a share in a goldmine. Then he backed out of the room with Theres, waved and slid around the corner.

For the rest of the day he might as well have been on the moon. Or Mars, if you prefer. Gravity had lost its power over him; he weighed twenty kilos at the most. Several times he took out the tissue with Paris' number on it, just to make sure it was still there. After unfolding it and folding it up again so many times, he thought the numbers were starting to look blurred, so he wrote them down on a piece of paper which he put in his wallet. Then he wrote them on another piece of paper which he put in his pocket.

He had never—never!—had anything like this happen to him; someone had...what was it called? Made *advances* to him. Never. He would invite her out to dinner. Where would he take her? No idea. He never ate in restaurants. He would have to...

That's where Jerry's head was at.

There were no further incidents with Theres during the course of the day, which was just as well because Jerry wasn't really there. Twenty kilos of his body mass, perhaps. The rest was floating somewhere out in space.

Theres got through that week and went out the following week with 'Nothing Compares 2 U'. It was Jerry who won *Idol.* A couple of days after she had given him her number, he called Paris. He had checked the restaurant pages in the newspaper, *Dagens Nyheter*, and suggested Dragon House, a buffet restaurant near Hornstull. All you can eat and so on.

They met up, they both ate enormous amounts of Thai and Chinese food, drank plenty of beer. Jerry found out that Paris was forty-two years old and had come to Sweden five years earlier when the father of her son, who was now nine, had got a job here. They had gone their separate ways three years ago, after the man started seeing a Swedish woman he was working with.

Paris had done all kinds of jobs both in the USA and in Sweden, and among other things had worked as a make-up artist on a local TV station in Miami. Hence her knowledge. She regarded herself as a survivor, and was absolutely categorical when it came to judging people and events. This was bad, that was good, he was an idiot, he was a sweetheart.

Jerry seemed to have the good fortune to fall into the sweetheart category, since he got a long hug before they parted. When he asked if he could ring her again, Paris said that she expected nothing else, honey.

The day Max Hansen's letter plopped through the letterbox, Jerry was standing on the balcony smoking as he devoted himself to detailed dreams involving going to bed with Paris. They had seen each other several times, he had been allowed to kiss her, and her lips had been a foretaste. He imagined it would be like falling into a feather bed. Allowing himself to be enveloped by her huge breasts, her round arms, burrowing down in her skin. Disappearing.

His fantasies had become so delicious that he felt caught out when Theres came out onto the balcony. His hands moved instinctively to hide his groin, even though there was nothing to hide but his thoughts.

Theres tilted her head to one side.

'Why are you embarrassed?'

'I'm not, I'm just having a smoke.'

Theres held out a piece of paper. 'Somebody says I'm good. Somebody wants to talk to me. You have to read it and tell me if it's all right.'

Jerry took Max Hansen's letter into the living room, sat down in the armchair and read it twice. He couldn't decide if it was empty words or a genuine opportunity. He might have been a little bit impressed by the mention of Stormfront, but at the end of the day it wasn't about that.

Jerry put down the letter and looked at Theres, who was sitting on the sofa with her hands folded on her lap like a patient saint.

'It's an agent,' he said. 'Somebody who wants to work with you.'

'What do you mean, work?'

'Sing. Fix things so that you can do that as a job. Sing. Make a CD, perhaps.'

Theres looked over at the CD rack on the wall. 'Am I going to sing on a CD?'

'Yes, maybe. Would you like that?'

'Yes.'

Jerry picked up the letter again, turning it this way and that as if he could suss out its weight and import through his feelings. This Max Hansen seemed to be genuinely interested in Theres, and the fact was their money wouldn't last forever.

After all, this was what he had fantasised about long ago. The chance of squeezing a bit of ready cash out of the force of nature that was Theres. Now the chance had come along, he wasn't so sure. A lot of polluted water had passed under the bridge since then. He folded up the letter, put it in the top drawer of the desk and said, 'We'll see.'

Somewhere inside he knew he would open that drawer again, that a new ball had appeared at the top of the slope, and that it would probably start to roll, with or without his co-operation.

Max Hansen, he thought. *Take a chance?*

4

At the beginning of November, Teresa was sitting on her bed with an empty sports bag next to her. She knew she ought to put something in the bag, but she didn't know what. Her train was leaving in an hour, and she had gone up to her room to pack. She glared at the empty bag.

Two days earlier Theres had emailed and asked if she could come over to Stockholm for a visit at the weekend. After a certain amount of difficulty Teresa had managed to book a train ticket on the internet, and had then presented her parents with a fait accompli. She was going to Stockholm on Saturday, could someone give her a lift to the station?

She was going to visit a friend. A girl. In Stockholm. Yes, she was absolutely sure it wasn't some dirty old man. They had met on the net and now they wanted to meet IRL. In real life. Yes, she would come home the same night and yes, she had checked on Google maps and knew exactly where she was going and how to get there. Svedmyra.

She didn't want to tell them it was the same girl they had all seen on *Idol.* Perhaps because they would think she was lying, perhaps they wouldn't believe her. Perhaps because she would be revealing something she wanted to keep secret.

Her parents knew how lonely she was, and presumably that was why they agreed. She gave them Theres' address and telephone number and promised to ring when she got there.

So far so good.

It was when she got round to trying to pack a bag that the whole thing ground to a halt. She had never travelled alone on the train before. You were supposed to have a bag when you were travelling, weren't you? But what was she supposed to put in it? What did she need?

Who am I?

That was another way of putting it. What did she want to take with her to Theres, what did she want to show, who did she want to be? She sat on her bed, staring at the empty bag, and she thought it was mocking her. The bag was her. Empty. Nothing. She had nothing to bring.

She went into the bathroom, did her best with some make-up and thought the result looked OK. She had learned to apply blusher so that her face looked less chubby from certain angles. She fluffed up her hair with a little mousse to create some air around her forehead. Kohl, eye shadow.

When she had finished Göran shouted from downstairs that they would have to go if they were going to catch the train. Without thinking, Teresa chucked in her map, her mobile and her MP3 player, her notebook and her black velour tracksuit. The tracksuit went in mostly because she needed something to fill up the bag.

On the way to the station, Göran asked more questions about the girl she was going to see, and Teresa told him the truth: that they had met on a forum about wolves, that they were the same age, and that she lived in Svedmyra. She lied or stretched the truth when it came to everything else.

Göran waited until the train came in, then gave Teresa a hug which she couldn't bring herself to return. When she was settled and the train was starting to pull out, Göran waved. She waved back without enthusiasm, and saw him turn away and head back to the car.

It only took a couple of minutes for the *journey* to sink its claws into her. She was travelling. She was sitting alone on a train going somewhere she had never been before. Between two points she was a *passenger*, a person who was on their way. A person who was free. She caught sight of her reflection in the window, and didn't recognise herself.

Who's that sitting there? Who can it be?

She took out her notebook and a pen, then sat there sucking the pen and occasionally glancing at herself in the glass. She would have loved to be the exciting stranger, sitting on the train and writing, but nothing came to her. Not a word. Her imagination had always been feeble, and now it had fainted dead away.

She wrote, 'I am sitting on a train...' but that was it. She wrote it again. And again. When she had been sitting there for ten minutes and filled two pages with the same six words, she looked at herself. The stranger.

Enough!

She shoved the notebook back in her bag and went to the toilet. She leaned against the washbasin for a long time, examining herself in the mirror. Then she wet her face, squirted liquid soap in her hands and washed herself thoroughly, scrubbing off every scrap of make-up. Then she wet her hair to flatten it down at the front, and dried herself with paper towels until her hair lay flat and shapeless.

She got undressed, pulled the black sweatshirt and the black velour tracksuit bottoms out of her bag and put them on. When she looked at the result in the mirror she was able to confirm that she looked bloody awful.

This is me.

When she sat down again the face looking back at her from the other side of the glass was familiar. That ugly cow had been right there with her all through her life, and now she was coming with her to Stockholm. Teresa opened her notebook and wrote:

Those who have wings fly
Those who have teeth bite
You have wings you have teeth
Make sure something happens
Use your hands, grip!
Use your teeth, bite!
Use your wings, fly!

Fly, fly, fly high one day
Fly high for fuck's sake

The streams of people at T-Centralen, the central subway station, terrified her. As she was going down the stairs from the platform she literally felt as if the waters were closing over her head. That she had a river in front of her, and she was at risk of drowning. Because she didn't even know which direction she was supposed to go in, she stepped into the river and allowed herself to be swept along until she reached the barriers leading to the tracks.

She handed over some money at a window and said, 'Svedmyra.' She was given three coupons and she asked where she should go, then she joined a new stream. She clung to her bag, feeling anxious all the time. There were too many people and she was too alone and too small.

Things were a bit better once she had boarded the train, checked that it was going to Svedmyra and found an empty seat. She could settle down, she had her place. But there were still too many people. Mostly adults with expressionless faces, surrounding her on all sides. At any moment an arm might reach out or someone might start talking to her, wanting something from her.

People kept trooping on and off, and by the time they reached Svedmyra the carriage was almost empty. Teresa stepped onto the platform and unfolded her map. She had made a cross by Theres' address, just like a treasure map.

There was a light covering of snow on the street, and she shivered in her thin sweatshirt. She pretended that she was a black hole: she wasn't actually moving—instead, the building where Theres lived was being drawn towards her, about to be sucked into her.

She found the right street and the right door was brought towards her. She kept the game going until she was standing in the lift pressing the button for the top floor, and then she had to stop. She suddenly felt nervous, and only her chilled skin stopped her from breaking out in a sweat.

Fly high for fuck's sake...

The lift carried her upwards.

It said 'Cederström' on the door, as Theres had told her it would. Teresa rang the bell and tried to arrange her face in a suitable expression, but couldn't come up with one and decided not to bother.

She didn't know what she had expected. Theres had written that she lived with 'Jerry', but hadn't explained who this Jerry was. The man who opened the door looked like the men who usually sat on the benches in the park, apart from the fact that the check shirt he was wearing looked brand new.

'Hi,' said Teresa. 'Does Theres live here?'

The man looked her up and down and glanced out onto the landing. Then he stepped to one side and said, 'Come in. You look cold.'

'I've got a jacket.'

'Right. You could have fooled me.' He gestured towards the interior of the apartment. 'She's in there.'

Teresa took off her shoes and walked through the hallway, keeping a firm grip on the strap of her bag. There was still a risk that the whole thing was a con. That the man who answered the door had sent the emails, and that something terrible would happen to her at any minute. She'd heard about that kind of thing.

When there was no one in the living room her heart started pounding. She listened, waiting for the bang as the front door slammed shut. It didn't come. The door to another room was open, and she saw Theres, sitting on a bed with her hands resting on her lap.

Everything simply fell away. The crowds of people that had frightened her, the anxiety about getting the wrong train, doing the wrong thing. The cold out on the streets, the brief fear of the man in the shirt. Gone. She had reached the cross on the map, she had reached Theres. She wasn't surprised that Theres didn't get up and come to meet her. Instead Teresa walked into the room, dropped her bag by the door and said, 'I'm here now.'

'Good,' said Theres, placing one hand on the bed beside her. 'Sit here.'

Teresa sat down next to her. In her head she had tried out and rejected a number of opening remarks, tried to visualise what she would say and do if their meeting went like this or that. This particular possibility hadn't occurred to her. That they would just sit next to each other without saying anything.

A minute or so passed, and Teresa began to warm up and relax. After the chaos of the journey it was really good just to sit still, not thinking. She registered that the room was bare, almost Spartan. No posters on the walls, no little ornaments tastefully or less than tastefully displayed. Only a bookshelf containing children's books, a CD player and a CD rack. Her own bag, thrown down by the door, looked like an intrusion.

'I wrote a poem,' said Teresa. 'On the train. Do you want to read it?'

'Yes.'

Teresa pulled her bag over. She opened her notebook and read through the poem one more time. Then she tore it out and gave it to Theres. 'Here. I think it's for you.'

Theres sat with the sheet of paper in front of her for a long time. Teresa glanced sideways at her and saw her eyes moving down the lines; when they reached the bottom, they went back to the top and started again. And again. Teresa squirmed, and in the end she couldn't bear it any longer, 'Do you like it?'

Theres lowered the paper. Without looking at Teresa, she said, 'It's about people being wolves. And birds. I think that's good. But there are ugly words too. Can you have ugly words in poems?'

'Yes, I think so. If it feels right.'

Theres read the poem once more. Then she said, 'It does feel right. Because the person is angry. Because they're not a wolf. Or a bird.' For the first time she looked Teresa in the eye. 'It's the best poem I've ever read.'

Teresa's cheeks flushed red. It was almost unbearable to meet the gaze of someone who had just said something like that, and the muscles in the back of her neck were shouting at her to turn her head away. But her eyes were steadfast and kept her head in place. In Theres' big, clear blue eyes there was not a hint of irony or expectation or any other emotion that aimed to provoke a reaction from Teresa. The only thing her eyes said was: *You have written the best poem I have ever read. There you are. I am looking at you.* That was why Teresa was able to maintain the contact, and after a few seconds it felt completely natural.

Theres pointed at Teresa's notebook and said, 'Have you written any more?'

'No. Just that one.'

'Can you write more?'

'Yes, maybe.'

'When you write I want to read them.'

Teresa nodded. Suddenly she didn't want to sit here any longer. She wanted to go home to her room and write poems, to fill the whole notebook. Then she would come back and just sit here and look at Theres while she read her poems. That was what she wanted. That was how she wanted things to be.

Jerry appeared in the doorway. 'So there you are. Everything OK?' Theres and Teresa nodded in unison and Jerry gave a snort. 'You look like…I don't know what you look like.'

'Laurel and Hardy?' suggested Teresa.

A grin spread across Jerry's face and he pointed at Teresa, waggling his finger. Then he stepped into the room and held out his hand. 'My name's Jerry. Hi.'

Teresa took his hand. 'Hi. Teresa. Are you…Theres' dad?'

Jerry shrugged his shoulders. 'Kind of.'

'Kind of?'

'Yes. Kind of.'

'He's my brother,' said Theres. 'He hid me when Lennart and Laila got dead.'

Jerry folded his arms and looked at Theres with a somewhat

anguished expression. Then he sighed deeply and seemed to give up. He cleared his throat, but his voice was still thick when he said, 'Would you like some juice? Or something? Biscuits?'

Teresa went to the toilet and used her mobile to ring home and tell them everything was fine. Then she sat in the living room and drank raspberry juice and ate a couple of chocolate brownies that were so old they were leathery. Jerry drank coffee and Theres ate apricot puree with a teaspoon out of a baby food jar. Teresa thought the whole thing was very uncomfortable. It felt as if Jerry was studying her and Theres all the time, as if he was trying to work something out. He was an unusual adult, and she liked him in a way, but she still wanted him to go away.

When they had finished eating and drinking, her prayers were answered. Jerry slapped his thighs and said, 'Right, girls, I have to go out for a while. And you seem to be getting on fine, so…I don't know exactly when I'll be back, but you'll be OK, won't you?'

When Jerry was ready to go, he waved Teresa over to him. She went out into the hallway and Jerry lowered his voice. 'Theres is a little bit special, as I expect you've noticed. If you find some of the things she says a bit strange, just…don't give it too much thought. You're not a telltale, are you? You're not the kind of person who runs around telling everybody everything?'

Teresa shook her head and Jerry chewed air in his closed mouth as if he were thinking, trying to reach a decision. 'It's like this. If Theres tells you anything…you mustn't tell *anyone*, you understand? Not your mum, not your dad, not *anyone*, OK? I'm relying on you.'

Teresa nodded and said, 'Yes. I know.'

The look Jerry gave her was so long and so penetrating that Teresa started to feel uncomfortable. He patted her on the shoulder and said, 'I'm glad she's met you.' Then he left.

When Teresa went back to the living room, Theres was sitting at the computer. She asked, 'Do you want to listen to some music?'

'Sure,' said Teresa, and crashed down on the sofa. She stretched out, free of the stiffness produced by having Jerry's eyes on her. It would be exciting to find out what kind of music Theres liked.

She didn't recognise the songs coming through the computer's speakers, but from the thin, synthetic sound she guessed it was something from the early eighties. Then again, what did she know. Maybe music was supposed to sound like that these days, she didn't really keep up. Anyway, she liked the intro, the melody. It came as a bit of a shock when she heard Theres' voice.

She couldn't pick up much of what Theres was singing, it just seemed like disjointed sentences with no connection, mixed with wailing in a lot of places. But it didn't really matter. The song had her hooked right away. It was catchy, melancholy, beautiful and happy all at the same time, and shivers of pleasure ran up and down Teresa's spine.

When the song came to an end Teresa sat up and called out, 'That was fantastic. It was...brilliant. What song was it?'

'I don't understand.'

'You know...what's it called?'

'It's not called anything.'

Then Teresa got it. The song was so self-evident and so immediately accessible that she had assumed she'd heard it before. But that wasn't the case. 'Did *you* write it?'

'Jerry wrote it. I'm singing.'

'Yes, I could tell. What's it about?'

'Nothing. I sing words. Your words are better.'

Theres turned and clicked on another track. The song began to play, and Teresa closed her eyes and leaned back on the sofa, ready to enjoy the experience again. When she heard Theres' voice it took her a couple of seconds to realise two things. One: the voice was no longer coming from the speakers, but from Theres herself. Two: she was now singing the words of the poem Teresa had given her.

Two warm hands grabbed her lungs and wrung them like floor cloths. It was a feeling of happiness so great that it was more like fear. She couldn't move. Theres modulated her voice and adapted the pauses so that the words flowed perfectly with the melody, as if they had been written together from the start. When the song reached its first crescendo and Theres sang, 'Fly, fly, fly high one day, fly high for fuck's sake', Teresa began to cry.

Theres pressed the space bar and the music stopped. She looked at Teresa, slumped on the sofa with tears pouring down her cheeks. Then she said, 'You're not sad. You're happy. You're crying but you're happy.'

Teresa nodded and swallowed several times, then wiped the tears from her eyes. 'Yes. I just thought it was so beautiful. Sorry.'

'Why do you say sorry?'

'Because...I don't know. Because I said it was beautiful even though I wrote it. But it's really because your voice is so fantastic.'

Theres nodded. 'My voice is fantastic. Your words are good. They go well together.'

'Yes. I suppose so. But it sounded much better when you sang it.'

'The words were the same. I have a good memory. Jerry says so.' Theres turned and clicked on a folder. She pointed at the rows of files filling the screen from top to bottom. 'We've made a lot of songs. Can you write words for them?'

They listened to a number of songs. Only a couple were as immediately appealing as the first one Theres had played, but there were melodies and moods among the other songs that also demanded lyrics. Fragments of sentences popped up in Teresa's head and she wrote them down in her notebook. She couldn't really get her head round what she was doing. It was possibly the most fun she had ever had in her whole life.

When they had listened to all the songs Teresa flopped against the back of the sofa, her brain exhausted. They had been busy for several hours, and towards the end she had started jotting down disjointed words to the melodies she was hearing, as if in a trance. She had always thought she hadn't got much imagination, but this didn't feel as if it had anything to do with imagination. She was just writing down what the music said.

It had started to get dark outside the balcony window, and Teresa gazed blankly at the top of a street lamp which was illuminating individual snowflakes as they fell. Suddenly she sat bolt upright. 'Shit! Shit, shit, shit!' She spotted the telephone on the coffee table. 'I just have to...can I...can I use your phone?'

'I don't know,' said Theres. 'I can't.'

The alarm clock next to the telephone was showing half past five. Her train had left ten minutes ago. She squeezed her eyes shut and pressed the receiver hard against her ear. It was Göran who answered. He sighed deeply when he heard what had happened. Then he offered to get in the car and come pick her up.

Teresa saw herself sitting next to her father for almost three hours, trying to avoid answering his questions because she didn't want this day to be questioned and subjected to explanations.

Theres was standing in front of her watching with interest as Teresa put her hand over the mouthpiece and asked, 'Could I stay the night?'

'Yes.'

Teresa had to ward off a few questions, but in the end it was decided that she would catch the train at one o'clock on Sunday instead. When she had hung up she was just about to start explaining to Theres that she didn't want to be a nuisance and so on, but Theres pre-empted her by pointing at the telephone and asking, 'Can you use that?'

Teresa had stopped puzzling over all the strange things about Theres, and simply answered, 'Yes.'

Theres took a piece of paper out of a drawer, handed it to Teresa and said, 'Ring this man.' Teresa read through the letter from Max Hansen, and saw that there was both a mobile number and a landline.

'What do you want me to say?' she asked.

'I want to make a shiny CD. With my voice on it. That you can use as a mirror.'

'He says he just wants to meet you. Discuss things.'

'I will meet him. Tomorrow. You will come with me. Then I'll make a CD.'

Teresa read through the letter again. As far as she could work out, it was the kind of letter every girl and boy with artistic ambitions dreamed of receiving. But she noticed it was dated ten days earlier. 'Have you had a lot of letters like this?'

'I've had one letter. That one.'

Teresa looked at the two short lines of numbers and tried to work out what to say when she had rung one of them. It was all too weird. 'Are you seriously telling me you've never used a phone? You're joking, right?'

'I'm not joking.'

Teresa pulled herself together and picked up the phone, keyed in the landline number. As it was ringing she glanced through the letter again. Apart from the fulsome words about Theres' talent, it had a businesslike tone. Teresa straightened up and tried to make herself bigger and more confident than she was. When a voice at the other end said, 'Max Hansen speaking', she cleared her throat with a deeper timbre than necessary and said, 'Good evening. I'm calling on behalf of...Tora Larsson. She has asked me to tell you that she would like to meet you.'

There was silence at the other end for a few seconds. Then Max Hansen said, 'Is this some kind of joke?'

'No. Tora Larsson would like to meet you tomorrow. In the morning.' Teresa thought about her one o'clock train and quickly added, 'At ten o'clock. Tell me where.'

'But this is just completely...why can't I speak to Tora herself?'

'She doesn't like using the telephone.'

'Oh, right, she doesn't like using the telephone. And can you give me one good reason why I should believe any of this?'

Teresa held the phone up in the air and said to Theres, 'Sing. Sing something.'

Without a second's hesitation Theres started to sing Teresa's poem.

It sounded even more beautiful a cappella, if that were possible. Teresa brought the phone back to her ear and said, 'Tell me where.'

She heard papers rustling at the other end, a pen moving across a sheet of paper. Then Max Hansen said, 'The Diplomat Hotel on Strandvägen—do you…does she know where that is?'

'Yes,' Teresa lied, trusting in the wonders of the internet.

'Ask for me in reception,' said Max Hansen. 'Ten o'clock. I'm looking forward to it. Really.'

Max Hansen's voice sounded different now. If it had been deliberately distant at the beginning of the conversation, now it sounded all too close, as if he wanted to crawl out of the telephone and whisper directly into Teresa's ear. When they had said goodbye, Teresa sank back on the sofa.

What the fuck have I got into here?

It was as if she had ended up in the middle of some spy story. The meeting at the hotel, brief messages, cryptic phone calls. She had no control, and didn't know whether she found that unpleasant or exciting. Once again there was the chance to take a leap, become someone else. Someone who could handle this situation. She would try.

Theres sat down next to her on the sofa. Teresa told her about the meeting, the time and place, and Theres merely nodded and said nothing.

They sat there side by side. After a while they both leaned back, almost simultaneously. One of them started the movement and the other completed it. Their shoulders were touching. Teresa could feel the faint warmth of Theres' body. They just sat there, not moving. The clock ticked on the coffee table.

Theres felt for Teresa's hand, and their fingers intertwined; they sat completely still, gazing into the dark rectangle of the TV screen where they could see themselves as two distant figures, sitting in a room far away. There was a faint overlap where their shoulders met, as if their sweatshirts were sewn together.

When Teresa looked at their hands after a long time, she thought the skin on her fingers was flowing out across the back of Theres' hand, and that the tips of Theres' fingers were beginning to melt into her own knuckles in the same way. She stared at their hands and thought it would take a knife, a sharp knife to separate them; there would be a lot of blood.

'Theres?'

After the long silence the single word was a big bird that flew out of her mouth and thudded around the room, bumping into the walls.

'Yes.'

'Who were Lennart and Laila?'

'I lived there. There was a house. I was in a room. I was hidden.'

'What happened?'

'I made them dead. With different tools.'

'Why?'

'I was scared. I wanted to have them.'

'Did you stop being scared after that?'

'No.'

'Are you scared now?'

'No. Are you scared?'

'No.'

And it was true. Some level of fear had been Teresa's companion for so long that she had been unable to see it, had accepted that it was as much a part of her life as her own shadow. It was only now that she caught sight of it. As it left her.

5

As soon as Max Hansen had ended the call and carefully stored the caller's number, he rang the Diplomat and booked one of the larger rooms he often used for business.

He found it difficult to sleep that night. So much was unclear about this Tora. He usually had a better handle on things before a crucial meeting, he would have had the chance to see how the land lay, suss out the situation, soften up the other party if necessary. This time he hadn't a clue; he hadn't even managed to speak to the lady in question. Which meant he had no idea how to plan his strategy. The hours of the night crawled by as he went through possible scenarios, parrying objections and considering manoeuvres that would lead to the desired result.

He was fairly sure that Tora Larsson was a genuine talent who could be a pretty good earner with a little moulding, a few nudges in the right direction. He was lucky to be first on the scene. So far so good. But then there was the other matter. Simply put, he wanted to fuck her. He wanted her signature on his contract and he wanted her body, at least once.

If Max Hansen took a step to one side and looked at himself objectively, he could see that he was a complete bastard. He wasn't stupid. But there was nothing he could do. His mouth went dry and his fingers began to itch as soon as he thought about the meeting with that cool little beauty. He had no choice. And he had long ago stopped taking that step to one side, and with a self-loathing that bordered on smugness had concluded: *You're a pig, Max Hansen. That's your nature, and the only thing you can do is keep screwing around.*

He wanted to screw young girls. Young girls didn't want anything to do with him in that way, he was under no illusions. But with the right preparation he could create a situation where young girls felt it was *necessary* to go to bed with him so that their dreams would come true. It was no more complicated than that.

He thought he had the situation more or less under control when he got up from his tangled sheets at two o'clock and took a sleeping pill. Twenty minutes later he was sleeping peacefully, and was woken by the clock radio at half past seven. He got up, groggy but determined, and began to gather together his paraphernalia.

At nine-thirty he was ready and waiting in room 214 at the Diplomat Hotel. During the past two years he had met seven wannabe artists here. Two of them had ended up on their backs in the fair-sized double bed, one had given him a half-decent blow job, and one had let him cop a feel before she drew the line. A reasonable success rate.

But this success rate depended on the fact that the ground had been prepared in advance. He had hinted at opportunities, coaxed half promises from girls who weren't exactly wet behind the ears, then cashed in. Tora Larsson would be a challenge.

He didn't really have any memory of the actual sex, since it had been over-written by the films he had made at the time, then watched over and over again. The number of times he had masturbated while watching himself having sex so far exceeded the number of times he had actually had sex that his real memories were not in his head, but on his DVD shelf.

The room was a good shape. When he mounted the camera on its stand, the viewfinder showed the generous floor space in front of the bed where the girls would do their little audition. When they had finished, he would zoom in on the bed while pretending to switch off the camera. All he could do then was hope for the best.

After setting up the camera he got out the champagne and put it in the bucket he had filled with ice from the machine in the corridor. Well, it was actually sparkling wine rather than champagne, the same thing at half the price, but he'd like to see the teenager who could tell the difference, even the experts are hard pushed to do that. Next to the bucket he placed two slender long-stemmed crystal flutes; they were the genuine article, and even came in their own case.

He took a shower without wetting his hair. He had arranged his hairstyle very carefully that morning: the eight hundred strands in his fringe had cost thirty kronor apiece and they were swept back to achieve just the right kind of tousled look. He snipped off a couple of nasal hairs, smoothed a discreet tinted moisturiser over his face, dabbed on a couple of drops of Lagerfeld.

He was forty-seven years old but on a good day, a day like this, he could pass for forty. He might be a pig but he was no dirty old man. Max Hansen looked at himself in mirror and did the usual pep talk, telling himself he looked pretty good, that there was nothing strange about a young girl getting it on with this guy. He winked at himself in the mirror. *Here's looking at you, babe.*

When he was dressed he sat down on the bed and waited, his mind an empty chess board, the pieces not yet set out. This was what it was all about: not taking anything for granted, being flexible. In this case his adaptability stretched to the point where he could accept it if he didn't even get to first base today. He wanted to go further with this girl, whatever happened.

At quarter past ten there was a soft tap on the door. Max Hansen wiped his palms on his trousers, smoothed down the bedspread and cast a final glance at himself in the mirror. Then he opened the door.

A strikingly unattractive girl was standing there. Small, deep-set eyes in a fat face framed by mousy hair plastered shapelessly to her skull. Her plump body was covered by a faded hoodie, and if the concept *unsexy* needed a material expression, here she was. Max Hansen almost took a step backwards.

'Hello,' said the girl. 'Are you Max?'

'I am. And who are you?'

The girl glanced at something just out of sight. Max couldn't help stepping forward and looking out, and there she was. The apple in the Garden of Eden, and all that. Clad in jeans and a T-shirt under a thin, open jacket, Tora Larsson's figure was more boyish than it had looked on TV, but the mere outline of the small breasts beneath the cotton fabric was enough to send a warm quiver through his groin. It was almost hard to believe she was old enough to take part in *Idol*.

Her face was small, dominated by the lips and two big blue eyes which gazed at a point just to his left, not blinking at all. Max had seen girls who were prettier, more beautiful, more exciting, whatever. But never anything as *attractive* as Tora Larsson, standing there in the semi-darkness of the corridor with her thin arms by her sides.

'Hi,' he said, holding out his hand. 'So you must be Tora?'

Tora looked at his outstretched hand without taking it, and the central plank of his strategy fell to pieces right there. In one single movement he withdrew his hand and gestured towards the room: 'Come on in.'

The other girl took a step forward and Max placed one hand on the doorpost, blocking her way.

'Hang on a minute,' he said. 'You're not Tora, are you?' The girl shook her head. 'No. So what exactly do you think you're doing?'

'I'm coming with her.'

'I'm sorry, but this is a matter of contract negotiations. It's a discussion between two parties. No outsiders. That's how it works.'

His authoritative tone made an impression. The girl looked at Tora, seeking support, and Tora said, 'Teresa is coming with me.'

Max decided to risk everything on one throw of the dice. Without more ado he said, 'Sorry, in that case we have nothing to discuss,' and closed the door. Then he stood just inside the room, his heart pounding. The doors were heavily soundproofed, and he couldn't hear what the girls were saying. He was *not* going to put his ear to the door. He tucked his thumbs inside his fists and squeezed hard.

After perhaps thirty seconds there was another knock at the door.

Max let out a long breath, waited for ten rapid heartbeats, then opened the door with an irritated, 'Yes?'

Tora was standing there this time. The other girl was sitting on the floor opposite the door. 'Teresa will wait,' said Tora, stepping into the room as the other girl glared at Max, who took out his wallet and held out a fifty-kronor note.

'Here. Go and sit in reception and get yourself a soft drink or something. Sorry, but that's the way it works in this industry.' The other girl took the note, but made no move to get up. Max closed the thick, heavy door as if he were sealing a bank vault. First stage completed.

Tora stood in the middle of the room, arms at her sides. She looked at the camera, but as Max was about to launch into his carefully prepared spiel, she had already turned her gaze to the champagne bucket. Max took this as an encouraging sign and said, 'Let's have a drop of bubbly, shall we? To celebrate.'

Tora watched as he filled two glasses. As he passed her a glass it almost slipped out of his sweaty hand, which had started to tremble on top of everything else. Tora's calm silence was confusing him. He had seen every possible variation: hysterical gabbling, rock-hard attitude (assumed or genuine), hesitant seductiveness or something close to panic. Everything but this. A visiting princess who knows that *all this is mine*, and barely tolerates the presence of others. It left him nonplussed, almost scared and really, really excited.

He clinked his glass against Tora's and took a large gulp. When she didn't move he said, 'Try it. It's absolutely delicious. Excellent label.'

Tora sipped the sparkling wine and said, 'No. It isn't delicious. It tastes bad.'

Something snapped inside Max Hansen and he slumped down into an armchair where he rested his cheek on his hand and simply looked at her. Then he clicked a button to start the camera. If nothing else came of this he would at least have a short film of her. Tora was standing in the middle of the floor with the glass in her hand, gazing at the window.

'Sing something,' said Max Hansen.

'What shall I sing?'

'Whatever you like. Sing "A Thousand and One Nights".'

Without hesitation Tora began to sing, and after just a few seconds it was as if a clear, cool stream was flowing through Max Hansen. Her voice washed away his anxiety, and he felt pure inside.

'There is no one in this world like you...'

When the song was over Max Hansen sat there with his mouth hanging open and realised that he had probably been crying; his eyes felt as if he had. The girl standing in front of him was immensely talented, there was no doubt about it. It wasn't just that she sang perfectly, there was something about the timbre of her voice that penetrated straight through the breastbone and squeezed, squeezed.

If only he could have been satisfied with that. He *wanted* to be satisfied with that. He was already exhausted, sated as if he'd had terrific sex. He should have simply rolled over and lit a cigar to celebrate. Not risked this.

But the little red devil that lived in his chest woke up and started swishing his tail around Max's nether regions, tickling where he could feel it the most. Max Hansen put his strategies to one side; after Tora's song he just couldn't do it anymore.

'Good,' he said. 'With a bit of practice I think you could be really good. I'd like to work with you.'

'Am I going to make a CD?'

'Yes. You're going to make a CD. I'll make sure of it. I'm going to make you a star. A big star. There's just one thing.'

Max Hansen knocked back the remains of the wine in his glass in order to combat the desert-dryness in his mouth. He didn't want to say it. He wasn't going to say it. He had his best chance for a very long time here, and he mustn't mess it up. But then the devil's forked tongue shot out and said the words for him.

'I need to know what you look like with no clothes on.'

There, it was said. The cards were on the table, and Max Hansen's body tensed as if expecting a blow. The expression, the howl from Tora that would crush all his hopes.

It happened so fast he almost didn't realise what was going on. Tora put her glass down on the bedside table, shrugged off her jacket, pulled off her T-shirt, stepped out of her trousers and knickers and stood there naked, two metres away from him. Max Hansen blinked. And blinked again. He didn't understand. He went over what had happened in the last few minutes, how it had come about that he was sitting here in an armchair with the girl he desired standing naked in front of him. The dialogue. What he had said. What she had said. He could see the pattern.

She does whatever you tell her to do.

It was that simple. Max Hansen's eyes drank in the smooth, slender body in front of him and if he had believed in God, if his prayers being answered had been a possibility, then the moment had come.

She does whatever you tell her to do.

A dizziness came over him. The possibilities. Go there, Tora. Sing here, Tora. Come here, Tora. Lie down here, Tora. Feverishly he tore off his shirt and vest, struggled out of his trousers and underpants and stood up, his arms spread wide. Tora looked at his erection. It wasn't too impressive, he knew that. Twelve centimetres, and even then you had to press the ruler right down to the root.

But that didn't matter now. Everything had become so simple when Tora just removed her clothes. They were like two children, innocents before each other's bodies.

'You're so beautiful,' whispered Max, falling to his knees.

The carpet rubbed against his kneecaps as he crawled towards Tora to bury his face in the blonde bush between her legs. When he was almost there she backed away half a step, bumping into the bed frame. She said, 'No.'

'Yes,' said Max Hansen. 'Come here, it's nice, I promise. Just a little...'

'No,' said Tora. 'Don't touch.'

Max Hansen grinned. *Don't touch.* This really was like a game. He couldn't remember when he had last felt so uncomplicatedly happy. Two naked bodies. Don't touch. Come on, a little bit, just a little bit. He shuffled forward and grabbed hold of her buttocks, buried his nose in her pussy and stuck out his tongue, sliding over the warm flesh inside.

He heard a crack, and a second later felt as if someone had slapped him across the back. His tongue was just slithering out again when a cramp shot through the muscles in his back, and he felt another blow. And another. He twisted his head around awkwardly, but couldn't see anything.

Strange, really, because it felt as if someone was standing there pouring warm water over his back. He looked up at Tora and saw that she was holding something in her right hand, although he couldn't work out what it was. In her left hand she was holding her champagne flute, which seemed to be missing its base.

That was what she was holding in her right hand. The base, with a piece of broken stem three centimetres long and dripping red with his blood. Tora raised the weapon again and Max Hansen cried out and curled up into a ball. A second later he felt a deeper blow between his shoulder blades. The glass spike penetrated his flesh and stayed there.

He screamed. The uneven surface of the broken stem must have damaged some nerve when it went in, because he started jerking as if he were having a fit. It was throbbing and pounding. He managed to raise his head to beg for mercy, but Tora was no longer there. He managed to haul himself to his feet with the help of the bed head. Throbbing, pounding. Then he heard the door opening.

6

There was something not right about that Max Hansen. Teresa had felt it as soon as he opened the door of the hotel room. Something wasn't quite right about the look on his face or the tone of his voice. Perhaps everyone in the music industry was like that, but she wouldn't have left Theres alone with him if it hadn't been necessary, and if Theres hadn't said that was what she wanted. She was going to make her CD.

However, there was absolutely no chance of Teresa going down to reception. As soon as Max Hansen had closed and locked the door, Teresa crept over and placed her ear to the door. She could hear the sound of voices inside, but not what they were saying. After a while she heard Theres singing 'A Thousand and One Nights' and felt a stab of jealousy. That was *their* song, somehow. Although of course Theres didn't know that.

And what if she had known? Would it have made any difference?

Teresa had a sentimental streak. She liked what was known as elegiac mood in poetry. A persistent, imprecise longing for what had been, even if it hadn't been particularly good. She was sometimes struck by a blissful melancholy when she saw *Bananas in Pyjamas* on TV, despite the fact that she hadn't really liked it when it was on the first time round.

Theres was the least sentimental person she had ever met. Only the present existed, and when Theres spoke about things that had happened in the past, it was as if she was reading aloud from a history book. Dry facts that had no relevance to what was happening now.

Teresa heard a scream from inside the room. She leapt to her feet and rattled the handle, banged on the door. When no one opened it, she banged again. A moment later the door opened and Theres was standing there, naked. There were streaks of blood on her stomach. One hand was red, and in the other she was holding a champagne glass without a base.

'What have you...what...'

Before Teresa managed to formulate a sensible question she caught sight of Max Hansen, disappearing into the bathroom. He too was naked, and before he locked the door she caught a glimpse of his back. A T-shaped object was sticking out in the middle of all the red, a tap that had been opened and let out the blood.

'Help me,' said Theres. 'I don't understand.'

If it hadn't been for the word 'help' Teresa would have taken to her heels. This was too much. But Theres had asked for help. Theres needed help. Therefore she had to help. Teresa walked into the room and closed the door behind her.

'Here,' said Theres, holding out the glass with the broken stem. 'Do you like this stuff? I don't. It tastes bad.'

Teresa shook her head. 'What...have you done?'

'I sang,' said Theres. 'Then I took off my clothes. Then he tried to eat me up. I wasn't scared. I knew I could make him dead.'

'Listen. Get dressed. We have to get out of here.'

When Teresa followed Theres into the room, she caught sight of the camera, the red light showing that it was recording. They had a similar one at school, and while Theres was getting dressed, Teresa rewound, and quickly looked through what had happened before she came into the room. Theres' refusal, Max Hansen's insistence, the result. She pressed eject, took out the DVD and slipped it into her pocket.

Theres was dressed now. The contents of the glass without a base had spilled out all over the bedside table. 'Come on,' said Teresa. 'We need to leave.'

Theres didn't move. There was the sound of running water from the bathroom. Teresa was beginning to get an odd taste in her mouth. The particular taste that comes when you are facing something completely unpredictable, a mixture of bile and honey. She didn't want to do this anymore. 'Come on,' she wheedled. 'We can't stay here.'

'Yes we can,' said Theres. 'I'm going to make a CD.'

'Not with him.'

'Yes. He wants to make a CD with me.'

'Before, maybe. Not anymore.'

'Yes, he does.'

Theres sat down on the bed and indicated that Teresa should come and sit beside her. Teresa wavered for a few seconds, but there wasn't really any alternative. She picked up the champagne bottle, tipped the contents into the ice bucket, tested its weight in her hand as a weapon, then sat down next to Theres. She handed her the bottle. 'Here.'

Theres didn't take it. 'What for?'

'In case he...tries to eat you again.'

'He won't.'

'But just in case.'

'If he does you can make him dead.'

They sat side by side. The intensity of the whimpering from the bathroom was lessening somewhat. Theres was probably right. That Max Hansen was an unpleasant character, but not particularly dangerous. A coward.

Teresa weighed the bottle in her hand. It was thick and heavy. The shape of the neck and the bulge at the top made it ideal for use as a club. She imagined what it would be like to bring it down on Max Hansen's coiffured skull, examined her feelings carefully. No. It wasn't unthinkable. Something within her actually longed to do it.

They were two defenceless girls. There was proof of Max Hansen's attempted attack on film. They would walk free on every count. She thought. But as Teresa sat there on the bed next to Theres, she felt anything but defenceless. On the contrary. She tried out a couple of mock blows with the bottle in her hand, looked at Theres, so calm and erect, her hands resting on her knees. Not defenceless.

We are invulnerable, thought Teresa. *We are the wolves.*

When Max Hansen emerged from the bathroom five minutes later, he was literally as pale as a corpse. Every scrap of colour had left his skin, and he had knotted a couple of bath towels around his chest and stomach as temporary bandages. He gave a start when he saw Theres and Teresa sitting on the bed.

'What the fuck…what the fuck are you doing here?' he said faintly, glancing at the bottle in Teresa's hand. He fumbled in his jacket pocket and took out his wallet, threw it on Theres' knee. 'Here. Take it. It's all I've got.'

Theres gave the wallet to Teresa, who didn't know what to do with it. She opened it and considered removing the money, but decided it was best not to, so she threw it back to Max Hansen.

'I'm going to make a CD,' said Theres.

Max Hansen swallowed. 'What?'

'I'm going to make a CD,' Theres repeated. 'I'm going to sing. You're going to help me.'

For a moment it looked as if Max Hansen was going to burst into tears. He swayed on his feet. Then he opened his mouth to say something, but no sound emerged. He was about to take a step towards Theres, but something in her posture stopped him.

'Is that…is that what you want?' he said eventually.

'Yes,' said Theres.

'So we can…we can just draw a line under this, and kind of…?'

Since Theres didn't reply, possibly because she wasn't familiar with the expression, Teresa answered instead. 'Nobody's drawing a line under anything. But you heard what she said, didn't you?' She patted her pocket and nodded at the camera. 'By the way, I've got the movie.'

'OK,' said Max Hansen. 'OK, OK.'

In the mirror Teresa could see blood seeping through the towels.

Presumably Max Hansen ought to go to hospital, if he was going to be in a position to help anybody with anything.

When Teresa got up, she realised her legs weren't quite as steady as her discussion with Max Hansen might have suggested. But she managed to get Theres to her feet, and placed the empty bottle on the table next to Max Hansen. She had to keep up the show for a little while longer.

And she succeeded. She would remember that moment for a long time, and how for once she actually managed to say the right thing in a difficult situation instead of thinking of it afterwards. As she and Theres headed for the door, Teresa turned back to the ashen, sweating figure.

'Don't call us,' she said. 'We'll call you.'

7

Teresa thought she was in a fairytale. The subway train rumbling along through the bowels of the earth was a magic train, and Theres by her side was a creature from another world.

Perhaps it was a way of dealing with the incomprehensible blood-splattered episode she had just witnessed, but from her final comment onwards her brain had decided that the whole thing was a fairytale in which she had been given a role.

Once upon a time there were two girls sitting on the subway. They were as different from one another as two girls can be.

'Theres,' she asked when they had gone a couple of stops. 'How come you killed those people you were living with?'

'First a hammer. Then different tools.'

'No, I mean why. Why did you do it?'

'What was inside. I wanted it.'

'And did you get it?'

'Yes.'

One of the girls looked like a fairy princess, but she was a dangerous killer. The other girl looked like a troll, but was as cowardly as a hamster.

'How does it feel?' asked Teresa. 'To kill someone?'

'Your hands get tired.'

'But I mean, how does it feel. Does it feel good or bad or horrible or...what does it feel like?'

Theres leaned closer and whispered, 'It feels good when it comes out. You don't feel scared anymore.'

'What is it that comes out?'

'A little bit of smoke. It tastes good. Your heart gets big.'

'Do you mean you feel braver?'

'Bigger.'

Teresa took Theres' hand in hers and examined it as if it were a sculpture and she was trying to understand the technique behind it. The fingers were long and slender; they seemed so fragile they might snap under the slightest pressure. But they were attached to a hand that was attached to an arm that was attached to a body that had killed. The hand was beautiful.

'Theres,' said Teresa. 'I love you.'

'What does that mean?'

'It means I don't want to be without you. I want to be with you all the time.'

'I love you.'

'What did you say?'

'I love you, Teresa. Let go of my hand.'

Without noticing, Teresa had squeezed Theres' hand tightly when she heard the words that had never been spoken to her before. She let go of the hand, leaned back and closed her eyes.

But in spite of the difference between them, they needed each other as the day needs the night. As the water needs the person who drinks it, and as the wanderer needs the water.

Teresa didn't know how the story went on, or how it would end. But it was hers, and she wanted to be a part of it.

8

When Jerry got back to Svedmyra, he was feeling happier than he had for a long time. Everything had gone according to expectations, even if Paris hadn't been the voracious lover he had hoped for. She had mostly lain still, gazing into his eyes in a way that paradoxically felt much too *intimate*. When he came she bit him hard on the shoulder, then began to cry.

It brought back so many things, she explained as they lay smoking afterwards. They would have to give it time. It would get better. Jerry stroked her curves and said that was all he wanted. Time with her. All the time in the world.

When he stepped into the lift her skin and her soft flesh were still there within him like a body memory. He had been woken by her hand on his penis, and had made love with her again, half-asleep, gently; with no tears. She was wonderful, he was wonderful, everything was wonderful.

He had been careless, he knew that. He had hardly given Theres a thought since he went home with Paris. But that was the way things were now; it would all work out, or it wouldn't. He was in love for the first time in his life, and if everything else went to hell, then so be it.

However, he still felt a stab of anxiety when he inserted the key and realised that the door wasn't locked. He walked in and shouted, 'Theres? Theres? Are you here? Theres?'

The DVD cases for *Saw* and *Hostel* were lying on the table in the living room. His own mattress was on the floor next to Theres' bed. Breadcrumbs and an empty baby food jar on the kitchen table. No note anywhere; he went around like a CSI technician trying to reconstruct the girls' activities before they disappeared.

He sat down at the kitchen table, swept the crumbs into his hand and ate them. There was nothing he could do but wait. He sat there looking out of the window, and the whole thing felt like a dream. Theres had never existed. The events of the last year had never happened. Would he really live with a fourteen-year-old girl who had killed his parents and who didn't exist in the eyes of society? The very idea was just absurd.

He slipped his shirt off his shoulder and studied the marks left by Paris' teeth, glowing red against his pale skin. *That* had clearly happened, at least. Which was a good thing. He got up and drank a glass of water, wondering what he ought to do, but came to no conclusion.

When the doorbell rang ten minutes later he was sure it was the police or some authority figure coming to put a stop to everything, one way or another. But it was the girls.

'Where the fuck have you been?'

Theres slunk into the apartment without answering, and Teresa pointed at her wrist, where she appeared to be wearing an invisible watch. 'I have to go. My train leaves in half an hour.'

'Yes, that's all very well, but where have you been?'

Teresa was on her way down the stairs, and answered over her shoulder, 'Out.'

When he went back inside, Theres was busy dragging his mattress out of her room. He picked up the other end and helped her to carry it, then sat down on his bed.

'Right,' he said. 'Start talking. What have you done?'

'We made songs. Teresa did the words. They were good.'

'OK. Then you watched horror films and then you both slept in your room because you got scared…'

Theres shook her head. 'Not scared. Happy.'

'Yeah, right. But what did you do this morning?'

'We went to see Max Hansen.'

'The agent, the one who wrote? What the fuck did you do that for?'

'I'm going to make a CD.'

Theres was standing in front of him, and Jerry grabbed hold of her hand. 'Theres, for God's sake. You can't do things like that. You can't just go off like that without me. You get that, don't you?'

Theres pulled her hand away and examined it, as if she wanted to make sure it was unharmed after the contact. Then she said, 'Teresa was with me. That was better.'

9

Teresa didn't know how much of her was sitting on the train to Österyd. It felt like less than half. She had left the essential parts in Theres' safekeeping in Stockholm, and the thing filling the seat on the train was no more than a functioning sack of blood and internal organs.

It was intoxicating and quite unpleasant. She was no longer in control of herself. The fine hairs on her forearms missed Theres' presence, the warmth of the body by her side. Yes. When she examined her longing, she discovered that was exactly how it looked: she wanted to be next to Theres. They didn't have to do or say anything, they could just sit next to one another in silence as long as they were together.

She had never experienced anything like it, this purely physical perception of a *lack*, an awareness that something big and important was missing. She wasn't blind. She realised that there was something significantly wrong with Theres, perhaps she even had some kind of brain damage. She didn't do anything in the same way as normal people, she didn't even eat normal food.

But 'normal'? What was so good about 'normal'?

The people in Teresa's class were more or less normal. She didn't like them. She wasn't interested in the other girls' tacky little secrets, she thought the boys were just stupid with their hoodies and their baseball caps, their pimply skin. None of them had *courage*. They walked like cowards and talked like cowards.

She could imagine them all in a deep hole, lined up just as they would be for a class photo, but with their hands and feet bound. She herself would be standing up at the top next to a huge pile of earth. Then she would throw one shovelful at a time into the hole. It would take many hours, but eventually it would be done. Nothing could be seen, nothing could be heard, and the world would be not one jot poorer.

Ten minutes before the train was due to arrive in Österyd, Teresa started to smile. She gave a big smile, she gave a little smile, she gave a medium-sized smile. Trained up her muscles as she constructed a role for herself.

When Göran picked her up at the station, the rehearsal was over. She was the lonely girl who had found a good friend at last. They had watched films and talked half the night and had a *brilliant* time. The smile and the glow around her were firmly in place, and Göran felt much better when he saw his daughter's changed mood. Teresa noticed how credible she was, and it wasn't really difficult because it was all true, on a simple level.

As soon as she got home she checked her emails and found a message from Theres in her Inbox, 'hi come back soon write more words to the songs'. Four MP3 files without titles were attached. Teresa opened them and found they were four of the melodies she had liked best.

She got to work. After working for a couple of hours she watched the clip of Theres on *Idol* several times, then carried on writing. When she was on her way to bed, she remembered the DVD from Max Hansen's camera. She took it out of her bag and stood there turning it over in her hands for a long time. Then she put it in an unmarked case and slid it into the CD rack.

The role she had invented for herself could also be used in school. She was less frosty if anyone spoke to her, and on the whole displayed a less pugnacious attitude. Not that anyone actually cared, but the friction lessened slightly.

To be fair, Johannes noticed the change in her, and when he asked she told him the same story she had dished up to Göran, with a little more detail. Friend in Stockholm, brilliant time and so on. She also let slip that they made music together. Johannes was pleased for her.

As far as her school work went, it was a different story. Her mind was elsewhere. She sat through an entire social studies lesson on the difference between Democrats and Republicans, and literally grasped *not one word* apart from the fact that someone called Jimmy Carter used to grow peanuts. He might have been a president of the USA. That was the sum total of her knowledge after a forty-minute lesson: that Jimmy Carter used to grow peanuts.

The fact was that the following sentence had suddenly come to her: *Fly to the place where wings aren't needed.* It was an exciting sentence, a good sentence. But clumsy. Impossible to find a rhyme. And what did it mean? That you should go to a place where you would no longer need to run away. Yes, something along those lines.

Fly to the place where you need no wings. Better. Rhymes with *sings. Go where your heart sings.* No, that was ugly. *Fly high until your heart sings.* Better.

She had scribbled down odd words and sentences on the sheet of paper with *Democrats / Republicans* written at the top. The information about Jimmy Carter and his peanuts had slipped through when she paused for thought, but she hadn't written it down. Then she started to play with the word *rings*. Rings in the water, on fingers, sitting in a ring. And so on. Then the lesson was over.

On the Saturday she caught the train to Stockholm again. Jerry had agreed to give Maria a call in order to lend credibility to Teresa's interpretation of the role. He told her *the girls had had a brilliant time together* and confirmed that Teresa was very welcome to stay with them any time, then he went off to see his girlfriend and left the two of them in peace.

They worked on the songs and watched *Dawn of the Dead*. In the evening they rang Max Hansen and arranged to meet at the hotel the following day, in the restaurant.

Then there was something Teresa wanted to do, but she found

it hard to ask. In spite of the fact that it was a completely normal thing between two friends, she felt embarrassed. Perhaps because they weren't just two friends. She sat there fiddling with her mobile phone, and couldn't quite bring herself to ask. As if Theres sensed her difficulties, she came straight out with it, 'What do you want to do?'

'I'd like to take a photograph of you.'

'How?'

'With this.' Teresa held up her phone, pointed it at Theres, then took a photograph and showed it to Theres on the display. Theres stroked the surface of the phone and asked how it worked. Teresa couldn't really explain that, of course, but they spent a while taking photographs and looking at the pictures. Theres even took a couple of pictures of Teresa which Teresa secretly deleted, because she thought she was so ugly.

10

The wound in Max Hansen's back had been stitched and was healing well, but the damage to his self-esteem was another matter. The incident in the hotel room had knocked him off balance. He spent four days shut in his apartment drinking heavily, looking through his old films and trying to masturbate, but without success.

He watched only the films featuring the most submissive and obliging girls, the ones who had got on their knees or spread their legs at the first hint. It didn't help. In the weary movements of their hands, in the passive acceptance of their bodies he seemed to see a threat that finished his erection before it had even started.

Tora Larsson had taken from him his only real pleasure. Drunk almost to the point of unconsciousness, he sat flicking through images of young, naked bodies and felt nothing but fear and a faint masochistic enjoyment of his own fear.

On the fifth day he woke up with a hangover that felt like being buried alive. Instead of a hair of the dog he took two strong painkillers and a long shower. When he had dried himself and put on clean clothes the situation had improved to the point where he merely felt like shit.

One thing was absolutely clear: Tora Larsson was his biggest opportunity for a long time, and he had no intention of messing it up. But she would pay for what she had done to him; she would literally pay, in hard cash.

Towards the afternoon, when he had had a couple of whiskies after all, just to restore the chemical balance in his body, his new strategy was ready.

This industry was killing him; it was time to pack it in. Tora Larsson would be his final project, and he would put everything he had into making her a success. She didn't seem to have a clue about anything, and he intended to amend his standard contract so that it gave him the maximum return.

Then people in the industry could say whatever they liked, piss on his hall carpet and encourage everyone to boycott him and whatever the fuck they could think of. He would rake up his money and put all this behind him, head off somewhere with a better climate, wash down his Viagra with cocktails with a little umbrella in them and live life for as long as life was there to be lived.

When Teresa rang him on the Saturday he was as nice as pie. He asked her to pass on his apologies, as far as he was concerned the whole thing was forgiven and forgotten, and now it was a matter of looking to the future. The world was their oyster and Tora was his number one priority.

During the afternoon he made some calls. A studio and producer posed no problems, but as he suspected his good name wasn't enough to persuade any record company to pay for a demo. However, he eventually managed to strike a deal with Ronny Berhardsson at Zapp Records, which was owned by EMI. They'd known each other for years, and Max Hansen had supplied him with a couple of artists who had at least recouped their production costs.

Ronny said Zapp could cover the cost of studio time, but the rest would have to come out of Max's own pocket. Ronny had seen *Idol*, and even if he wasn't quite as enthusiastic as Max, he agreed that the girl had potential. It was worth a shot.

As Max Hansen got ready to leave for the meeting, he was careful not to omit a detail he had forgotten last time. He took Robbie with him.

Robbie was a sun made of metal, a happy face the size of a five-kronor piece surrounded by five stubby points. Max had won it at the

Tivoli theme park in Copenhagen when he was eight years old, on a family visit with both sets of grandparents.

He could no longer remember why he had called the little smiley sun Robert, later shortened to Robbie, but it had accompanied him throughout his life as his lucky charm. The last thing Max did before leaving the apartment was to kiss Robbie on the nose and tuck him in his jacket pocket.

Wish me luck, buddy.

He got to the restaurant fifteen minutes before the agreed time, ordered sashimi and read through the contract he had prepared the previous evening. It gave him the rights to fifty per cent of all Tora's income from future recordings and appearances. He was hoping that the girl or girls would have so little idea about this sort of thing that fifty–fifty would sound perfectly reasonable.

He would of course need the signature of a parent or guardian, but his intention was to get the project moving first, so that this person would feel obliged to accept his terms if the whole thing was to go ahead. The scheme was not without risk; there was a reason why he'd brought Robbie along.

Max had finished his sashimi and begun to worry that the meeting would be a wash-out when the freak appeared by the entrance to the restaurant. Teresa, that was her name. Max Hansen got up and went to meet her.

Then Tora appeared, and Max had to turn to Robbie's other particularly useful quality. The sight of that beautiful creature sent a stab of fear through him. He hadn't thought he would react like this, but a week of brooding darkly on what had happened in the hotel room had got into his bones. He started to shake and pushed his hand into his jacket pocket, clasped his hand around Robbie's protruding points. The fear in his heart shot down his arm and gathered around the pain in his hand. A seemingly relaxed pose: left hand in his jacket pocket, right hand outstretched, hello there, welcome. They sat down at the table.

Teresa did the talking and Max relaxed a little, loosened his grip on Robbie. He set out his plan. They would make a demo featuring two songs: a cover of something Tora sang well, plus a new song. He knew several pretty good songwriters and would gather together a few possibilities. At that point he was interrupted.

'We've got songs,' said the freak.

'I'm sure you have,' said Max. 'But we can look at those later. We need to adopt a completely professional approach at this stage.'

The freak placed a cheap MP3 player with earphones on the table and ordered him to listen. She was rather rude. He extricated his left hand from his pocket, holding it so that the red indentations in his palm wouldn't show, sighed meaningfully and put the earphones in.

He knew roughly what he was going to hear. Once upon a time it had been cassettes, then CDs, and more recently MP3 files that young wannabes had sent him. They fell into two categories: feeble variations on whatever happened to be current, or mournful ballads accompanied by guitar. By and large.

Teresa pressed play and it took Max Hansen three seconds to realise this was something that had been recorded at home using a music program, without any great finesse. Guitar, bass, percussion and a clumsy synth track. When Theres began to sing he thought he recognised the song, although he couldn't quite place it.

> They say that you will never fly
> They say that you're too young
> They say that you must always listen
> To all their rules and strictures
> But if you have wings you'll fly...

It was a good song. Actually, it was a *really* good song. The production was crap and the lyrics needed a bit of work, but the melody was immediately appealing and of course Tora sang perfectly. By the time he heard the first chorus, Max Hansen had already decided that he could perhaps save on the cost of a songwriter. This song showed off Tora's vocal range and potential beautifully.

He had to keep up the pretence. Before the song came to an end he pulled out the earphones and shrugged. 'Well, I suppose it might do. It might be OK with decent production. We can probably work with what we've got here.' Max Hansen took out the contract and placed it in front of Tora along with a pen. 'Right, I need your paw mark on this piece of paper.' He turned to the last page and pointed to the line at the bottom. 'Just here.'

Tora looked at the line, then at the pen. Then she said, 'How do I make a paw mark?' She turned to Teresa. 'Can you do it?'

Max forced a smile and slipped his left hand into his jacket pocket, where he rubbed his thumb over Robbie's face. 'A signature, I mean. You need to sign here. If I'm going to carry on working with you so that you can make a CD.'

Teresa pushed the contract back across the table. 'We can't do that.' Robbie found his way back into Max's palm, pressing against the skin until it was almost punctured. Max closed his eyes, concentrated on the pain, and managed to remain calm.

'Listen, my dear,' he said to Tora. 'This is your *chance*. Trust me, I'm going to make you a star, you're going to earn money and have fans, the whole shooting match. But you have to sign this piece of paper, or that's the end of it.'

'I don't want money,' said Tora. 'I want to make a CD.'

'And you *will* make a...' Max Hansen broke off. 'What do you mean, you don't want money?'

'She means what she says,' said Teresa.

After some negotiation it emerged that what Tora wanted was a deal where Max Hansen gave her cash in hand. There was no need for paperwork or registration or the allocation of rights. Max Hansen was to act as if he were her guardian, but without any written proof.

It was risky. Max Hansen would never even have considered it if it hadn't been for his plan: *take the money and run.* He could cash in bigtime here before it came to light that he had no right to. After all, everyone would just assume the paperwork was in order.

'OK,' he said, 'we're agreed,' as if it was perfectly normal not to have a signed contract between artist and agent.

So Max Hansen put his papers away, forbore from rubbing his hands and explained how things would work over the next few weeks. The biggest fly in the ointment was that Tora refused to do anything unless Teresa came along, which meant he would have to book studio time at the weekends. He hoped the girls' irritating symbiosis would wear away as time went by; Tora was too talented to drag a troll on a chain along behind her. But for now he would just have to live with it.

All communication was to be via email, and he had no problem with that. He was quite happy to avoid the hassle of trying to explain himself to parents or brothers or whoever.

When they had said goodbye and talk soon, Max sat there for a long time staring straight ahead. Then he took out Robbie and pressed him to his lips, whispering, 'Well done, buddy.' When a waiter came to ask if there would be anything else, Max ordered a small bottle of champagne. Well, sparkling wine. The same thing for half the price. That was his theme tune.

11

The following weekend they recorded the demo in a studio on Götgatan. A series of emails had criss-crossed between Theres, Teresa and Max Hansen. A background tape to the song 'Fly' had been prepared, and the decision had been made to cover Abba's 'Thank You for the Music'.

Teresa felt small and lost in the soundproofed basement rooms. She didn't know what Max Hansen had said to the studio technicians and the producer, but it was obvious that everyone regarded her as an irritating hanger-on and barely tolerated her.

This was partly down to Theres. Even when she was due to go in and record her vocal track, she refused to do anything unless Teresa went in with her. Teresa was told not to make a sound. Not to rustle, not to move, not to breathe audibly. Preferably not to exist.

Theres was familiar with the technology involving headphones and the microphone from her home recordings, and as far as Teresa could judge she sang perfectly on the very first take. The warnings about audible breathing were superfluous, since Teresa was holding her breath most of the time in any case.

The producer's voice came over the speakers, asking Theres to put a little more emphasis on this phrase, hold back in the first verse and so on. Theres did as she was asked, and after two more takes the producer was happy.

After another hour or so they played the raw mix. Teresa couldn't understand this business of a 'raw mix'. It already sounded like something you might hear on the radio, and a shiver ran down her arms when she heard the first lines and thought: *That's my song. I wrote that.*

Faced with a result, something similar seemed to occur to the studio people, and they looked on her with a slightly kinder expression. A guy in his twenties turned to her and said, 'Good lyrics, kid,' and Teresa had to stare at the floor because she was blushing. She could handle nastiness; kindness and praise were tricky.

The song continued, and even though it sounded much more like a real song than it had before, Teresa felt something was missing; it had lost something from the simple version they had recorded in Svedmyra. She couldn't for the life of her put her finger on what it was, and didn't dare to say anything because she knew she would be waved away. Presumably they knew what they were doing.

Then they moved on to 'Thank You for the Music', and when Theres had sung the last line, 'For giving it to me...', the people on the mixer desk were sitting motionless and open-mouthed. Then the producer switched on the speakers so that Theres and Teresa could hear the spontaneous applause.

Max Hansen was satisfied, and announced they were 'onto a surefire winner'. When Teresa asked if they could have a copy of the raw mix on CD, he said it was impossible because they didn't want to risk it getting out before the whole thing was finished. It would also be a good idea if they deleted the version they had at home, to make sure there couldn't be any unnecessary leaks. Teresa said of course, without the slightest intention of doing so. Max Hansen gave Theres a five-hundred-kronor note. He would be in touch as soon as things started moving.

After the comparative calm of the studio it was something of a shock, in spite of everything, to emerge onto Götgatan, which was busy with Sunday shoppers and people out for a stroll. Teresa breathed in the cold air and tried to clear her brain. Then she felt a hand come down heavily on her shoulder; she caught a movement at the corner of her eye and turned around just in time to catch Theres, who was on the point of falling over.

People gave them odd looks as they stood there clinging tightly to one another, with Theres' face pressed into Teresa's chest. Teresa whispered, 'What is it? What's the matter?'

Theres' body shuddered as she let out a single long breath of air that went right through Teresa's top and spread warmth across her skin. She held Theres more tightly and they stood there without moving for a long time. Then Theres straightened up just enough for her mouth to come away from the fabric, and said, 'They eat.'

'Who? The people in the studio?'

'They take. They eat.'

Teresa groped for Theres' hand to support her, and found that the hand was clutching the note Max Hansen had given her. When Teresa touched her she opened her hand and the crumpled note fell to the ground. Teresa looked at it, lying there in the wet and the dirt, and a fierce rage flared up in her stomach as she saw how it all worked.

They take. They eat.

In an email Max Hansen had indicated that he would very much like to see the film Teresa had taken from his camera destroyed. Teresa had replied that she had thrown it away. But she still had it, and she remembered exactly what she had seen. How he had wanted to exploit Theres, take something from her, eat her, swallow her, documenting the whole thing so that he could relive it all over again.

The same thing had happened in the studio, only in a way that was deemed generally acceptable. Theres had something they wanted. They would suck it out of her, package it up and sell the result to the highest bidder, and the only thing Theres got was that bit of paper lying in the slush.

They take. They eat.

Teresa hadn't seen it. She had been misled by the way the people at the studio had behaved as if it were all a matter of course, and the simplicity with which Theres seemed able to sing just about anything.

She hadn't understood. That it cost. From Theres' behaviour in public places she had realised that Theres found it difficult to be surrounded by adults. Now she had spent a whole day in that situation. In cramped, silent rooms.

When Teresa tried to hug Theres again, she made a feeble attempt to pull away. Teresa let go, and caught her eye instead. Theres' eyes were a pale, transparent blue, not unlike the zombies in *Dawn of the Dead*. As if someone had stuck needles in them and sucked out the colour.

They take. They eat.

Teresa bent down and picked up the five-hundred-kronor note. She ignored Theres' half-hearted resistance and led her towards Medborgarplatsen.

'Come on,' she said. 'We're taking a taxi.'

Teresa had never hailed a taxi before, but the driver seemed to find it perfectly natural as she waved at him, and stopped to let them climb into the back seat. Teresa told him the address and showed him the crumpled five-hundred-kronor note, just to be on the safe side.

Theres shuffled as far into the corner as she could, wrapped her arms around her body and closed her eyes. She looked so small and pitiful that Teresa was overcome by a new feeling: tenderness. She wanted Theres to rest her head on her knee, she wanted to stroke her hair and whisper: *everything's fine, you're safe, I'm here.*

Instead she simply sat there with her hands clamped between her thighs watching Theres, who appeared to have fallen asleep. An enormous, tranquil happiness came into her body. Grew. And grew. When they passed the Globe Arena she felt as if she might disintegrate with happiness. She had never seen the Globe before. She had never been in a taxi before. She had never sat beside the sleeping form of someone she loved before. She had been living in the shadows.

For the want of any other chance of contact with Theres, she took out her MP3 player and listened to 'Fly' at full volume, *their* version.

It wasn't that it was better than the one that had been recorded in the studio. It was *infinitely* better.

Theres had recovered somewhat by the time they got back to Svedmyra, and was able to make her way up to the apartment without help. Outside the door she stopped, turned to Teresa and said in a weak voice, 'I'm not going to make a CD.' Then she opened the door.

Jerry was home. When he asked what they'd been doing, Theres just shook her head and disappeared into her room, where she flopped down on the bed and fell asleep again.

As Teresa headed for the door of the apartment, Jerry blocked her way. He folded his arms and said with a menacing air of calm, 'I want to know what you two are up to.'

'Nothing.'

'Teresa. If you want to come here to visit Theres again, then I want to know what you're up to. Whatever it is. Just don't lie.'

'My train leaves soon.'

'I noticed you turned up in a taxi. Take another taxi. Otherwise you're not welcome here anymore.'

'That's not your decision.'

'Yes, it is.'

Teresa had to tip her head back so that she could see Jerry's face. It wasn't as closed and harsh as his voice suggested. More troubled. She asked, 'Why do you want to know?'

'Why do you think? Because I care about Theres, of course.'

'So do I.'

'I believe you. But I want to know what you're doing.'

Teresa wasn't capable of making up a story, that had never been her strong point. So she told him. She left out the part with Max Hansen in the hotel room, and gave a brief account of their songwriting and today's studio session. How exhausted Theres had become.

When she had finished she looked Jerry in the eye. There was neither displeasure nor pleasure there. They stood like that until Teresa just had to look away. Then Jerry gave a brief nod and said,

'OK. So now I know. Shall I ring for a taxi?'

'Yes...please.'

While Jerry was making the call Teresa went over to the bedroom and stood for a while, resting her head on the doorpost, watching the sleeping Theres. A cold, slimy unease writhed in her belly, where happiness had bubbled such a short time ago.

Never to see you again.

Jerry could make that decision, as easily as taking a breath. He could lock the door, unplug the phone or move away with Theres, and they wouldn't be able to do a thing about it. They had no power over themselves.

'I think it's probably time you made a move,' Jerry said behind her.

Teresa detached herself from the doorpost like a piece of ivy being ripped off a wall. She went towards the front door with her head lowered; she wanted to ask, 'Can I come again next weekend?' but her pride made it impossible. Instead she straightened her back, looked at Jerry and said, 'I'll be back next weekend, OK?'

Jerry shook his head and grinned. 'Of course. What else would you do?'

Teresa didn't really understand what was behind his remark. There was something odd about it. But she grasped the fact that she could come back. Since she was about to burst into tears of relief, she quickly turned away, opened the door and ran down the stairs.

When she got home she locked her bedroom door, took out Max Hansen's DVD and watched it. She had expected—had been afraid, to some extent—that the sight of Theres' naked body would have some effect on her. That was partly why she hadn't watched the film apart from the glimpses while it was still in the camera.

But it didn't happen. She thought Theres was beautiful with and without clothes, and that was all there was to it. When Max Hansen's bare backside came into view, Teresa began to wonder whether she might be asexual. The whole business of sex just seemed unnecessary and ugly. Max Hansen down on his knees, Theres backing away,

Hansen grabbing hold of her, pushing his face into her crotch. So undignified.

However, she watched what followed with keen interest. Theres picking up the glass and snapping the stem. Then beginning to hack at Max Hansen's back with the spike of glass, as devoid of emotion as a carpenter hammering in a nail. It was something that needed to be done, and she did it without even spilling the contents of the glass in her other hand. When Max Hansen realised what had happened and began to scream, she didn't even look at him as she went to open the door.

You're totally sick, Theres. You are the wolf above all other wolves.

She played the sequence over and over again.

At the beginning of December Teresa walked into the classroom and saw that five of the girls had gathered around her desk. In the middle sat Jenny, showing them something on her mobile. No. Teresa felt in her pockets. She'd left her phone behind when she went out at break time. It was *her* mobile Jenny had in her hand.

When the girls caught sight of Teresa, Jenny held up the mobile. The display was showing one of the photos of Theres.

'Who's this, Teresa? Is she your girlfriend?'

Jenny turned the mobile back to face her and scrolled through the photos. Caroline said, 'She's *really* pretty. How did you get such a pretty girlfriend?'

Teresa didn't respond, and made no move to take the phone, because she knew exactly what would happen. Jenny would run off, throw it to someone else, and Teresa would just end up feeling worse than she already did. She didn't give a damn what they said, but she didn't like them talking about Theres. She didn't like it at all.

'Hang on a minute!' Johanna said suddenly, pointing at Teresa's mobile. 'It's *her*! The girl who was on *Idol*! Do you *know* her?'

Teresa nodded, and Jenny, aware that the situation was slipping out of her hands, said, 'Of course she doesn't. And in any case she was useless. Absolutely fucking useless. Worst thing I've ever seen.'

Teresa went and stood on the opposite side of the desk. Then she cleared her throat and spat straight in Jenny's face. Jenny squealed in disgust and wiped Teresa's spit out of her eye. Then she did something Teresa wouldn't have expected of her. Her eyes narrowed; she hissed, 'You disgusting little bitch, what the fuck do you think you're doing?' and jumped over the desk and scratched Teresa's face with her long nails.

It didn't really hurt, and Teresa kept her head. In her mind's eye she saw Theres with the spike of glass. How calm she had been. It was all about calmness. Calmness and ruthlessness. When Jenny went for her again, hands scrabbling wildly, Teresa leaned back a fraction to gather her strength, clenched her fist and punched Jenny in the face as hard as she could.

So simple. Jenny fell backwards with blood pouring from her smashed nose. The other girls were frozen to the spot, and Teresa picked up her mobile and put it in her pocket. So simple. Everything is actually very simple.

After Jenny had been carted off to the hospital, Teresa had to have a long conversation with the Principal and the school counsellor. In many ways the conversation was like the lesson on the Democrats and Republicans, except that Teresa was unfortunately unable to make notes. She had already begun to transform her experience with Jenny into a song with the working title 'Mush'. It was about things that had a solid form in everyday life, but which had to be turned into mush if you wanted to live.

She was also preoccupied with her new insight into the concept of simplicity. You usually know what to do in a given situation, but doubt, cowardice or misguided concern for others gets in the way. Moving her hand and body back, then shifting her weight forward and delivering the blow had been the obvious thing to do. The problem was how to apply this same simplicity to situations that were not about violence, that could not be solved with violence.

Listen to your heart.

Yes, in a way it was an incredibly banal insight. But perhaps the most banal insights were the greatest of all, if you were really capable of living by them. It could well be true, and Teresa's thoughts continued along these lines as the Principal and the counsellor droned on with their questions.

She answered in monosyllables, in a tone of voice she hoped sounded authentic. 'Don't know', 'Don't know', 'No', 'Yes'. The role this time was *girl shocked by her own actions.*

Fortunately she had scratches on her cheek, which helped with her interpretation of the role. She had seen red, she hadn't known what she was doing. Eventually she was allowed to go back to her lesson.

When she walked into the classroom everyone fell silent as she sat down at her desk. She glanced at Micke, and the hint of a smile flitted across his face. She took out her exercise book and scribbled down the fragments of 'Mush' that had come to her. She already knew what melody they would fit.

12

If a journey of a thousand miles begins with a single step, then many things that end up being of major significance start out as a cool idea. Someone is bored and tries out some small idea just to pass the time. And before you know it we have Pacman, nylon stockings, the theory of gravity or the idea for *The Lord of the Rings*. A professor is sitting in his study one gloomy day. He takes a piece of paper and jots down, 'In a hole in the ground there lived a hobbit.' He doesn't know what a hobbit is, or what kind of hole it is. But it's a jolly little sentence—what might come next?

The weekend after the incident with Jenny, Theres and Teresa were sitting around on Saturday evening with nothing to do. They didn't feel like watching a film, and they had spent so much time working on songs that they'd run out of steam. Teresa had taught Theres to play noughts and crosses, but after a few trial games they were so unbearably even that each round became simply a matter of who could hold out the longest, and it was always Theres.

Theres seemed to lack any capacity for boredom, and as they sat opposite one another at the coffee table with a round of noughts and crosses between them that already covered half a page, Teresa began to feel a desperate urge to come up with something, anything, new.

Then it came to her. 'I've got an idea,' she said. 'Shall we make a video?'

Max Hansen hadn't been in touch for several days, and it seemed as if Theres' career in music was over before it had begun. They might as well mess about a bit on their own, it didn't really matter after all.

They dug out a dark blue sheet which they hung on the wall in Theres' bedroom, and mounted some small lamps for the lighting. In a drawer in the kitchen Teresa found a light-rope which they suspended from the ceiling so that it would make Theres' eyes sparkle when she looked up at it.

Teresa fastened her mobile to the back of a chair with duct tape, then adjusted the height by putting a few DVDs under the legs of the chair so that Theres' face just filled the screen. Then she began recording and started the song on the computer.

Theres couldn't grasp the concept of miming; she just sang the song. Perhaps the lip synching worked better that way, and in any case it wouldn't be a problem to remove the sound from the film and add the pre-recorded track instead. The real Theres' voice blended perfectly with the pre-recorded version as she sang the whole song.

> Fly, fly away from everyday things
> Fly, fly away and put aside your wings
> Fly, fly away from ties that bind
> Fly to me, fly to me...

Teresa never got used to it, she was just as spellbound every single time. When Theres had finished singing it was a long time before Teresa could bring herself to lean forward and switch off the camera.

They had done some work on iMovie in school, and Teresa knew the basics of how to edit and add sound. As she was about to replace what Theres had just sung with the pre-recorded version, she stopped. Instead of removing the new version completely, she simply lowered the volume.

The new version sounded different, but still toned perfectly with the old one. The quality on the mobile's microphone was much worse, but the tinny, metallic sound in the background somehow made the song fuller, more exciting. Teresa wasn't musical...What was that called?

'Theres,' she asked. 'What you sang just now. You weren't singing the same thing, were you? You were singing a harmony, weren't you?'

'I don't know. What's a harmony?'

'I think what you just sang was a harmony.'

'That's the way it should be. Sometimes.'

Teresa experimented, making Theres' voice from the mobile louder and softer in different places, removing it from the verse and making it significantly louder in certain parts of the refrain until Theres said that was the way it should be. They played the result on full screen with sound and picture, and everything fitted together in a way that was difficult to define. It just worked.

Theres' calm, expressionless face, only her mouth moving as she sang the dramatic words to the natural melody, occasionally supplemented by the electronic voice that seemed to come from another world. It fitted.

Teresa leaned back in her chair and folded her arms across her chest as she looked at the frozen image of Theres on the screen. 'Shall we post it on the net?' she said. 'On MySpace or something? Somewhere that people can watch it?'

'Yes. People can watch it.'

Teresa spent a while sorting out a MySpace account for her old alias Josefin. As she was about to post the video, she came across a problem she hadn't considered: who was she going to put down as the singer, and who was behind the song? Theres was already known as Tora Larsson, and what about Teresa? Did she want to expose herself to possible derision? That was always a risk when you put yourself out there in some way.

The cursor flashed, demanding a name in the box for artist and originator. Teresa juggled with words. Tora Larsson, Teresa, Theres, Larsson, Tora, Teresa, Larsson…

Te…sla.

'Tesla,' she said.

'What's that?'

'We are. That's what we're called, the two of us together. Tesla. Is that OK?'

'Yes.'

Teresa keyed in the name and the title, 'Fly', and sent the package off to the incalculable storage area that is MySpace. Then she logged out, switched the computer to standby mode and shrugged.

'We can check later,' she said. 'If anyone's watched it. Anyway, it's done now. Although I don't suppose anyone will be interested.'

In a hole in the ground there lived a hobbit.

13

Two days later, twenty people had watched and listened. Four days later it was three hundred. When Teresa went up to Stockholm the following weekend and they checked the number of hits together, it had reached two thousand. Without exception the comments were positive, and some enthusiasts had sent the link to every single person they knew. Virtually all of them seemed to be young girls.

A couple of hours before Teresa was due to go home on Sunday, they checked again. The number of people who had listened to the track was up to four thousand, and the video had been given the honour of a place on the banner as 'most played', which would presumably guarantee even *more* hits.

Just as Teresa was about to leave for the station, Max Hansen rang; he was absolutely beside himself. Someone had told him about the video clip, and how the hell could they possibly have done something so bloody stupid? They'd ruined everything now. All the work he'd put in, all the money he'd invested to get the *right* version released, and they'd just killed all his efforts stone dead with this fucking awful recording that absolutely anybody could get hold of for free.

Max Hansen was so angry that his voice was breaking, and it was impossible to work out if his screams were rage or just distress.

'But it doesn't matter,' said Teresa.

It was rage. Max Hansen roared with a fury that made it difficult to hear what he was saying, and Teresa had to hold the receiver away from her ear.

'You have no fucking idea! You think all you have to do is record a song and next week you're on *Tracks* and you get to be on TV, you're so fucking stupid I could kill myself! Let me tell you what you're going to do. You're going to go into your account and take down that fucking video right now, because otherwise I don't know what I'm going to—'

'Bye,' said Teresa, and put the phone down. When it rang again she pulled the jack out of the wall.

The Christmas holidays arrived, and 'Fly' continued to grow exponentially. As more people watched they told others to watch, and when those people had watched they mentioned it to others. Soon the video was also on YouTube, attracting even more hits.

At first Teresa had tried to follow all the comments, lapping up the praise and delighting in the fact that so many young girls found consolation in the song and thought the lyrics were 'fantastic', but ignoring the sexual allusions and derogatory remarks from boys and girls who somehow felt threatened by Theres' appearance.

But it all got too much.

One day when she was sitting reading yet another post along the lines of *wasn't she the girl who was on* Idol *and why does she look so peculiar and who is she and what are the words really about*, she suddenly realised that was enough. She just couldn't read one more word.

A large part of her life and her thoughts had begun to focus on the lyrics she had written, the little video they had made in a couple of hours, and she couldn't help it: she regretted it.

She had finally done something that would *show those bastards*, and her name wasn't even there. She tried to convince herself that it wasn't important, that she didn't care because she was above such things. But it wasn't true. Even if she had no desire to stand in the spotlight, she wanted people to *know*. Know that it was *her*, Teresa Svensson, that girl there, that little grey girl, she was the one who wrote 'Fly'.

She felt as if her brain was boiling to the point of disintegration as she read all the positive comments that were about her, but without one single person being aware of that fact. She just couldn't cope anymore.

Göran and Maria had decided to try something new, and had booked a chalet in the mountains for a week over Christmas. Teresa hadn't wanted to go and had tried to come up with a good reason why she had to stay at home, but a couple of days before they were due to leave, she changed her mind. She needed to get away. Away from the computer, away from the regrets.

After only two days she had withdrawal symptoms. Since she didn't like skiing, she had nothing to do apart from reading the poetry books she had brought with her, listening to music and playing games on her mobile. She loathed the whole environment, with all these outdoor types packing their skis into their roofrack capsules in the mornings, her contemporaries with their over-sized snowboard clothing and something unbearably *sporty* about the way they moved. If she was an outsider at school, she was a complete alien here.

Her brothers soon made friends and hung out with them, while her parents set off on cross-country skiing expeditions. On the third day Teresa decided the only way to survive mentally was to get out her notebook and start writing a couple of new songs.

One evening when the family had had dinner in the hotel and were passing reception on the way back to their chalet, Teresa heard the song. A group of young people aged about seventeen or eighteen were sitting on the sofas around a laptop. She could see Theres' face on the screen, and 'Fly' could be heard through the small external speakers. The teenagers sat motionless, staring into Theres' slightly blurred eyes as she sang.

Olof nudged her shoulder and nodded over towards the group. 'Have you heard that? It's brilliant.'

'I wrote it,' said Teresa.

'Sure you did. You and Beyoncé. Why the fuck are you saying that?'

'Because it's true.'

Olof grinned at Arvid and twisted his index finger at his temple, and the family headed for the exit. Teresa stayed where she was, her fists clenched, staring down at the floor. The song faded away and the teenagers began to make comments. One girl said it was *like the best song ever*, and another wondered why there weren't more. One of the boys brought the discussion to an end by playing a clip where a drunk fell out of a window.

Teresa sat down in an armchair a little way off and picked up a discarded copy of the evening paper, *Aftonbladet*, in order to distract herself. On page seven there was a feature article with the headline, 'Who is Tesla?' pointing out that the song 'Fly' had now scored almost a million hits, despite the fact that nobody really knew who the artist was.

Suddenly and without warning, Teresa's head caught fire. The next moment a thick fire blanket was thrown over her. Darkness enveloped her, and she could hardly breathe. Her lungs contracted and lost all strength. Searing pain sliced through her still-burning head and she was pressed down in the armchair, incapable of moving.

That was how Göran found her fifteen minutes later. He walked into reception, looked around and spotted Teresa, slumped in the armchair. 'There you are. Where did you get to?' Teresa opened her mouth to reply, but her tongue refused to co-operate. Göran leaned over her, tugged at her hand. 'Come on. We're all going to have a game of Yahtzee.'

Teresa had felt bad many times, been unhappy and spat out the word *angst* without really knowing what it meant. Now she knew. If she had been capable of thought she would not have referred to the state she was in as angst, but would have believed that some latent illness had suddenly and violently struck her down. But angst was what it was. Pure, sheer panic, paralysing every muscle in her body. Göran had to more or less carry her back to the chalet.

Teresa hardly slept that night; she lay staring into the darkness until the grey light of dawn brought the frost patterns on the window into focus. She didn't want any breakfast, and Maria forced her to take two painkillers before the family set off on their respective adventures.

Only when they returned in time for dinner did Göran and Maria start to worry. They found Teresa in exactly the same position as they had left her, lying on her side in bed, her eyes fixed on the sign that said waxing skis inside the chalet was not permitted.

Maria placed a hand on her forehead and established that she didn't have a temperature. 'What's the matter, sweetheart?'

Maria's voice sounded strange to Teresa's ears. The volume was normal, but it didn't sound as if it was coming from somewhere nearby. This was probably because the person who was speaking was far away, and the voice was electronically enhanced. So there was no point in responding, and in any case the question didn't make any sense.

'Has something happened?' asked Maria.

Same again. The question had nothing to do with her. It was being directed out into empty space, and the room Teresa took up in that space was insignificant and shrinking. She was slowly being crumpled up like a sheet of paper covered in writing, weighed down by words of no value. Soon she would be a white ball, and would roll away out of sight.

During the night, as Teresa once again lay staring out into the darkness, 'Fly' passed one million hits on MySpace.

14

Christmas didn't turn out the way Jerry had hoped. He and Theres celebrated Christmas Eve at home with Paris and her nine-year-old son Malcolm. He was a lively boy who found it difficult to accept Theres' cool, distant attitude. He wanted to show her all his toys, and was furious when Theres didn't react as he expected. In the end he went into a major sulk and refused to be anywhere near her, let alone speak to her.

Paris did her best to keep things cheerful, and Jerry played and joked with Malcolm while Theres sat and stared at the Christmas tree as if it was a riveting movie. Things were bearable, but it was painfully clear they were never going to be one big happy family.

The success of 'Fly' had not yet reached its climax. Jerry had seen the video, thought it was nicely done, and hadn't given it another thought. He was just grateful that Theres hadn't used her real name.

On Boxing Day a feeling of gloom overcame him. He had probably been nurturing a stupid hope that he would be able to bring the two half families together into one unit, that the spirit of Christmas would wave its magic wand over them. But it didn't happen. His real fear was that Paris would decide to end their relationship because it had no future. She said she loved him and wanted to be with him, but the doubt was gnawing away.

So he wasn't exactly in a buoyant mood as he sat watching an old John Wayne western when the doorbell rang on Boxing Day. He'd had a couple of beers, and he could almost feel the liquid swilling around inside him as he hauled himself out of the armchair and went to answer the door

His first thought was that it was a salesman of some kind. The carefully arranged hair, the salon suntan, the suit, the practised smile. Some bloody mobile subscription or...vacuum cleaners. Yes. Jerry's first impression was that the man had come to sell him a vacuum cleaner. Then he introduced himself as Max Hansen.

'Right, yes,' said Jerry. 'So that's who you are. Right.'

As Jerry took his outstretched hand, Max Hansen said, 'Now I don't know how much Theres has told you...' There was an element of anxiety in the way he asked the question that Jerry didn't understand. When he shrugged his shoulders and said he knew fuck all, Max Hansen seemed relieved.

'I have tried to ring,' he said. 'But perhaps there's something wrong with your phone.'

'It's not plugged in,' said Jerry. 'I think it's meant to be like that.'

Max Hansen asked if he might possibly come in, and Jerry asked what it was about. Max Hansen asked once again if he might possibly come in, and Jerry repeated his question. If you bang your head against a wall, who screams first, you or the wall? Answer: you. So Max Hansen gave up and quietly explained why he was there.

As Jerry no doubt knew, Tora had recorded a song which had become an enormous hit on the internet. But she had also made another, professional recording, and Max Hansen now wanted to release this version as a single.

'OK,' said Jerry, beginning to close the door. 'Best of luck.'

Max Hansen inserted his foot in the door and Jerry had an unpleasant flashback which didn't improve his mood.

'You don't understand,' said Max Hansen. 'We could be talking about big money here. The problem is that no record company is prepared to release the single until I have the documentation to prove that I have the right to act for Tora. Are you her guardian?'

Max Hansen's voice had taken on an aggressive tone. It would of course have been no problem to slam the door on his foot and force him to remove it, but talk of big money couldn't be completely ignored. Jerry had enough to manage for another year or so, but that was it.

'No,' said Jerry. 'I'm not her guardian. She hasn't got a guardian. There can't be any documentation. What do you suggest?'

Jerry had opened the door just enough for Max Hansen to lean forward and whisper close to his face, 'That I fake all the paperwork. That you don't make a fuss. And then you'll get the money on the quiet.'

Jerry thought it over. He had realised that Theres' non-existence in the system caused insurmountable problems. What the vacuum cleaner salesman was offering was a solution that circumvented all that: money floating down out of the blue without him needing to get dragged into anything.

'OK,' he said. 'You do that. But I'll be keeping an eye on you.'

Max Hansen removed his foot. 'You do that. I'll be in touch.'

Jerry closed the door with an unpleasant feeling in his body. Someone was walking over his grave. Yes. At some point in the future something was happening that he couldn't foresee. Max Hansen had been a bit quick with his idea of faking the documentation. But what could Jerry have done? Max Hansen could fake away to his heart's content, there wasn't a chance in hell that Jerry would go to the police. His only little trump card was that Max Hansen didn't know that. At least, he didn't think so.

But it didn't feel good, and when Theres asked him who had been at the door, and he told her it was a vacuum cleaner salesman, he felt a clinking in his breast like thirty pieces of silver.

Theres spent most of her time at the computer, and when Jerry asked her what she was doing she said that girls liked the song and wrote to her, and she wrote back. Jerry wondered what had happened to Teresa, and was told that she had disappeared. That she didn't answer messages. Theres didn't appear to be upset or concerned about this, but as always it was hard to know.

The day before New Year's Eve the doorbell rang, and Jerry

opened it briskly. He was expecting more wheeling and dealing from Max Hansen and had decided to play the heavy and hope for the best. But out on the landing stood a frightened little girl aged about fifteen who almost fell backwards down the stairs when he flung the door open.

'Hi,' said the girl, so quietly that it was difficult to hear. 'Is Theres home?'

'Who are you?'

The girl gabbled her reply like something that must have been repeated many times, 'My name's Linn sorry if I'm disturbing you.'

Jerry sighed and stepped to one side. 'Welcome Linn-sorry-if-I'm-disturbing-you. Theres is in there.'

The girl quickly kicked off her shoes and padded off to Theres' room. Soon after that the door closed. Jerry stood in the hallway looking at Linn's tiny red trainers.

Something told him he was witnessing the birth of a monster. As it turned out, he was absolutely right.

15

The family came home early from the mountains when Göran and Maria finally realised that Teresa's condition wasn't something that could be cured with painkillers. She wasn't catatonic, but she wasn't far from it. She refused to eat anything for two days, and when Göran and Maria asked in despair if there was anything she might fancy, she came out with just two words: 'Baby food.'

So they bought baby food. Teresa ate a few spoonfuls when she was fed, drank a little water, then curled up in her bed and stroked the nose of an old cuddly toy until it was threadbare.

Göran and Maria were ordinary people. It had never occurred to them that one of their children might suffer from problems that came under the heading 'psychiatric', and it wasn't stupidity or negligence that stopped them from contacting the Psychiatric Service for Children and Adolescents. It just wasn't on their radar.

For reasons they couldn't work out, their daughter had suddenly become very, very unhappy. *Depressed* was a word they could say, but without any real understanding of the concept. Depressed just meant very unhappy. But time heals all wounds, even invisible ones, and a person who is very unhappy will cheer up sooner or later.

A few days passed, Teresa ate small portions of baby food, drank water and lay in her bed. It was only when she gradually began to talk that they realised they might need some help after all.

It was Göran who was sitting by her bed trying to get her to drink a little more water when Teresa suddenly said, 'There's nothing.'

Perhaps he should have been pleased that she was talking at long last so they could work out what was wrong, but what she said wasn't exactly something to celebrate.

'What do you mean?' he said. 'There's...there's everything. Everything exists.'

'Not for me.'

Göran's eyes darted around the room as if he were searching for something to hold up as real, as evidence. He fastened on a bowl of yellow plastic beads, and a distant memory drifted up like a mist, struggling to find a solid form, and failing. Something about yellow beads and existing. Something about Teresa and another, better time. Teresa mumbled something and Göran leaned closer. 'What did you say?'

'I have to go to the other side.'

'What other side?'

'Where you become dead and are given life.'

Three hours later Göran and Maria were sitting with Teresa between them in a room at the psychiatric service centre in Rimsta. Teresa's temporary descent into leaden misery was one thing, but her talk about dying crossed a line. They couldn't ignore that.

Göran and Maria's ideas about psychiatric care were somewhat exaggerated. They had expected a lot of white, and silence. White coats, white rooms, closed doors; so they were positively stunned when the person who greeted them was a perfectly ordinary middle-aged woman in street clothes. She showed them into a room which looked considerably less sterile than a normal doctor's surgery.

A long conversation followed, during which Göran and Maria described the period leading up to Teresa's present condition as best they could, and explained what had finally made them contact the psychiatric service. Teresa didn't say a word.

Eventually the doctor turned to her and asked, 'How do you feel? Are your parents right to think you want to take your own life?'

Teresa slowly shook her head without saying anything. When the doctor had waited a while and was on the point of asking a follow-up question, Teresa said, 'I have no life. It's empty. I can't take it. No one can take it.'

The doctor stood up and went over to Göran and Maria. 'Would you mind waiting outside for a while so that I can have a little chat with Teresa on her own?'

Ten minutes later they were called back in. The doctor was sitting next to Teresa with one hand resting on the arm of her chair as if establishing some kind of ownership. When Göran and Maria had sat down she said, 'I think we're going to let Teresa stay here for a couple of days, then we'll see how we get on.'

'But what's the matter with her?' asked Maria.

'It's a little early to say, but I think it would be helpful if we could talk a little more with Teresa.'

While they were waiting Göran had read through some of the information leaflets in the other room, including one on suicidal tendencies in young people. He was therefore able to ask, 'Will you be keeping her under observation?'

The doctor smiled. 'We will, yes. You can feel completely reassured.'

But they didn't feel reassured. As Göran and Maria were driving home to fetch some things for Teresa, Maria launched into a long and mildly hysterical monologue, the key point of which was *what they had done wrong.*

Göran, who had got some idea from the information leaflets, tried to reassure her that depression was often a purely medical condition, a chemical imbalance for which no one could be blamed, but Maria didn't want to hear that. She went through the last few months with a fine-tooth comb, and reached the obvious conclusion: it was those trips to Stockholm. What had she actually been doing there?

Göran, on the other hand, maintained that Teresa had been much happier since she started spending time with Theres, but to no avail. The trips to Stockholm were the element in Teresa's life that had changed, and in some way they were at the root of the problem.

As Maria packed a bag with clothes, books and her MP3 player in Teresa's room, Göran stood looking at the bowl of yellow beads. When he picked one up and held it between the thumb and forefinger of his right hand, his left hand found its way up to his collarbone. And he remembered.

If I didn't exist, then nobody would be holding this bead.

Picking her up from the childminder. The afternoons at the kitchen table. All those necklaces made from plastic beads. Where did they go?

There's nothing.

Göran's stomach contracted and he began to cry. Maria asked him to stop.

16

Teresa was taken into care. People were taking care of her. They passed like shadows outside the window of her eyes. Sometimes their voices reached her, sometimes food was pushed into her mouth and she swallowed it. Right at the back of her consciousness sat a very small Teresa who was perfectly aware of what was happening, but her clarity of mind did not reach the big body. She vegetated. She waited.

From time to time there were periods when her brain worked as it should. She would think, she would feel. It was the emptiness that was the problem. She couldn't remember how it had felt not to be empty, to have a wall of flesh and blood to protect her from the world. It no longer existed.

Her situation could be described as a state of constant *fear*, overshadowing everything. She was afraid of moving, afraid of eating, afraid of speaking. The fear came from the emptiness, from being utterly defenceless. If she reached out a hand it might crack like an eggshell when it touched the world. She kept still.

After a few days of fruitless discussions, they started to give her pills. Small, oval pills with a groove in the middle. The days and the weeks flowed together, and she didn't know how much time had passed when a glimmer of light began to seep into her immense darkness. She remembered the feeling of a fire blanket being thrown over her. Now she could see a tiny gap. The voices around her became clearer, the contours more defined.

For a few days she simply lay, sat or stood looking out through that gap, registering what was happening around her and taking it in. She was neither happy nor sad, but there was no doubt that she was *alive*.

Eventually she opened the gap a little wider and stepped out. She wasn't exactly a butterfly emerging from its chrysalis, but she was transformed. She was Teresa the empty one, but she wore her shell and pretended that she was alive in a way that convinced even her. Sometimes she even thought it was real.

She carried on taking the medication, which she had discovered was called Fontex and was the same as Prozac, and went for counselling. She could remember the old Teresa now, the way she had been, and that was the role she played. Once again she did it so convincingly that she sometimes believed it herself.

At the end of February, almost two months after she had been admitted, she was allowed to go home. In the back seat of the car she sat and looked at her hands. They were her hands. They were attached to her body, and they belonged to her. She understood that now.

Two weeks before she was discharged, her class teacher had come to visit and brought her some school books, and Teresa had worked hard. The school work itself was no problem; the reading and the mathematical problems flowed straight into her mind and were dealt with rapidly, since they were no longer disturbed by the skeins of expectation and anxiety which are part of flesh and blood human beings. In two weeks she covered everything she had missed, and more besides.

When she went back to school the others kept a certain distance, which she regarded as completely natural. Jenny, who was about to undergo yet another operation to straighten her nose, spat out, 'Oh look, the local headcase. Home from the loony bin, are you?' but fell silent when Teresa looked at her.

Johannes and Agnes had been to visit her the day after the teacher came, and they made no attempt to avoid her in school. During one break time Teresa told them a little bit about life in the psychiatric unit and the difficulties that arose on a ward where any object that could be adapted for suicide had been removed. Amusing anecdotes.

She watched them as she talked, and a voice inside her head said: *They're so lovely. I like them so much.* It was true, and at the same time it wasn't true, because she needed to say it to herself, trying to establish a fact that she knew ought to be there, but that she just couldn't feel.

It was easier with Micke.

A couple of days after she came back, as she was ambling around the playground during break, she saw him standing smoking outside the gym equipment storeroom. She went over and took the cigarette he offered her, took a couple of careful drags and managed not to cough.

'How are you?' asked Micke. 'I mean, are you a real psycho now?'

'I don't know. Yes, I suppose I am. I have to take pills.'

'My mother takes pills. Loads of them. She sometimes flips out completely if she forgets to take them.'

'What do you mean, she flips out?'

'Well, once she went completely...she started yelling that there was a pig hiding in the oven.'

'An ordinary pig?'

'No, a cooked one. Although it was still alive and it was going to jump out and bite her.' Micke looked at Teresa. 'But that's not the same as what you've got, is it?'

'Don't know. Maybe it could be if I work on it.'

Micke laughed out loud and Teresa felt...not happy, but totally *unpressured.* Micke didn't make any demands. Even Agnes and Johannes felt like a threat. They expected a certain kind of behaviour from her, she had to conform. Micke, on the other hand, seemed to have a more relaxed attitude towards her since she became a psycho. That was something.

It took three days after she had been discharged before she felt able to go near the computer. During the long period in the unit she had been weaned off it. As she looked at the big metal box, the screen and the keyboard, she thought she was looking at a *source of infection*. If she pressed the power button, the sickness would come pouring out.

But Theres. Theres.

Teresa took a deep breath, sat down at her desk and opened the lid of Pandora's box, logged into her email account. Tons of spam had come in during her absence, and in amongst all the rubbish were five, no six, messages from Theres. The last one was dated six weeks ago.

She opened them and read them. Each message was only one or two lines long, and apart from the first two, they were all short questions. Why didn't she write, why didn't she reply. In the last line of the last message Theres stated simply, 'i'm not writing any more'. The rest was spam.

A feeling of sorrow began to rise up inside Teresa, but was stopped before it became painful. Sometimes she thought she could *see* the medication working in her body. What she saw was a chainsaw; the blade shot out and sheared off the top and bottom of her emotional register. The crown and the roots. Leaving her with a bare trunk to drag around.

She read the last message again, and clicked on reply. Then she wrote:

> I've been ill. I was in hospital. I didn't have a computer.
> I couldn't write.
> I'm back home now. I miss you. Can I come over at the weekend?

She sent the message, then sat on her bed and read through Ekelöf's 'Voices Under the Earth' three times. She understood every single word.

> I long to move from the black square to the white.
> I long to move from the red strand to the blue.

She flicked back and forth through the paperback edition of his collected poems. She hadn't had it with her in the unit, because she had never really got Ekelöf. Now she found that almost every poem spoke to her, and that he had suddenly become her favourite poet. Gunnar Ekelöf. He knew.

> This creature, Nameless
> comes to life in a closed room
> With no other opening but the gap
> through which he is forced to emerge
> Now he is on the move
> is empty in
> a fulfilled world

Amazed, she read on and found other poems that struck a chord, other descriptions of things with which she was already familiar. It was almost difficult to put the book aside while she checked her messages. Yes. Theres had replied.

> good that you're home come here soon

Joy gathered itself, ready to make a huge leap in her breast. Then the chainsaw was there, slicing through her happiness as it fled, so that it fell down between her ribs and landed as a mutilated little stump of pleasure. But pleasure nonetheless.

It took a couple of long conversations with Maria, in which Göran was on Teresa's side, before she was given permission to go. Teresa, forced to resort to a ploy that was beneath her dignity, said, 'It's the only thing I enjoy.' Maria gave in, and Teresa felt vaguely grubby. But she was allowed to go, that was the important thing. As long as she remembered to take her tablets.

This was Maria's new hobby horse. Since Teresa's stay in the unit her attitude had changed from being completely ignorant and therefore deeply sceptical of psychiatric drugs to regarding Fontex as God's gift to mankind. It was thanks to the pills that Teresa was back home and functioning, that they didn't have to have a depressed child. Teresa wasn't quite so sure, but for the time being she carried on taking them three times a day.

On the Saturday she packed her tablets, her new-found friend Ekelöf and her MP3 player. Bright Eyes had been a constant companion during her illness, and by this stage she knew every nuance, every remarkable sound on the tracks on 'Digital Ash in a Digital Urn'. He still had it.

The train journey was a means of transport, nothing else. She had a distant memory of previous journeys when she had felt anxious or excited or wistful. Not any more. When she had written to Theres that she missed her it was, like so many other things, true and not true. She was sitting on a train. She would be reunited with Theres, and what had been divided would become one again. This was right and proper, but no reason for anxiety or hope. It just was.

But still. When she got off at Svedmyra and reached the shop on the corner where she could look up at Theres' balcony, it was like *colour.* As if a little colour had come into her empty space. What colour? She closed her eyes and tried to work it out, because this was a welcome feeling, a real feeling.

Violet.

It was dark violet, tending towards purple. She hoisted her bag up on her shoulder and headed for Theres' door, dark violet Teresa.

It was Jerry who answered. He seemed irritated, but when he saw Teresa he gave a big smile and even touched her shoulder, almost ushering her into the apartment.

'Hi Teresa,' he said. 'It's been a while. Theres said you'd been ill—what's been the matter?'

'I...'

Teresa went blank whenever she tried to describe what had happened in simple terms. She had never been given a neat diagnosis that she could just trot out. Jerry waited for a while, then asked:

'Was it something to do with your head?'

'Yes.'

'OK. But you're better now?'

'Yes. I'm better now.'

'Cool. Theres is in there. There's been so much going on around here, it's just crazy. You wouldn't believe it.'

Teresa assumed he was referring to all the fuss about 'Fly'. She hadn't read any newspapers, or listened to the radio or gone on the internet for over two months, and had no idea what had become of the little song they had put together in a different life.

As Teresa approached Theres' room, she thought there must be a television on somewhere. She could hear the murmur of voices talking quietly. Behind her Jerry said, 'Squeeze in, as they say.' Teresa stopped dead in the doorway, and every scrap of colour drained away from her. Regardless of what she had hoped or not hoped would happen when she came to visit Theres, she hadn't expected this.

The room was full of girls of Teresa's own age. Theres was sitting in the middle of the bed with a girl on either side of her, and five more were sitting on the floor. They were all looking at Theres, who seemed to be finishing an explanation with the words, 'You will die. First. Then you will live. Then no one can touch you. Then no one can hurt you. If anyone wants to hurt you, you must make them dead. Then it is yours.'

The girls sat open-mouthed, listening to the words flowing in a rhythmic stream from Theres' mouth. If Teresa hadn't been so shocked, she would have been carried along too. She had been there, she had been the one to whom Theres directed her words. The girls in the room were like her, and they had replaced her. She couldn't see any faces, just a shapeless group of enemies.

Theres caught sight of her and said, 'Teresa.'

Teresa whispered, 'Theres'—more of a whimper than a reply—and the chainsaw started up with a furious roar, hacking and cutting to chop off the lead weight that was dropping through her body, trying to drag her down, down. Down on her knees, down on her face, down through the floor, down into the ground.

I am nothing. Not even to you.

One of the girls sitting on the floor got up and came over. She was an emo girl about the same age as Teresa. Black hair with a pink fringe, full-on eye make-up, a piercing in her lower lip and stick-thin legs in skinny jeans. 'Hi. Miranda.'

A fragile hand was extended towards Teresa. The nails were painted black. Teresa looked at the outstretched hand. It was all about to go wrong. She could feel it. Chainsaw and medication or not: the fire blanket was about to be thrown over her. It was here in the room with her now.

'Are you Teresa?' asked Miranda. 'I really love your lyrics. All of them.'

Teresa couldn't shake the hand, because her arms were locked around her stomach as she concentrated on trying to breathe.

Your lyrics. All of them.

Theres had played the songs to these girls. *Their* songs. Their secrets.

She clutched her bag tightly and rushed to the door, ran down the stairs and carried on running until she reached the subway station. The train rumbled in and Teresa sat down on the disabled seat right in the corner, making herself as small as possible.

It was over now. It was really over now, and the only voices that existed were the voices under the earth:

> I became the last piece of the jigsaw
> The piece that doesn't fit anywhere, the picture complete without me.

ALL THE GIRLS

I

What does it take to break a person?

Torturers and interrogators would be able to provide statistics. This many nights without sleep, this many needles, this much water, this voltage of current on this many occasions.

But there is considerable variation in people's ability to withstand torture. Sometimes one can achieve the desired result simply by showing the instruments and explaining what is to be done with them. Sometimes it takes weeks; one may be forced to restart a heart which has given out from the pain, and even then one may not manage to break the subject down.

However, it is presumably possible to discern some kind of average. This many needles, this many blows to the soles of the feet, before most people are sufficiently destroyed to give up what they once held most dear.

But in everyday life?

After all, even a normal life contains its quota of pain and disappointment. The difference is that these are not mechanically applied, but are mainly to be found on the emotional plane, and are therefore even more unpredictable. Some people seem able to tolerate just about anything, while others fall apart at the least setback. You never know. Something which is devastating to one person can be no more than a shrug of the shoulders to another, who in turn is shattered by something that others perceive as trivial.

On top of all this, the situation can vary from day to day, even for the same person. It must be hell to be a torturer with only the instruments of everyday life as your resources for finding the breaking point.

Teresa did not fall down dead, nor did she do anything to make that happen. She shuffled her clumsy body along, bought a ticket at the central station, rang home and asked to be picked up in Österyd. Then she sat and stared at the arrival and departure board. She didn't read anything, she didn't listen to any music, she didn't think.

If anyone who didn't know her had seen her getting on the train, that person would have seen a girl getting on the train. If anyone who knew her had seen her taking her seat, that person would have seen Teresa taking her seat. After all, nothing had really happened from the world's point of view, except that a girl had given up all hope. Hardly even worth mentioning.

When she arrived in Österyd, she didn't do a very good job of playing the role of herself. Göran was worried, and asked if she'd taken her tablets. She had taken her tablets. She would always take her tablets. That was what she would do from now on: she would eat, drink, sleep and take her tablets.

When she sat down at the computer in her room, she didn't weigh up the pros and cons. She simply did it. She knew Theres' password, and she hacked into her email account. As she suspected there were hundreds of messages from a couple of dozen addresses. Girls who had heard 'Fly' and got in touch with Theres, and Theres had replied and invited them to Svedmyra.

The tone of the messages became more reverential as time went on. It was clear that these girls looked up to Theres as an idol in the original meaning of the word. An icon, a focus for prayer.

From a few odd sentences such as, 'I'd kill my parents too if I only had the nerve' and 'I feel as if I grew up in a cellar too', Teresa realised that Theres had told them. Everything she had shared only with Teresa was now public property. At least for those who worshipped Theres.

Teresa took out the DVD of Max Hansen in the hotel room and sat for a long time, looking at herself in its shiny surface. She would post the film on the net. She had no idea what the consequences would be, but in the end it would probably harm Theres. Create problems for her. Make her into something other than the lovely girl singing the beautiful song that wasn't even her own.

Teresa slipped the DVD into the computer and double clicked to open it. Click, click. A few more clicks and everything would change for Theres.

Instead she took out the DVD, meticulously scratched it all over with a ballpoint pen, then threw it in the waste paper basket. She took out her mobile and deleted every picture of Theres. She logged into her own email account and deleted all the old messages from Theres. A new one had arrived an hour earlier. She deleted that one without even reading it.

Then she leaned forward on her chair, rubbing her temples as she tried to delete the images of Theres from the hard drive in her brain. It was more difficult, and the effort made her start thinking about Theres. She would have to live with the images. They would probably fade, little by little.

2

The images did not fade. Teresa lived through the days and weeks that followed with a Theres-shaped space inside her that just grew and grew. In the end the space was the same shape as her body, and it was empty. The emptiness was nothing new, it was the emptiness that had put her in bed, sent her to the psychiatric unit and given her pills to take.

But even emptiness has its topography, its smell and its taste. This was a different emptiness. It echoed with Theres, and it hurt. Sometimes it felt as if Teresa consisted only of pain and absence, as if they were what kept her upright.

She tried out what remedies she could think of. She tried self-harming. Sitting in the old cave where she used to spend time with Johannes, she cut herself with pieces of glass she found in the forest. It gave her a moment's relief, but after a few days she gave up. It didn't last.

She tried starving herself, hiding away the food served up at the kitchen table, until she was found out. Then she started sticking her fingers down her throat in the bathroom after she had eaten. That brought no relief either, and she gave up the experiment.

She tried taking more tablets, eating more food, drinking more soft drinks. The soft drinks helped a bit. The moment she put a glass of cold Trocadero to her lips everything felt OK, and went on feeling OK for the first few gulps. She drank more fizzy drinks.

While all this was going on, she kept up with her school work. She developed the trick of creating a tunnel from her head to the teacher or the book. As long as she managed to keep the tunnel intact, she could maintain her concentration.

At the end of March there was the class party. Not the kind that's arranged by the school, where the adult gaze damps down the festivities, but a *real* class party. Mimmi's parents had gone to Egypt for a week and she had the house to herself. Perhaps the party was a kind of revenge; Mimmi would have liked to go with them but she had to stay at home because of her poor grades.

The whole class was invited, along with a few other people, and it didn't occur to anyone to exclude Teresa. Jenny might have her hangers on, but not everyone thought it was a bad thing that her nose had been rearranged, and despite the fact that Teresa didn't have anyone she could call a friend, a few people at least had a silent regard for her as the dark point that allows the rest of the picture to shine. She could come to the party.

Teresa went to the party for the same reason she did everything these days. Because she could. Because it was there. Because it made no difference what she did in any case. She might as well sit on a sofa at Mimmi's house as on a chair in her bedroom.

As she approached the house she heard 'Toxic' pulsating through the walls, and through the living room window she could see a couple of Britney clones moving slowly, like water weed in an aquarium. Jenny and Ester. Teresa felt neither unease nor anticipation, but an exhaustion came over her. She just didn't have the strength.

She put down the plastic bag containing a bottle of Trocadero and two cans of beer and sat down on the steps. 'Toxic' was followed by that song by The Ark that everybody thought was going to win Eurovision next weekend. Teresa sat listening, surrounded by cheerful pop songs about angst, then got up to go home. She heard a whistle behind her.

The light was on in the garage and the door was open. Micke was sitting just inside, waving her over. He had a cardboard box next to him. As Teresa went over, he pointed at her plastic bag. 'What have you got?'

Teresa showed him her cans of beer and her Trocadero. Micke shook his head and told her to sit down, then took a bottle out of his box, opened it and handed it to her. Teresa looked at the label. Bacardi Breezer with melon.

'I thought it was only girls who drank this stuff,' she said.

'What the fuck do you know about it?'

'Nothing.'

'Exactly.'

Micke clinked his bottle against hers, and they drank. Teresa thought it was delicious, even nicer than Trocadero. When they had emptied the bottles, Micke said, 'Okaaay. So are you ready to partaaaay?'

'No.'

Micke laughed. 'OK. Let's have another then.'

He gave her a cigarette, and this time Teresa didn't even have to make an effort not to cough. The alcopop had smoothed a soft channel in her throat, and the smoke slid down without prickling.

'You know what, Teresa,' said Micke. 'I like you. You're kind of weird. You're completely different from...Chip 'n' Dale, for example.'

'Chip 'n' Dale?'

'You know. Jenny and Ester. Chip 'n' Dale. With their bunches and all the rest of it. Bling-bling and the whole fucking Christmas tree thing going on.'

Teresa hadn't thought it could happen; she was so completely unprepared for the laugh that burst out of her that she started coughing as it collided with a swig of alcohol on the way down. Micke thumped her on the back and said, 'Nice and calm, nice and calm now.'

They finished their cigarettes and emptied their bottles, and the incredible thing was that that was exactly how Teresa felt: nice and calm. Bearing in mind all the different kinds of alcohol Göran had at home, it was strange that Teresa had never considered it as a drug to ease her troubles. She looked at the bottle in her hand. Strange, bordering on idiotic. This actually *worked*.

She didn't feel drunk, just elated; she couldn't remember when she had last felt like this. When they got up to go in and join the party, Teresa grabbed hold of Micke's hand, and he moved away with a grin.

'Get it together,' he said. 'You're cool aren't you?'

No, Teresa wasn't cool. But it didn't really matter. She stayed a little way behind Micke as they went up the steps and into the party, then they split up. Five minutes later Teresa sneaked into the garage and quickly knocked back another Bacardi Breezer. Then she went inside again.

Johannes was sitting on his own on the sofa, and Teresa flopped down next to him.

'Hi. Where's Agnes?'

Johannes folded his arms. 'She's coming later. I think.'

'Why isn't she here now?'

'How the fuck should I know? I don't know what she's doing.'

'Of course you do. You're an item.'

'And what if we're not? Are you pissed, by the way?'

'No.'

'You sound pissed.'

'I'm just a little bit happy. Aren't I allowed to be a little bit happy?'

Johannes shrugged, and Teresa grabbed a handful of cheese puffs out of a bowl, munching them as she sank back on the sofa and looked around the room. With a few exceptions they weren't too bad after all, the people in her class. She looked at Leo and remembered the time he helped her fix her bicycle chain when it came off. She looked at Mimmi and remembered they'd quite enjoyed doing a Swedish project together. And so on.

For the first time in ages a faint longing stirred inside her. She wanted to *join in*, if only a little bit. Get closer, be part of things, do what the others did. A part of her knew that she actually didn't want to and couldn't anyway, but *right now* that was the way she felt and because it was pleasant, she stayed with the feeling.

'I sometimes wonder,' said Johannes, who hadn't spoken for a while.

'What?'

'What would have happened if I hadn't moved house.'

Teresa waited for him to go on. When he didn't, she helped him out. 'You turned into a bit of a dude after that.'

Johannes gave a stiff little smile. 'Not really. I just did what I had to do to fit in, kind of. Sometimes I think...shit, if only I'd been able to stay there. We had fun sometimes, didn't we?'

'Do you really think about this?'

'Yes. Sometimes.'

Teresa swallowed a lump of soggy cheese puffs. Then she swallowed again and said, 'Me too.'

They were sitting close together. By this stage Teresa was so familiar with every form of sorrow that she could pick the different kinds with the precision of a car spotter. As soon as they got close, she could identify the model. This was melancholy. Grieving for something that has been and can never be again.

But it was a pleasant sorrow, a Moomintroll sorrow so unlike the one she carried around in her everyday life that she welcomed it like a warm, woolly blanket. There was an ache in her breast, and when Johannes put his arm around her, she leaned her head on his shoulder.

Johannes.

She closed her eyes and gave herself up to her dizziness and her lightly borne melancholy. She was almost happy. There was a flash and she opened her eyes. Karl-Axel had crept up close and taken a picture of them with his mobile. Johannes didn't seem to care, and Teresa closed her eyes again.

Johannes. If only everything had been different.

That time on the rocks. If she had let him put his tongue in her mouth, if she hadn't pushed him away. If he hadn't moved house, if she hadn't...perhaps she wouldn't have got so fat, perhaps she wouldn't be taking the pills now, perhaps...

'Hi.'

Teresa opened her eyes again. Agnes was sitting next to her on the sofa. Even though Johannes didn't take his arm away, Teresa sat up straight as if she had been caught in the middle of some forbidden act. Or thought.

Agnes was looking shyly at Johannes. Teresa couldn't understand how anyone could resist such a look; she would gladly have sacrificed a finger to look like Agnes for *just one day.*

No. Not one day. One week. One month. Her little finger for one month. Not her index finger. Her index finger for one year. Her whole hand for her whole life? Her left hand, in that case.

Johannes touched her shoulder. 'What's the matter?'

Teresa didn't know how long she'd been sitting there caught up in thoughts about looks and body parts, but when she came out of them she could feel that something had changed in the atmosphere between Agnes and Johannes, and she was sitting between them like a third wheel. She got up and went into the kitchen.

On the worktop she found half a glass of red wine and knocked it back. She thought it tasted peculiar, as if it had been mixed with spirits.

Her right hand for Johannes. Special offer—one kidney, her right hand and twenty kilos of flesh. Shylock. The Merchant of Venice. A pound of flesh. What does that mean?

She went for a wander around the house. People were sitting in groups, and she felt slightly sick when she realised they were just talking lumps of flesh. Jenny was posed unnaturally against a door frame, twisting a strand of hair around her finger as she talked to Albin, whose hand was resting on her hip.

They're going to fuck. Everybody's going to go off and fuck.

Teresa's gaze locked onto Jenny's hip, and she thought about the set of exclusive chef's knives she had seen on a magnetic holder in the kitchen. Shylock. If she sliced away Jenny's hips, Albin wouldn't have anything to hold onto.

'What are you looking at, headcase?' Jenny hissed at her and Albin adopted a stance that suggested he would defend his fuck if necessary. Teresa pulled a face at them and wobbled into the living room. Agnes and Johannes were snogging the face off each other on the sofa. Teresa hadn't really thought they were capable of such a thing. Particularly Agnes, who was always so cool when it came to expressions of affection, but now she was half lying on top of Johannes, her tongue slurping away in his mouth as her hand squeezed his inner thigh.

Teresa stood staring at them. Johannes seemed to be having some difficulty keeping control of his hands; a couple of fingers slipped inside the waistband of Agnes' jeans at the back, but didn't dare go any further. They were among other people, after all. Instead they rubbed themselves against one another, licking and sucking and enjoying themselves inside their bubble of arousal.

Teresa stared. Alternate streams of hot and cold liquid flooded her body. The stereo was playing that song about dying.

> We're gonna die at the same time, you and I
> We're gonna die-ie-ie-ie-ie-ie-ie-ie-ie...

She tore herself away. She moved through the house as if she were underwater, towards the front door. There was only one thing she wanted. She managed to get down the steps and over to the garage, where she fell to her knees next to the box, took out a bottle of Bacardi Breezer and drank. Relief, for a few seconds. She emptied the bottle in thirty seconds then remained on her knees for a long time, swaying back and forth with her head in her hands.

'For fuck's sake, are you pinching my supplies?'

Micke was standing in front of her, a drunken smile playing around his lips. When Teresa opened her mouth to apologise, he waved dismissively and said, 'It's cool. What's mine is yours and all that shit.' He leaned against the door frame and lit a cigarette. When he offered Teresa the packet, her eyes filled with tears.

'Micke. You're so bloody nice. So kind.'

'Sure I am. You want one or not?'

'Can't you fuck me? Now?'

Micke gave a snort. 'Pull yourself together. You're pissed.'

'I'm not pissed. Everybody else is pissed. They're all pissed and they're going to fuck.'

Micke was standing directly in front of her. Teresa placed one hand over his crotch, squeezed his cock. Micke waved her hand away half-heartedly, but when she began to rub she could feel him growing hard.

'For fuck's sake, Teresa. Pack it in.'

But she didn't want to pack it in. She wanted to be fucked and snogged like everybody else and she wanted to be close and part of it all. Through the water billowing all around her and making everything blurred, she shuffled forward on her knees. She watched her hands like two alien fish as they undid Micke's belt and pulled down his zip.

When she took his semi-erect cock in her mouth, Micke groaned out loud. A couple of thrusts in and out and he was completely hard, and there were no more protests. He placed his hand on her head, buried his fingers in her hair and pressed her towards him.

For a little while she enjoyed the unfamiliar feeling. The warm piece of flesh in her mouth, the sounds Micke was making. Then the veil of water was drawn aside, and she saw what she was doing. This wasn't her. Not here, not like this. She couldn't breathe. She wanted to stop now, she wanted to go home.

She tried to pull away, but Micke whispered, 'Don't stop, don't stop', pressing her head closer so that his cock touched the back of her throat. A violent wave of nausea crashed through her body, surging up until she vomited. Alcopops, red wine and cheese puffs spurted out of her in a red slop that went all over Micke's cock, hands and jeans, and the garage floor. He backed away towards the wall, shaking the revolting mess off his hands as he yelled, 'What the fuck are you doing? That's so fucking disgusting!'

Teresa collapsed and threw up again, a pool forming beneath her on the cement floor. On the edge of her vision she could see Micke ripping off a long length of kitchen towel from a holder on the wall. When had wiped the worst of the mess off himself, he handed her a bundle.

'Here. This wasn't such a good idea, was it?'

Teresa wiped her mouth as she mechanically shook her head. An acrid stench hit her nostrils and she blew her nose and took a couple of deep breaths. She heard a snigger and turned towards Micke, who was looking out into the garden.

It took a couple of seconds for her eyes to adjust to the darkness. Then she saw that there was a little group standing behind a low shrub five metres away from the garage. Jenny, Albin and Karl-Axel.

Micke said, 'What the hell are you doing, you fucking idiots?'

Karl-Axel held up his mobile. 'Nothing. Just made a little film. Real hardcore stuff. It's just that the ending's a bit disgusting.'

Teresa hid her face in her hands. She heard the sound of running footsteps, screams and laughter. When she raised her head a long time later, she was alone. She got to her feet and looked around. Her red vomit splashed up the walls, the pool at her feet made the garage look like a slaughterhouse. A slaughterhouse.

She rang Göran on her mobile and asked him to come and pick her up. Then she went and sat on the pavement and waited for him, staring down through the grating over a drain. Behind her the party went on.

3

Somewhere there has to be rock bottom, a limit to how far a person can fall. It is possible that Teresa had reached this point when she woke up at half past eight on Saturday morning. She started the day by going to the toilet and spewing up everything that hadn't already come up. Then she lay in her bed with her arms around her belly and just wanted to die. Really die. Be obliterated, not exist any more, not take one more step in this world.

She had thought it was unnecessary to remove all sharp objects from her room; her problems had never had anything to do with taking her own life. Now her thoughts were focused on nothing else. She lay there wondering whether she had the strength or the courage to sharpen a pencil and hold it upright on the desk in her clenched fist, then slam her head down onto the point so that it penetrated her eye and went into her brain.

No. It was too gruesome, and there wasn't even any guarantee that she would die. But she wanted to die. Her memories of the previous evening were blurred and disjointed, but she remembered the most important bits, which made her want to fill her mouth with earth, cover her body with earth.

The bottle of Fontex tablets was on her bedside table. She knew they weren't an option, that they wouldn't work. Otherwise she wouldn't have been allowed to have them there. Out of habit she reached for the bottle to take her morning tablet, but let her hand drop.

If she stopped taking her tablets, perhaps she really would become mentally ill. Perhaps they would come and take her away. Lock her up. It was an alternative to dying, and almost the same thing. Only the earth in the mouth was missing, but you could always eat that anyway.

That was the way her thoughts went on Saturday morning.

When she got up to go to the toilet again, Maria was sitting in the armchair on the landing, knitting. She never usually sat there. She was keeping watch.

'Hi,' said Teresa.

'Hi. Have you taken your tablet?'

'Mm.'

Sitting on the toilet, she made her decision. She really would stop taking her tablets, she would see if she went crazy. Give it a month. If that didn't work she would come up with a way of killing herself that didn't feel too horrible. Her hope was that she would go mad without actually noticing.

Just after twelve she went downstairs to keep up appearances. She ate a bread roll with cheese; it tasted like ash. The radio was on in Olof's room because he was listening to *Tracks*. As the song that was bubbling under this week was introduced, Teresa stopped in mid-bite to listen to Kaj Kindvall: 'A studio version of a track that's already had considerable success on MySpace and YouTube has now been released. The artist calls herself Tesla, and apart from a couple of appearances and an early exit from the latest series of *Idol*, we don't know too much about her. Perhaps that will all change now. This is "Fly".'

The song began, and Teresa resumed her chewing. They had added strings and made the song more showy. It no longer had anything to do with her. She finished her sandwich and had a glass of milk. Then she felt sick and had to go and throw up again.

At three o'clock her mobile beeped to tell her that she had a message. It said, 'Film of the year! Check this out!' A film clip was attached.

Since she already had her face pressed firmly to the ground, she had a look. The picture quality was surprisingly good. Karl-Axel's father had an excellent job. He gave his son excellent presents. For example an excellent mobile with excellent definition and excellent video and sound recording. The film might even have been even more excellent and more detailed than Teresa's crappy mobile was capable of showing.

They had been standing there right from the start, and they had filmed the whole thing, right from Teresa's, 'Micke. You're so bloody nice. So kind.' Teresa saw and understood. No shadow would fall over Micke. He was a boy, and she had practically attacked him. Forced herself on him, then thrown up all over him.

She knew how it worked. The film would spread. Right across the world. In a couple of days people in Buenos Aires would be sitting laughing at the most disgusting thing they had ever seen, then they would send it on to their friends. She couldn't quite take it in.

Teresa sat down at her desk; her hands were ice-cold. Her mobile rang. She automatically pressed the reply button and put it to her ear.

'Yes?'

'Teresa? Hi, it's Johannes.'

'Hi, Johannes.'

There was silence at the other end. Then Johannes sighed, making a crackling sound in her ear. 'How are you feeling?'

Teresa didn't reply. There was no simple answer to that question.

'I saw the film,' said Johannes. 'Well, not all of it, but...I just wanted to...I feel really sorry for you.'

'Don't.'

'But I do. It's not right. You've had such a...I just wanted to say that...I'm here. Just so you know.'

'How are things with Agnes?'

'What? Oh, fine. And she says the same.'

'Are you back together?'

'Yes. But Teresa, try to...try...Oh, I don't know. But I'm here, OK? And Agnes. And we're very fond of you.'

'I know you're not. But thanks anyway. It was kind of you.'

Teresa rang off. When the phone rang again she rejected the call. She lay down on her bed and stared up at the ceiling.

Something gets dirty. A towel. Then it gets dirtier. And even dirtier, so dirty that it begins to fall apart. It is trampled in the mud, picked up, rolled into a ball. There is a breaking point in the state of dirtiness where the object that is dirty ceases to be itself. It becomes something else. The towel no longer looks like a towel, it cannot be used as a towel, it is not a towel. The same thing applies to a human being. Oh, the capacity for reflection might get in the way, the capacity to miss what that person once was. Human, detergent-scented, usable.

But it disappears, very gradually. It disappears.

During the afternoon and evening she received a number of suggestive or downright unpleasant text messages which she saved after reading them. The telephone rang twice; the first time it was somebody making slurping noises, the second time somebody whispering, 'Don't stop, don't stop.'

When Teresa went to bed, she was incapable of sleeping. She tried reading some Ekelöf, but couldn't concentrate for more than two lines at a time.

She re-read the disgusting texts: *have a nice weekend slag; suck and swallow; World Championship in cock sucking and spewing,* along with those who had made a little more effort.

She couldn't get enough. It was two o'clock in the morning when she sat down at the computer to see if she had received any emails. She had. More of the same from unfamiliar addresses; the little film had already spread far and wide, and had fired certain people's imagination and limited ability to articulate their thoughts.

There were several messages from Theres as well, spread over the past few weeks. When she opened one of them she almost expected it to contain some variation on the cock/suck/spew theme.

'you must come here you have to be here' one of them said. In another, older message, 'why did you run away tell me why you didn't stay'. The oldest, apart from the one she had deleted, said, 'jerry says you misunderstood i don't understand how you misunderstood you have to tell me'. The most recent message had arrived on Friday evening while Teresa was at the party, 'you have to write i don't like it when you're gone'.

Teresa copied the phrases from fourteen messages in total and pasted them in chronological order into one single document, which she read over and over again. If she had still had the ability to cry, she would have done so. Instead of tears a couple of phrases by Ekelöf welled up and forced their way out.

She clicked on reply, and at the top of the message she wrote, 'I live in another world, but you live in the same one.'

She looked at the sentence. That was really all she had to say. But still her fingers began to move over the keys. She imitated Theres' elided style, which made it easier to write. She didn't make any effort to be anything other than honest.

> Theres. I haven't gone. I exist. But I don't exist. Everyone wants to hurt me. Everyone hates me. I ran because I love you. I want you to be with me. Not with other people. You don't know how unhappy I am. All the time. I'm empty. There is nowhere I can be. Forgive me. I live in another world now.

She sent the message. Then she went back to bed. Her own darkness melted into the darkness of the room, and she fell asleep.

When she woke up at nine o'clock, there was a reply from Theres in her inbox.

> you must live in this world you must come to me now would be good but next weekend jerry is going to america so you will come then i will show you what to do

For a message from Theres, it was practically a novel. As usual there was a fair amount that needed interpreting, but that didn't bother

Teresa. She had written, and she had received a reply. She would go to Stockholm, and she would go without any particular hopes. It wasn't an act of will that made her think that way. It was simply a fact.

4

On Sunday afternoon, when Teresa was taken ill, nothing could have been more welcome. Her temperature shot up above thirty-nine degrees and it felt cool and refreshing. Her body was exhausted, her thoughts pleasantly fuzzy. All of her real pain was absorbed in the inconsequential aching of her muscles, and as her temperature approached forty degrees and the fever made her body levitate from the sheets there was even a hint of pleasure.

She took some ibuprofen and her temperature came down during the night, allowing her to sleep, but it was still so high when Maria checked on Monday morning that there was no question of Teresa going to school. As if she would have anyway. She switched off her mobile and lay in bed, doing nothing but savouring her illness, giving herself up to it. That was what she had.

All the time she was conscientiously taking her pills out of the Fontex bottle and throwing them away. When Maria pressed her to take her tablet, she hid it under her tongue until Maria had left the room.

Her temperature was back to normal on Thursday morning and Maria thought she could go back to school, but Teresa said, 'No. I'm going to stay at home and rest today and tomorrow. I'm going to Stockholm at the weekend.'

'You are *not.*'

'Yes, I am.'

'Last time you came home a complete wreck and now you've just been ill, so if you think I'm letting you go off there again, you're wrong.'

'Mum. There's nothing you can say or do to stop me. Because it doesn't matter. If you don't let me go, I shall just lie here in bed until I die. I won't eat. I won't drink. I'm serious.'

It didn't surprise Teresa that Maria actually listened to what she said, because something had happened to Teresa's voice. She wasn't speaking from her mouth any longer, but from her sternum, and she could only say what was true. Maria could obviously hear this too. For a long time she just stood and stared at Teresa. Then she vacated the dangerous plateau on which they found themselves and inclined her head. 'Right!' she said. 'If that's the way it's going to be, then you can pay for your own ticket.'

On Saturday morning Göran gave her a lift to the station. They didn't speak much in the car, and the few words Teresa did say just seemed to make Göran uncomfortable. Teresa understood. It was her voice, she could hear the timbre herself. Perhaps this was how ghosts spoke, or vampires: creatures without a soul.

The train took her to Stockholm and the subway took her to Svedmyra and the lift took her to Theres' door. She felt nothing. When Theres opened the door she walked past her into the apartment and sat down at the kitchen table. Theres sat opposite her.

Teresa had no desire to say anything, but she had come here, after all. She said, 'Is Jerry in America?'

'Yes. With Paris. Why are you unhappy?'

'Because of what I wrote.'

'I didn't understand.'

'There's a lot you don't understand.'

'Yes. A lot. Do you want some food?'

'No. Your song is on *Tracks*.'

'I know. We'll listen. To see if it wins.'

'What does it matter if it wins?'

'Then more people will want to listen to it.'

'Why do you want more people to listen?'

'My singing is good. Your words are good. Why are you unhappy?'

'Because I'm fat and ugly and lonely and nobody likes me. For a start.'

'I like you.'

'Perhaps. But you like so many people.'

'I like you best.'

'What do you mean?'

'There are lots of girls. But I like you best.'

'Is anyone coming today?'

'Not today. And not tomorrow.'

'Why not?'

'I'm going to be with you. Why are you unhappy?'

Teresa got up from the table and took a walk around the apartment. It was like revisiting a place you've been away from for so long that everything has become unfamiliar. There was the computer they had played on. There was Theres' bed where they had sat, the sofa where they had watched horror films. Everything was true and not true. They belonged to someone else. Next to the computer lay her own notebook with lyrics in it. She read a couple of them and couldn't understand why she had written them.

At twelve o'clock she helped Theres put the radio on, then they sat in silence on the sofa as song after song was played. Teresa listened behind the music, behind the words. There was nothing there. Yet another song was introduced as a really great track from an exciting new band, and the only thing it expressed was its complete lack of content.

It was a few minutes away from two o'clock when a crackling, buzzing sound was heard. The jingle for this week's Bullet: the highest new entry, 'Fly', by Tesla. The song had gone from nowhere straight to number two, beaten only by The Ark with 'The Worrying Kind'.

When Teresa switched off the radio, Theres said, 'We didn't win.'

'Maybe next week.'

'What do you mean?'

'It doesn't matter.'

'Why are you unhappy?'

'Can you stop asking me that?'

'No. I want to know.'

Teresa took out her mobile, scrolled through until she found the clip from the garage, pressed play and gave it to Theres, who held the little screen close to her eyes as she carefully followed the course of events. When it was over she gave the phone back to Teresa and said, 'Being sick is not good.'

'Is that all you've got to say?'

Theres pondered for a couple of seconds, then asked, 'Why did you do that? With the boy?'

'I was drunk.'

'You'd been drinking alcohol.'

'Yes.'

'Alcohol is not good. Why are you unhappy?'

Something had been silently building up and now Teresa jerked as a clearly audible 'click' reverberated through her body. A switch was flicked on, a hatch opened. She leapt to her feet and *screamed.*

'Why can't you understand *anything*? Can't you understand that's just about the most disgusting, ugly, revolting thing you can do and it's on film and it's *me* who's doing it and every single fucking person in the entire fucking world can watch it and see how ugly and how completely fucking disgusting I am throwing up all over his cock and I already felt like shit beforehand and I thought I was totally empty then I had a drink so I wouldn't be empty any more and then that happened and it turned out that it's actually possible to be *even more* fucking empty. It's possible to be so fucking empty that you really don't exist any more and I don't exist any more and this isn't me standing here and this isn't me talking and you don't know me any more and I don't know you.'

During this entire screaming monologue, Theres sat straight-backed with her hands resting on her knees, listening attentively.

When Teresa flopped down in the armchair, her face bright red, and wrapped her arms tightly around her body, Theres said, 'Those were good words. That you wrote.'

'Which fucking words?'

'I live in another world, but you live in the same one.'

'And do you understand what that means?'

'No. But I laughed.'

'I've never heard you laugh.'

'I've started.'

'What do you mean, you've started?'

'Some of the girls laugh. Then I laugh too. Sometimes. Otherwise they get scared.' Theres looked over at the window. 'We're going now.'

'Going where?'

'I'll show you what to do.'

Five minutes later they were standing by the loading bay at the back of the local shop, which had closed at two o'clock. Teresa looked at the hammer Theres had brought with her from home, and which was now dangling from her hand.

'Are we going to break in?'

'No. He's coming now. I know.'

Just as Theres uttered the last word, the door opened and a man in his forties came out. He looked remarkably like Teresa's English teacher. The same sparse beard and slightly bulging eyes, the same clothes: jeans and a check shirt. In his hand he was holding a small metal box, presumably the day's takings. He caught sight of Theres and Teresa as soon as he opened the door.

'Hi girls, and what—'

He didn't get any further before Theres smashed the hammer into his temple. He staggered backwards a couple of steps into the shop, then went down full length on his back. Theres grabbed the door before it swung shut, and walked in. Teresa followed her. She had not yet begun to feel anything.

The heavy metal door closed behind them, and the room was

in semi-darkness. Only the light from the shop windows filtered in through a doorway. Teresa found the light switch, and a couple of fluorescent tubes on the ceiling came on. The man was lying on the floor with his mouth open, one hand pressed to his temple. A small amount of blood was seeping through his fingers.

Theres gave the hammer to Teresa and said, 'Make him dead.'

Teresa weighed the hammer in her hand and looked at the man. She tried a practice blow in the air. The man started to scream. Inarticulate noises at first, and then with words.

'Take the money! There's almost eight thousand! Take it and get out of here! I've never seen you, I don't know who you are, my mother's ill, she needs me, you can't, please don't do anything stupid, just take the money...'

Theres found a roll of packing tape and tore off a strip, which she wound twice around the man's mouth. Teresa was surprised that he offered no resistance, but his hands were moving in an odd, jerky way. Presumably the blow to the head had sabotaged something to do with his bodily functions. The man snorted and snot ran out of his nose and down over the packing tape. It looked a bit like *Hostel*. That was probably where Theres had got the idea of the tape from.

Teresa took a step towards the man and his feet scrabbled on the floor as he tried to move backwards. She raised the hammer; asked herself how she felt. Then she held it out to Theres.

'I can't.'

Theres didn't take it. 'No. You have to do it.'

'Why?'

'You say you're empty. You need to.'

Theres turned to face Teresa and looked her in the eyes. Teresa gasped. She stared into those dark blue voids as Theres' voice flowed into her ears. 'You make him dead. Then you take him. There will be a little bit of smoke. Red smoke. You take it. Then you're not empty. Then you'll be happy and you'll want to do things again.'

Theres' voice had taken on something of the same quality as Teresa's; it was coming from a different place in her body, not from her mouth, and everything she said was true. When Teresa turned back to the man, he had managed to turn on his side and grab hold of something on the floor. A Stanley knife for opening boxes. He was holding it up with the blade pointing at Teresa as he tried to get to his feet. His eyes were staring insanely and snot kept spurting out of his nose.

Teresa gritted her teeth and raised the hammer. The man's hand flew out and the blade sliced through her top, making a superficial cut on her stomach. The movement overbalanced the man, and he fell on the floor again. Theres stamped on his hand until he dropped the knife.

Teresa looked at the blood tricking down towards the waistband of her trousers, drew her index and middle fingers through it and stuck them in her mouth. It turned red inside, and the colour billowed up in her head until that too was red on the inside. Colour. She had colour. When she ran her tongue over her teeth, it felt as if they had been sharpened into points.

She quickly squatted down and slammed the hammer straight into the man's forehead. There was an echoing crunch and a sound like a heavy foot stamping on a frozen puddle. The man's body arched upwards and his hip brushed against Teresa's hip before he collapsed and lay flat on his back again. His hands and feet were shaking, and the blood vessels in his eyes burst.

The smells. Teresa was aware of the smells. The sweat of fear from the man's body, the iron smell of the blood and all around her a miasma of storeroom odours, floating through the air. Rotting bananas, fresh mushrooms, printer's ink and stale beer from the container of cans for recycling. She recognised them all, she could identify them and tick them off. They melted together with the red, cascading colour inside her head and became one single experience, one single thought going around and around: *I'm alive. I'm alive. I'm alive.*

She hit the man on the temple, on the head. She smashed his teeth and she knocked out one eye. She hit his forehead as hard as she could several times until a hole opened up in his skull, and she was able to creep close to him, quivering with excitement, and watch the lone thin curl of smoke rise from deep inside. No, she didn't see it, but she knew it was there, she could smell it; sense its presence.

She drew back her lips and growled softly as it flowed into her and became a part of her.

They took a walk through the closed shop. Teresa picked up a bar of chocolate, took a bite without opening it, then threw it away. She opened a packet of crisps and ate two, then poured the rest all over the contents of the freezer. She barked and bit off a piece of Falun sausage, chewed it to a soggy mess then spat it out over the tomatoes. Meanwhile Theres fetched two plastic bags and filled them with as many jars of baby food as she could carry.

They went back to the storeroom. An irregular pool of blood had flowed from the man's head, and on the edge of the pool lay the hammer. Teresa picked it up, went over to the sink and rinsed it under the tap. She caught sight of herself in the mirror.

Her face was spattered with blood and a few small, more solid lumps of human tissue were stuck to her cheeks. Streaks of blood had trickled down over her forehead from her hair. She turned to Theres.

'Theres. Do you think I'm beautiful now?'

'Yes.'

'Would you like to kiss me?'

'No.'

'That's what I thought.'

The cut on her stomach had begun to hurt, but was no longer bleeding. However, both her top and the knees of her trousers were so blood-soaked that no one could have seen her without getting suspicious. She washed her face, then they waited until it was dark before they left.

The last thing they did was to take the notes from the cash box. Then they walked back to Theres' apartment at normal speed. They didn't meet a single person on the way.

5

That night Teresa dreamed about wolves.

First of all she was a human child, a helpless little creature cast out into the forest. Out of the darkness the pale eyes approached, creeping towards her between the trunks of the fir trees. Paws moving silently across the carpet of needles. The circle closing in. She wanted to run, but had not yet learned to walk.

Then rough tongues were licking her body all over. They were in the lair, and the wolves licked and licked her skin. As the tongues rasped over her stomach, it hurt so much that she cried out. Layer after layer of skin was peeled away, and the pain was unbearable. Then the fur began to appear beneath the skin. The pain diminished and the wolves left her.

A small amount of moonlight shone in through the opening of the lair, and she saw herself from the outside. She was lying on the earth floor, wet from the wolves' saliva, trembling with cold because the sparse fur was not yet able to protect her.

The scene changed, and from the all-seeing perspective of the moon she saw a wolf running through the forest. A crippled or sick wolf with its fur in clumps, a pitiful creature terrified of the least sound. She was in the moon and in the wolf at the same time, she was drifting in the sky and crawling over the ground through the same pair of eyes.

Then time must have passed, because the ground was covered in snow. She was racing through the forest, and every leap was an expression of joy. There was strength in her muscles, and she saw that her front legs were covered in thick, smooth fur. She was following a trail of blood. Dark patches were visible in the snow at irregular intervals, and she was hunting a quarry that was already injured.

She dashed up a hill, the snow whirling up around her paws. When she reached the top she stopped and stood, her tongue hanging out. She was panting and her breath turned to smoke in the cold air. In front of her the pack was gathered around the injured deer whose hooves still moved beneath the mass of grey fur.

The leader of the pack turned to her. The deer stopped moving, a blown eye reflecting the sky. As the whole pack turned like one single creature, focusing their attention on the lone wolf, she showed her submissiveness. She exposed her throat and lay down on her back, waving her paws; she was a wolf cub, lowest in rank of them all.

They moved closer. She whimpered like the cub she now was, displaying her helplessness, not knowing if they were coming to accept her into the pack or to rip her to shreds.

6

'Theres? When you dream—what do you dream about?'

'I don't know how to do that.'

'Don't you dream?'

'No. How do you do it?'

Teresa was lying on the mattress next to Theres' bed, watching the dust bunnies quiver as she breathed out. She rolled onto her back. The T-shirt she had borrowed from Theres was so small that it stopped just above the wound on her stomach. She ran her hand over the scab that was beginning to form, and it hurt. She stroked it again. If it hadn't been for the cut, she would have been able to fly. Tell herself she hadn't done what she had done.

But the cut was there. Inflicted with a Stanley knife, the kind used to open boxes. By someone who worked in a shop. Who was now dead, beaten to death with a hammer. By Teresa. She stroked the cut and tried to make the act real. She had done it, she would never be able to get away from the fact that she had done it. So it might as well be real. Otherwise everything would be wasted.

'How do you do it?' Theres asked.

'It just happens,' said Teresa. 'You can't make it happen. It's not something you can learn. I don't think so, anyway.'

'Tell me how you do it.'

'You sleep. And pictures come into your head. You don't have any control over it, it just comes. Last night I dreamed I was a wolf.'

'That's not possible.'

'In a dream it is.' Teresa propped herself up on her elbow so that she could see Theres, who was staring up at the ceiling. 'Theres? Do you ever imagine stuff? I mean, do you have, like pictures and actions in your head that you think about?'

'I don't understand.'

'No, I didn't think you would.' Teresa blew out a puff of air and the dust bunnies danced away under the bed. 'That thing we did yesterday. To the man in the shop. Do you think about that?'

'No. It's over. You're happy now.'

Teresa curled up as best she could in Theres' clothes, which were much too tight. They had shoved her own blood-soaked clothes into two plastic bags and thrown them down the rubbish chute the previous evening.

Happy? No, she wasn't happy. She was a stranger to herself, she was presumably still in shock. But alive. She could feel that she was alive. Perhaps that was the same thing as being happy, according to Theres' way of looking at things.

Teresa opened and closed her hands. There was a little bit of coagulated blood underneath the nail of one of her little fingers. She stuck her finger in her mouth and sucked and licked until the blood was gone. Her hands felt bigger, stronger than the previous day. Capable hands. Terrible hands. Her hands.

It was just after eleven, and her train was due to leave at two-thirty. Every normal activity, such as getting on a train and showing her ticket, seemed absurd. She felt so light, as if she would have floated away like a helium balloon if her heavy hands had not been keeping her on the ground.

She looked at herself. Theres' clothes made her look like a sausage stuffed into a skin that was too small. This was a minor problem under the circumstances, but she couldn't go home looking like a clown. There would be questions if nothing else.

'Theres,' she said. 'I think we're going to have to go into town.'

In H&M on Drottninggatan Teresa grabbed the first suitable pair of jeans, a T-shirt and a sweater in her size, then went to the changing room and put them on. When she came out she saw that two girls aged about twelve were edging towards Theres.

'Excuse me,' said one of them. 'You're Tesla, aren't you?'

Theres pointed at Teresa, who had come over and was standing next to her. 'We,' she said. 'I sing. Teresa writes the words.'

'Right,' said the girl. 'Well, anyway, I think "Fly" is absolutely brilliant.' She chewed her lip, trying to think of something else to say, but seemed unable to come up with anything. Instead she offered Theres a notebook and pen. Theres took them. Then nothing happened. The girls looked anxiously at one another.

'She wants your autograph,' said Teresa.

'And yours, I suppose,' said the girl.

Teresa opened the book at a blank page and wrote her name. Then she gave the pen to Theres, who shook her head. 'What am I supposed to write?'

'Just put Tesla.'

Theres did as she was told, then handed the book back to the girl, who pressed it to her chest and turned to her friend, who hadn't said a word from start to finish; she had just gazed at Theres with big eyes. She had nothing to add. Then the girl who had done the talking did something totally unexpected. She gave a little bow. The other girl did the same. The gesture seemed so out of place that Teresa laughed out loud.

Then Theres laughed too. Her laughter sounded unnatural and barely human, more like something you might hear from a laugh bag in a joke shop. The girls stiffened and scurried off towards the accessories department with their heads close together, whispering.

'Theres,' said Teresa. 'I think you should give up laughing.'

'Why?'

'Because it sounds weird.'

'Aren't I any good at laughing?'

'That's one way of putting it. No.'

At the till Teresa took out her wallet; she didn't recognise it, because it was so fat. Then she remembered. The takings. The metal box they had broken open with a screwdriver. Seven thousand eight hundred kronor, mainly in five-hundred-kronor notes.

But it wasn't real money. You worked for real money, or you were given it, as a gift or as pocket money, a little bit at a time. This was a bundle of bits of paper that had been lying in a drawer, and had ended up in Teresa's wallet. She was disappointed when the assistant told her, after scanning and tugging off the security tags, the amount she had to pay for the clothes. She would have liked to give away more of the bits of paper, got rid of them.

Drottninggatan was packed. Street vendors were demonstrating battery-driven toys and rubbish made of plastic and glass. They were all made of flesh and blood. A well-placed blow could make the flesh burst and the blood pour out.

Teresa didn't feel too good. She would have liked to hold hands with Theres for support. The feeling of being so light that she might blow away was starting to become acute. It was just like when she had had a high temperature; perhaps she still had it. She felt hot and dizzy.

In a side street Teresa stopped outside a shop window. It was a shoe shop, and in the window there were a couple of dozen different designs of Doc Martens, heavy boots with a high lace-up. A bright red pair with thick soles had caught Teresa's eye.

She had never been interested in clothes, never had any *style*. When the girls in her class sat sighing over the latest magazine and some jacket that was just 'sooo cool', she didn't understand it at all. It was a jacket, it looked more or less the same as any other jacket. She had never seen an item of clothing and simply known that it was right.

But now she was standing here, and the boots were *glowing* at her. They were hers, to the point where she could have stuck her hand through the glass and taken them. Going through the normal procedure of making a purchase felt unnatural, but she did it. When it turned out that they didn't have any in her size, she asked if she could try on the pair in the window, and they fitted perfectly. Of course. They were made for her feet, and cost only three bits of paper.

When they got outside, the world looked different. As if the extra height the soles gave her changed her perspective totally, even if it was only two centimetres. Teresa *walked* differently, and therefore she *saw* differently. The boots gave weight to her entire body, and whereas before it had felt as if people could pass right through her, now they stepped aside, the crowds parting before her.

A plump woman in folk costume was playing a reedy tune on a recorder. Teresa went and stood directly in front of her. The woman's eyes were weary, and she was so small that Teresa could have swallowed her with one bite. Instead she placed one of the bits of paper in the hat that was on the ground in front of the woman. Her eyes opened wide; a long harangue of gratitude in some East European language came pouring forth. Teresa stood motionless, unmoved, tasting the moment and her own weight.

'Now you're happy,' said Theres.

'Yes,' said Teresa. 'Now I'm happy.'

They took the subway to Svedmyra. The weight of the boots worked even when Teresa wasn't standing up. Sitting there next to Theres, who had settled deep in the corner as usual, a protection zone was formed around them, and no one came to sit in their square.

'Those girls,' she said to Theres. 'The ones who come to visit you. What are they like?'

'At first they're happy. Then they say they're unhappy. And scared. They want to talk. I help them.'

Teresa looked around the carriage. Mostly adults. A few girls and boys of their own age were sitting with earphones in, tapping away on their mobile phones. They looked neither unhappy nor scared. Either they were hiding it well, or they were just a different kind of person from the ones who found their way to Theres.

'Theres, I want to meet those girls.'

'They want to meet you.'

Two police cars were parked outside the local shop; blue and white tape between the lamp posts cordoned off the street. As Theres and Teresa went past they could see there was an ambulance round the back, by the loading bay. Teresa resisted an impulse to try to peer in through the window—*the perpetrator always returns to the scene of the crime*—and carried on with Theres towards her apartment. When they were out of earshot, she said, 'You do realise we can't say anything about this, don't you? Not to those other girls either.'

'Yes,' said Theres. 'Jerry said. You go to prison if you get into trouble. I know.'

Teresa glanced back at the shop. The loading bay was hidden from view, and she didn't think anyone had seen them going to or from the shop. But she wasn't sure. If it hadn't been for the boots, her knees might well have given way. Instead she kept on walking, her footsteps firm and steady.

She didn't have much time if she was going to catch her train after saying goodbye to Theres, but she stopped dead when they got to the apartment.

Something was wrong.

She looked around the hallway. The clothes hangers, the rug, Jerry's clothes, her own bag. She had a distinct feeling that someone had been here. Perhaps the rug was slightly out of line, perhaps a pen had been moved on the hall table. Something. They had left the door unlocked, and anyone could have got in.

And could still be here.

Something that would have felt horrible just a couple of days ago now happened quite naturally. Teresa went into the kitchen and fetched the biggest carving knife, then marched through the apartment with the knife held in front of her, ready to attack. She opened every wardrobe, looked under the beds.

Theres sat on the sofa with her hands on her knees, following Teresa's movements as she secured the area. Only when Teresa was convinced no one was hiding anywhere and came back to the living room did she ask a question: 'What are you doing?'

'Someone's been here,' said Teresa, putting the knife down on the coffee table. 'And I don't understand why. It bothers me.'

Her train was leaving in twenty-five minutes, and she would need to be lucky with the subway if she was going to catch it. But still she stood absolutely motionless for ten seconds, breathing in through her nose. Sniffing the air. There was something there. A scent. Something she couldn't place.

She grabbed her bag and told Theres to lock the door behind her. Then she raced down the stairs and ran all the way to the subway station. She saw a train coming in, and just managed to slip through the doors before they closed.

The train to Österyd was full, and she got on two minutes before it was due to leave. Since she didn't have a seat reservation, she pushed her way through to find an empty space. As she moved into the next carriage, she became aware of the same scent again. She stopped and sniffed, looked around.

A group of men in their forties and fifties were sitting on one side of her. There were a few beer cans on the table, and they were talking loudly about someone called Birgitta on reception, and whether she had fake tits or not. The scent of aftershave was coming from the men, and suddenly she knew.

There was an empty seat in the buffet car, and the counter hadn't opened yet. As soon as she sat down she heaved her bag up onto the table so that she could get out her mobile and ring Theres. She found her phone, and at the same time discovered that something else was missing. With gritted teeth she hit speed dial, and when Theres answered she said, 'It was Max Hansen who was in your apartment. And he's pinched my MP3 player.'

7

Max Hansen was on a steep incline. He had lost his grip, and he was sliding. Downwards. It didn't matter to him, because there was a conscious decision behind it. He was being carried to the bottom of his own free will; he was completing his downhill race in slow motion, as if he were enjoying a skiing holiday. There was pleasure along the way, and he hoped he would be able to brake before the crash came.

The catalyst, the first shove in the back had happened on Christmas Day.

He had dedicated Christmas Eve to drinking and grinding his teeth at Tora Larsson's stupidity. The record company lost interest in his master tape once they found out about the video clip on MySpace. His cash cow had escaped from her stall, and was offering her udders to anyone who wanted a drink. Free to everyone, come along and have a taste.

There was absolutely nothing he could do. The fact that there was no contract, the gamble that was going to make his fortune, had instead become his misfortune. It had been a calculated risk, but he couldn't have imagined that it would go down the pan in this particular way, and that bothered him. In his drunken misery he had taken out Robbie and was on the point of hurling him from the balcony, but managed to stop himself.

Before he passed out on the sofa he spent a long time weeping and patting Robbie's shiny nose, begging for forgiveness for what he had almost done.

On Christmas Day he rang Clara. She was a Danish woman he thought he had pulled at Café Opera a year or so ago. He had hauled out what Danish he could still remember, talked jokingly about their homeland, then taken her back to his place. It had all been just a bit too easy, and when it was all over, it turned out she expected payment. She got her money and Max got her phone number.

In spite of the fact that Clara, at around thirty, was a bit old for him he had used her services a couple of times. Since he wasn't particularly attracted to her, it had to be a hand job or a blow job, which was cheaper anyway.

This time she made it clear that she would be charging holiday rates, in other words a supplementary fee of five hundred kronor as it was Christmas Day, but there was nothing Max could do. He needed her.

When she arrived at his apartment he had already sunk a couple of whiskies and was feeling sentimental. He tried speaking Danish to her, the childish expressions he remembered, but Clara made it very clear that she just wanted to get this over with. She wanted to get home to her daughter.

So Max took off his clothes and sat down in the armchair. Clara started working on him with her hand. Her practice was not to work with her mouth unless he was wearing a condom. But of course the first task was to get it up so that she had something to put the condom *on*. She kneaded and stroked, and whispered encouragement in Danish.

Not a twitch. Not a tingle. Nothing.

He had never had problems with Clara before. On the contrary. The fact that everything was clearly agreed from the start and that there was no uncertainty about it usually relaxed him; usually, he would get a hard-on as soon as she touched him. Not this time. It was just like when he watched his films. He had lost something after the experience with Tora Larsson. At that moment, as he sat staring at his dormant cock, he realised it would never come back. He was impotent.

Clara sighed and scrabbled at his pubic hair with her fingers. 'Come on, there's a good boy, up you get for Clara.' Max pushed her hand away and threw his head back. There was a faint cracking noise and suddenly he knew what he wanted.

'Bite me,' he said. When Clara didn't react, he pointed to his shoulder. 'Bite me hard. Here.'

Clara, who presumably wasn't entirely unfamiliar with the scenario, shrugged her shoulders, leaned over him and nipped his shoulder. Max whispered, 'Harder.' She bit harder, almost drawing blood, and something soft and pleasant flooded through Max's body. He told her to bite him in a couple of other places. When she didn't want to do that any more, he told her to slap him across the face. And again, harder.

His ears were ringing and his penis was still lying there like a trampled snake, but he had the same sense of satisfaction, of peacefulness, as after intercourse. When he paid Clara she said she wasn't all that keen on this kind of thing, but she had a colleague called Disa who was more of a specialist. She gave Max Disa's number. Merry Christmas.

After she left, he sat in the armchair and examined his feelings. So this was what it had come to. This was the way of things now. Max closed his eyes and let go of what he had been, or what he thought he had been. Began to slide. There was no point in keeping up a respectable facade or chasing after the status that might lead him to his sexual pleasures. Let go.

Let go.

The following day he went to the address—he had only sent letters there to that point—and had the conversation with Jerry. He was going to salvage what could be salvaged by whatever means were available. As if on cue, Ronny from Zapp Records rang the day before New Year's Eve; they were still kind of interested, in spite of everything. The huge popularity of the song couldn't be ignored. A professional recording had its value. Was it Max who owned the rights?

He played the tape. They could draw their own conclusions.

Then things began to happen. The song became a big hit, and the interest in Tesla was huge. Unfortunately Max hadn't been paid any big advance. The royalties would trickle in, but that was a long way off and Max was in a hurry. He was on thin ice; he had to grab as much as possible before it gave under him.

The record company wanted a whole album, and they were prepared to cough up a decent amount of money in advance. Other companies got in touch, and after several conversations back and forth with Ronny, Zapp were ready to cough up so much they were on the point of haemorrhage. Everything was going Max's way, and he slithered along on the treacherous ice and threw himself down the ski run and any other metaphor he could think of to describe the basic problem: he didn't have the songs.

He hadn't even managed to establish contact with Tora Larsson. He had phoned, he had written, he had emailed both her and the freak without getting any response. He knew they had more songs, but how the hell was he going to get hold of them if they refused even to *answer*?

It was so frustrating he thought he was going to lose his mind. One day he sat for a long time, staring at Disa's telephone number. Clara had told him the woman was a dominatrix; she would bring her gear round and hurt him any way he wanted.

Max tried to picture the scenario. Bound, perhaps. A whip flicking across his back. The pain. He saw himself and his own thoughts, and only then did he realise what he was actually looking for. He fumbled with his arm and felt at the scars on his back, the ones he could reach.

Something decisive had happened to him that day in the hotel room with Tora Larsson. It had been terrible, but when he closed his eyes and stroked the smooth surface of the scars, he realised he missed it. This was what he wanted to experience again.

This is not good. Pull yourself together, Max.

He weighed up his options, and considered them one by one. There was Jerry and the contract and legal procedures, the use of intermediaries or a straight Tesla copy, letters he could write, phone calls he could make. In the end, Ockham's Razor won out: *If several possibilities exist, choose the simplest.*

He needed Tora Larsson's music. She didn't want to give it to him. When you were on the downward slope anyway, the solution was obvious.

He bought a scruffy second-hand Canada Goose jacket, a pair of thermal trousers and a warm hat. Then he started to watch the front door of Tora's apartment block. This was a tricky exercise, because there wasn't anywhere to hide, and it would arouse suspicion if people saw him wandering up and down the street for too long.

Ockham again. He bought a six-pack of beer and sat down on a bench a hundred metres from the door. Because he was in full view, he became invisible. An old drunk that nobody wanted to look at. He couldn't manage more than a few hours a day, but he had Robbie in his pocket: his luck had to be in at some point, for fuck's sake.

During the course of five mornings he saw neither Jerry nor Tora leave the apartment. What he did see was girls going into the apartment block; sometimes he caught a glimpse of them or Tora up at the window. He came to the conclusion that Jerry wasn't home.

Sometimes his mobile rang. Girls he had made a half-hearted play for ages ago or more recently, old acquaintances who wanted to check out the situation. Presumably the word was out that he was the man behind Tora Larsson, and he had become someone it might be worth keeping in touch with. He could hear the clink of crockery or the murmur of conversation in the background when they called from restaurants or cafés, the impersonal, obsequious tone in their voices.

He sat on his bench and shivered, held the phone well away from his ear and said Hi and How's it going and Cool, and he despised every last one of them. They were little pack animals, lemmings gathering kudos as they hurtled towards the abyss, squeaking as they ran.

He raised his can of ice-cold beer to Tora Larsson's window. He loathed her and he respected her. As he sat here on his bench and she wandered around her apartment, there was a bond between them, an invisible trail of blood running from his feet to her door, through her letterbox and into her body. A shudder ran down his spine as he thought about it.

Finally, on the sixth day, Tora came out with the freak. Max gripped his beer can with both hands and stared down at the ground as if he was too drunk to look up when they walked past him, just a few metres away. He watched them disappear in the direction of the subway and waited a few minutes before entering the building and taking the lift up to her apartment.

With stiff hands he took Robbie out of his pocket and pressed him to his forehead. Then he tried the handle. The door wasn't locked. He just stood there for while staring into the wide-open apartment as if he was afraid a trap might suddenly slam shut. He just couldn't be this lucky.

He steeled himself and slipped into the hallway, closing the door behind him. Quietly he said, 'Hello? Anyone home?' No reply and no time to lose. He headed for the computer in the living room and bit his lower lip when he saw that it was switched off. He started it up, whispering, 'Come on, come on, come on, please…'

His luck was out. He needed a password to get into the system. He tried 'Tora' and 'Tesla' and a number of other words. Finally he hammered in 'fuckinghell', but that particular curse didn't work either. He shut down the computer and went hunting.

In a bag in the hallway he found what he was looking for. He recognised the cheap MP3 player from his second meeting with Tora. He started to sweat in his thick jacket as he scrolled through the playlists, and under 'Theres' he found 'Fly' along with another twenty or so songs. He put the earphones in and was able to confirm that he had struck gold.

Theres?

He slipped the MP3 player in his pocket and stood by the door, unsure what to do next. The girls had gone off somewhere on the subway; he was bound to have some time left.

Theres?

This was probably his only chance to find out something about the girl who had come to rule his life. He undid his jacket so that he could cool down, locked the door from the inside and started searching the apartment with fresh eyes.

In the drawer of the bedside table next to what was presumably Jerry's bed, he found a folder with documents relating to the sale of a house. Jerry had inherited it from his parents, Lennart and Laila Cederström. The estate inventory indicated that they had both passed away on the same date. Max vaguely recognised the name Lennart Cederström, but couldn't place it. Something to do with music. He stored the name in his memory.

In the desk drawers he found more rubbish, the kind you might expect. Old bills and guarantees, documents from *Idol* and the very first letter he had sent. What struck him as he went through rental agreements and bank statements was that there wasn't a single document anywhere relating to Tora. Nothing from any school or authority, no mementoes.

Her own room was spartan, like a cell in a refugee hostel. A CD player, a few CDs and Bamse the Bear comics. A bed. On the bedside table lay an ID card. Max picked it up and studied it carefully.

Angelika Tora Larsson. So far, so good. But there was absolutely no chance that the girl in the photograph was the Tora he knew. He held the card up to the light, looked at it side-on. Someone had altered it. The card was battered and scratched, but it was obvious that something had been done to the numbers indicating the date of birth.

Angelika. Tora. Theres.

He wasn't one jot closer to understanding who the girl calling herself Tora Larsson actually was, but two things he did know. One: there was something very suspect going on here. And two: he ought to be able to use it to his advantage.

He had been in the apartment for over an hour, it was almost eleven o'clock and he decided not to tempt fate any longer. Before he left he checked that everything looked just the same as when he arrived. He closed the door behind him and listened to make sure no one was coming up the stairs, then hurried down and out into the street. As he headed for the subway he noticed that there were a couple of police cars parked outside the shop, right next to the bench where he would no longer need to sit. He was done here. He had found what he was looking for, and a lot more.

As soon as he got home he poured himself a large celebratory whisky. Then he transferred the songs from the MP3 player to his computer, and sat down to listen to them.

Gold. Pure gold. Five of the songs were definitely in the same class as 'Fly', and the rest were perfectly OK. The lyrics weren't always that brilliant, but he couldn't think of many Swedish artists who wouldn't be proud to be associated with this album.

Yes, album. He had already started thinking about it like that. The files that were now on his computer would have to be run through the desk a few times, the production had to be sorted out and they needed to be tidied up a bit, but he had everything he needed for a real smash.

However, there was a problem. Tora Larsson would never agree to the project, and he didn't know what she might do when she found out what he was up to. It was a dilemma, to put it mildly.

With the help of the computer Max started checking the information he had found in the apartment. He soon discovered that no one with Tora's ID number existed. However, Angelika Tora Larsson did exist, and she had the same number if you altered just one digit.

Max found the really juicy information when he did a search on Lennart and Laila Cederström. He read the articles about the Swedish pop stars who had been brutally murdered, their son Jerry, and the strange room the police had discovered in the cellar. He put this together with what his back knew about Tora's capacity for violence, and suddenly his dilemma was no longer a dilemma.

He no longer had a problem; it was Tora Larsson who had a problem. He could do exactly what he wanted, and she wouldn't be able to say a word.

8

On Monday morning Teresa went to school. Heads turned to look at her as she got on the bus. She went straight to the back, and sat with her feet in their Doc Martens on the back of the seat in front of her. People looked at her and sniggered. As soon as she looked them in the eye, they looked away.

Eight members of her class had arrived before her. They were standing around waiting for the first lesson to start. One of them was Karl-Axel, the documentary film maker. Teresa was completely calm inside as she met his gaze from some distance away. She walked steadily along the corridor, the boots giving her footsteps weight and power.

When she was a couple of metres away from the group, Karl-Axel grinned and said, 'Morning *Teresa*', then grabbed the side of his cheek and pulled it in and out a couple of times so that it made a smacking, slurping noise. A couple of the lads gave a dirty laugh.

Teresa could have sat down right at the end of the bench outside the classroom and ignored the whole thing. Someone would say how disappointing it was that stuffed cabbage leaves weren't on the lunch menu today, someone else would say they hoped she hadn't eaten too much for breakfast. Something along those lines. She could have sat there with her eyes firmly fixed on the floor, pretending she couldn't hear them. But she had thought the situation through, and it just wasn't an option.

Instead she grinned back at Karl-Axel as if he done something really clever, then took a step forward and kicked him in the groin. The boots had a reinforced steel toe-cap, and her aim was more or less perfect. Karl-Axel went down as if a stopper had been pulled out, doubled over on the floor and started shaking before he even worked out how to yell. His mouth was opening and closing, and all the colour had left his face. Teresa leaned over him.

'What are you saying? What is it you're trying to say, *Karl-Axel*?'

Something between a squeak and a whisper emerged from Karl-Axel's mouth, and Teresa thought she heard him say, 'Only joking...' She placed her foot on his cheek, pressed his face down on the floor and turned to the others.

'Anyone else feel like joking?'

Nobody volunteered, and Teresa removed her foot. The sole had left a pattern on Karl-Axel's cheek. His body jerked as he pressed his hands to his groin, making inarticulate hissing noises. She looked at him and felt no pleasure. He was just a scared, pathetic little boy, and she actually regretted kicking him quite so hard.

But there was nothing she could do about that. Teresa sat down on the bench and folded her arms, waiting for this minor incident to be over. There would no doubt be more, but she had gone back to her idea about simplicity, and her plans for the day were simple. As soon as someone said or did something derogatory about her, she would kick them. The girls on the shin, the boys on the cock, if possible. That was all.

Several more students arrived, and Karl-Axel was still refusing to get up. Whispered conversations took place as the new arrivals were told what had happened.

Agnes arrived only a minute or so before the lesson was due to begin. By that time Karl-Axel had managed to struggle up into a sitting position, leaning against the lockers. She tilted her head to one side and asked, 'Why are you sitting there?'

Karl-Axel shook his head, and Patrik said, 'Teresa kicked him. Between the legs. Really fucking hard.'

Agnes turned to Teresa with the hint of an ambiguous smile on her lips. At first Teresa thought it was a kind of approval, but when Agnes didn't sit down next to her as usual, she suspected it was just for want of anything else to do.

Teresa's plan succeeded beyond all expectation. Everyone in the class avoided her, but nobody said anything else during the course of the day. Not even Jenny managed to come out with a spiteful comment when Teresa was within earshot. She concentrated on her inner wolf, and remained unmoved.

It was only during the lunch break that her defences wobbled. Nobody came to sit by her, but as she sat there with her lunch she could feel the eyes on her, hear the whispers. What was Dirty Teresa going to do with the food? What was Puky Teresa going to stick in her mouth now?

She looked at her plate, on which two pieces of crumbed fish lay next to four potatoes with a few slices of tomato around the edge. A lump rose from her stomach, stuck in her throat and turned to nausea. She could kick anyone who stood in her way, but she couldn't eat this.

She thought about getting up, going over to the slop bucket, scraping all the food off her plate and leaving the dining room. Everybody laughing behind her back. Oh what fun they would have.

Smoke rose from the plate. The quarry's flank ripped open, the steaming blood meeting the cold air. She cut a piece of potato and bit through the skin. Her jaws tensed as she chewed through muscle and sinew. The dying twitches of the crumbed fish, then the bite that extinguished all life. The red juice of the tomatoes, running down her throat. Not a scrap would be left for the crows.

When she got up and carried her empty plate over to the counter, the white skeleton she handed over had been scraped clean. A successful hunt, a meal which would keep the body alive for the rest of the day. She had won.

And so it went on. Day after day Teresa went to school in her red boots, fearing nothing and no one. Nor did she feel any longing or regret. When she met Micke, she nodded to him and he nodded back. There was nothing to say, and she was done with emotions. They had died along with her childhood, spilt in red pools on a cement floor.

She could have grieved, but did not do so because her emotions had been replaced by *perceptions*. Her senses were at full stretch; liberated from her brain's struggle with itself, Teresa experienced every impression with much greater intensity.

She could walk down corridors and enjoy the murmur of voices behind closed doors, the colours of the cupboards and the walls, the smell of paper, cleaning materials and drying clothes. She could enjoy all the impressions that, taken together, made her a part of the world, someone who was walking around and who was *alive*. Such an obvious fact that she had managed to ignore for fifteen years: she was alive.

Therefore, she did not grieve for what she had lost, but instead rejoiced at what she had gained and what she had become. It was that simple. It may not have showed on the outside, but she was *happy*.

On Tuesday evening she spent a while exchanging emails with Theres, making plans for the weekend's meeting with the other girls. They settled on Sunday at twelve o'clock, but as Jerry was back it couldn't be in Svedmyra. They could meet outdoors, but where? They would give the matter some thought; nothing was decided.

Teresa surfed various sites on wolves, read some new posts on the forum, and ended up on an auction site where someone was selling a wolf skin. The starting price was six hundred kronor; the auction was due to end in a couple of hours, and so far nobody had put in an offer.

She looked at the photograph of the grey pelt, laid out on an ordinary kitchen table. Once upon a time it had been part of a real wolf, the hunter of the forest. Muscles had worked beneath that fur, it had rubbed up against other coats, loped across the snow and howled beneath the stars. If someone bought it, it might end up on the floor in front of a fire, something soft for the kids to sit on.

Without giving it any further thought, Teresa put in a maximum bid of one thousand kronor. Five minutes later she went back and raised it to two thousand. That was all the money she had in her account. She had given the bits of paper from the metal cash box to Theres.

She lay down on her bed and read some Ekelöf. The rapport she had felt when she came out of hospital was no longer there, and she caught herself thinking Ekelöf was *weak*. A weakling. A little worm of a writer. But still. She read these lines several times:

> The silence of the deep night is great
> It is not disturbed by the rustle of the people
> eating one another here on the shore

It was the word 'rustle' she liked. That was all. A rustling sound as flesh is consumed.

She put down the book and lay with her hands behind her head, missing her MP3 player. She didn't like the idea that Max Hansen might be sitting wearing her earphones at this very minute, listening to the songs she and Teresa had made together. She didn't like it at all. It was like knowing there was a pig in the wardrobe, a snout snuffling around among your clean clothes.

Her mobile rang, and when Teresa answered she expected to hear that slimy voice from the depths of the sty, but it was Johannes. After a few introductory phrases he asked how she was, and she said she was absolutely fine.

'It's just that I've got a feeling you're...I don't know, that you're *not there*, kind of.'

'I haven't gone anywhere. I'm here.'

'So why are you avoiding me, then?'

'Am I?'

'Yes, you are. Do you think I haven't noticed?'

'What does it matter? You don't want anything to do with me.'

There was a long sigh at the other end of the phone. Then Johannes said, 'Teresa, just stop that. You're my oldest friend. Don't you remember what we said? That we'd be friends. No matter what.'

Teresa had a strange, rough feeling in her throat, but her voice sounded perfectly normal when she replied, 'We said a lot of things. When we were little.'

'Are you thinking about anything in particular?'

'No.'

Johannes gave a snort, as if he were smiling at some memory. 'I just thought about that time…when we were lying in the cave, do you remember? When we said we were going to be dead?'

The rough feeling in her throat had begun to take on the form of a lump, and Teresa said, 'Listen, I've got things to do.'

'OK. But can't you come over one day, Teresa? It's such a long time since we had a proper chat. And listen, we can play Tekken! I've got a…'

'Bye Johannes. Bye.'

She ended the call. Then she wrapped her arms tightly around her stomach and leaned forward, then down as far as she could until there was a rushing noise in her head and it started to hurt. She straightened up and it flowed away. Her skull emptied as the blood poured back down her body and her anxiety abated.

She tore a sheet of paper into tiny, tiny pieces which she pushed in her mouth and chewed. When the paper had turned into a soggy ball, she spat it out into the waste paper basket. She was grateful that she was alone. Her defences were weak; if anyone had wanted to harm her, this would have been the perfect opportunity.

It was quarter past eleven, and the auction was over. She checked her messages and found an email from the website telling her she had won. No one else had put in a bid, and the wolf skin was hers for six hundred kronor.

She knew exactly what she was going to do with it, and where she was going to suggest for Sunday's meeting.

9

'He wrote. Max Hansen.'

'What did he write?'

'That he knows. About Lennart and Laila. And the room. When I was little. How they ended up dead.'

'So what's he going to do, then?'

'An album. With our songs.'

'No, I mean what's he going to do with what he's found out. About you.'

'Nothing.'

'What? Is that what he wrote, that he's not going to do anything at all?'

'If I don't do anything, he won't do anything. That's what it said.'

They were sitting right at the back of the number 47 bus from Sergels Torg. A few families with children were sitting towards the front, but the seats closest to them were empty. It was the middle of April, and the streams of tourists heading for Djurgården had not yet got under way. Teresa leaned forward, resting her elbows on the full rucksack at her feet as she tried to think.

It was hardly likely to be in Max Hansen's interests to reveal what he knew about Theres; it was just an empty threat.

Or was it?

The girl who grew up in a cellar and turned into a cold-blooded murderer. It was just the kind of story people loved. Teresa had never thought about Theres' story in that way before, but she could see it now. The newspaper screamers. Day after day. A story that would run and run, and plenty of free advertising for the album. Could Max Hansen be such an evil bastard? Could he?

As the bus crossed the bridge Teresa straightened up and took a deep breath, drumming the heels of her boots on the floor. It was pointless to speculate. She would concentrate on what was happening now.

Twelve girls had said they were coming. The youngest was fourteen, the oldest nineteen. Theres had told her a little bit about each of them, but Teresa found it difficult to separate the monosyllabic accounts and link them to the names. Miranda and Beata and Cecilia and two Annas and so on.

She remembered Miranda from that time in the apartment, and Ronja was the name of a girl Theres said had tried to kill herself three times, once by eating glass. That had stuck in Teresa's mind, because it was so extreme. Ronja. No doubt her parents had had something else in mind when they chose the name.

They got off outside Skansen. Teresa heaved the rucksack onto her back and headed for the Solliden entrance. Theres didn't follow her. She was stuck outside the main entrance, gazing up at the sign. When Teresa turned back, Theres asked, 'Is this Skansen?'

'Yes.'

'What is it?'

'A zoo. And some old buildings, that kind of thing. Why do you ask?'

Theres frowned. 'I'm going to sing here.'

'What? Or rather...when? How come?'

'I don't understand. Am I going to sing to the animals?'

Teresa looked at the big, ornate letters above the entrance. She knew there were concerts here sometimes, and so of course...

'Just hang on a minute,' she said. 'When are you going to sing here?'

'In the summer. Max Hansen wrote. Sing Along at Skansen. Good publicity.'

'*You're* performing at Sing Along at Skansen?'

'Yes. Otherwise he'll tell about Lennart and Laila.' Theres' tone of voice altered slightly, and Teresa sensed that she was just regurgitating something Max Hansen had written when she went on, 'Then Jerry will go to prison. I'll end up in the loony bin with all the other nutters. Why am I going to sing to the animals?'

Teresa took off her rucksack and put it on the ground. Then she sat down on it and asked Theres to sit next to her. She took her hand.

'OK,' she said. 'First of all. You're not going to sing to the animals. There'll be people there. Thousands of people. Adults and kids and teenagers. It's shown on TV. Millions of people watch it. That's what it's about, OK? Sing Along at Skansen.'

Theres nodded. Then she shook her head. 'That's not good. A lot of people is not good. I know.'

'No. And secondly. You are not going to end up in a loony bin. And if you do, I'll be coming with you. We're both just as screwed up, OK? Whatever happens to you, happens to me. That's just the way it is. But this business with Max Hansen...I don't know what we're going to do.'

'We'll have to make him dead.'

Teresa laughed. 'I should think he'll be bloody careful around us from now on. But we'll have to think of something.'

'Yes. That's good. Now let go of my hand.'

Teresa didn't let go. When Theres tried to pull away, she held on more tightly. 'Why don't you like it when I take your hand?'

'You're not to take my hand. It's my hand.'

The leap of logic distracted Teresa, and Theres pulled away and stood up. Teresa stayed where she was, looking at her own hands. *Take my hand.* People took things from one another. She was not to take Theres' hand. Of course.

She hoisted up the rucksack again and went ahead of Theres along Sollidsbacken, outside the railings. On the miniature map she had printed off from the internet the distances had looked quite short, but when they reached the Solliden entrance she realised they had almost a kilometre still to go. A bus passed on Djurgårdsvägen; presumably the buses went all the way. She would bear that in mind for next time. If there was a next time.

They turned off onto Sirishovsvägen. Teresa looked at her map, and once they had passed the Bellman gate they walked another hundred metres along the wire fence, peering through the netting.

'They're not here,' said Theres.

Teresa looped her fingers through the wire and slowly scanned the terrain. She had imagine a more open area, but the wolf enclosure was a landscape of trees with new leaves, bushes and stones strewn over hillsides. Their natural environment. She knew there should be seven wolves in there, but there was no sign of any of them.

Her gaze stopped at an oddly shaped rock, and she gasped. It was a block of stone, but its strange shape was due to the fact that there was a wolf lying right on top. It was lying completely still, looking in their direction.

'There,' she said, pointing it out to Theres. 'There.'

Theres stood right next to her, pressing her body against the fence so that she could get as close as possible. They were caught in the wolf's field of vision, and a faint breeze was blowing towards their backs. Presumably the wolf had picked up their scent. Teresa's stomach flipped over. *Right now you're thinking about us. What are you thinking? How do you think?*

They stood there for a long time, clinging to the fence and looking at the wolf looking back at them. They were together. Then the wolf began to lick the fur on its paws, and left them.

'Why are you unhappy?' asked Theres.

Only then did Teresa discover that her eyes were wet, and tears had run down her cheeks.

'I'm not unhappy,' she said. 'I'm happy. Because I've arrived.'

They spread blankets on the ground in front of the wolf enclosure. Before Teresa pulled the wolf skin out of her rucksack, she glanced over at the rock. The wolf had left its post, which was a good thing, because as she placed it in the centre it felt like a kind of blasphemy. As if she were not worthy.

She and Theres sat down on the blankets with their backs to the fence and waited. In the message calling everyone to the meeting, they had explained that Teresa who wrote the lyrics would also be coming. She didn't feel like Teresa who wrote the lyrics. She was a little lone wolf, and a strange pack was moving closer.

'Theres?' she asked. 'Have you played them all the songs?'

'Yes.'

'Have you told them about yourself?'

'Yes.'

'Lennart and Laila and...everything?'

'Yes. Everything.'

It was as she suspected, and there was really only one question she wanted to ask. She was afraid of the question because she was afraid of the answer, but she asked it anyway.

'Theres. What is it that makes me different from them?'

'You came first. You wrote the words.'

'But otherwise we're similar?'

'Yes. Very similar.'

Teresa lowered her head. What had she thought? That she was unique and the only person in the whole world with whom Theres could have contact, the only person who could love Theres? Yes. That's exactly what she had thought, until she walked into Theres' apartment and found the pack gathered. Now she had the final confirmation that she had been an idiot.

Very similar.

The first group of seven girls was approaching from the bus stop. There was *one* consolation to be found in Theres' painful honesty: perhaps the pack wasn't as alien as she had thought. She watched the seven girls, and even from a distance there was already something she recognised in their movements, the way they walked, as if their footsteps might damage the ground.

Teresa undid her boots, pulled the laces tighter and said, 'But they haven't made anyone dead, have they? None of them?'

'No.'

'And do you think they could?'

'Yes. All of them.'

Teresa looked at the little group who had now reached the fence, and her eyes narrowed. A new plan took its first uncertain steps in her brain. Then she waved and smiled.

All of them.

When the girls came over to say hello, Teresa felt *elevated* in a way she had never experienced before. She was treated with respect, as if she were giving an audience. She couldn't help it; she enjoyed it. She had never been the focus of so much positive attention.

They praised certain phrasing or individual lines, some said that her lyrics described exactly how they felt themselves, and that they wished they could write like that. After a few comments in that vein Teresa sought refuge in false modesty, and said that it wasn't really anything special, anyone could have...and so on.

In spite of the fact that the other girls regarded her as an authority, they still spoke the same language. It was a different matter with Theres. They treated her like something made of the finest porcelain, speaking quietly and not daring to touch her. When Theres spoke they listened, their bodies tense with concentration.

What Theres said was nothing remarkable, but of course Teresa knew how it worked. Theres had the ability to say exactly the right thing to the right person, the self-evident truth that that particular person needed, expressed with that elusive, subjugating tone in her voice that made it into more than truth, into The Truth.

After exchanging greetings and chatting for a while, the girls sat down around the wolf skin and immersed themselves in their own thoughts, or ventured some tentative comment.

Teresa hadn't expected it, but when they were all assembled and she looked around the group—how they sat, the way they moved their hands, how they looked—she concluded that she was probably the strongest person there. She had nothing to be afraid of.

On the other hand, she was the one who had known Theres the longest, the one sitting by her side. What would she have been without Theres? A little grey mouse, scurrying along by the wall and trying to be invisible. Maybe. Or maybe not. In any case, she looked at the others with tenderness in her eyes. When little Linn started to look as if she might burst into tears, Teresa felt no jealousy as Theres crept over to her and whispered in her ear until she was calm again.

Apart from Ronja, none of these girls would pick up much support in the voting for prom queen. Several of them were a few kilos overweight, like Teresa, and about half had piercings: lips, nose or eyebrows. Beata's appearance was Asiatic, and she was the only one who seemed to have naturally black hair; both Annas, Linn and Caroline had different-coloured roots.

Only Cecilia was actually fat, and she hid her body in coarse military clothing, but most of the others were dressed in bulky clothes that hid their shape. As for make-up, it covered the entire spectrum—from Melinda, who had birds' wings drawn in pen at the corners of her eyes, to Erika who wasn't wearing any make-up at all, and who was so colourless in general that she was almost invisible. Teresa guessed that hardly any of them were joiners: they wouldn't be members of any club or society.

But Ronja was the exception. She was the oldest in the group at nineteen, and looked like the sporty type: football, probably. She was wearing Adidas trousers and a windbreaker, she was slender and her hair was blonde and straight. A more athletic, socially adept version of Theres. Not the prettiest girl in the class, but a perfectly acceptable candidate to wear the crown. And she was the one who ate glass.

A common denominator united them, and it was probably only Teresa who was aware of it: the *scent* of the girls. They all smelled more or less the same. Hardly any of them used perfume, and those few did so sparingly. But that wasn't the scent they had in common, it was what lay beneath it. Fear.

It had been Teresa's own bodily odour for so many years that she recognised it immediately. She could probably have sniffed her way to each and every one of these girls if they were on the same bus. A bitter, sweetish smell with a hint of flammable liquid. Coca-Cola mixed with petrol.

As the girls shuffled closer to one another and the conversations got going, there was a change in the air around them. The security of the pack made the scent diminish. Their bodies, their skin, ceased to exude fear as the conversations intertwined to form a single, unified melody.

'...and I can feel the whole thing just falling apart...my mum's got a new bloke and I don't like the way he looks at me...they said I couldn't come even if I paid...he came home in the middle of the night and he had a knife...and even though I try my best in every way...shook my little brother and he ended up with brain damage... have to wear earphones all the time so nobody can hear...and when I'm walking along, it's as if it's somebody else walking along...that I was completely worthless, that I had no chance...tried to hide under the bed, which was just so fucking stupid...the music I listen to, my clothes, how I look, everything...that noise, when I hear that noise I know...as if I didn't exist...little tiny pinpricks all the time...just to walk away, leave it all behind...nobody but me...'

Teresa turned towards the enclosure just in time to see the wolf clambering up onto his rock once more, folding its paws in front of it then looking down on the group of girls with its ears pricked, as if it were listening to their conversations. Teresa turned back to the others and pointed.

'That wolf,' she said. 'It's looking at us. It's wondering who we are. Who are we?'

The conversations died away, and they all looked up at the grey figure lying calmly watching them. Judging by the size, Teresa guessed it was a female.

'Because we are something, aren't we?' she went on. 'Together we are something, although we don't know what it is yet. Do you feel it too?'

While the girls were talking, Theres had sat there humming quietly to herself, but now the humming turned into words, flowing out of her mouth like a song. Her gaze was turned inwards, and her hands hovered in front of her as if she were carrying out some complex invocation of which her voice was a part. In a second they were all swept up in its rhythm, and several of the girls began to sway in time with the melody of her speech.

'All those who are afraid must stop being afraid. No one has done wrong. No one will be alone. The big people want us. They will not have us. I do not understand. But we are strong now. I do not understand we. We. We. I am small. We are not small. We are the red that comes out. We are what they want. No one will be allowed to touch us.'

When the flow of words ceased, there was absolute silence, and all the girls sat gazing into space with unseeing eyes. Then the silence was broken by a muted clapping. It was Ronja, bringing her palms together three times, applauding.

Teresa pulled the wolf skin towards her and took the plate shears out of her rucksack. She cut a strip off the skin and gave it to Linn, who whispered, 'Thank you,' and rubbed the coarse fur over her cheek. Teresa carried on cutting and handing out strips until everyone had a piece. Some put it in their pocket, but most sat stroking the grey, dense hair as if it really was a body they held in their hands.

'From now on,' said Teresa, 'we are the pack. Anyone who harms one of us, harms us all.'

The girls nodded and stroked the wolf skin they now shared. Suddenly Ronja laughed out loud. She rocked back and forth, howling with laughter and waving the strip of skin around. Teresa looked at her, listened to the sound of her laughter and recognised something from her time in the psychiatric unit, from the other inmates. Ronja was a combination of letters, a diagnosis. She had some kind of mental illness that Teresa couldn't put a name to.

When Ronja had finished laughing, she kissed the piece of skin several times, then knotted it around her arm with the help of her teeth before turning to Teresa.

'You said just now that we are something, although we don't know what it is yet. I can tell you what we are. We're a gang of losers who like your songs. And we're dangerous. Seriously fucking dangerous.'

10

Over the next few weeks the group tried to find its direction. Apart from Theres and Teresa's songs, there wasn't much that linked them, no interest or activity on which to focus. They only thing they had was the feeling of necessity, the sense that they needed to meet and be together, but in every other way they were a drifting pack with no definite goal.

All of them wanted to be close to Theres. A contradictory mixture of the urge to defend and take care of this fragile girl, and the urge to venerate and fear her as something sent from heaven. They thirsted for her words, her voice when she occasionally sang, her mere presence.

And they thirsted for each other. Gradually they all spoke of the scent Teresa had been aware of during their first meeting. This was the only group where they felt safe. The fear that ruled their everyday lives faded away when they sat down together.

Teresa had begun to regard these Sunday gatherings as her real life, and the group as her family. The other days of the week were merely incidental; she longed constantly for the weekend when she would be with *her family.*

And yet there was something missing. Ronja said they were more like an encounter group than a pack. They all had their piece of wolf skin, some had even sewn it on their jackets, but where was this pack actually going, what was it going to *do*?

The third time they met, Linn, who had begun to pluck up

the courage to speak, told them that she sometimes pretended she was dead. She mentioned it in passing, but struck an unexpected chord. It turned out that they had found a very clear common denominator. *All of them*, every single one of the girls, played that particular game.

So they began to play it together. Lying on the grass outside the wolf enclosure, they held each other's hands, closed their eyes and whispered chants such as: 'The grass is growing through our hearts', 'Our bodies are rotting and the worms are eating us from the inside', 'We are sinking through the earth and all is silent'. They could lie like that for a long time, and when they rose from their graves it was as if the world had become more alive.

Theres said it was good, but not right. When Teresa asked what she meant, the reply was that Teresa already knew.

Yes. She knew. But it was not the kind of knowledge she could share with the others. Irrespective of how much she valued their affinity, she dared not trust them in the same unconsidered way that Theres did.

Teresa would have liked to tell them, talk about her own experience and show them the scar on her stomach. How she had come to life and how her senses had been heightened, how ever since she had lived in a *present* that had not been accessible before. How this allowed her to sit in the group and really be there, to leave the group and still feel the quiver of life in the rustle of the leaves, the smell of exhaust fumes and the play of colours.

But she dared not tell them. The others were not in the same place as her. When they met it always took a while before they found their common voice, before the fear was driven out. The other six days of the week were stuck firmly to them, and in spite of everything they were just other people with parents and classmates.

So difficult to stay alive! She often thought about it, and remembered what she had been like. Never really *there*. She had caught sight of herself only in fleeting glimpses between her troubles and her thoughts, as someone who breathes and lives and can experience the moment. Then it was gone.

So different now. Teresa would have liked to tell them. But it was too dangerous. Yet.

THE DEAD GIRLS

1

The album that was released in the middle of May was a bit of a hotch-potch. Because they wanted to surf the wave created by 'Fly', the producer, the musicians and the studio techs had only a couple of weeks to create a finished product from the bare MP3 files.

Max Hansen tried both the carrot and the stick to get Theres into the studio so that her singing could be professionally recorded. He promised five- and six-figure sums, he threatened her with the police, psychiatric care and throwing her to the ravening dogs of the media, but it was no use. Either his threats were transparent, or she was incapable of grasping the misery he could unleash on her head.

He thought it was probably the former. Either Theres or the freak realised he couldn't reveal what he knew without implicating himself. Oh, he was ready to do that, but he wanted to wait for the right moment. The moment when he was a long way away from Stockholm, and his only problem was where the money would get the best return.

Despite the fact that the album had been a rush job, it was enthusiastically received. Not one reviewer failed to comment on the poor sound quality; but on the other hand Tesla's voice had a tone and a timbre that made up for the defects. The production also left a great deal to be desired, but there too the technical aspects were counterbalanced by the quality of the songs. There was no doubt whatsoever that this Tesla, whoever she might be, was a new artist to be reckoned with.

Given what Max Hansen had found out about Theres, he dared not meet her without other people present, but he couldn't get hold of her by phone or email. Therefore it was impossible to arrange any interviews or photo shoots.

However, just a few days after the album had been released, he came to realise that what he had thought was a weakness was in fact a strength. There was a huge appetite for information about this new star in the Swedish music firmament, but none was forthcoming. Just when Max Hansen had begun to draw up strategies to create fake quotes and interviews, he noticed the change of tone in what was being written about Tesla.

Her silence was interpreted as seriousness, and her absence from the public arena was seen as enigmatic. After an article in *Aftonbladet* which interwove acclaim for Tesla as the great new hope for Swedish music with unabashed speculation about her, other newspapers jumped on the bandwagon. The clips from *Idol* were analysed and pronounced magical, Tora Larsson's terse responses were interpreted and commented upon. Journalists turned and twisted what they knew, and got nowhere; and the result was a genuine mystique surrounding Tesla. Something exciting.

Max Hansen couldn't have timed the whole thing any better if he had planned it. It was a three-stage rocket. First the speculation, then Sing Along at Skansen, then...the bomb. A week or so after Sing Along he would drop the bomb, and if that didn't boost the already-high sales figures, then he didn't know what would.

But there was a defect in the rocket's construction.

Tesla's appearance at Skansen was set for June 26; she was appearing on the same bill as The Ark. Everything was poised for success, and Max Hansen had emailed her all the information. All sorted except for one small point: he had no idea whether she was intending to turn up.

Swedish Television had been after him for her details so that they could contact her directly, but Max Hansen had referred to the girl's well-known shyness, and said that all communication was to go through him, and that he could guarantee that she would be there for both the rehearsals and the show, no problem.

But in fact: mucho problem.

The uncertainty gnawed away at him, and Max Hansen began to consider desperate measures.

2

Insofar as it is possible to become a different person from the one we are born, Jerry came home from the USA a different person. His focus on the future had changed, his view of the past had changed, and for once he had not been kicked in a new direction, but had taken the step himself.

It happened on the third day of his visit. Paris' parents lived in a small house on the outskirts of Miami, and Jerry, Paris and Malcolm had gone shopping at a Wal-Mart that made the Flygfyren complex in Norrtälje look like a sausage stall. If the car park had been emptied of vehicles, it would probably have been possible to land a plane on it.

It was unusually humid for April. Paris had told him this was nothing compared to summer, but for Jerry it felt positively tropical. A pressure grew in his skull as they pushed their way among the crowds in the air-conditioned shopping mall, and when they emerged into the car park with their over-stuffed bags and the heat hit them, Jerry was overcome by dizziness.

The car was parked several hundred metres from the entrance, and as they walked across the vast expanse beneath the blazing sun, his legs gave way. The bags landed on the asphalt and he fell to his knees. He bent down, clutching his head with his hands as the sweat poured down his back. He was embarrassed, but he just couldn't get up. It felt like a failure, a confirmation of what a pathetic specimen he was.

Paris' parents had welcomed him, and he had almost managed to forget that he had let Theres down in order to make the trip possible.

He felt bad about leaving her alone, but there had been no alternative. He just had to go with Paris. Now, down on his knees on the burning asphalt, it was as if God had punished him. Struck him over the head with his sun club in order to bring him to his knees and make him realise what a shit he was.

He felt Malcolm's arms around him, the weight of the child's body against his back as the boy embraced him from behind and shouted, 'Jerry, Jerry, what's the matter? Please get up Jerry, please!'

The thin, anxious voice cooled him down a little and he looked up in time to see Paris bend down and caress his cheek. The sun was directly behind her head, and made her black hair shine like a halo as she said, 'Darling, what happened? Are you OK?'

Jerry straightened up. He was still on his knees squinting into the sun as he looked into Paris' eyes. The words that came out of his mouth needed no thought:

'Paris, will you marry me?'

'Yes.'

'What did you...what?'

'Yes. When you get up off your knees we can go find the priest, if that's what you want.'

Jerry gradually managed to get to his feet, but Paris hadn't been serious about going to find the priest right away. Yes, she wanted to marry him, but she wanted a proper wedding. If she had said she only wanted to marry him as long as it was on top of Mount Everest dressed in deep sea diving gear, Jerry would have started investigating the possibilities. A proper wedding was a piece of cake.

When they got back to Sweden they started making plans, and they decided to get married in Miami in the middle of July, because Paris was the one who had family. It was fun to think about, but basically it was nothing more than a technicality. The key thing had happened in the car park outside Wal-Mart.

Jerry had been down for the count several times in his life; he knew what it meant to be on his knees in both a physical and mental sense. But no one had ever put their arms around him and said *Please get up Jerry, please* with genuine anxiety in their voice. And no one had ever caressed his cheek, called him darling and asked him if he was OK. No one had ever actually cared whether he got up or not.

But the miracle had happened in that blazing car park, and how could it not change him? There was a future that looked bright, and when he thought about his murky past, there was a point to it after all, because it had led him to *now*.

If Ingemar Stenmark's race hadn't interrupted his performance on the guitar, perhaps he wouldn't have got so lost in his teens, and then perhaps he wouldn't have been interested in Theres. If Theres hadn't been found and hadn't killed his parents, then she wouldn't have been living with him. If he hadn't played the guitar, if he hadn't found that wallet, if Theres hadn't been so violent...in the end everything had led to Paris and his collapse in the car park. And so it was all good.

Perhaps his new-found happiness made him take the difficulties with Theres less than seriously, but it seemed as if she too had sorted herself out. She was communicating with her friends, and seemed to be adapting to a more normal life.

The only cloud on Jerry's horizon was Max Hansen. A week or so after Jerry got back from the USA, Hansen was on him like a leech, trying to force Theres into the studio. Jerry discovered that Max Hansen was aware of Theres' background, because he used it as a threat. Jerry asked Theres if she wanted to sing in the studio again, and she said no. Max Hansen refused to take no for an answer, and Jerry changed to an unlisted phone number.

The album still came out, and Jerry entertained many evil thoughts about Max Hansen when the telephone started to ring despite the unlisted number. Journalists asked about Tesla or Tora Larsson, and Jerry said he had no idea what they were talking about. After five calls he unplugged the phone, threw it in the bin and got himself a mobile with a pre-paid card.

At the end of May Jerry received an envelope. It contained ten one-thousand-kronor notes, and a letter which explained in an aggressive tone that he would get another twenty thousand if he could just guarantee that Theres would turn up at Skansen on the morning of June 26. It would be in his best interests to contact Max Hansen immediately to confirm that he would take care of the matter, otherwise things could get very nasty indeed.

Jerry put the ten thousand kronor away for the wedding, and asked Theres what she wanted to do. She said she didn't know, and he had to be satisfied with that. What else was he supposed to do? Shove Theres in a sack and carry her off to Skansen? The only thing he could do was keep his fingers crossed, say a prayer and hope for the best.

These days his contact with Theres was mostly limited to practical matters. She had her own life and he had his. He made sure there was baby food in the fridge, and he paid the bills. Apart from that she had to look after herself, while he spent more and more time at home with Paris and Malcolm.

Jerry was so far gone in his new, positive attitude to the world that he didn't even think twice when he heard by chance at the end of May that the man who used to run the local shop had been robbed and murdered. It was just a tragic story that for once had nothing to do with him.

3

Just about a week after the album was released, Teresa got an email from Max Hansen. The message said, 'Read these and think carefully. June 26. Confirm.'

Attached were a number of newspaper articles about Lennart and Laila, a copy of the estate inventory showing Jerry as the heir, the ID information on Angelika Tora Larsson, and a copy of Theres' application form for *Idol*.

Max Hansen wanted to show that he had everything stitched up, and even though it didn't come as a surprise that he knew what he knew, it had the desired effect. The very thought that he could ruin their entire lives with one click of the mouse was abhorrent, and for the first time Teresa was really frightened. She sent a long message to Theres, going through various scenarios and weighing up their options, and came to the conclusion that it would probably be best if Theres said that she would perform at Skansen. At least that would buy them the time until then to come up with something.

The *something* was a given. The problem was how they could get close enough to Max Hansen to carry it out, then get away without being discovered. Teresa was filled with longing. The man in the shop had been thrown into her path, she had done what she had done and hadn't felt good about it until afterwards. Max Hansen was a different matter altogether. She was looking forward to it, and this time she was going to enjoy it from beginning to end. If she got the chance.

Her fingers had begun to itch in an unpleasant way, and from time to time she had a hungry feeling in her stomach. Her awareness of life had begun to be sullied by images forcing themselves on her unannounced. She could become fixated by the back of someone's head on the bus, imagining a tool in her hand, yearning to strike a blow. When she was alone in the library with the librarian one afternoon, she worked out ways of killing her. Ask for some unusual book, follow her down to the storeroom. A brick, a length of pipe. Bang on the head, bang again. Again. Open. And then the red smoke, to taste it, to get close again.

She had continued to throw away three Fontex tablets a day, picked up a new prescription and carried on throwing them away. She had been for follow-up meetings at the psychiatric unit and had played her role effectively; they felt she was so well she ought to be able to come off her medication by the summer.

But she knew that her normal behaviour was nothing to do with being 'well' in the usual sense of the word. She was secure and harmonious, yes. She was happy with both herself and her life, yes. So far so good, ticking the boxes on the psychiatrist's list. But the *reason* for her excellent results was something only she and Theres knew about. The fact that she was a murderer, that she was a wolf, that she had cast normal human considerations aside.

If she had explained all this in the doctor's pleasant office, she would have been locked up for the foreseeable future rather than being pronounced more or less fit and well. Teresa knew that she was not well in the conventional meaning of the word, but she was perfectly fine on her own terms, and that was what mattered.

The problem was...the abstinence.

It got so bad that she could sit at the kitchen table watching Olof shovelling down sandwiches as he read some games magazine, and she would find herself studying the back of his neck, glancing from his hairline to the marble rolling pin and back again. One day when Maria wasn't very well and spent the day at home on the sofa listening to old Dean Martin records, Teresa stood gazing at her mother, lying there with her eyes closed, as her fingers caressed the knob on the end of the poker.

That kind of thing.

Regardless of how good Teresa was feeling these days, and regardless of the fact that Dean Martin was singing that you couldn't go to jail for what you were *thinking*, she would have liked to pass on these particular fantasies. But they forced their way in, and she couldn't shake them off.

When Teresa picked Theres up in Svedmyra four days after Max Hansen's message, they still hadn't come to any decisions. It was just two weeks until June 26, and Teresa had checked the news on the internet every morning, fearing that Max Hansen would have gone public with what he knew. It hadn't happened yet, but the feeling in Teresa's stomach told her it wouldn't be much longer.

They talked on the subway and they talked on the bus to Djurgården. Whispering, because there were a lot more people now than when they had come out here the first time. Their conclusion was that they would say yes to Max Hansen. Whether Theres would actually turn up on the day was another matter. Teresa certainly had no intention of being Max Hansen's mouthpiece and trying to persuade her.

As usual they had turned up a while before the others, and as they approached the place near the wolf enclosure they could see three men sitting there. On previous occasions other people had got there before them, and the entire group would then use the simple and effective method of staring at the intruders until they moved away.

The men were in their twenties, and had no blankets, beer or musical equipment with them, so Teresa presumed it wouldn't be too long before they left. For the time being she and Theres spread the blankets out a little further up, sat down and carried on talking.

Three shadows fell over their spot. They had been so absorbed in their conversation that they hadn't noticed the three men coming over. As soon as Teresa looked up at them she could see that something was wrong, in spite of the fact that the light was behind them, and immediately afterwards came the scent, clear and unmistakable: *threat*.

All three men were standing with their hands in the pockets of baggy tracksuit tops, and they had arranged themselves so that Theres and Teresa were trapped between them and the fence.

The one in the middle crouched down. Beneath his thin trousers Teresa could see the contours of pumped-up leg muscles; his upper arms were as thick as her thighs.

'Hi,' he said, nodding at Theres. 'You're Tesla, aren't you?'

Theres, who appeared completely unmoved by the attitude of the men, nodded and came out with her usual response, 'We. I sing. Teresa writes the words.'

'Yeah, right.' said the man. 'Because you're such a pretty girl.' He nudged Teresa's shoulder, as if she were something in his way. 'Why would you bother with a bag of spanners like her otherwise?'

'I don't understand,' said Theres.

'No. It does look that way, like you don't really get it.'

'What do you want?' said Teresa. 'Get lost. We haven't done anything to you.'

The man pointed at Teresa. 'You. Shut the fuck up. It's her I'm talking to.' He gestured to one of the other men, who came and crouched down next to Teresa, while the first man went over to Theres.

The man who was now so close to Teresa that she could smell the mouthwash on his breath held up his big hands, showing her the weapons at his disposal. He looked less than intelligent, bordering on mentally challenged, and Teresa had no doubt that he did exactly as he was told. Out of the corner of her eye she could see some of the other girls approaching, but they were some distance away.

'You sing well,' said the first man, towering over Theres. He pointed into Skansen. 'And you're going to sing here in a couple of weeks, aren't you?' When Theres didn't reply, he said it again, but with greater emphasis. '*Aren't you?*'

When the men first came over Teresa had quickly considered the possibility that they had something to do with Max Hansen, then dismissed the idea as being too over the top. But it was actually true. He had found himself some muscle to carry out what his written threats had failed to achieve.

When Theres still didn't reply, the man grabbed her under the arms and lifted her with no effort, pinning her up against the fence with her face on a level with his, her feet dangling several centimetres off the ground. Teresa tried to get up, but her gorilla placed his heavy hands on her shoulders, pressing her down while snorting as if he were calming a horse. The girls had broken into a run, but they were still at least a hundred metres away.

The first man pulled Theres closer, then thrust her back against the fence, making the wire netting rattle. *'Aren't you?'* Theres drew back her lips, exposing her gums, and the man laughed. 'Growl as much as you want—are you going to do as you're told, or what? I need an answer!'

He shook Theres so that her head banged against the fence. Tears of rage scalded Teresa's eyes as she scratched the gorilla's arms: she was making no more impression than a swarm of midges. She would have kicked, screamed, fought to the very last drop of blood, *and she couldn't even get to her feet*. It was unbearable.

'Yes!' she yelled. 'Yes! She'll be there! Leave her alone! Let go of her!'

The man who was holding Theres nodded. 'I want to hear it from you, little girl. I'm asking you nicely—now are you going to do what you've been asked to do?'

The two Annas, Miranda, Cecilia and Ronja had arrived. The third man walked towards them, his arms raised. 'OK, OK. Let's just stay here girls, nice and calm now.'

Ronja aimed a kick at his kneecap, but he kept his balance, grabbed hold of her and threw her down on the grass. The other four stood irresolute, staring at Theres who nodded and said, 'Yes. I'll sing.' Two seconds later her teeth had closed on her attacker's eyebrow.

His roar brought everything to a stop. His friends, completely paralysed, followed what was happening over by the fence with their mouths agape. The man spun around as if he were dancing with Theres, at the same time trying to push her away. When he succeeded it was at the expense of a few grams of body weight. Theres spat something out of her mouth and blood poured down into the man's eye as he held her at arm's length.

He bellowed like an injured animal, and hurled Theres at the fence with all his strength. She bounced against the wire and fell head first on the ground. As the man gathered himself to deliver a kick to her stomach, the one who had been holding on to Teresa shouted, 'We weren't supposed to hurt her!'

The man came to his senses, pressed one hand to his injured eyebrow and contented himself with tipping Theres over onto her back with the toe of his shoe, whereupon he grabbed hold of her crotch with his other hand and hissed, 'You need to be bloody careful from now on. I might come back and play with you again one of these days!'

Then they left. They were followed by curses and empty threats, mainly from Ronja and Teresa, but they left. All the girls gathered around Theres, whose lip had split. Her mouth was smeared with a mixture of blood and saliva, and no matter how she struggled, a billowing mass of arms and hands covered her, stroking and wiping and supporting. Only when she put her arms over her head and shouted, 'Stop touching me!' were the helpful limbs withdrawn, and the girls stood with their hands empty, not knowing what to do with them.

'Fuck!' said Ronja. 'Fucking hell, fuck fuck fuck! There were *more* of us!'

She ripped off a low-hanging branch and started whipping the tree trunk as curses poured from her lips and her body jerked as if she were having a fit. Teresa thought she might flip into real hysteria, but after a minute or so she threw down the branch, hit herself on the head with clenched fists a few times, then lowered her hands and exhaled.

The rest of the girls had arrived, and they all stood around with their heads lowered during Ronja's outburst, some of them stroking their piece of wolf skin as if to console something within themselves, to apologise. When Ronja came and sat down on the blanket, her hands still shaking, Teresa said, 'OK?'

Several times they had discussed spending a whole weekend together, and now it had become absolutely essential. They could talk and identify themselves with wolves as much as they liked, but when it really mattered they had not acted as a pack, but had splintered into individual, frightened little people. It could not be allowed to happen again.

Beata's parents had a little place in the forest outside Åkersberga. They wouldn't be going out there until July, and Beata knew where the key was. The problem was that it was a good five kilometres from the nearest bus stop. However, it turned out that both Anna L and Ronja had passed their driving test, and that Anna actually had a car.

None of the others had thought of themselves as the kind of group where someone had a driver's licence, but when it turned out to be the case, a heady feeling of liberation quickly took hold. They had a place to be, they had a way of getting there. Together they had resources and opportunities which they lacked when they were alone.

Teresa was sitting as close to Theres as possible without touching her while the others made plans for the coming weekend. Times, food, sleeping bags and so on. Theres seemed unmoved by the incident with the men, and only her swollen lower lip bore witness to the fact that something had happened. She didn't join in the discussion until the question of food came up. The girls were discussing pasta and yoghurt when Theres said, 'I don't eat that kind of food.'

As usual, the slightest utterance from Theres brought all conversation to a halt. Everyone turned to her, some with an embarrassed expression as if they were ashamed of having forgotten about her for a few minutes.

Cecilia asked, 'So...what do you eat, then?'

'Stuff in jars. It's called Semper. And Nestlé.'

'You mean like…baby food? Why do you eat baby food?'

'I'm little.'

'We'll sort it,' said Teresa. 'No problem.'

There was a brief silence as the group digested this new information. Then Linn looked around and stated with unusual firmness, 'In that case, we'll all eat the same thing.'

Some laughed with relief at this elegant way of slicing through a knotty problem, and the planning took another direction. What flavours, what size jars, how many, and who could do the shopping?

By the time they parted, everything was decided. The following Friday afternoon they would take the subway, the Roslagen line, then the number 621 bus to Grandalsvägen in Åkersberga. Then Anna L would run a shuttle service in her car to transport them to the cottage next to Lake Trastsjön. They would bring sleeping bags and bedrolls, they were going to eat baby food for two days and they were going to become a real pack.

The other girls waved as they headed for the bus stop, leaving Theres and Teresa sitting on the blankets. Teresa went for a little walk, found the lump of flesh Theres had bitten out of the man's eyebrow, and ground it into the soil with the sole of her boot. Then she sat down again.

'Will it be OK?' she asked. 'Next weekend?'

'Yes,' said Theres. 'It's good. They will stop being afraid. Like you.'

Teresa had to wait for a long time before Theres turned to look at the wolf enclosure, and couldn't see what she was doing. She quickly leaned over and kissed her on the cheek.

'Sorry,' she said. 'Thanks.'

4

Everyone is actually called something else.

On the Tuesday evening before school broke up, Teresa stood in front of the bathroom mirror trying to find her other name. She had grown up as Teresa, heard people say it to her thousands of times. But was that really her *name*?

She had thought about it before, but it had come back to her when Johannes rang a couple of hours earlier. Once again he maintained that she was behaving very strangely, that he could tell something was wrong, and couldn't they meet? He had used the name *Teresa* over and over again until Teresa felt as if the person he was talking to was a complete stranger. It was no longer her. However, she put the phone down with a horrible feeling that he was right. That she had lost herself, gone astray. Or rather: that this *Teresa* he was talking to had lost herself. But was she actually Teresa any more? Was that her name?

Those were her thoughts as she stood in front of the mirror, studying her face and searching for a clue. She thought her eyes had hardened, literally. As if the eyeball was no longer a jelly-like lump filled with fluid, but was made of glass, hard and impenetrable.

'You are weird,' she said to herself. 'You are hard. You are weird. And hard.'

She liked the words. She wanted to be those words, wanted them to fit her like her boots, to wrap themselves tightly around her like her boots and become her.

'My words. Weird. Hard. Words. Hard. Weird.'

Urd. Urd.

Her body said yes, in spite of the fact that she didn't remember. Where had she heard the word before? Was it a name? She went to the computer and opened Wikipedia.

Urd. The original and possibly the only goddess of fate in Norse mythology. One of the three Norns. With her sisters she would spin and cut the threads of life, and her name came from the Icelandic word for unlucky fate.

Everyone is actually called something else. I am called Urd.

This wasn't something she intended to tell other people, and she wasn't going to try to get them to use it. But within herself she would know. Just as the boots fitted themselves to her feet and enabled her to walk firmly and steadily, so the name would anchor her inside, and would consume all her uncertainty.

'Urd!'

On Wednesday she got through the end-of-term celebrations with her eyes wide open, and yet firmly closed. The summer dresses and chirruping voices, the off-key singing, the odd tear at the thought of saying goodbye for the summer—none of it had anything to do with her.

It had nothing to do with Urd, and she did not see it. Her thoughts were with the pack.

5

On Friday afternoon Teresa went over to Svedmyra to collect Theres. Some of the others joined them on the subway, and more of the girls were waiting at the bus stop. By the time they got on the 621 only Malin and Cecilia were missing.

After they had exchanged a few texts, everything went according to plan. Anna L came and picked them up a few at a time. Her little car was so rusty it was almost impossible to talk while they were travelling, because there were holes in both the silencer and the floor. Anna yelled that she had bought it on the internet for three thousand.

What Teresa had imagined when Beata said her parents had a little place in the forest couldn't have been further removed from reality. The house, tucked in among fir trees, might once have been a cottage but it had been renovated and extended so many times that it was more like a mansion—albeit an oddly proportioned and over-decorated one. The closest neighbour was half a kilometre away, and on the slope leading down to the lake all the trees had been felled and the stumps removed to create a lake view thirty metres wide, leading down to a jetty.

While Ronja took the car to pick up Malin and Cecilia, who had come on the next bus, the others went exploring with Beata. An old garage had been converted into a workshop with two carpentry benches, and Beata explained that her father spent most of his time there in the summer. Hence the over-the-top ornate carving on the outside of the house. Her father could devote an entire week to making a spectacularly ugly frieze just to avoid spending time with her mother.

When they came out of the workshop Teresa spotted a half-rotten door that seemed to have been thrown away on a slope, and to be disappearing gradually into the ground. She went over and saw that although there was moss growing around the rusty handle, it actually was a door, because it was surrounded by a frame.

'The root cellar,' said Beata. 'Spooky.'

Theres had come over, and when Teresa started to tug at the handle, she helped. They had to struggle to rip out the grass that had taken root in the rotting wood, but eventually they managed to open the door and a chilly breath of earth, iron and decay came at them from underground. Without any hesitation Theres walked down three steps and disappeared in the darkness.

'Theres?' shouted Teresa. 'What are you doing?'

There was no reply, so Teresa swallowed and went down the steps through an opening that was so low she had to crouch. The temperature dropped by several degrees, and when she had got through the opening and her eyes had begun to grow accustomed to the gloom, she saw that she was in a surprisingly large room. She could stand up straight, and each wall was at least two metres away.

From the darkest corner she heard Theres say, 'This is good.'

Teresa took a step in the direction of the voice, and eventually she was able to make out Theres, sitting on a low wooden box with her back to the wall. The box was rectangular; Teresa sat down next to her, looking over towards the opening and the world outside, which suddenly seemed far away.

'What do you mean, good?' she asked.

'You know.'

They could hear the voices of the others in the other world as one by one they descended into the cold, musty room. As soon as they were in they started speaking in whispers. Sofie had a small LED on her keyring, and swept the blue light slowly around the space.

The stone walls were damp and a few rotting tools lay in a heap in the corner nearest the door, their iron parts rusting. The earth floor had been flattened and here and there some kind of white sprouts were sticking up, which Teresa found disgusting. Apart from that, she thought the room was...good. Very good.

When Sofie shone the light on the box Theres was sitting on, Teresa noticed that the entire front was covered in faded red letters that said, WARNING! EXPLOSIVE MATERIAL! Her stomach flipped and she asked Beata, 'Is there dynamite or something in here?'

'No,' said Beata, 'unfortunately. It used to have potatoes in it. Ages ago. Before that, I don't know.'

Teresa wrinkled her nose. A minor disappointment. Not that she had any definite plans, but the very thought of having explosives at her disposal was appealing. Miranda seemed to share her feelings because she said, 'Shit, that's a shame. Just imagine if we'd had some dynamite.'

There was silence for a while, and they stood together in the darkness surrounded by the smell of mould, each thinking privately of the use they could make of something that could blow everything to kingdom come. Then they heard Ronja's voice from up above.

'Hey, where is everybody?'

A minute or so later, Ronja, Malin and Cecilia were down in the cellar as well. They had all arrived. Teresa closed her eyes, feeling the presence of the others' bodies around her, the breathing and the small noises, the beat of their pulses and the shared scent that drove the musty smell away. She took a deep breath through her nose and straightened her back. Theres said, 'Close the door.'

Teresa expected protests. *Cold, horrible, scared of the dark* and so on, but none came. She didn't know whether it was because they had all been seized by that same feeling of immediacy and togetherness, or because Theres had said it. But nobody raised any objections as Anna S and Malin pooled their strength to pull the heavy door shut, and suddenly it was pitch dark. Teresa opened and closed her eyes, but there was no difference.

Yes. There was one difference. When they had been sitting in total darkness for a minute or so, it was as if the others' bodies moved even closer, so close that they began to dissolve and flow through her. She could hear them, she could feel them, she could taste them, and in the enclosed darkness they became like one body, several hundred kilos of flesh waiting, breathing.

'We are the dead,' said Theres, and an almost inaudible gasp went through the mass as every heart stopped and listened. She had said it. Now it was true.

'We are in the darkness. We are beneath the earth. No one can see us. We do not exist. Little One is here. Little One came from the earth. Little One was given eyes. And a mouth. Little One could sing. Little One became dead. And lived again. Little One is here. Death is not here.'

When Theres had uttered the final words everyone let out a long breath together. Teresa got up and made her way through the bodies. When she reached the door she had to brace her back against it to push it open. Sunlight poured in.

One by one the girls emerged, blinking in the gentle evening light. They looked at each other, saying nothing, drifting off in different directions or gathering in small groups. Five minutes or so passed.

Then it was as if a slow, rolling wave moved through the air, reaching them one by one. Happiness. Linn found some early wild strawberries and started threading them on a blade of grass. Soon several of the others began to do the same thing. Ronja found a football that was virtually deflated, and she, Anna L and Sofie started to play, passing it to one another. And so on.

Teresa sat on a chopping block watching them. She had almost forgotten Theres until she saw her come up from the cellar and peer across at the others. Teresa went over.

'Hi.'

Theres didn't respond. Her eyes were dark, and she was not squinting because of the light; her eyes were narrowed in disapproval.

'What's the matter?' asked Teresa.

'They don't understand.'

'What is it they don't understand?'

'You know.'

Teresa nodded slowly. She was standing beside Theres. She was the one who had the knowledge. That was the way it should be. Unfortunately it wasn't true.

'No,' she said. 'I don't know, actually. I thought it was terrific when we were down in the cellar together. You did something. Something happened.'

'Yes,' said Theres, looking at the other girls as they raced around. 'Together. Not now. Not Cecilia. Not Ronja. Not Linn. Not Malin...' She kept going until she had listed every single name, and finished off with, 'Not you.'

'So what do you think we should do now, then?'

'Come with me.'

Theres turned and went back down into the cellar. Teresa followed her.

When they went into the house a while later, the others had unpacked the baby food and sorted the jars into groups according to content. Vegetable puree was the most popular, but nobody was very keen on meat with dill, and they pretended to quarrel over the jars as spoons criss-crossed so that everyone could try the different flavours.

They were sitting in a circle on the floor and Teresa joined them, while Theres went and sat alone at the kitchen table, opened a jar of beef stew and stuck her spoon in it without a word. The cheerful atmosphere ebbed away and everybody kept glancing at Theres, who shovelled down the khaki coloured slop until she had emptied two jars, her face completely expressionless.

Even Teresa, who had sat with Theres in the cellar and talked until they shared the same conviction, couldn't understand her behaviour. She had never seen Theres like this in the group, and was just about to pass on what she had said when Theres exploded.

She got to her feet, picked up a baby-food jar in each hand, and hurled them at the wall. When Beata said, 'Hey—' Theres *screamed*, letting out one single, piercingly clear note. It was like having a dentist's drill thrust into your ears, and everyone curled up, their arms over their heads. Theres' voice jumped up an octave until the frequency sliced through flesh and made the bones vibrate. The girls just sat there, curled up, rigid with tension as they waited for it to stop.

The scream broke off abruptly, and the silence that followed was almost as unpleasant. The girls lowered their arms and saw Theres sitting at the kitchen table once more, staring at them as silent tears rolled down her cheeks. None of them dared go over to comfort her.

Slowly Theres got up from the table, pulled open a drawer containing tools, and selected an awl. She stood in front of them and drove it into her right arm with such force that it stuck fast. She pulled it out and blood welled up. When she put the awl in her right hand and squeezed it, her palm was already sticky and red. She drove the awl into her left arm, showed it to them and pulled it out again. At no point did her expression change. Only the tears continued to flow.

Perhaps her vocal cords had been damaged by that high-pitched scream. When she spoke her voice seemed impossibly deep for her slender body.

'You don't understand,' she said. 'I can't feel it.'

She put down the awl and went outside.

The girls stayed where they were on the floor. Someone picked up a jar that had fallen over, someone dropped a spoon, and those who had started crying because Theres was crying gently dried their tears. Teresa picked up their scent, and the scent was shame. They were all ashamed and did not know why, did not understand what they had done wrong.

Teresa put her jar of apricot puree down on the floor and got up. 'I'll go and help her.'

Someone in the group whispered, 'But how?'

'There's something we're going to do.'

When she got outside Theres was already on her way back from the garden shed with a spade. They passed one another without speaking, and in the shed Teresa found another spade, which she took round to the front of the house, to the grassy slope leading down to the water.

The sun had set but was resting just below the horizon, and the sky was pale violet as they drove their spades into the ground and began to dig. Theres' arms and hands were bright with half-dried blood; there was a sticky sound as she let go of the spade and grabbed hold of it again, and the effort made the blood start welling up once more from the small, deep wounds. If she was in pain, she gave no indication of it.

Beata's father had done a good job, and it was easy to scrape away the top layer of turf and soil until they had a rectangle thirty centimetres deep and two metres by one metre wide. Then they hit rocks. By this time the other girls had come out. Erika found another spade in the garage, and Caroline and Malin found two trowels. Everyone helped, without asking what they were doing. When they reached bigger stones, Beata fetched a crowbar which she and Malin used to loosen them, then they lifted them out. The hole grew quickly.

Theres worked with her eyes fixed on the ground. Her lips moved as if she were talking to herself, silently. When they had reached a depth of one and a half metres, Teresa rested her arms on the handle of the spade. 'Well?'

Theres nodded, threw the spade out of the hole and swung herself up. Teresa had to drive the spade deep into the ground and use the handle as a step to climb out.

When they were all gathered around the hole, no one could avoid seeing what they had created together. A grave. They stood close together looking down into the hole as if they were taking part in a funeral where only the crucial element was missing.

Ronja smiled and said, 'Who are we burying?'

The twilight had deepened, and as Sofie was the only one with a torch, Teresa turned to her. 'Fetch the box. From the cellar.' When Sofie had gone off with Cecilia, others were sent to fetch a hammer, nails and some rope.

The box that used to contain explosives had the same dimensions as a small coffin, and at each end there was a loop of rope attached to an iron mounting so it could be lifted. Teresa opened the lid and tipped out a few shrivelled potatoes and some soil. She banged on the sides with her fists and discovered that the rough planks were sound. It would hold. The hammer, nails and rope had been found.

Teresa looked around the group. Several of the girls were shuffling on the spot and their faces, wearing an expression of deep concentration, glowed pale and white in the darkness of the twilight.

'Who wants to go first?'

Some of them had perhaps thought that it was a game, some had expected something else, some might have understood exactly what was going to happen, but when the words were spoken the pale ovals turned toward Teresa, eyes opened wide with fear and several shook their heads. 'Noooo...'

'Yes,' said Teresa. 'That's what we're going to do now.'

'Why?'

'Because that's the way it has to be.'

A few of the girls came forward and touched the coffin, imagining themselves enclosed in the narrow space, between the unforgiving planks of wood. Some took out their pieces of wolf skin, clutching them tightly in their hands or sucking them unthinkingly as they plucked up courage. A long time passed without anyone volunteering. Then Linn stepped forward. 'I'll do it.'

A faint sigh of relief ran through the group. Teresa gestured towards the coffin. Linn climbed in and sat with her arms wrapped around her knees. 'What are you going to do?'

'We're going to nail down the lid,' said Teresa. 'We're going to lower you into the grave and shovel earth on top. And there you are.'

'How long for?'

Theres had yet to speak. She went up to Linn and said in that strange, dark voice, 'Until you are dead.'

Linn hugged her knees more tightly to her chest. 'But I don't know if I want to die. At the moment.'

'Until you are dead but can scream,' said Theres. 'Then you scream.'

'But what if you can't hear me?'

'I will hear you.'

Linn was so small that there were several centimetres to spare on either side of her and six centimetres above her head when she lay down in the coffin, crossed her arms over her chest and closed her eyes. The others stood there at a loss as Teresa lowered the lid and hammered a nail into each corner. Then she cut two five-metre lengths of rope and threw them to Caroline and Miranda.

'Thread those through the loops. Lower her down.'

They did as they were told, but when they had threaded the rope through, made another loop and begun to lift the coffin towards the hole, Anna L started wringing her hands and looking around anxiously, 'Is this OK? Can we do this? This isn't a good thing to do, is it?'

'It's good,' said Theres. 'It's very good.'

Anna L nodded and fell silent, but her hands continued to twist around one another like two small tormented animals as Caroline and Miranda lowered the coffin into the grave. When it reached the bottom, they stood holding the loops of rope in their hands. Teresa indicated that they should lay them over the edge of the hole.

Theres picked up a spade and started throwing the soil on top of the coffin. The lumps hit the coffin with dull thuds. After eight shovelfuls the lid was no longer visible, and Anna L said, 'That's OK, isn't it? Surely that's enough now?'

'Get in your car,' said Theres, 'and go away.' She continued shovelling earth into the hole. Anna L didn't move, and Teresa grabbed the second spade to help out. Then Sofie took the third. In a couple of minutes the grave was half-filled in.

Theres gave her spade to Malin and said, 'Everybody must help. Everybody must join in.'

Miranda dropped to her knees and picked up one of the trowels, while Cecilia took the other. Those who had no tools shovelled the earth in with their hands, several weeping as they did so.

The coffin wasn't big enough to fill the space left by the stones and turf they had removed. When they had shovelled in all the earth, it was still a few centimetres below the surface. Theres went to the end of the grave and crouched down, staring at the black rectangle.

'Linn has become dead,' she said. 'Linn was a little girl. A nice little girl. Now she is dead.'

The sobbing increased in intensity and several of the girls covered their faces with their hands. The sky was now deep violet with a single blood-red cloud drifting across the lake from one shore to the other. Slowly, slowly as if it wanted to make time pass even more sluggishly than it already was. A loon cried out, making them all shudder. If death had a call, then it sounded exactly like that. If death had a shape, then it was that black rectangle gaping in the ground. Linn's grave.

The atmosphere was so petrifying that none of them could even get out their mobiles to check how much time had passed. It might have been five minutes, it might have been fifteen when Theres lowered her head, as if she were listening to a sound from the grave, then said, 'Now.'

Teresa wasn't sure, but she thought she had heard it too. It was more of a squeak than a scream; it was impossible to work out where it came from, and it was barely even human. But it had been there, and as soon as Theres said, 'Now,' they all grabbed spades and trowels and crowded around the grave to remove the soil as quickly as possible.

There were still a few centimetres of soil left when Ronja grabbed one loop of rope, Anna L the other, and both of them pulled. The coffin was lifted out of the hole along with a layer of earth which trickled over the lid when it almost tipped over the edge.

'Linn?' Anna L called out, banging the end of the coffin with her hand. No response; Teresa pushed her aside so that she could use the other side of the hammer to jemmy out the nails, while Anna babbled away, 'Linn, Linn, little Linn, Linn?'

The lid came off. Linn was lying just as they had left her, apart from the fact that the arms crossed over her chest now ended in two clenched fists. Her face bore an expression of exalted peace. The girls were standing just as still as Linn was lying, and they were all as silent as Linn, apart from Anna L who was babbling again: 'We've killed her, what have we done, we've killed little Linn.'

Theres went over to the coffin and stroked Linn's hair, caressed her cheek and whispered in her ear, 'You must stop being dead. You must live.'

Someone screamed as Linn's eyes opened. For a moment time stood still as she and Theres looked deep into one another; then Theres grabbed her hand and pulled her into a sitting position. Linn looked at the others, wide-eyed. Then she got up and moved her hands slowly, floating over her body.

The loon called again, and Linn turned her head in the direction of the sound. Then she looked up at the first star of the evening as she took a breath so deep it seemed it would never end.

Someone asked, 'How...how are you feeling?'

Linn turned to the others. She opened and closed her hands a couple of times, looked at her palms. Her face was just as peaceful as when she lay dead.

'Empty,' she said. 'Completely empty.'

'Is it terrible?' Teresa asked.

Linn frowned as if she didn't understand the question. Then she said, 'It's empty. It's nothing.' She went over to Theres and put her arms around her. Theres allowed it to happen, but did not return the embrace, and they all heard as Linn whispered, 'Thank you. Thank you so much.'

The sun had risen above the tree tops on the other side of the lake by the time it was Teresa's turn. She had waited until last because she wanted to see the others before she herself was transformed.

About half the girls had reacted like Linn when they died and were restored to life. Several were now sitting gazing out over the lake, or moving slowly and dreamily like the morning mist drifting across the water. They were all exhausted. None of them wanted to sleep.

An outside observer, a friend or relative or parent—especially a parent—would surely have been afraid, would have asked what terrible thing had happened. Because something terrible had happened, after all. Each and every one of them had been part of something dreadful.

But was it evil?

It would depend who you asked. Teresa couldn't imagine a single person, institution or authority who would give their blessing to what they had been doing for the past five hours.

Except Theres.

Theres said it was good, and they all followed Theres' star. Therefore it was good.

Not all of them had succeeded. Both Malin and Cecilia had started screaming as soon as the coffin was lowered, and continued to scream as the earth was shovelled into the hole. It was no more than half-full before those at the top had to start digging it up again. Both were hysterical and completely unreachable when they got out, collapsing in a heap and sobbing, sobbing.

Cecilia's large body had consumed the oxygen much too quickly, and she was almost unconscious by the time four of them hauled the coffin up. When she came round she was inconsolable. She had wanted to stay much longer, and counted this as yet another of her failures.

Anna L stayed down as long as anyone else, but when the coffin came up and Theres leaned over her, she pushed her aside and said she was going for a walk. She was away for a good hour, and when she came back she had picked a bunch of flowers. She went down to the jetty and threw them in the water, one by one.

Ronja hadn't screamed. When perhaps twenty minutes had passed, those who had already been down started talking quietly about how long the air might last. Then, without any particular hurry, they dug up the coffin, still without any signal from Ronja. When the lid was lifted she acted more or less the same as Linn, except that it took longer to wake her. By this stage everyone except Miranda and Teresa had been down, so the fact that Ronja appeared to be dead didn't cause any panic.

Ronja explained her behaviour by saying that she had completely forgotten she was supposed to scream; it had never occurred to her. As soon as the coffin reached the bottom she had accepted that she was dead, and that there was nothing more to be done. The others nodded in recognition despite the fact that, unlike Ronja, they had managed to hang on to some small instinct for self-preservation.

Teresa stretched out in the bottom of the coffin. They had rinsed it out after Caroline threw up, but there was still a sour smell lurking not far from Teresa's nose. She folded her arms over her chest and made an effort to shut down her senses as Linn and Melinda closed the lid, but the blows of the hammer still echoed through her head like thunderclaps, amplified in the enclosed space.

She opened her eyes and saw a tiny amount of light coming through a crack near her feet. Then she could feel in her stomach that the coffin was being lifted. And lowered. After an unfeasibly long time, bumps along her back told her that she was now at the bottom of the hole. She heard the first thud as earth hit the lid; she closed her eyes, her breathing slow and shallow.

She could hear the spades being driven into the pile of earth, then immediately afterwards a couple of thuds. Spades in, thud, thud. Spades in, thud, thud. There was a rhythm to it, and she counted the blows. When she got to thirty she noticed that she could no longer hear the spades, and that the thuds were growing fainter. She managed to count another thirty, then there was silence. Complete silence. She didn't know how much earth there was left to shovel in, but inside her chest she could feel the weight already lying on top of her.

The space between her chest and the lid was no more than six centimetres. There was no way she would be able to get out, however much she might want to. If she tried to force out the nails, the weight of the earth would make it impossible. She had been deserted. She had been given up. She kept her breathing slow and shallow.

No light through the crack, no voices, no spades, no thuds of earth. Nothing. She had already lost all concept of time. She knew she hadn't been lying there for half an hour. But she had no idea whether it was three minutes or ten, because there were no reference points.

She started to count inside her head. When she got to a hundred, she gave up. She was usually good at counting in seconds, but even the concept 'second' had lost its meaning. Perhaps she had been counting far too slowly; or far too quickly, she didn't know.

So she let go. Although she hadn't been aware of it, her whole body had been tense; she only realised this when she relaxed. She let go and gave herself up to the darkness and the silence and the absence of everything that she was.

Another incalculable period of time passed. Her breathing was slow and shallow. Something moved. A faint noise. At first she thought it was an insect or worm that had ended up in the coffin with her, and she tried to pinpoint the sound. Her hands moved over the sides of the coffin. A rough, mute nothingness.

But the sound. The movement.

The space just about allowed her to roll over onto her side. Her shoulder pressed against the lid as she turned her back on the direction she thought the sound was coming from. She put her hands over her ears. She could still hear it. Something was moving through the earth. Digging. Getting closer.

Her heart began to beat faster, and she was no longer able to control her breathing. The air was forced out of her in panting, jerky breaths as the thing that was moving through the earth slid along the side of the coffin. She could hear it, she could feel it right through her body.

It was getting warmer. Sweat broke out along her hairline, and the air had ceased to contain what she needed. She twitched as if she had been given an electric shock, twitched again, and panic wasn't far away. She was surrounded by earth on all sides, lying in complete darkness, had no air, and something had dug its way through to her and was working its way in. She was going to scream. Despite the fact that she hadn't reached that point, she was going to scream.

She drew thin air into her lungs and at the same time the other thing pushed its way in, crept in behind her back and lay behind her, spooning.

Urd.

She exhaled without screaming. She felt herself being embraced by the soft, forgiving, no-longer-frightening darkness. Urd was lying beside her. Urd was her. Urd did not scream.

Teresa?

Not there anymore. Never had been.

Out of the darkness pictures emerged, her life.

She saw herself being buried in the ground, but the coffin was empty. She saw her computer, saw herself sitting at the computer, keys pressed down like a self-playing piano. No one was there. A hammer struck, blood spurted over a cement floor, vomit spewed over another cement floor, but the fluids came out of the empty air and the film speeded up.

Theres sitting alone on the subway, talking to someone who didn't exist, Göran waving off a train with no passengers on it, a bicycle without a rider moving along a gravel track, Johannes playing Tekken by himself, being kissed by an invisible ghost, dry leaves whirling around in the cave between the rocks where no one had ever been. Clothes collapsing in heaps in the garden, in rooms, on the streets. Collapsing as the person who had worn them disappeared.

It stopped at a yellow bead. A child's fingers holding a little yellow bead. *If I didn't exist, then nobody would be holding this bead.* The yellow bead was there, half a metre above the surface of the table. Then the fingers holding it disappeared and the bead dropped through the air, bounced a couple of times and lay still.

The only thing that remained of all of this was that single yellow point. No. The only thing that remained was that single yellow point *and the eyes that saw it*. Then the eyes disappeared, the bead disappeared and everything went white. Chalk white. Searing, burning phosphorus-white. A whiteness so dazzling and painful that it was an ear-splitting scream.

They stood together on the jetty in the dawn light, fourteen girls. It was five o'clock in the morning, but the sun was already high in the sky, pouring its light down upon them. The morning mist had dispersed, and the lake was dead calm.

The jetty was small, and the girls stood close together like a flock of birds, sharing each other's warmth, allowing a new kind of energy to flow between their bodies. Their eyes were empty, their senses wide open.

Teresa's throat was still hurting from the scream she hadn't even known she'd let out, but like the other girls she was still, drinking in the soft light of the morning, the smell of mud, reeds and water coming from the lake, the long sustained explosion of birdsong in the trees, the closeness she felt with the other girls, and the space all around her.

Teresa moved away from the group and went to stand at the very edge of the jetty. She picked up a rusty nail, looked at it and threw it in the water, following it with her eyes as it sank. Then she turned to the group and said, 'We were the dead. We need life.'

6

Things had changed for the better for Max Hansen following the success of Tesla. He had even begun to rethink his plan to burn all his bridges and head for the tropics.

The incident he had arranged outside Skansen had produced the desired result. The boys had reported back that Tora now said yes, and the following day he had received an email confirmation. Perhaps it no longer made good business sense to make her infamous with all those revelations. Time would tell if it was enough just to make her famous. That would allow him to remain in the country.

Because the country, or rather the city, had begun to show him its most friendly face; it was almost like the '80s all over again. People wanted to talk to him, discuss future projects or offer their services. Max Hansen—last chance—had rapidly and amusingly become a player again.

He wasn't a fool. He knew that popularity like this was temporary and could vanish overnight, but as long as it lasted he was enjoying being back in the warmth, lapping up the strained smiles and good wishes, relishing every dutiful pat on the back.

He had started going out again. Café Opera, Riche, Spy Bar. Many of the musicians had been replaced by the suits who called the shots, or young men in scooped T-shirts who called themselves producers just because they could handle Autotune. It wasn't like the good old days, but there were still plenty of people who wanted to hang out with the powerful, and Max Hansen was once again someone who counted.

This particular Saturday he had started at Café Opera. Two girls who called themselves Divinity and played electroclash were throwing a release party for their new album in one of the side rooms, and Max had been invited. He thought the music was close to unbearable, so after knocking back a couple of free mojitos, he discreetly slipped back into the main room.

It was no more than half full, which would have been unthinkable on a Saturday night twenty years ago. Max said hello to a producer with EMI, an art director with Sony, and a session guitarist who was a little *too* eager to chat to him, so he excused himself and went over to the bar, where he ordered a glass of white wine. He stood there with his back to the counter, the ice-cold glass in his hand, enjoying the satisfying feeling of being, if not king, then at least a little prince in this particular kingdom. He'd missed it.

'What are you drinking?'

A young girl had appeared beside him. Max raised his glass and gave a casual shrug. 'Just white wine. The night is young.'

'I prefer bubbly,' said the girl.

Max Hansen looked at her more carefully. She was in her twenties; probably a bit young to have even got in. Not exactly stunning but reasonably pretty, and dressed in a tracksuit top that could be regarded as hip hop at a push. Straight, medium-length hair and a narrow face. She reminded him a little of Tora Larsson, in fact, but without the baggage. So Max Hansen beamed at her and said, 'Well, I'm sure we can do something about that. What's your name?'

'Alice.'

'As in Wonderland?'

'Yes. As in Wonderland. That's where I come from.'

There was something dangerous in Alice's eyes that Max Hansen liked. She was probably not one of those girls who lay motionless on their backs staring at the ceiling like they were sending up a prayer to God and their mother. She looked like the kind of girl who might be up for all kinds of things.

Max Hansen ordered a bottle of sparkling wine and as the girl sipped at her glass and looked at him through half-closed eyes, he suddenly felt suspicious. This was going a little too well. He was under no illusions about his own attractiveness, so how come this girl was so obviously flirting with him?

'Do you know who I am?' he asked.

'Of course,' said Alice. 'You're Max Hansen. Tesla's manager. Isn't that right?'

'Yes. Do we know each other?'

'No. But I'm a singer too. Among other things.'

OK. So now they knew where they stood. It was that glint in her eye that had made him misjudge the situation. Alice was simply one of those girls. They had started to circle again recently.

When Alice asked, 'Have you got any tips on how to make it as a singer?' he no longer had any doubts. This was where they started, almost without exception. So Max Hansen poured himself another glass of bubbly and launched his usual routine.

It took Alice quarter of an hour to empty her glass, and when Max Hansen made a move to pour her the last of the wine, she placed her hand over the top and said, 'No thanks. I'm driving.'

'And where is it you're driving to?'

'Home.' Her gaze swept up and down his body in a way that made his balls tingle. 'Do you want to come with me?'

The Ford Fiesta parked behind the national theatre was one of the scruffiest cars he had ever seen, and certainly the scruffiest he had ever sat in. When Alice turned the key in the ignition, it sounded like an entire Formula One starting grid, and there was a faint whiff of petrol fumes, as if there might be a hole somewhere.

Alice drove along Birger Jarlsgatan towards Roslagstull, and as they passed Stureplan Max bent down and pretended to adjust his shoelaces. His taste for young girls was no secret, but a young girl in a roaring heap of metal like this was a step too far, and he didn't want to be seen. Only when Alice turned onto Roslagsvägen did he relax, leaning back as best he could on the hard seat.

He glanced over at Alice, whose gaze was fixed firmly on the road. Nice profile. Well-defined chin and jaw line, but the shape of her nose softened what could have been an angular look. He was attracted, no two ways about it.

But there was a problem, of course. Just a couple of evenings ago he had brought home a lady he had known for quite some time for a couple of drinks. They had never got past the drinks. As soon as they sat down next to each other on the sofa Max realised nothing was going to happen, because his body made not the slightest response to her tight top and slit skirt. He had had to pretend that he'd never had anything else in mind, just a couple of drinks with an old friend.

However, that woman had been almost twice as old as Alice. He was hoping things would go better now he was back on home territory, so to speak.

To scope out the lie of the land, both hers and his own, he placed a hand on Alice's thigh and squeezed tentatively. She let it happen—so far, so good. But what about Max? The engine screamed and the car rattled so much that it wasn't easy to tell. He searched for the tingle in his crotch he had felt when she looked at him; he squeezed harder and checked again.

Nothing. It wasn't there.

The car was clattering past the lights of Mörby Centrum as Max Hansen's heart sank. This whole noisy, smelly, uncomfortable journey was pointless, and was about to end in embarrassment and a lonely taxi ride home.

He felt a sudden pain in his forearm as Alice pinched him, and he removed his hand from her thigh. She reached out her hand and pinched him again, harder this time. Max laughed and said loudly, almost yelling to be heard over the engine, 'Do you like that sort of game?'

'Absolutely,' said Alice. 'That's the best kind.'

Max Hansen settled back in his seat. Maybe the evening wouldn't end up so badly after all.

He had expected Alice to live in a small apartment somewhere like Täby, but when they passed that turn-off as well, he asked her where they were heading.

'To Wonderland,' she said, and he had to be content with that. It was often the way with young girls. They liked to appear a little mysterious, and he had nothing against that; quite the reverse, in fact. Particularly if they played the role as well as Alice. It gave the whole thing the feeling of an adventure, of heading out into the unknown.

When they turned off in Åkersberga and drove through an enormous housing estate, Max started to worry that it would be one of *those* occasions. Perhaps she lived with her parents, and he would have to sit and make conversation. If that was the case, he wasn't setting foot through the door.

But they left the houses and set off along a smaller road leading into the forest. Every time he thought they had arrived there was another bend, and the car's feeble headlights would have struggled to show them the way through the tunnel of trees if there hadn't still been light in the sky.

But this was unknown territory, and no mistake. He hadn't seen a house for several minutes, and was beginning to feel uncomfortable when Alice turned into a narrow driveway at long last, and switched off the engine.

'Here we are!' she said, clapping her hands.

When he stepped out of the car, Max Hansen's ears were still buzzing as if he'd just come out of a concert, and the petrol fumes had made him feel slightly nauseous. He just had time to think *this had better be fucking worth it* when he sensed a movement and a rustling sound behind him. The next moment a black plastic bag was slipped over his head, and his legs were kicked from underneath him. He went down, hitting the back of his head so hard on a stone that he was seeing stars as he was lifted by many hands.

7

While Ronja was in Stockholm, the others got the garage ready. They had spread plastic sheeting over the floor, and the two carpentry benches stood side by side in the centre. It was fortunate that Beata's father was so interested in woodwork, because it meant that a wide selection of tools was neatly displayed along the wall.

Teresa chose from the awls, chisels and knives, and left aside the pliers and saws. After all, this wasn't about torture. Not primarily. She cut thirteen pieces of paper from two sheets of A4, and wrote a name on each.

At about ten o'clock those who were going to collect Max Hansen went and hid behind the woodshed. It was quarter to eleven before they heard the unmistakable sound of the car engine coming along the track. The members of the group waiting in the garage stood listening in the darkness; they heard the sound of the engine being switched off, a car door opening, then not much else. They had expected yelling and a struggle, perhaps even an attempt to escape, and had prepared for all these eventualities. But all they heard was a rustling sound, then silence.

They had talked through the whole thing during the day. They had slept for a few hours, close together in their sleeping bags on the kitchen floor, and eaten some baby food, then Teresa told them about what had happened in the shop. What she had done and how she had felt afterwards.

She didn't even consider whether or not telling them was a risk. She was going to tell them now, and she told them. The whole story, from the moment when she and Theres were standing in the loading bay right up to the purchase of the red boots the following day, and how they had come in handy at school.

Then she put forward her suggestion, which was no longer a suggestion but more an explanation of what they must do now. Theres supported her, and there was never any discussion as to *whether* they should do it, only *how* they should do it.

Ideas were quietly put forward and rejected or accepted in the same simple way as they had planned the whole weekend. At an early stage Ronja had offered to act as bait, and once that was sorted out, the rest was largely a matter of technicalities. The woodshed, the plastic sheeting, the tools. Not even when the details were settled and the whole thing began to seem real did anyone react with revulsion or reluctance to take part. This was what they had to do, end of story.

As Teresa stood listening in the garage, she wondered if it had gone wrong from the start. Hadn't Ronja even managed to get hold of Max Hansen? Teresa had brought some newspaper articles so that Ronja could see what he looked like, and he had mentioned that he usually frequented Café Opera. But that didn't mean he had been there tonight, of course.

Teresa had begun to consider other options when she heard the sound of running footsteps, and Sofie pulled open the garage door. Behind her came Ronja, Caroline, Anna S and Melinda carrying a limp body wrapped in black plastic, which they dumped on the workbenches. Teresa switched on the fluorescent light and set to work.

She had expected more resistance from Max Hansen, but the man was just feebly moving his legs, and all Ronja had to do was press down on his shoulders to keep him in place. Teresa freed his arms from the plastic and fastened his hands in the clamps on the workbench. Only when she made the final adjustments to tighten the clamp around his right hand did she hear a muted scream from inside the sack. Meanwhile Cecilia had grabbed hold of his legs; she and Linn bent them over the edge of the benches and tied his feet to the base with thin rope.

They all took a step back, arranged themselves in a circle around the benches, and contemplated their treasure. Max Hansen was gradually coming round. His body jolted back and forth as best it could, fettered at every corner. The sack rustled as he jerked his head, billowing in and out as he screamed, inhaled, then screamed again.

'Let me go, what's going on, who are you, what are you doing?'

Teresa picked up a Stanley knife and sliced through the bag over his face. His skin was bright red with exertion and fear. His eyes opened even wider when he caught sight of Teresa.

'Hi,' she said. Theres passed her a wide strip of gaffer tape and Teresa placed it over his mouth. She thought it was a shame she wouldn't be able to hear him scream, but it wasn't worth the risk. Three of the others cut off his clothes, then stepped back.

Everything had gone according to plan—slightly better than expected, actually. The fact that Max Hansen had banged his head might well have saved those charged with bringing him in a split lip or a black eye. Now he was lying in the correct position. Ready for use.

Teresa found his naked body just as repulsive as when she had seen it on film. A flabby, calloused lump of pale flesh. Seeing him lying there now, it was difficult to imagine that he had been a real threat to them for a while. She couldn't help smiling. Then giggling.

She was still giggling when she fetched the pieces of paper with names on, and a staple gun. Max Hansen jerked and squealed like... yes, *like a stuck pig* when she stapled 'Melinda' to his shoulder. Teresa said, 'Lie still.'

Human beings are strange. They always struggle, to the bitter end—no matter how hopeless the situation is. With the tiny, tiny amount of movement Max Hansen had with his fettered arms and legs, he kept on trying to twist out of the way as Teresa rapidly stapled 'Linn' and 'Cecilia' to his thighs. There was the sound of splashing on the plastic covering the floor as he wet himself, and Teresa had to walk around the puddle as she moved across to fix 'Anna S' to his other shoulder.

She continued until all the names were stapled to his body, like a blanket made of pieces of paper. Ronja had to help hold his head so that she could finally fix her own name to his temple. Theres fetched the tools laid out on the bench at the side, and handed them out to the girls.

With their weapons in their hands they closed the circle around Max Hansen more tightly. His eyes darted from their faces to the tools, back and forth, back and forth until something happened. His body, which had been tensed in an arc, as far as he could manage it, suddenly relaxed. The expression in his eyes altered, and his head sank back.

Teresa couldn't believe what she was seeing, but obviously the others could see it too, because they stopped dead and just stared, like her. Slowly, slowly Max Hansen's cock began to rise. His eyes were looking up at the ceiling. The expression in them was hard to read because the tape over his mouth distorted his features, but Teresa thought she could see...yes, *peace*.

She looked from his stiff cock to his face. She shook her head and said, 'Do you understand what's going to happen?'

Max Hansen nodded faintly, his eyes still fixed on the ceiling, without losing that expression of tortured bliss.

Teresa thought it was best to start with a safe bet, so she nodded to Ronja, who had a small, sharpened screwdriver and whose name was fastened just above Max Hansen's right hip bone. Ronja stepped forward, pulled a face at the defiant erection, and without further ado drove the screwdriver straight through her piece of paper, all the way to the handle.

Max Hansen screamed through his nose, snot spurted out, sweat poured down his forehead and his body quivered for a few seconds before becoming still once more. The erection didn't subside, but remained sticking up about three centimetres below the handle of the screwdriver; it was about the same thickness.

It was Linn's turn next. She had to stand on tiptoe to stab through the label below the right collarbone with her slender chisel. Max Hansen's back squelched sweatily against the bench as he reared up and fell back down. Blood was trickling out of his wounds and dripping slowly onto the plastic.

Teresa had worked out that if they left the tools in place, it would take longer for him to bleed to death. She had also made sure she chose thin, short spikes and blades. He wasn't going to die until everyone had done what they had to do and played their part.

Caroline was the sixth in line, and when she drove her knife through the label in the inside of his right thigh, Max Hansen let out a completely different kind of groan as he ejaculated with such force that the semen spurted into his face and over his head. Miranda, who had been standing behind the bench, squeaked in disgust and wiped her top with a cloth.

By this stage a fairly large pool of blood had begun to gather on the floor, and Teresa waved the girls forward more quickly so that they would all have their turn before it was over. Max Hansen's penis finally collapsed and he was hardly even twitching as he was stabbed now.

In the end only Anna L, Cecilia and Teresa remained. Theres had said that she would prefer to watch, and was following the procedure curled up on the workbench at the side, humming 'Thank You for the Music'.

Anna L stepped forward. She had been given a fine awl, because her label was dangerously close to the heart. She frowned, raised the awl and looked at Max Hansen's eyes; only the whites were visible now. Then she shook her head and lowered her hand. With tears in her voice she said, 'I can't. This is crazy. It's wrong. You can't.'

Theres jumped down and went over to her. 'Do you want to sit in your car?' she asked. Anna L shook her head as tears welled up in her eyes, and she said, 'I just can't.'

'You can,' said Theres. 'You have to.'

'But this is crazy.'

'It isn't crazy,' said Theres as she gripped her wrist, moved the hand holding the awl to the correct position, 'it isn't crazy at all', then she thrust Anna's hand down so that the awl went in halfway. Theres banged it with the palm of her hand, hammering it all the way in, then climbed back onto the workbench. Anna L crouched down by the wall with her hands over her head as Cecilia drove in a long nail.

Max Hansen's body was limp, perforated in thirteen places and white from loss of blood. Shafts and handles stuck up through sticky pieces of paper, moving in time with his shallow breathing. A film covered his eyes as the pupils rolled back into place, and his gaze fixed on Teresa. He moved his head as if he wanted to say something, and since Teresa didn't think he could possibly have any strength left to scream, she pulled off the tape. He looked at her and whispered, 'Teresa...' She leaned closer to his marble-grey face. 'Yes?'

Max Hansen's lips didn't move and the consonants were no more than faint puffs of air. 'That was fantastic. That was fantastic...that was fantastic...that was fantastic...'

'Just one thing,' said Teresa. 'That stuff you've got on Theres. Is it going to get out?'

Max Hansen made a movement with his head, the hint of a shake, a no, then he carried on whispering, 'That was fantastic...that was fantastic...'

Teresa shrugged her shoulders. 'Glad you thought so. Bit of a shame, though. You might change your mind now.'

She picked up the drill that had been charging all day, pressed the button. The bit, which was the thickness of a little finger, was spinning around at twenty revolutions per second. She showed it to Max Hansen, revved the motor a couple of times then pushed it into the label attached to his temple.

And at long last came the scream she had longed for.

The girls gathered around the body, which was twitching like a landed fish as the blood spurted, with dwindling force, from the hole in the temple. Theres stood at the top and stroked the sticky hair from Max

Hansen's forehead. She said, 'Come closer.'

They moved right in, fourteen girls. A rattling came from Max Hansen's throat, then the body lay still. The blood stopped flowing from the temple, and as if that little black hole were a point of higher gravity, they were all drawn closer, as close as possible, as thin wisps of smoke extended like cobwebs.

They breathed in collectively, inhaling the essence that had been Max Hansen and incorporating it with the circulation of their own blood. But it was so little, much too little. Several of them moved their lips closer to the hole to force out something that was no longer there, almost kissing Max Hansen's lacerated skull in order to lap up the very last bit.

They straightened up and the light in the garage was so bright, the iron-rich smell of blood so strong, and the sound as their feet stuck to the plastic and pulled free sliced through their ears. Their breathing was uneven as they returned to their wide-open bodies.

'We are here,' said Theres. 'Now we are here.'

8

Many spent the night crying. Their senses were open wounds, their perceptions too powerful. They consoled and held one another, shared sleeping bags or lay caressing each other's faces without speaking.

But in spite of the tears and the need for comfort, the underlying feeling was one of *happiness*. A different kind of happiness. A happiness so great, so piercing, that it had something of grief in it. Because it couldn't last forever, it was far too intense for that. They could keep it alive together through the closeness of their bodies and their shared experience, but at some point it must fade and die. So: the grief.

It was yet another sleepless night, and before dawn they went out under cover of darkness to clean up. A group of them carried Max Hansen's plastic-wrapped body down to the grave and threw it in along with his clothes, then filled the hole with earth and stones before carefully replacing the turf and stamping it down. Within a couple of weeks the turf would have grown into the surrounding grass. The others tidied up the garage, washed all the tools and scrubbed the work benches.

When dawn came and they had restored everything to its original state, they gathered on the jetty to watch the sun rise. Linn still had tears in her eyes, but not for the reason the others thought. When they had allowed the first rays of the sun to warm their faces for a while, Linn folded her arms, turned to Teresa and said, 'Next time *I* want to use the drill.'

It was perhaps not quite the last thing Teresa had expected, but almost. Linn's little face looked so sulky that Teresa burst out laughing, and soon several of the girls were laughing. Linn looked around, her expression furious.

'What are you laughing at? I got practically *nothing*!'

The laughter quickly died down and there was silence as they looked at each other. They no longer needed to talk as much in order to communicate, and it appeared that several of them had been thinking along the same lines as Linn.

Next time. There was going to be a next time.

At about twelve o'clock the shuttle service to the bus stop began. Theres had had a long conversation with Anna L, and Anna said she did want to be involved in the future, but that she would need the others' help. She would get it; that was the whole point of being a pack rather than fourteen girls. They gathered around her, they held her and shared their strength with her. Ronja offered to drive her car to Mörby so that she could travel on the bus with the others.

This turned out to be a valuable experience, because it was only on the bus that the experience finally seemed to settle within her, as they took up the whole of the back of the bus together and Anna found herself in a familiar environment, but no longer defenceless and afraid. No, she was sitting here now with *her family*—who had been buried and risen again, the hungry sharp-toothed ones, her sisters in the pack who would defend her. Then at last happiness came to her.

'You all kind of *belong* to me, don't you? And I belong to you. We're together in this. Seriously together. We can do anything at all, and we'll never let each other down, will we.'

It wasn't a question, it was a statement, and Anna took a deep breath and flung her arms wide, as if she had only just fully risen from the grave.

They parted company at different places along the way, having decided to meet again the following Sunday in the usual place. Teresa went on to Svedmyra with Theres. In spite of the fact that they were alone for the first time in over twenty-four hours, they didn't say much, didn't discuss what had happened or the others' reactions. It wasn't possible, because the others no longer were *the others*. It was not possible to talk about them as if they weren't there.

They went their separate ways at the front door of Theres' apartment block. As Teresa turned to head back towards the subway station, Theres said, 'It was good.'

'Yes,' said Teresa. 'It was very good.'

On the subway and then on the train home, there was just one word going round and round in Teresa's head, jerking and bumping about like a fish in a bowl that was far too small.

Urd. Urd. Urd.

Voices under the ground. On one level she knew that it was an image created by her oxygen-starved brain as she lay buried. On another it was real and true. Urd had come to her, lain down behind her and then put on her thin skin like a close-fitting suit. Urd was no longer merely her name. Urd was her.

9

Teresa woke up in her own bed at six o'clock on Monday morning feeling like a calf about to be turned out to pasture. The barn door had been opened after the long winter, and before her lay green meadows, flowers and the bright summer. There was a word for it: *joyfulness.* As she stood at her window wide awake, gazing out over the garden, she felt full of joy, and her whole body, not just her legs, was full of energy.

When the household began to wake up an hour later she lay down on her bed and pretended to be half-dead. She rubbed her eyes hard for a long time to make them look terrible, and when Maria came in Teresa explained that she felt awful and just couldn't get up, couldn't do anything. This was accepted with a sigh and a shrug, and Teresa was left in peace.

It was like that poem by Bob Hansson she had read a year or so earlier. The man who phones work and explains that he can't come in. Why not? Is he ill? No, he's far too healthy, but he might be in the following day if he feels worse.

She lay in bed impatiently waiting for the others to go off to work or to see friends so that she could be alone. When the house was finally empty, she got up. The first thing she did was to go down to the kitchen and pour herself a glass of water.

She sat for a long time looking at the clear liquid in the glass, enjoying the play of the surface and the spectrum of colours on the tablecloth when she tilted the glass and allowed the light to break up.

Then she raised the glass to her lips.

A shudder ran through her body as the water slipped into her mouth. It was smooth and cool and crept over her tongue and palate like a caress. And they say water doesn't taste of anything! It tasted of earth and iron and grass. Saltiness and sweetness in thin layers, the taste of depth and eternity. When she swallowed it was like receiving a gift, being able to taste something so delicious. And she still had plenty left in her glass.

It took her five minutes to finish the water, and when she went out into the garden afterwards she was so overwhelmed with the happiness bubbling up from the impressions flooding into her body that she had to sit down on the steps for a while. She closed her eyes, put her hands over her ears and concentrated only on the scents, the scents of early summer.

To think that people can walk around on this earth and not be aware of what is around them. What a waste. They might just as well be robots, soulless automata moving between work, the bank, the shop and the TV until their batteries run down.

Teresa had been just the same, but that person now lay crumpled in a grave. She was a goddess, and perceived things with the senses of a goddess. She was Urd, the primitive one.

And so her day passed. She wandered through the trees, gently running her hands over leaves and stones; she walked like Eve through Paradise, knowing that everything was hers, and everything was good.

She woke up feeling happy on Tuesday as well, and another day passed in a state of joyful awareness that might have burst her chest open if she hadn't divided it into manageable parts, one or two senses at a time. Towards evening it slowly began to slip away from her.

She could hear the voices of her parents and her brothers again. Of course they were no longer her parents or her brothers: her family was thirteen people who were not present. But she knew what they were called, these people sitting around the dinner table with her.

Their inane babble about trivialities was a grating distraction and the food did not taste as good as it had done the previous day, when she had eaten very little and had had to conceal how much she was enjoying each bite of potato—the poor appetite fitted nicely with the impression of illness she wanted to maintain.

Tuesday evening was different. She pretended to feel weak and exhausted, closed her eyes and tried to recapture the feeling. It was there, but much fainter. She excused herself and went up to her room.

When she woke up on Wednesday another little bit had disappeared, and by Thursday morning she was being honest when she said she didn't feel well. She told herself her senses were still stronger, but she was beginning to feel pretty much like an ordinary person. And that felt like an illness compared with the way things had been at the beginning of the week.

Friday and Saturday were the direct opposite of Monday and Tuesday. She felt ill, as if she was constantly quivering inside, but she had to pretend to the family that she was feeling much better so they wouldn't stop her going to Stockholm on Sunday. It was stressful and difficult, and she collapsed at night into uneasy sleep filled with nightmares.

They would have had to bind her hand and foot to stop her going. She would have run away, hitch-hiked, caught the train without a ticket if necessary, but it was simpler if the others believed she was feeling OK. So at night she lay there tossing and turning, and during the day she walked around with arms folded or fists clenched in her pockets to hide her shaking hands, and all the time she smiled, smiled, smiled and spoke nicely.

Only when she was sitting on the train on Sunday was she able, at last, to drop the act. She slumped in her seat, flowing like jelly over the rough upholstery. When an elderly lady leaned forward to ask if she was all right, she went and shut herself in the toilet.

She looked at herself in the mirror. She looked every bit as sick as she had pretended to be on Monday: cold sweat, pallor; lank, greasy hair. She splashed her face a few times with cold water, dried herself with paper towels, then sat on the toilet and breathed deeply until some of the weight inside her chest disappeared.

She looked at her hands and forced them to stop shaking. Soon everything would be better. Soon she would be with her pack.

10

Just being with Theres on the subway, then the bus, made Teresa feel better; by the time they were lying on the blankets outside the wolf enclosure, her body was able to soak up the warmth of the sun. The shivering that had gripped her over the last few days diminished, and she was able to talk without having to control the shake in her voice. She could do it. With Theres beside her, she could do it.

She lay on her stomach gazing into the enclosure, but couldn't see any of the wolves. She took her piece of wolf skin out of her pocket, waved it around and stroked it like a talisman.

'What are you doing?' asked Theres.

'I want them to come. The wolves.'

'Why?'

'I want to see them.'

There was silence for a while, then Theres said, 'Here they come.'

Teresa peered among the tree trunks and rocks, but there was no sign of any grey shape. When she turned to Theres to ask her where they were, she saw that Theres was looking over towards the far end of the fence, where the rest of the girls were approaching in a group.

'I thought you meant the wolves,' said Teresa.

'We are the wolves. That's what you said.'

Yes. That's what she'd said. But the pack creeping along the narrow track was no more wolf-like than she was right now. They came and sat down, shuffling close to each other on the blankets with Theres at the centre. An inaudible whimper hung in the air along with a scent indistinguishable, to Teresa, from her own. The scent of exhaustion and nagging pain.

It turned out that the others had felt much the same over the course of the week. To begin with, a joyous, crackling proximity to life that felt indestructible, as if it would last forever, then the slow change to fever and despair as the feeling dissolved.

Like Teresa, the others found consolation in the group, relief in simply being close to one another, but the voices echoing between them were weak; *empty* in a ghostly way.

'...I thought that now, at long last...and then when it disappeared, I saw myself...I mean, you're like, *nothing*...I haven't done anything, I'm never going to do anything...as if I was invisible...nobody's going to remember me...everything will disappear...it's as if you're too small to be heard...when it disappeared, all I had left was empty hands...'

This went on for a good five minutes, a low whimpering made verbal, until Theres yelled, 'Quiet!'

The voices broke off abruptly. Theres was holding both hands up in front of her, the palms facing outwards as if she was stopping a runaway train, and she shouted again, 'Quiet! Quiet!'

If they could have pricked up their ears, they would have done so now. They were sitting in a huddle around Theres, who straightened up and looked from one to the other. They were focussed on her lips, waiting for a few words that could free them. A suggestion, an order, a telling-off. Anything.

When Theres opened her mouth, they were so intently anticipating some pithy, vital truth that it took them a couple of seconds to realise that she was *singing*.

> I'm nothing special, in fact I'm a bit of a bore
> If I tell a joke, you've probably heard it before
> But I have a talent, a wonderful thing
> 'cause everyone listens when I start to sing
> I'm so grateful and proud
> All I want is to sing it out loud...

By the time she had got that far most of them had recognised the song, and even if they didn't know the words to the verse, they knew the chorus. Theres' pure, clear voice, so perfectly pitched, resonated through their bodies like a giant tuning fork, guiding them to the right note as they joined in.

> So I say thank you for the music, the songs I'm singing
> Thanks for all the joy they're bringing...

Theres sang the song all the way through, the others helped out in the choruses, and the music was like morphine. The pain in their bodies eased, flowed out through the notes, and as long as the song went on there was nothing to fear. In the silence after the final words died away, they heard distant applause. People walking their dogs had stopped in various places and one of them shouted, 'Yay! Sing Along at Skansen!' before moving on.

Theres pointed towards Skansen and said, 'That's what I'm going to sing. There. The day after tomorrow. You will all come. Then it will be over. It will be good.' She got up and went over to the fence, leaned against the wire and let out a low growl, trying to entice the wolves without success.

'What do you mean, over?' said Caroline. 'What does she mean, it'll be over? I don't understand what she's talking about.'

Teresa looked towards Skansen, imagining the Solliden stage somewhere far beyond the trees, just as she had seen it on TV. The crowds, the singers, the camera cranes and 'Stockholm in My Heart'. The wall of young girls, just like them and very different from them, pressed against the barriers right at the front as they sang along. Theres standing on the stage. The rest of them in the audience. Among all those people.

'Ronja?' said Teresa. 'Do you remember asking me where we were actually going, what we were going to *do*?'

Ronja nodded and shrugged her shoulders. 'We've done stuff.'

'No,' said Teresa. 'We haven't done anything. We have only prepared ourselves.' She glanced at the sign on the wolf enclosure:

Do not feed the animals, then waved her hand towards it, towards Skansen. 'But we are going to do something. We are going to feel good forever. And no bastard is ever going to forget *us*.'

11

Hitachi DS14DFL.

Weight 1.6 kg. Total length 210mm. Ergonomic, rubber-coated handle. 13mm chuck capacity. 1,200 revolutions per minute.

Teresa had searched for over an hour to find the right tool. It had to be battery operated, and have a slender handle which would suit small hands. It mustn't be too big or heavy, but must be able to run a reasonably thick drill bit. It had to be available to buy all over the place. And it had to look *good*.

Behind the nondescript name Hitachi DS14DFL she found the answer. A slender tool with a long-lasting heavy duty lithium-ion battery. The handle looked inviting: she longed to hold it, to extend her arm with a sharp, whirling point.

She clicked on the group containing the other girls' email addresses and forwarded the product information along with details of a number of different shops where the machine could be bought. They could improvise when it came to other tools or weapons, but their claws would be the same.

Sunday had become Monday while she sat at the computer searching for this: for the tool that would free them, at long last, from these lives in which they had never asked to be imprisoned. The moon was high in the sky outside her window, and soon she would be gone.

The itch in her body would not let her be. She paced the strip of moonlight on the floor of her bedroom, thinking about her mother and father asleep in their beds, thinking about the drill, thinking about the axe in the cellar. The only thing that stopped her was her reluctance to start a chain of events that would prevent her from being there on Tuesday.

Her fingers were tingling, the soles of her feet were burning and she was panting like a starving animal as she forced herself to quit the pacing before she woke everybody up; a knock on the door, a curious head poked into her room, and this particular night could end in disaster.

She sat on the bed and did something she hadn't done for several months: she took her medication. She stuffed three tablets in her mouth and swallowed them without water. Then she sat still, hands resting on her knees, breathing and waiting for something to happen.

When there was no change after half an hour and her body was still being torn apart, she sat down at the computer and wrote a letter. She used the language Theres would use, because it helped her gather and simplify her thoughts. When the letter was finished she printed out four copies and placed them in envelopes on which she wrote addresses she had looked up on the internet.

Then she stood by the window looking at the moon, hugging herself and trying to survive the night.

On Monday she caught the bus to Rimsta and bought the chosen drill with the last of her savings. On the bus back she sat there holding the box close like a lifebuoy, and when she got home she unpacked the drill and placed it in the charger.

She planned and visualised, tried to think herself into the situation. She watched clips from Sing Along at Skansen on the net to see how the audience was deployed, the big tree in the middle, where the cameras were. She was afraid.

Afraid that her courage would fail when it came to the crunch, afraid that she would miss her opportunity because of the cowardice and the human frailty that still chafed away somewhere inside her.

That evening, Johannes rang.

The voices of her parents and her brothers had been reduced to meaningless background noise, whether they were speaking to her or not. She had nothing to do with them. So how come Johannes' voice could still be *heard*?

'Hi Teresa.'

Teresa. That name. She did remember it, she knew that in some way it meant her. Yes. When Johannes said it she could remember that other girl. Before Theres, before 'Fly', before Max Hansen and before Urd. Poor little Teresa with her poor little poems and her poor little life.

She spoke in Teresa's voice. It was still there. In a way it was pleasant to speak in that voice. *Teresa* wasn't suffering from this tearing hunger, *Teresa* didn't have a bloody task to carry out. *Teresa* was Johannes' friend, and always would be.

'Hi Johannes.'

She lay down on the bed, closed her eyes and had a perfectly normal conversation with Johannes. They talked about Agnes, about people in school, about the alterations to the library. For a while Teresa pretended that these things were important, and it was nice.

After a while they slipped into talking about memories. Teresa allowed herself to be led, without resisting, to their cave, their bike rides, the places where they went swimming, the sheep. They talked for over two hours, and when Teresa picked up the drill and weighed it in her hand after saying goodbye, the whole thing seemed impossible.

She lunged, raced the motor and simulated resistance, her limbs flailing as she screamed, 'Urd!'

Urd.

She managed to get a few hours' sleep that night, lying in bed with the drill and squeezing the wonderful, soft grip that fitted her hand as if it had been made for her.

12

A person can think murderous thoughts and hide them behind a smile, she can fantasise about blood flowing and brain matter splattering as she eats her muesli, humming quietly to herself. But even if nothing concrete shows on the outside, people around her will notice something sooner or later. It leaks out like radiation or osmosis, seeping out of her very being.

Teresa's parents had started to be afraid of her. You couldn't put your finger on anything definite that she said or did, but there was a kind of shimmer around her, a black aura that made them feel uncomfortable as soon as she walked into a room.

When Teresa asked for a lift to Österyd more than an hour before the train was due to leave, no one asked any questions. They knew she was going to Stockholm to meet that friend of hers, but that was all they knew. If she wanted to go to Österyd first, then she could go to Österyd.

Teresa's rucksack looked heavy, but when Göran offered to help her carry it she just looked at him in a way that made him lower his hands. They got in the car in silence, and they drove into Österyd in silence. When Teresa told him where she wanted to be dropped off, Göran said, 'Isn't that where Johannes lives?'

'Yes.'

'Are you going to see him?'

'Yes.'

'Oh good! It might...brighten you up a bit.'

'I hope so.'

Teresa got out of the car and grabbed her rucksack, then stood there with her head lowered. She didn't close the door. When she looked at Göran a flash of pain passed through her eyes. He leaned over the passenger seat and held out his hand. 'Sweetheart...'

Teresa backed away from his touch and said, 'I'm not sure if I'm going to Stockholm. It depends. I'll ring you if I don't go.' Then she slammed the door shut, turned away and walked towards the door of Johannes' apartment block.

Göran sat there with his hands resting on the wheel. When Teresa had disappeared inside he let out a sob and lowered his head. His forehead hit one of the horn buttons, and the sound made him jump and look around. A man of about his own age with two supermarket carrier bags in his hands was standing looking at him. He waved, started the car and drove off.

Teresa hesitated before ringing the doorbell. This could be very, very painful. She hadn't even turned around when she left her father, but before she could do anything else she just had to say goodbye to Johannes. Then whatever was going to happen could happen.

Her thumb hovered over the white plastic button as if it was wired to those Cruise missiles that could start a world war. The worst thing was that she didn't know *which* action would start the chain of events: to push or not to push.

She pushed the button. No roar of engines going through twelve litres of rocket fuel per second, no terrified screams from the entire population of the world. Just a quiet *ding dong*, then footsteps in the hallway.

Johannes opened the door looking exactly the same as Teresa thought he had looked ever since *his* transformation. A pink T-shirt and khaki shorts, and he already had a tan even though the summer had hardly started. His eyes sparkled, and before Teresa could stop him he had flung his arms around her.

'Teresa! It's so good to see you!'

'You too,' she mumbled into his shoulder.

He took a step back, still holding onto her arms, and looked her up and down.

'How are you? You don't look too good, actually.'

'Thanks.'

'Oh, you know what I mean. Come in.'

Teresa took her rucksack with her into the living room and sat down in an armchair. The apartment looked like it had been decorated by several different people, all with appalling taste. Nothing matched anything else, and a standard lamp that looked like a valuable antique was standing next to a huge plastic flower on a Perspex box.

Johannes had mentioned how busy his mother was these days, how she didn't have time to bother about what the apartment looked like.

Teresa looked around and asked, 'Has Agnes' mother been here?'

Johannes laughed out loud and told her a long story about how Clara, Agnes' mother, had reacted the first time she came to dinner, how she had paused in front of a picture of a weeping child and eventually said, 'Well, that's certainly...a classic.'

When Teresa didn't even smile at his anecdotes, he sighed and sat down on the sofa, tucked his hands between his knees and waited. Teresa shuffled forward to the edge of the armchair, as close to him as possible. Then she said, 'I've killed people.'

Johannes grinned. 'What are you talking about?'

'I've killed two people. One by myself, and one with other people.'

His smile grew rigid then disappeared as he looked her in the eye. 'You can't be serious.'

'I am serious. And today I'm going to kill some more.'

Johannes frowned as if she were telling him a joke he just didn't get, then he snorted. 'Why are you saying this? Of course you're not going to kill people. Of course you haven't already killed people. What's going on, Teresa?'

She opened her rucksack. On the dark brown coffee table she placed the drill, a hammer, a carving knife and a small pair of bolt cutters. 'These are the tools we're going to use. The others have got the same. More or less.'

'What others?'

'The others who are going to be with me. My pack.'

Johannes got up and walked around the room, rubbing his scalp. Then he came and stood next to Teresa. He looked at the tools, then at her. 'What are you talking about? Stop it, Teresa. What's the matter with you?'

'I can't stop it. But I'm scared.'

'I'm not fucking surprised. What are you scared of?'

'That I won't be able to do it. I'm the one that has to go first.'

Johannes stroked her hair, shaking his head at the same time. Then he knelt down in front of her and said, 'Come on. Come on,' and put his arms around her again, holding her tight as he whispered, 'Listen, Teresa. You haven't killed anyone and you're not going to kill anyone and you have to stop talking like this. Why would you kill anyone?'

Teresa pushed him away and said, 'Because I can. Because I want to. Because it makes me alive.'

'You *want* to kill people?'

'Yes. I really, really want to. I long to do it. But I don't know if I dare. I don't know if I'm...ready.'

Johannes sighed and raised his eyebrows, then said in a tone which suggested he was prepared to play along a little bit, 'So how will you know if you're ready, then?'

'By killing you.'

'You're going to kill *me*?'

'Yes.'

'Er...when?'

'Now.'

A shadow passed over Johannes' face as he tired of the game. With a swift movement he picked up the hammer and held it out to Teresa, still kneeling in front of her. 'Go on then, kill me. Do it.'

'You don't believe me?'

'No.'

Teresa raised the hammer and said, 'Are you brave enough to close your eyes?'

He looked her in the eyes. For a long time. Then he closed his eyes. His eyelids were thin, delicate and completely relaxed. He wasn't screwing his eyes up at all, his breathing was calm and even, and there was the hint of a smile on his lips. His cheeks were covered in fine, downy hairs and he was her best friend and the only boy she had perhaps actually loved. She said, 'Bye then,' and slammed the hammer into his temple.

She kept on hitting him until only a tiny bit of life remained. Then she picked up the drill and opened him up. The battery was fully charged, and it took her only a couple of seconds to drill through the skull. Johannes' legs jerked in a series of final cramps, kicking over the plastic flower. Then she bent over him and took what had been the essence of him.

When she got up her path was clearly marked, and she knew she had the strength to follow it. There was nothing left. No further considerations, nothing to return to. She was entirely happy as she closed the door behind her and walked down the stairs, through the odours of frying food, cleaning products and dust warmed by the sun, tickling her nostrils.

In the box outside the railway station she posted the letters addressed to the four main national newspapers: *Dagens Nyheter, Svenska Dagbladet, Expressen* and *Aftonbladet*. The letters were all exactly the same, and she had written them because she could.

> Hi,
>
> Today at Sing Along at Skansen we are going to kill a lot of people. We might die too. You never know.
>
> You will ask why. Why, why, why. On the news placards. In the papers. Big thick letters. WHY? A sea of lighted candles. Pieces of paper with messages. People

weeping. And over and above everything: WHY?

And this is our answer (wait for it now): BECAUSE!!!!

Because the tide of death is rising. Do you realise the tide of death is rising? In our schools. On Idol. In H & M. It is rising. Everyone knows. Everyone feels. No one realises.

Today it will overflow.

We were the nice little girls down at the front. We screamed and wept on cue. We worshipped ourselves when you made us into stars. We bought ourselves from you. 'High five,' you said. 'Congratulations!'

The tide of death is rising. Thanks to you. It's all thanks to you. You have deserved it all.

Goodbye
The wolves of Skansen

There wasn't really anything she wanted to say. She had made up a reason because it felt appropriate. If you're going to do something magnificent then you might as well come up with a magnificent reason, it makes things tidier. She had sat at the computer and put herself in her own position. If a group of girls were about to do what they were about to do, what might a nice farewell letter look like?

Then she had written it. If everything went the way she had planned it, the letter would be examined to the point of exhaustion, and every single word would be analysed. But she didn't mean anything. She imagined herself and made things up. When she read through what she had written, she found it was all true. But it wasn't about her. Nothing had ever been about her. Perhaps that was the reason.

EPILOGUE

'We wait until the first chorus. Then we begin. Spread out.'

Teresa 19.47, 26/6/2007

I

Mother says I was a dancer before I could walk

Robert Segerwall has earned his place in the VIP seats after thirty years' hard labour in the service of entertainment at Swedish Television. He is one of the people the camera lingers on when the singing starts. He is wearing a loose beige linen jacket, and gives the impression of both relaxation and upright character. He was actually in the running to take over when Lasse gave up. He is not bitter, he loves his free summers.

When the first blow strikes his arm, for a moment he is angry that someone has ruined his jacket. Then comes the pain, and the blood. When his wife of twenty-five years starts screaming at his side, he realises that the danger is real.

He turns to his attacker, but has no time to do anything before a slash across his throat monopolises his attention. The blows that come after this are irrelevant.

She says I began to sing long before I could talk

Everyone knows that when Linda Larsson does something, she does it properly. That's why she claimed her spot at the Solliden stage at ten o'clock this morning. If she's going to Sing Along at Skansen, then she's going for the full experience. She has eaten the picnic she brought with her, she has watched the rehearsals. She is planning to write about it all in her blog, and has been making a few notes.

When she hears the angry buzzing behind her, she thinks it is an unusually large wasp. She also knows that the best thing to do in that case is to sit perfectly still. Not to start waving her arms about. She looks down at her notepad and wonders whether to write something about the wasp.

Then comes the sting in the back of her neck. The pain is indescribable. Her fingers spread and are suddenly ice cold. She opens her mouth to scream, but something is blocking her windpipe. Blood spurts over her notepad and her hand flies up to her throat where it is penetrated halfway by a rapidly rotating drill bit. Then the drill is torn out and she just has time to grasp what has happened before she loses consciousness.

And I've often wondered, how did it all start?

Despite the fact that they haven't got to the bit where the audience joins in, Isailo Jovanovic can't help singing along. This is the third time he has been to Sing Along at Skansen and, however integrated he might feel after seventeen years in Sweden, he just doesn't know the *songs*. Every year it's Evert Taube—and you don't hear those songs much in Belgrade. But Abba, that's different. When he was a teenager Isailo and his friends used to swap tapes; Isailo had his first kiss to the sound of 'Fernando'.

He knows he has a decent tenor voice, and even though the people around him are not singing, he joins in with the girl up on the stage. He has never heard anyone sing like that, and it is a pleasure to hear his voice blending with hers.

He can hear the distant sound of people screaming, and assumes that the girl is some kind of idol. This isn't important to him as he enjoys the way her voice interweaves with his.

In the middle of his joyous singing he receives a blow to his jaw, a terrible blow on his chin. Something breaks in his lower jaw and he is hurled to the ground. In a couple of seconds his mouth is full of blood and fragments of tooth. He doesn't understand. This is not the Sweden he knows.

Then he sees the hammer being raised, and holds up his hands in self-defence. His head is ringing and he is unable to focus. A blurred figure takes a step to one side, then comes an annihilating blow right on the top of his head.

Who found out that nothing can capture a heart like a melody can?

Johan Lejonhjärta is in seventh heaven. He came to Sing Along at Skansen for one thing, and one thing only, and that thing has happened. Ola Salo touched him. Johan has adored Ola Salo from the very start, and Ola was one of the reasons why he dared to come out of the closet eight years ago, leaving Kisa and moving to Stockholm.

When Ola fluttered past the sea of spectators as he sang 'The Worrying Kind', Johan stretched out his hand. And Ola didn't just touch his hand. He took it for a moment and looked Johan in the eye as he sang 'Be good for goodness sake'. The words and the touch burned into Johan.

He knows it's ridiculous. He is thirty-two years old, and thinks he has been touched by a divine being. He has photographed his hand with his mobile, he has turned the words 'be good for goodness sake' over and over in his head like the words of a guru, a guideline for life. He knows it's ridiculous and he couldn't care less and he gives himself up to his happiness.

When he hears the screams around him they are filtered through his own experience, and he interprets them as screams of happiness and excitement. He loves Abba too, and the girl up there is a wonderful singer, but that's not important right now.

He works as a carpenter and recognises the sound behind him for exactly what it is. A drill. And yet he does not link the sound with the agonising pain in his back, because it is just too far-fetched. Only when the second blow comes does he realise that the rev count of the drill is slowing down at the same time as he feels a quivering pain through his skeleton.

When he turns around the drill is pushed into his chest, and he coughs up blood as one lung is punctured. The drill is pulled out and he opens his mouth to stammer out a plea, a prayer. For a fraction of a second he can see the rotating spiral before it becomes blurred and disappears into his eye.

Well, whoever it was, I'm a fan

Elsie Karlsson has seen them come and go. She was here back in Egon Kjerrman's day, but she'd go for Bosse Larsson if she had to choose. There was nothing wrong with Lasse, nor this new chap, but Bosse Larsson knew how to spread a sense of *wellbeing* like no one else. Things weren't so over the top in those days.

You can usually get a seat if you arrive about two, but today there must be something particularly popular on, so Elsie has had to sit on her wheeled walker. To tell the truth, she wishes the show would end, because she's really tired. You might think one of these young people would offer her their seat, but times have changed.

This is a nice tune, and the girl who is singing is very good. As far as Elsie can remember the girl wasn't there for the rehearsals, which is unheard of. Or perhaps Elsie has forgotten. That happens more and more often these days.

Some kind of commotion over by the seating attracts her attention. A few people have got up and are running away. Odd. Things are usually very orderly and controlled once the broadcast has begun, people hardly dare cross their legs. But now people are running around and screaming in a quite unprecedented way.

She doesn't understand what has happened until she is lying on her back and hears her hip bone crack. The wheeled walker has been pulled from underneath her. It hurts so much that the grinding of her jaws leaves her false teeth askew inside her mouth. Her glasses must have fallen off, because she can hardly see.

A thin figure is leaning over her with something in its hand. Elsie believes that people are intrinsically good, and assumes that this is someone who is going to help her, that whatever the figure is holding in its hand is something that can save her. Then comes the blow directly to her forehead, and everything goes black.

Inside her head, in some corner which is still conscious, she hears a sound like an angry insect. It is coming closer.

So I say thank you for the music, the songs I'm singing

At first Lena Forsman thought it was a bad idea. Going to Sing Along at Skansen on a first date. It felt like a family thing, not something for two people who met on the internet. But it's gone well, really well.

There was so much to talk about as they fumbled their way towards an understanding of one another, and so far Peter seems to be a real gem. Self-confident without being arrogant, funny without being stupid. Not bad looking, well dressed, and as for the thinning hair, she actually thought it was sexy. On him anyway.

He had bought her raspberries from one of the girls who went around selling them before the live broadcast, and when 'Some Day I'll Come Sailing Home' started up, he put his arm around her shoulders and half-jokingly swayed along in time. The arm had stayed there as a little girl came on stage and sang that fantastic Abba song.

The mixing desk hides the middle of the stage from where they are standing, and since she can't see anyway, and since the girl is singing so beautifully, Lena closes her eyes and gives herself up to the pleasure of the friendly arm around her shoulders, the warm summer evening and the special moments life can still bring, moments like this.

She hears hysterical screams and smiles at the memory of herself when she was like that, when she was fourteen years old and went to see Abba at Gröna Lund; she almost fainted when Annifrid looked her in the eye for that fraction of a second, and she screamed until her throat hurt.

Suddenly Peter's grip tightens around her shoulders. He is squeezing so hard that she gasps and opens her eyes, just as his hand is torn away from her. She sees him fall at her feet, clutching his head. He begins to twitch and shake, and her first thought is: *Is he having an epileptic fit?*

Then she sees that blood is beginning to seep from beneath his right hand. She doesn't understand what has happened, but leans over him and says, 'Peter? Peter? What's the matter?'

His eyes are staring at a point immediately behind her. They widen and he opens his mouth to say something. The next moment a blow to the back of her neck brings her down, and she falls onto his body. She just has time to catch the aroma of Old Spice before another blow extinguishes all perception.

Thanks for all the joy they're bringing

Ronnie Ahlberg doesn't know what the hell to do. He is in charge of the camera ten metres to the left of the stage, and from his metre-high wooden podium he has a good overview. What he is seeing is not what happened during rehearsals. Through his headset he has just been told to run pictures of the audience in the seated area, but what is happening down there isn't exactly ideal material. People are out of their seats and running, and there seems to be some kind of mass exodus going on.

Still, his job is not to look for reasons, but to find camera angles. Since the audience in the seated area has decided to depart from the script for some reason, he turns the camera towards the standing area behind the barriers, where the kids are still behaving as they should, holding their mobiles up in the air to film the show and waving banners with 'TESLA RULES' and 'TESLA GIRLS JAKOBSBERG'.

He hears a voice in his ear. Abrahamsson, the picture editor, sounds almost on the verge of tears in the outside broadcast truck. 'What's going on out there, Ronnie? Half our monitors are fucking useless.'

Ronnie's camera is about to go the same way. The kids have started behaving oddly too, and the 'TESLA RULES' banner ends up on the ground just as the crowd at his feet begins to move away from the barrier. He is just thinking of angling his camera up towards the stage and the girl who is singing, because at least she's standing still, when a powerful blow to his knee makes his legs give way beneath him.

He tries to stop himself from falling by grabbing hold of one of the levers on the camera, but a blow to the other knee sends him tumbling from the platform, executing an involuntary stage dive backwards into the sea of running people.

His face, arms and hands are trampled underfoot as he hears a high-pitched whining noise—it sounds like a camera flash charging—coming closer to his ear.

Who can live without it? I ask in all honesty, what would life be?

No, Sing Along at Skansen is not Kalle Bäckström's scene, he was quite clear on that point after enduring a song by The Ark, some old farts' song, and now that kid who was on MySpace. He only came because Emmy was supposed to be here. And now he can't get hold of her!

He has spent the last ten minutes standing next to the portable toilets fifty metres behind the back row of seats, texting. He asked Emmy where she is, and she told him she was down the front. Whereabouts down the front, he asked her, and now he's waiting for the reply.

OK, OK. If necessary he's going to push his way through the crowd just so he can stand next to her and rub himself up against her. She's the prettiest girl in the class, and when she said, 'Are you coming to Skansen on Tuesday?', he might have misinterpreted it slightly. As if it was a date. But she was here with three girlfriends, and he hasn't even managed to find her yet.

He is standing there staring at his phone, using the power of the mind to try and make a reply from her appear, when he realises something is going on. People are screaming and waving their arms in the air down at the front, and one or two are running past him. He lowers his mobile and stands on tiptoe so that he can see better.

The crowd in front of him is *expanding*. The entire audience begins to swell towards him as if it was escaping from a pressure cooker. Slowly at first, then faster and faster. He is standing on the slope leading down from Solliden, right in the middle of the valve itself, and the boiling mass of people is cascading towards him.

He can't understand what is going on, and stands there with his mouth open as the wave approaches. When it is just a few metres away he finally comes to his senses, hurls himself into one of the toilets and locks the door. Thousands of footsteps in headlong flight thunder past outside the door, and the toilet shakes as bodies fall from the horde and crash into the thin plastic walls.

He sits down on the seat and carries on texting, searching for Emmy, but there is no reply.

Without a song or a dance, what are we?

'Event Security' it says on the back of Joel Carlsson's red T-shirt. That's the name of the company he works for, and that has been his job description for the last ten years. Event security. A friend at the gym put him in touch with them, and he's stayed because he enjoys his job. Particularly when it comes to Sing Along at Skansen.

Rock concerts can be hard work: overheated venues, loud music and kids getting crushed and passing out. At sports events there are the drunks and hooligans to deal with. Sing Along is like a holiday by comparison, and within the company this particular job is allocated as a reward for long and loyal service.

Walking around spraying water on teenage girls who have got a bit sweaty, but who mostly just laugh and think it's cool, telling people who are already pretty calm to calm down just a little bit more and stop trying to move forward. It's very rare that Joel has to take a hard line or remove anybody.

But tonight there's something wrong. When that Tesla walked on stage and started singing, you could have heard a pin drop in the audience at first. What a voice! People stood there with their mouths just hanging open, like they were bewitched. Joel took the opportunity to have a bit of a breather, drink some water and do some stretches while he enjoyed the song himself.

Then he hears the scream. It comes from somewhere in the seated area, oddly enough. He is dazzled by the lighting rig as he scans the audience and sees that some people have got to their feet. In the middle of the live broadcast, for fuck's sake! He waves angrily at them to sit down, but they take no notice. Instead more people stand up, and he hears more screams.

Inappropriate noises *and* inappropriate movement. His job, among other things, is to prevent exactly this, and he looks around to see if he can pinpoint the source of the problem.

Something is going on behind one of the close-up cameras, over by the VIP seats. If there is anywhere he would expect things to be perfectly calm, it's in that area. A-list or B-list celebrities sitting like lighted candles, just waiting for the camera to focus on them. But now there are screams and movement and the place is full of people getting up and *running*.

Joel scuttles along below the stage where the little girl is still standing and singing, in spite of the fact that the music has stopped. When he reaches the VIP seats the entire area closest to the stage is already empty, apart from two people. Joel catches sight of something on the ground, and stops dead.

Fucking hell.

Robert Segerwall, that old guy who used to be big on TV, is lying in a pool of what must be blood, and blood is still pouring out of a wound or a hole in his temple. Joel is about to hurl himself towards Segerwall, but then realises he can do more good elsewhere.

Prioritise, Joel. Prioritise.

What he at first took to be a quarrel is a struggle for life and death. He recognises Robert Segerwall's wife, but not the young girl she is fighting with. Or whatever you would call it. The older woman is tearing at the air, trying to scratch the girl's face, but Joel can see that this is a battle she is going to lose. In one hand the girl has a long knife, in the other a drill.

Joel doesn't get there in time. Just as he takes his first stride towards them, the hand holding the knife shoots out. Joel couldn't have done it better during his training with the elite Coastal Rangers. The blade slices across the woman's neck and she staggers backwards, her hands pressed to her throat.

At last she seems to realise that flight is the only possibility. As she is trapped between the young girl and Joel, who is moving forward, she wobbles up the steps leading to the stage, blood gushing down over her chest.

Prioritise.

He has to stop this girl before she does anything else. He reaches her in two rapid strides and twists the knife out of her hand. She gets in one blow to his head with the drill before he knocks it out of her hand. He locks her arms behind her back, yelling, 'What the fuck are you doing, are you insane?'

The girl relaxes in his grasp and says calmly, 'I am not insane. I am sane. I am perfectly sane.'

So I say thank you for the music, for giving it to me.

As Eva Segerwall takes the last step onto the stage, there is unfortunately nothing left within her to let her know that her dream has finally come true.

It is twenty-three years since she set aside her ambitions as a singer to support her husband in his TV career. But oh, what dreams she had! To hear Bosse Larsson say her name one day, to tread the boards here in Solliden beneath the birch trees, to stand on this very stage!

And now she is standing here, incapable of savouring it. Her life is pouring out through her throat, splashing around her feet as she staggers towards the angelic figure standing behind the microphone, still singing.

For a second their eyes meet, and Eva becomes even more afraid than she already was. There is no help to be found there. The big blue eyes gaze at her without sympathy, they do not even seem to notice the cascades of blood covering her light summer dress. She coughs up more blood and totters, on legs which are about to give way, towards the left, past the stage entrance, past the empty seats where the orchestra were sitting, past the flower arrangements and out onto the jetty.

And there she sees an escape route at last. Through misty eyes she sees the waters of Mälarviken glittering far below. She throws herself in that direction but hits an invisible wall, falls backwards and just lies there, gives up.

2

I've been so lucky
I am the girl with golden hair
I want to sing it out to everybody
What a joy! What a life! What a chance!

The orchestra had stopped playing long ago; Theres stood alone on the Solliden stage and sang the final verses a cappella, even though there was no longer anyone listening. Down below her feet there was utter chaos.

Thirty or so people lay dead or dying on the seats and on the ground. A woman had managed to escape onto the stage with blood pouring from her throat and had run into the Perspex screen protecting the stage from the wind coming off Mälarviken. She was just lying there in a heap on the jetty, over by the standing area. Theres put the microphone back in its stand, went over to the woman and drank her.

Some members of the group had been grabbed by security guards or other adults, some had been knocked over and trampled underfoot as the audience panicked and fled, some were still standing or crouching next to their latest victim, sucking up their life.

Theres went right to the end of the jetty, threw back her head and *howled*. For a moment everything stopped as the heart-rending sound froze the summer evening to solid ice. Then the other girls answered. Bloody faces looked up and teeth were bared, the girls who had been caught filled their lungs with air, and Linn, who was lying next to the barrier with a broken leg, dragged herself into a sitting position and joined in.

The same howl rose from fourteen throats, a rising and falling note with a single message.

We exist. Be afraid of us.

Then more guards arrived, more capable hands to help drag away and render harmless the wild animals that had insinuated themselves in among human habitation.

Teresa had managed to get to the side of the stage, and as the other girls were running away or being captured, she called Theres over. Together they ran towards the wolf enclosure. They passed groups of people standing, sitting or lying at what they judged to be a safe distance from the danger. Moans and weeping from both children and adults filled the air.

Teresa saw a man with his arms around two people who were presumably his wife and son, and a thought struck her. A detail they had never mentioned when they were planning for this day.

'Jerry?' she asked. 'Is he here?'

Without slowing down Theres replied, 'I told him he wasn't allowed to come.'

Presumably he had seen it on TV, presumably he knew by this stage what had happened. But he hadn't been here, there was no risk that he was one of the dead. In some way that was a relief.

They ran, and the people allowed them to pass. A young voice yelled, 'She's the one who was singing!' but that was all they knew. Theres and Teresa ran side by side until they reached the enclosure.

Before the show began, when everyone was gathered in Solliden, Teresa had used the bolt cutters to make a hole about the size of a door in the fence, so that their grey sisters and brothers would have the opportunity to join in.

None of them had taken that opportunity, but as if the wolves had sensed the atmosphere of the hunt that pervaded the area, several of them had emerged from their lairs and hiding places and were now warily circling the area near the breach, baring their teeth and growling. Teresa looked at them and shook her head.

'They didn't come to us.'

Theres stood with her neck extended, watching the shaggy figures that were watching her. Then it happened. At first Teresa couldn't work out what was tickling the back of her hand. When she looked down she saw that it was Theres' fingers, fumbling for hers. She grabbed Theres' hand and held it tightly. They stood for a long time, side by side in front of the door, squeezing each other's hands.

Then Theres said, 'In that case, we will go to them.'

'Thank You for the Music'
Music and Lyrics by Benny Andersson and Björn Ulvaeus
Printed by permission of Universal/Union Songs Musikforlag AB,
Stockholm, Sweden.

With special thanks to ABBA, for inspiration.